BRIAN KERR

DAUGHTERS
of the
CROSSLANDS

Sero Sed Serio
PORTLAND, OREGON

Published by Sero Sed Serio, Portland, Oregon.

briankerrbooks.com

Printed in the United States of America
ISBN (Paperback): 979-8-9996189-0-0
ISBN (Hardcover): 979-8-9996189-2-4
ISBN (eBook): 979-8-9996189-1-7
Library of Congress Control Number: 2025915926

First Edition

10 9 8 7 6 5 4 3 2 1

For Braeden and Coraline,
who are finally old enough to read this,
and for James,
who has been old enough for years.

And for Julie, who remains my favorite.

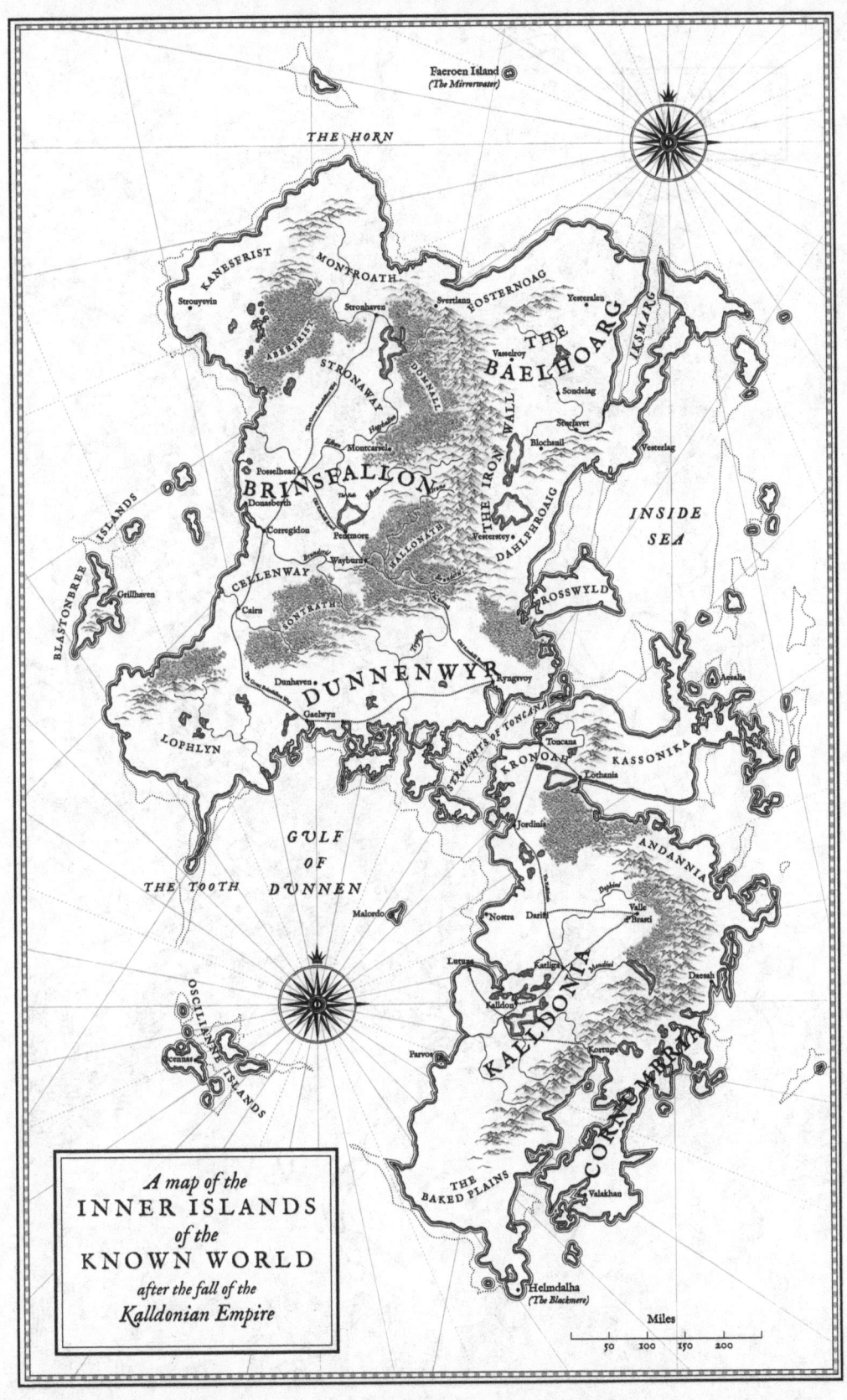

Facroen Island
(The Mirrerwater)

THE HORN

KANESFRIST
MONTROATH
Strouyevin
Stronhaven
Svertlang FOSTERNOAG
Yesteralen
IASMARG

STRONAWAY
Vasclroy
THE
BAELHOARG
DORNALL

Hognden
Sondelag
INSIDE
SEA

Montcarvelo
Mhs
Stovlavet

Posselhead
BRINSFALLON
Vesteovery
Blochaull
Vesterlag

Donaeberth
Penemore
Vesterovery
DAHLFEROAIG

Corregidon
Wayburry
HALLONATH

CELLENWAY
ROSSWYLD

Cairo
SONTRATH

Dunhaven
DUNNENWYR
Ryngvoy

BLASTONBREE
ISLANDS
Grillhaven

Gaelwyn

Lesala

LOPHLYN

STRAIGHTS OF TONCAN
KRONOAB
Toncasa
KASSONIKA
Lothania

Jordinis
ANDANNIA

GULF
OF
DUNNEN
Daphini

THE TOOTH
Valle
d'Braeti

Nostra
Darist

Malordo

Latuna
Katliga
Mandini

Kalldon
Daesah

OSCILLANTE ISLANDS
Cennas
KALLDONIA
CORNMBRAE

Parvos
Kortaga

THE
BAKED PLAINS
Valakhau

Helmdalha
(The Blackmere)

A map of the
INNER ISLANDS
of the
KNOWN WORLD
after the fall of the
Kalldonian Empire

Miles
50 100 150 200

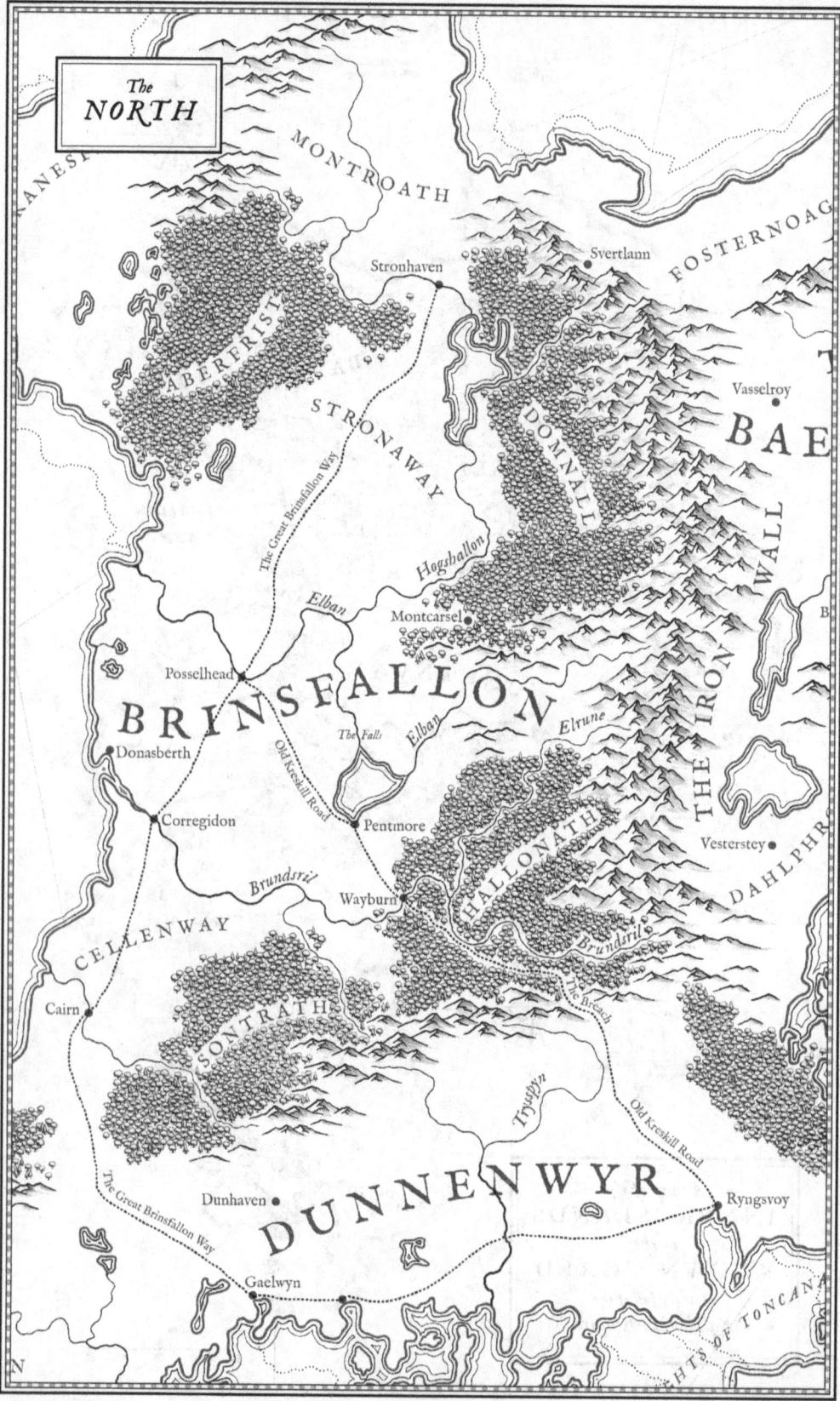

The
NORTH

MONTROATH

KANES...

ABERFIST

Stronhaven

Svertlann

FOSTERNOAG

Vasselroy

BAE

STRONAWAY

DOMNALL

The Great Brinsfallon Way

Hogsfallon

Elban

Montcarsel

Posselhead

THE IRON WALL

BRINSFALLON

Donasberth

The Falls   Elban

Elrune

Old Kreskill Road

Pentmore

HALLONATH

Vesterstey

DAHLPHR...

Corregidon

Brundsril

Wayburn

Brundsril

CELLENWAY

SONTRATH

The Breach

Cairn

Tysbyn

Old Kreskill Road

DUNNENWYR

Dunhaven

Ryngsvoy

The Great Brinsfallon Way

Gaelwyn

...HTS OF TONCAN...

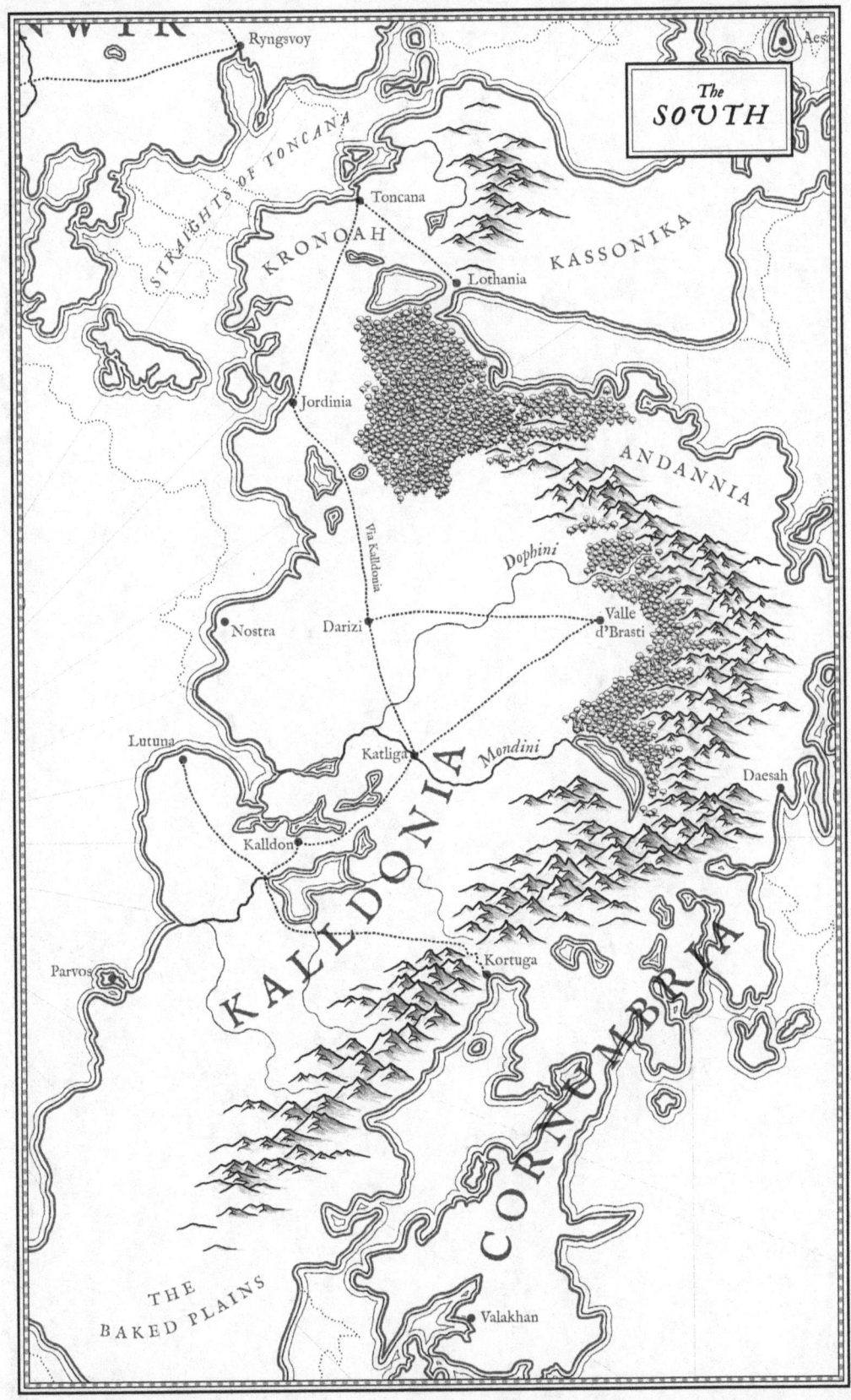

PART ONE

THE LAMPFLAME on Senya's mantel quivered and then righted itself as it yearned for rough wood rafters less than an arm's reach overhead. Retrieving her ladle from its hook, she dug deep into an iron pot over the hearth. The seething stew heaved. With three good stirs, she pulled to fill a wooden bowl, set the ladle against the pot's lip, and placed the steaming bowl on a modest table in the middle of the room. Several straps of smoked meat and braided garlic dangled above. Turning back to the fire, she crouched with a firm grip on a sharp iron poker and plunged its hooked tip into the core of the coals, shoving them tight to the center. Flames rose and swirled in response. Satisfied, she leaned the poker beside the hearth and dropped a fresh log on the fire.

Stepping to her sideboard, Senya moved a pair of root vegetables out of her way and sliced off a chunk of yesterday's bread. Firelight splashed trembling light over the clean stone floor. Her narrow bed lay in shadow to one side. Retrieving her mug of herbal brew, she stepped to the table and sat.

Her day had been long and exhausting. Out in the lambing shed since well before dawn, she'd struggled to help two of her favorite ewes manage their labors, and proved helpless while a third passed away immediately after giving birth. Three others had agonized for hours before pushing out a collection of puny sickly lambs. So much worse than usual. A few had managed to stay alive, but even those were born weak and feeble. It had taken everything in Senya's waning power to keep them breathing. She'd sung. She'd nursed. She'd scooped sludge from mouths and struggled to clear tiny airways. Nothing had worked, not like it used to.

She ate slowly, trying her best to savor the stew. The fire swayed and churned, coals pulsing with fresh heat. A sharp unease had plagued her all through the day, growing worse into evening and the coming dark. As dusk had fallen, she'd caught flickering movement out of the corner of her eye—a figure, standing among the trees, just beyond sight. A woman, maybe. Pale skin. Shining blue eyes and a long gray cloak. A second woman had appeared several paces from the first, and both seemed to shimmer and glint. When Senya had spun to get a better look, to shout and ask their business, both had vanished back into shadow.

Hockby had followed her gaze and asked if she'd seen something. But she'd only stood and stared, hesitant to speak.

"Just the fog playing tricks," she'd said.

This sense of dread wasn't anything new to Senya. Strange and disturbing visions had come to her ever since she was young—shifting glimpses of faces and voices flashing into view and then disappearing, typically things only she could see, brought to her from the living and the dead alike. A body walking upright but not quite alive, maybe a wraith of some kind, maybe something else. Sometimes she would witness an event before it occurred. She never talked much about any of it. Better to keep quiet. People found her odd and different enough already, and mentioning this sort of thing just made her that much more of an outsider.

Hockby had been good to her though, even when she'd first arrived at this remote settlement, worn out and guarded, nearly three years ago. He'd remained her friend ever since. Hockby was a good man. He took her seriously, but some things were better left alone.

The fire hissed and cracked. Senya finished her stew and ran the spoon along an empty edge to retrieve the last loose bits of meat. Stepping to a cupboard beside the table, she rinsed her bowl in a bucket and wiped it clean. Set it back in the cupboard to dry.

A loud knock at the door shattered the quiet. Stepping cautiously, Senya paused and listened. This was awfully late for visitors. Almost nobody came all the way out to visit her in this cramped little house, nestled next to the stone sheepfold wall. She preferred it that way. This remote corner of a remote settlement gave her just the right kind of solitude.

She waited. No footsteps creaked her timber porch. No sounds on the stony path beyond. She heard no voices, no movement outside. Nothing but a breeze in the trees. She slid open a narrow viewport in the door.

A tall woman in a long gray cloak stood at the edge of the lamplight, pure white and completely hairless—as if formed from the strange night mist itself. A chill ran down Senya's spine.

"Who are you? What do you want?"

"I am sorry," the visitor replied. Keen sapphire eyes glowed in the dim, both pupils vertical black slits—eyes of a cat, made for shadows. "I realize my arrival is somewhat... un... orthodox..." She spoke slowly, as if rising from a deep sleep. "You are Senya, yes?"

"I might be."

"Sorry, of course..." The woman glanced down to her left. One hand idly reached across to tug at her opposite elbow. "I am not well versed in... pleasantries. I do apologize." She returned her gaze to Senya. "I am called Cevellica. I have come for your brother."

"My brother?"

The woman's long pale fingers pulled at the fabric of her gray sleeve. "Yes," she said. "For Raedwin."

For Raedwin.

Her brother's name sounded so unfamiliar and odd when spoken in this woman's heavy, disjointed accent—not as though from a foreign land, but as if speaking itself was a foreign act. Senya slid the viewport closed.

"My brother is not here," she answered through the door. She'd not seen her twin in a long time and had lost the thread of his whereabouts years ago.

"Sorry... not *for*..." The visitor hesitated. "I have come... on his *behalf*. To ask... a favor..."

Raedwin had so often drifted, asking questions that were better left alone, looking for answers and dabbling in things well beyond his control, wandering into places prudence would never normally allow. He liked to push the boundaries between this world and the other, between knowledge and insanity, between safety and menace and simple misfortune. None of it ever seemed like a good idea, and Senya had told him as much every chance she'd gotten. They'd argued about it nearly all their lives.

"Please," Cevellica begged through the closed door. "I realize this must be most... disconcerting... but I am hoping you will at least listen to what I have to say..."

Senya had long suspected Raedwin's dubious paths would eventually come to something like this—a confusing plea sent through vague and mysterious channels in the middle of the night. Raedwin was never about simple, practical approaches—a letter from the village post or word from a friend in the daylight like everybody else. Or reaching out to her himself. Of course he would send disturbing news of some disastrous end via some ethereal messenger who made no sense. Raedwin had finally gone too far, and this was how he'd chosen to communicate.

"He needs your help."

Senya's breath caught in her throat. *Of course he does*. Her heart hammered.

"He has become lost," Cevellica added. "Forces conspire against him. You are his twin sister. His blood. The only one who might be able to reach him. To take his hand and bring him to the light. Guide him away from trouble, and bring him home."

Senya's forehead fell to the door. She let out a long, uncertain breath and shook her head, rolling it against the wood.

"I'm sorry," she said. "I don't think I can help you." Her voice emerged muffled and weak. "Raedwin doesn't live with me anymore. This is not his home."

She was met with silence. No sounds of the visitor retreating nor of stepping forward onto the porch planks. Nothing.

Senya had seen all of this before. Raedwin needing help was nothing new. Always excited about what the unknown could bring, her brother had gotten into plenty of trouble in the past, his curiosity plaguing him all throughout their childhood. Tighter and tighter spots, with messes that grew trickier for Senya to fix as the years went on. Venturing out time and again, no matter the consequences. After their mother had passed, he'd had almost nothing left to hold him back.

Far to the north in Stronhaven, a cranky old alchemist had caught him stealing an instrument of some great value, and by the time Senya had arrived to deal with it, the man held her brother strapped to a chopping block, ready to take his hand. Senya had intervened and promised her own hand instead. The man had inspected his prize with a lewd grin, groped her as he jeered, and agreed to the exchange immediately. But as soon as he'd freed Raedwin, they both had run. They'd sprinted through the muddy streets, out the city gates, and south into the countryside with nothing but the belongings they held in hand. They kept running, away from Stronaway and the Far North altogether. They'd never returned and never looked back.

Maybe they were both still running.

Senya waited. Roof timbers moaned with a gust of wind off the lake. She slid open the viewport again.

Cevellica remained as before, unmoving. "Your brother is trapped," she said slowly. "Held. Lost. And those who wish ill of him will soon be in complete dominance..."

Senya swore in silence. "I'm sorry," she called. "I've never really been able to help him, so I don't think there's any way I can really help you. Not anymore."

"I realize this is unpleasant, but the needed task is quite simple..." Cevellica's words came carefully controlled, managed, as if set by a predetermined script.

"Nothing is ever simple where my brother is concerned," Senya said.

"Which is why we have come to you. We have tried many other avenues... but all have..."

"All have failed, and I'm your last great hope?"

Cevellica nodded. "Yes, perhaps..."

"Well, maybe not."

The woman's face twitched as her head cocked to the side. She frowned. "You really do not wish to help?"

"Whether or not I wish to help doesn't matter. I wish a lot of things, especially for my brother. But I can't help you. It never matters what I wish. I told you. I've never been able to help Raedwin in the past, and I don't see how I can help him now."

Maybe her brother had fully gotten lost this time, and maybe some catastrophe was indeed headed his way, but what did it matter? What could Senya do now that was any different from a lifetime of failed attempts to keep him safe? Years ago, he'd alluded to a plan to go somewhere south beyond Cellenway, maybe past Dunnenwyr as well, to find some new rumored knowledge hidden away down there. Maybe that was Cevellica. Maybe it was someone else. He never would tell her exactly where he was, and Senya had long ago lost her sense of him. The feeling of his presence had faded away over time and then eventually had gone fully dark. She'd sensed nothing of his whereabouts in well over three years.

Her worry over him had risen to panic at first and then diminished to simple concern, which resolved over time into a vague, settled sense of loss. She couldn't be sure if it was her own diminishing abilities at fault or if the same was happening to Raedwin. In any case, he would do what he did, and there was not much she could do about it. Maybe it was better that way.

She had to let him go. She had to. Sooner or later, Raedwin had to live or die in whatever way he chose for himself. She didn't want to battle with him anymore. Or have to save him again. She didn't want any more messengers in the middle of the night. She wanted a safe little home and a small quiet life and never to have to look away. Sometimes she wanted to erase all the things she had ever seen and all the places she had ever known, maybe forget who she was to the eyes of this world, and remain a little lost.

"I am sorry," she said finally. "Thank you for your concern for my brother. But I have to ask you to leave now. I am going to close this window. Please do not come back."

And with that, she slid the viewport closed.

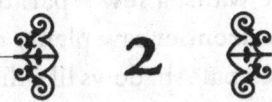

2

THE LITTLE LAMB must have died in the night. Senya saw no sign of life as she drew near—no flick of an ear, no tail wag. Only yesterday she'd seen this same lamb run free over ragged strips of remaining snow, dancing on unsteady legs. Healthy and happy. High piercing bleats ringing in the breeze. The first lamb of the season born, and now just the latest one to die.

Crouching to examine limbs and snout and eyes, she found no blood or wounds. No sign of injuries. Nothing but his little black face with a few black spots over delicate hooves, his body stretched across a fleeting patch of early sun.

Hockby approached from the lakeshore. "That same fox, you think?"

Senya shook her head. "No tracks. Not a scratch on him. Like he just lay down, took a nap, and that was it."

Hockby stood tall and lean. Years of laughter had wrinkled the corners of his kind eyes, and a short, uneven beard braced his ready smile—blank now as he stared at the lamb on the ground. "Probably the cold. Abandoned by its mother, I suppose. Shouldn't have been out on its own like this."

Senya's role here was simple—keep the lambs alive and stay out of the way. She was typically pretty good at both. She'd seen plenty of death around all the farms she'd served over the years and knew all the ways to stave it off. But somehow she'd missed any recent signs of sickness and disease. The weather had been dry and mild, so maybe she'd just lost focus. Been distracted. Clearly she hadn't culled properly. Maybe she'd been too gentle with the ewes, or too harsh. Either way, she should have known better.

"It's not your fault," Hockby assured her.

Senya glanced at the morning fog gathering over the water and slowly creeping up the slope to climb the rocky bluffs above. Her weakening talents were not what they used to be. She couldn't hide that fact forever.

"You did what you could."

The morning watch had reported glimpses of a strange lone figure on a ridge outside the sheepfold. Maybe two. Even with nothing more than torchlight along the walls, a few separate watchmen had sworn to it. Brinsfallon's eastern frontier saw plenty of peculiar folk and odd events, but nobody had seen pale shadows like these before. Ashen figures cloaked like smoke and fog. Ghosts maybe. Certainly more than just the fog playing tricks.

Then somebody claimed to have seen Senya's curious pale visitor in the night, and word had quickly passed to the Clanmother. They were not quite sure what they'd witnessed exactly—a woman in a shimmering gray cloak loitering outside Senya's door, clearly pleading, asking for something. Lingering longer than expected, the interloper had disappeared from sight soon after.

Senya remained silent. She rose. Nothing moved along the high sheepfold wall. Darkness pooled under huddled branches. A fresh breeze pushed the fog, causing misty fingers to split apart and then join again to settle among the pine groves like itinerant spectators waiting for some hidden doom yet to come.

The Clanmother had called for a search of the nearby hills. Keen weapons and fierce dogs could generally deal with the occasional bandit or whatever hungry creature wandered out of the Hallonath, but she needed to make sure no unseen threat was gathering without their knowledge.

"We ought to get the rest of them in," Senya said. "Keep an eye out. See if we've got any more trouble on the way."

"I wouldn't have guessed this little guy to end up out here," Hockby said, still staring at the lamb. "All full of piss and vinegar just yesterday."

"If you want to get started, I'll find a good spot for him outside the fold, up the hill a bit. Away from everything."

Hockby agreed, and they got to work. Both had plenty to do without distractions from vague suspicions nobody but Senya could feel. She needed to focus. The ewes were ready, and more lambs would come soon enough.

❦

Whispers simmered through the settlement all day. These sightings. The dead and dying livestock. Senya had awakened some kind of demon from the Underworld, they cried. The Clanmother denounced such worries as nonsense and called for calm. But she ordered a double watch overnight nonetheless.

Senya's flame-colored eyes were usually the first thing that made people talk. Often they would gape and gasp. Some would mutter among themselves. *The look of a Brohndai*, they'd whisper—just like those immortal men of the Far North who had roamed all the known lands before their banishment by the late empire. She had the same orange eyes and the same nearly black skin. Telltale signs. But nobody had seen a real Brohndai in decades.

You don't belong here, people would say, either directly with words or in silence without.

Senya had long since given up trying to explain herself. Nobody cared who or where her father was, or who her mother had been. Nobody wanted to know about fallen immortality and what that might mean. They only cared that she was different. A slight, unassuming woman, she was good with sheep and livestock as well as a ready hand in the garden. And she had an uncanny ability as a healer, for people as well as animals. Skills which gave her dependable worth. Out here among the fortified farms on the Brinsfallon frontier, she'd at long last found a place that welcomed her, a place that finally felt a little bit like home.

But today, rumors and easy talk quickly put the whole settlement on edge. Cautious of Senya and wary of everything she said, they began to separate from her and kept their distance. By way of answer, she held her head down and concentrated on her work, ignoring the idle and pointed talk. She refused to pay heed and be distracted by nonsense. She would not stand by and let more lambs die on her watch.

As evening fell, Hockby joined with a few of the most loyal fieldhands in her house at the edge of the sheepfold. Hockby's wife, Brin, brought their new baby along. They ate and spoke of Winter's passing and the coming Spring, keeping quiet about the sheep they'd lost. They stayed silent about rumors of any visitors. Senya sat and watched the child's round pink face near the crackling fire, happy sounds gurgling as his tiny hands wrestled meaning from the air. He crawled to the edge of the light, his fat round fingers reaching to examine the gyrating shadows flickering across the floor.

"You'd make a good mother," Brin said softly.

Senya smiled. "Oh, I don't think that's in the bones." She loved children, but motherhood probably wasn't for her.

"You're young. There's still time."

Senya let out a laugh. "You're very kind," she said. "But I'm not as young as I appear." In truth, she had seen more winters than any mother she'd ever known, including her own. Her time for having children had likely long since passed.

"You have such power of life in you. I think you would shine."

Senya shook her head, forcing another smile. "Maybe I used to, but not so much anymore." In any case, men were not for her. She'd tried all that before. The lives of men were too fleeting, their love too short. She was satisfied to remain as she was, a mother to sheep and goats on this narrow slice of windswept lakeshore. She worked hard to keep it that way.

"The time will come," Brin assured. "You will find your voice. You just need to let yourself free."

Senya said nothing. She watched the baby crawl across the floor, soft palms slapping stone. The fire popped.

"Someone like you shouldn't hide out here forever," Brin added quietly.

Senya turned to her. Brin was a lovely woman. Red curls dangled playfully over plump cheeks. Young, unblemished skin. Firelight reflected in her friendly wide eyes. Senya gave her a smile.

"Not many see me like you do," she said.

They spoke no more about it. Senya's cozy home emptied once the meal was finished and the day's tales had been told. She thanked them all and sat in silence near the hearth. After a time, she rose and stepped over to her bookshelf. Pulling out a particular volume, she took it to the table and sat.

It was an old copy of the *Black Book of the Baelhoarg*, rendered by the Brohndai scribes of Yesteralen in the long years before their banishment by the empire. The book had been part of her family since they'd lived in Storlavet, and maybe for years before that. Her mother used to read from it almost nightly, with Senya and Raedwin huddled over oil lamps near the kitchen fire. Stories of myth and legend as well as lessons of life and death.

She let the covers fall open to somewhere in the center, the pages landing where they may—finally settling at the very end of the epic *Boneshine Song*, an ancient and tragic tale of heroic adventure shared between two siblings. She scanned the words in front of her:

> *And so the spent ashes of his wandering misspoken life*
> *Strayed well past the true course*
> *Written deft and plain upon his early palm.*
> *His last drawn breath exhaled to quiet, and then gone,*
> *Sent forth as nothing more*
> *Than flame-fueled ash and buried dust.*
>
> *His beloved sister was left alone then,*
> *Deserted and lost, crying mournful tears*
> *Misplaced into the empty mouth of tomorrow's vanished hope.*
> *She, born of shining bones and acts of faith,*
> *Built from inborn truths spirited by the long-dead journey*
> *Held fast within the living bedrock of her own beating heart.*

She read the words over and again, almost hearing the sound of her mother's voice in the telling, with Senya and her brother lying next to one another at her feet. The whole of it came across like some kind of symbol, the book falling open to this particular page, like a message from the Knowing herself. Raedwin adored symbols and hidden, coded languages, but Senya was never so sure of such things.

She returned the book to the shelf. The world could go on the same for years, and then everything changed all at once. A pattern repeated, over and again, since before the first light illuminated the earth's long, cold beginning.

3

SENYA HAD nearly fallen asleep in her chair next to the fire by the time the second knock came to her door. Startled fully awake, she rose. It wasn't likely to be Hockby or one of the fieldhands at this hour—they would've just waited until tomorrow—but it wasn't likely to be anybody else either. She stepped to look out the viewport.

Cevellica stood outside the lamplights' reach, just like the night before. A pillar of embodied mist in the dim.

"I asked you not to come back," Senya called. "I thought that part was clear."

Cevellica said nothing. She held up an intricate brass plate dangling from a small stout ring. A circular band pivoted around a central pin, lined with markings and measurements that aligned at points to delicate engravings on the face underneath.

Raedwin's star taker.

Senya immediately recognized the device, one of her brother's most cherished belongings when they were young. He'd bought it from a strange withered old woman at a market stall in Corregidon—a transaction that had taken every last coin he'd been able to muster at the time.

Cevellica gave a firm nod. "You know what this is," she said. "That much is clear from your eyes…"

Raedwin had claimed the device had been made by ship captains of Old Kortuga. They would use them to find their way at sea, he'd said, long before the Kalldonians had forced their empire on all the known world. Senya was never quite sure she believed that story.

"I have brought it to show our connection," Cevellica added. "We felt some sign would be appropriate, to ease your mind. We are colleagues, of a sort, your brother and I."

"People are talking. They don't much like night visitors around here."

"I am sorry. This is important."

"To you? Or to me?"

"To Raedwin." The visitor opened her mouth as if to add something else but instead drew in a sharp breath, as if stung.

Thin and awkward in her heavy gray cloak, Cevellica appeared to be both young and old in the lamplight, as if separate from time itself. She was tall and quite beautiful, if a little ominous. Her face twitched slightly as she waited, a pleading glint to her eye. She seemed to be offering her best effort at a benign smile.

Senya sighed. "You're not going away, are you?"

Cevellica hesitated and then gave a tentative shake of her head.

"He really sent you?"

"We have journeyed quite far to find you," she said slowly.

"I'm sorry... who is *we*?"

"Yes. I apologize. We are a group of seekers... a gathering of like minds in Kalldonia who question doctrine... patterns of rigid rules."

"Kalldonia? Hells. How did you find me all the way up here?"

"We have put forth... considerable effort. You have not been easy."

Senya almost laughed at this. She had never been easy, that much was true. Neither had Raedwin. Two sides of a dirty, misused coin. "All right," she said. Reluctantly, she invited the woman inside. Whatever this was all about, there was no use in trying to sort it out through a narrow viewport night after night, inviting plenty more suspicion.

Cevellica handed Raedwin's star taker to Senya as she stepped into the room. "I will attempt to remain direct," she said. "And not waste your time any more than necessary."

Senya set the star taker on the table and went to the fire. Lifting her iron poker, she nudged logs together to further brighten the flame. She stood back.

"I have known your brother for quite some time," Cevellica said. "And we have worked together for years. We are almost like family." That last word caught in her throat as if she had not wished it to emerge. Her hand flew up awkwardly and tugged at the edge of her earlobe and then at the fabric of her hood. "I am sorry. Family is not the appropriate word... You are his twin sister. I am nothing by comparison."

"No, it's fine," Senya said. "Here, come and have a seat by the fire." She gestured to an empty ladderbacked chair.

Cevellica suddenly turned away with a start. Instead of taking a step toward the hearth, she slid her feet awkwardly sideways, keeping her eyes on the floor. She moved to settle on a bench next to the table. Facing away from the flames, she struggled to address Senya while avoiding the fire.

"As you know, Raedwin journeyed far to the south several years ago," she began. "We heard of him long before he knew of us, and we extended certain invitations. After a time, he came at last to find us. And as I said, we shared beliefs that no arbitrary rules should hold bearing over the truth of our existence. Your brother seeks these same things as well. He searches for truths, even now. A thirsty mind, not easily quenched. We found him to be a kindred spirit. Probing and learning, pushing to discover." Her gaze fell to the floor as her hand idly caressed the worn edge of the table in a way that was strangely sensual.

"Crassica is the headmost among us," she said at last. "And she became very close to your brother indeed."

The visitor glanced at Senya and tried to smile again, but her bared teeth shone like a snarl in the firelight. She didn't openly show any weapons, but Senya held the iron poker just in case. She did not sit down.

"But now..." Cevellica shook her head as her voice trailed off. "It is an unpleasantness I bring, and for that I am sorry. Your brother asks many deep questions, over and again, and he seeks until he finds answers. Wanders until truths become clear."

Wanders until truths become clear. That did sound exactly like her brother.

"He tests, but reality itself proved too limiting. And so he has gone inside himself. To study and see. He has..." Cevellica held her feline eyes on Senya, glittering blue in the dim light. "He has stepped through a passage into the Crosslands between living and dead."

"He did *what!*?"

"Like a trance, in a way. Or like sleep. A living dream, maybe. He has retreated inside himself and gone into the Crosslands. He is locked away.

Lost. He is held there, immovable. Not awake, but not asleep. Not much alive, but not dead. Unable, or unwilling, to return."

Senya shook her head. "The Crosslands," she repeated flatly. The passing world. A place souls traversed in one of two ways, depending upon one's worth among the living. Their mother used to warn them at bedtime not to be enticed by gentle invitations brought by creatures of that place, mostly to keep Senya honest and to keep Raedwin from wandering off in the night.

Senya straightened and pinned her eyes on the visitor. "Just because my brother stumbled and fell while doing something stupid doesn't mean I'm about to follow you all the way down to Kalldonia to help him. You should know that up front."

"No, sorry... not Kalldonia..." Cevellica said earnestly. "You must join us nearby, in Pentmore. We have come to you for this. We have journeyed far, and we are already here. Come to the city and meet with us, the others I am with. You would simply need to lie down and sleep. We will help you enter the Crosslands and guide you. Help to locate Raedwin. Guide him away from disaster. Soon they will have him..."

"They?"

Cevellica remained quiet for a long time. Senya wasn't sure the woman had heard, but then she drew in a sharp breath and shivered. "Darkness," she said in a wavering voice. "Confusion. It is difficult to explain. But you must convince him to come home before it is too late."

Convince him to come home. As if Senya had ever been able to convince her brother of anything.

"Your body will not need to go anywhere. Only your mind. Your spirit. We could do it right here, if you would like, but I am not sure those around you would much appreciate our presence."

Senya had to admit that last part was plenty true.

Cevellica sat upright and twisted her shoulders to better face Senya. "Your brother has delusions beyond what I have told. He has created a whole series of false images inside the Crosslands. He has created false friends, and a woman to love. A tower of great wonder, with workers to help him make and build. But none of it is real. All is feigned. An act, like a child's make-believe. And soon this misadventure will meet a level of failure and cataclysm for which our Raedwin is not yet prepared."

Senya stared into the flames. "You are all children," she said in a low voice. "Playing with toys that are too big for you."

Cevellica smiled. "Perhaps that is true, yes. Toys too big for us, yet the truth remains…"

"The truth?"

Cevellica paused, her mouth open.

"The truth is I don't know if any of what you say is real," Senya said. "I don't know who you are. You say forces are aligned against my brother, that he's done these things, and somebody is out to get him, but any *they* you speak of is no different from *you*, as far as I can tell."

"I speak… truth…"

"Maybe you do, maybe you don't."

"He needs your help…"

"And it would be really great if I could give that help, wouldn't it? That'd be tidy for everybody. And I'd love nothing more than to be able to go and pull my brother out of the Crosslands or wherever he is and bring him home and have everything be okay, finally and maybe forever, or whatever it is that he wants. But I know him. Even if I could find him in the Crosslands and get him to come out of whatever trance he's fallen into, this wouldn't be the end. Not for him, and not for me. There will always be something else. Something he finds a little too exciting around whatever next corner he comes to. Something new and shiny and full of intrigue. Raedwin will never be done with any of this."

But as Senya spoke, she knew she couldn't completely ignore him. Raedwin was still her brother. Still her one and only, no matter how much distance and past missteps lay between them. She would never be able to just let him go. She already knew that much. And as strange as all this came across, as odd and awkward as the invitation had been, Senya knew there was at least some truth to all this—despite her suspicion that it wasn't exactly the same truth Cevellica was selling.

The truth, the real truth, was that Senya needed time to think. She picked up the star taker and offered it back to her guest.

"No." Cevellica waved it away. "You must keep it. At least consider what I have said."

Senya bit at her cheek. "Of course."

"Please," Cevellica said, worry spreading over her porcelain face. "He is your brother."

A sharp slice of anger rose in Senya. "Yes, I'm aware he's my brother." A brittleness came into her voice. "But I am curious… did he ever tell you what happened right before he left me behind, ten years ago now? If you are so close in your group down wherever it is you all live, it seems that little detail might've come up. Did he say what happened between us?"

Cevellica sat in silence. She gave no answer.

Senya stepped toward the fire. "Years ago, I had a love, a good man," she said. "Sidmor was his name. He didn't care what I was or where I'd come from—he was unquestionably good. Until my brother—my beloved brother—decided to take him under his wing and train him in a little bit of alchemy. Teach him dazzling feats of market-stall sorcery. Plenty of easy coin to be made on the side, he said. Sidmor was ready, he said. Tried to convince me his few months of fumbling experiments or whatever they'd done together had actually amounted to anything worthwhile."

Senya let out a long, uneasy sigh. "But Sidmor was not ready," she said. "Not at all. And the explosion they conjured took his jaw off and opened the left side of his skull. Did Raedwin tell you all about that? Did he ever mention the name Sidmor to you? To anybody? Did he tell you that was the last time I saw him? Ten years ago, up in Posselhead. The day my love died."

Cevellica made no move to answer.

"His blood left such a strange burnt pattern on the worktable that I'd almost mistaken it for some new fabric they'd created together. Some invented textile. But that's not what it was, was it? Did he tell you any of that?"

Cevellica shifted in her seat, struggling to avert her eyes from the fire and look directly at Senya, her face placid. She said nothing.

Senya's voice lowered to almost a whisper. "That's what Raedwin's experiments come to. Things like this. All of it. They come to pain and anguish and ruined lives." She turned back to the fire. "So I'm sorry if I don't jump right up to help you. I need some time to think. My brother is probably beyond my help anyway. He always has been. I don't have anywhere to bring him back to, and I have nothing to entice him with. This isn't his home. It's barely mine. So I'm afraid you'll have to sort out how to free him on your own."

The woman considered this for a long, silent moment. "Okay," she said at last, resigned to Senya's resistance. Clearly hoping for a change of mind, she described the place in Pentmore where they would wait, in a particular warehouse down along the water. "We will remain there for many days," she said. "We will wait for you. As will he. But please consider this… time does pass, and his trouble grows."

Senya gave no answer. Abruptly Cevellica stood, nodded awkwardly, and walked out the door, leaving in much the same way she'd arrived—without preamble or warning. In the moment it took Senya to follow and wish her a safe journey, the woman was gone. The misty night pulled in close and dense, reclaiming her as one of its own.

Senya closed and locked the door. She returned to the hearth. The brass star taker gleamed on the table next to her, pulsing in the reflected firelight.

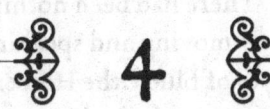

4

SENYA WAS summoned to appear before the Clanmother just after dawn. The previous evening's guard had reported more gray figures in the day's waning light, and a nervous anxiety surged through the settlement. She weaved her way down the rocky slope into the heart of its central cluster of buildings. A fine rain fell. Hacking their meager colony out of the wilderness east of Pentmore generations before, the first men and women had fortified the place with layered walls of sturdy wooden poles carved to blade-sharp points at every tip. Torches along its toothy rim flourished orange light against the gray morning.

Senya arrived early. No need to prolong the inevitable. The edges of the Great Hall's thatch roof dripped quietly while a pair of torches blazed at either side of heavy wooden doors. She entered.

The room was spacious. Hewn rafters braced the high ceiling, pulsing with emberglow from a central firepit. An old woman crouched in a shadowy corner, chewing quietly on a root. At intervals she spat into a frothy bowl. Noticing Senya, an apprentice grabbed a long pole candle and went about lighting several oil lamps. He placed three fresh logs onto the embers. Smoke pots smoldered with flower of wakefulness, pushing a sweet and pungent haze through the room.

Two men and a woman burst through the heavy doors. The Clan-mother, followed by the Horsemaster and Guardmaster. They spread and joined Senya around the central fire. Although not an old woman, the Clanmother's grim face showed many years of hard struggle. A long pair of scars ran from inside her hairline across her forehead and down her cheekbone.

"Thank you for coming," the Clanmother greeted. She asked Senya to repeat everything she'd seen of her visitor once again, pushing for a detailed description. Her voice was strangely detached, as if pondering something else entirely. "Did she shift with the lamplight? Or did her clothing contain tricks of light and shadow?"

Senya shook her head. There had been nothing like that. Nothing but Cevellica's awkward way of moving and speaking.

"A pale woman with eyes of blue," the Horsemaster muttered, almost a growl. "Ghostlike movements, cloaked in gray." His stiff beard barely moved as he spoke.

"Harbinger of the Underworld," the Guardmaster added in a low voice. He closed his eyes and whispered words of warding.

"She was no ghost," Senya assured. That much was clear. But she knew where this was heading.

"The Hallonath is full of many dark and evil things," the Horsemaster added. "Some as subtle as the mists themselves."

"She didn't come out of the Hallonath," Senya argued. "She came from Pentmore. Her name is Cevellica."

The Clanmother held out both palms in a sign of peace, as if pushing some invisible force away. "We cannot sustain this," she said directly to Senya in a measured, concerned voice, bringing the discussion to a close. "A siege has not yet been laid, and my people are ready to split apart."

My people. Placing Senya firmly on the outside.

The Clanmother's face was kind but impassive. "This fear... is a disease."

Senya nodded stiffly and glanced between them. Faces unmoving in the flickering firelight. Her own worth quickly fading, right along with her abilities.

"Since when," she said at last, "do you let fear run things inside these walls?"

A long silence fell. Flames crackled in the firepit. "Since always," the Clanmother said in a steady voice. "Look around you. Fear is what built this place."

As afternoon fell into evening, Senya went to stand at the edge of the headlands where the rocky land met the broad reach of the lake. Waves marched in from the moody hills on the far shore, creasing the uncertain water in wide shifting bands. Rain threatened.

As kids, Senya and her brother had endured suspicion and talk whenever they remained too long in any one place. Their mother had done her best to protect her strange orange-eyed twins who did not seem to age, moving from town to town, from village to city to remote waypoints and outposts. The road became their home as much as anywhere else. Quickly learning to share thoughts and emotions with one another, speaking without opening their mouths, Senya and Raedwin could sense the whereabouts of one another from rather great distances. They would toss silent words back and forth like colored balls in play until both laughed aloud, making their poor, protective mother ever more nervous.

But all of that was ages ago. After their mother died, Senya had tried to settle down on a quiet little farm tucked against the sea near Donasberth and simply live her life in peace. She'd rather see than be seen, rather listen than speak. She loved the idea of an untroubled evening by a roaring hearth far more than going out with Raedwin to dig up some lost tomb, looking for an artifact that explained the end of the world.

But she hadn't lasted at that farm, nor at the one after. Or the three after that.

She wished their father were here. He would understand the wider picture of what was happening. He would know what course to take, or at least how to weigh the potentials for each direction available. But her father was far to the north, having long ago fled with the rest of the Brohndai to Faeroen Island, distant and hidden in the icy North Sea—a flight she had never been interested in following.

She found a dry place to sit among the rocks near several small pools. Her reach was much stronger the more she could immerse herself in water. Back when she could connect with Raedwin, the seashore had been where she would see him best. Hear him and join with him. Laugh alongside him.

Slipping her toes in the icy water, she sat back and let her feet settle among soft weeds, taking time to completely calm herself, to root her center in earth and sky while remaining deeply bonded to the water.

She closed her eyes and reached. Working to calm and steady her breathing, she watched and listened, stretching her perception. It had been so long since she'd tried to find him. Low waves ebbed and flowed. Water moved against her skin.

Still nothing, the same as last time. Nothing but clouds and confusion.

When the vision finally came, it hit like a surging flood in a flash, powered by something well beyond her, beyond anything she'd ever experienced before. It pulled her across the green valleys of Brinsfallon, over the mountains to the hideous broken bones of Dunnenwyr, and then farther south, across the Straits, all the way to Kalldonia.

She barely breathed. The vision came from outside, *toward* her rather than *from* her, as if pushed by some unseen force. Not the way her connections with Raedwin had ever worked before. Dry golden lands unfolded to a forest bracing distant mountains. A ruined ancient keep stood atop a bluff. Six crumbling towers. The seventh, a shining spire of iron and glass.

And then she saw him.

Raedwin was there. Obscured. Eyes blinded. A powerful hidden cage hung over the towers, over the fortress, over the land—a cage that held her brother in and kept Senya out. Quietly he moved underground through shadowy tunnels, unseen.

Trying to hide.

A woman joined him at the edge of a crumbling wall. She was pale and hairless, with smooth skin and piercing blue eyes, similar to Cevellica. Yet this woman was clearly different. Older. A sadness poured from her, a loss as deep as any Senya had ever known. She reached and took Raedwin's hand as they stood together at the edge of a great abyss.

Another presence was there, a third, hidden somewhere deeper—a spirit with great power, holding the Sight far keener than Senya's own. Gazing out from beneath the towers, from inside the bluff itself, seeking something, sweeping northward to Cairn and then Corregidon, shifting focus, ever searching, desiring. The gaze held, almost as if speaking to someone or something there, and then it beckoned eastward, toward Pentmore.

Toward Senya.

She broke the vision with a start and pulled her feet from the water. The glimmer of Raedwin faded, taking with it the flickering hope and familiar color of her brother's lifelong energy.

That presence, that gaze. *What was that?* Had it tried to show her something? Was it Raedwin, reaching toward her himself? No, this was something else, something new. Something dangerous.

Senya's heart pounded. Right or wrong, truth or lies, something was happening. Maybe Raedwin really was trapped in the Crosslands between the living and the dead. Maybe he had somehow been able to reach out through shared memories and demand that she listen.

Her breathing came quick and labored. Sweat beaded on her brow, chilling with the cool lake breeze. She'd never had some other vision reach toward her, not like that. She shivered and hugged her knees to her chest. The sun had long since set. Darkness fell around her.

That was him she'd seen. It was clearly him. Unchanged and alive, but something was wrong. Something was off. Raedwin was trying to hide, held in place, moving like a rat in a cage, detained either by his own will, his own choices, or something else. Someone else. Whatever it was, however he had positioned himself, one definite thing was clear—her brother had indeed gotten into a peculiar and powerful kind of trouble. Whatever was happening, Raedwin had not been hidden from her Sight by any choice of his own.

It took two days for the full Council to gather in the Great Hall. Low light from seven lamps danced across the rough wooden beams. Muted discussion floated throughout, punctuated with rushed voices and harried gestures. Opinions flashed and countered. The watch had reported five different figures at separate intervals over the last three days. Several had sworn to it. The loose coalition of order inside the settlement's walls had already begun to slip and unravel.

Senya sat in the shadows to one side. Folded into her long riding cloak with its hood pulled low, she listened, churning with her own silent thoughts.

"This… visitor," the Clanmother broke in. She held her gaze on Senya for a long minute as if waiting for her to form the next words herself. "You must, of course, realize what she was…"

Senya said nothing. She knew when to keep quiet.

"A Vallahnir," the Guardmaster cried. "Of the Crosslands!"

A hiss ran through the room, followed by murmuring rustle. *"Dark powers,"* they whispered under their breath. "What has she brought among us?" someone shouted.

Born of the very core of the Everliving Tree—the Great Unseen Oak—in all the legends and ancient tales, Vallahnir were said to be evident only at the very end of one's life, beautiful pale women come to usher the dying through the Crosslands to the Everlife or the Underworld. Ghostly heralds of death itself.

Senya sighed. "Now we're talking night fables and children's stories?"

The Clanmother stiffened. "Telling a story to children does not render it false."

Senya shook her head, almost unable to continue. She understood Vallahnir as well as anybody outside Faeroen Island, except for maybe her brother. Wrapped in gray mist, Vallahnir were elemental, not physical. They were not of the living world and did not knock on people's doors to sit by the fire and have a chat.

"She was flesh and bone," Senya said. "I could touch her well enough."

But had she touched her? Had she actually reached out and brought skin to skin, or had she only held Raedwin's star taker? Cevellica was clearly strange enough and rather ethereal, but a *Vallahnir*? There was no way. Senya would've known. She would've sensed it. If this were true, she would've seen.

"She told me my brother was in trouble," Senya offered. "Like I already told you. That's all."

But if Raedwin had indeed dabbled in places beyond the boundaries of the living and truly become lost inside the Crosslands, then what better messenger for such a thing than an embodiment of the Crosslands itself?

"They want me to come to Pentmore," she added. "To help bring him back."

"They?" the Guardmaster said sharply.

The room erupted into several speaking at once, each demanding to be heard. Senya said nothing.

Was she really so blind? Had she really lost so much of her perception? Her skills? Cevellica had been right there, right at her table. She was no ghost. Vallahnir did not take physical form and shape. And what would a Vallahnir have to do with Raedwin anyway? Or with her?

The discussions continued on without her. "Senya is just one young woman," someone said. "It's those ashcloaks we should fear. How many might there be?"

"She's in league with Dark Arts," said a second.

"Or a victim of them."

"She cannot stay here."

"We cannot send her away with nothing!"

"But we cannot allow her to remain, can we?"

The voices all blended and blurred together. A general din erupting and then subsiding. A vote was called and cast. Soon the Clanmother raised her hand.

"The decision is made," she announced. "But we must discuss the means."

"This is no small thing," Hockby said, his voice exhausted from pleas of clemency. "We may be sending Senya to her death."

"Death may come to all of us if she stays," a hard-faced woman barked to his left.

"Let us not roll back into argument," the Clanmother said. "The Elders have spoken. The vote has been cast." She turned to face Senya in the corner. "I am sorry, but you must leave us. Go where you feel is best. We cannot harbor you any longer."

Harbor you. As if her worth here was nothing more than the space she'd occupied for the past three years. As if all the work she'd done for these people never existed.

"Okay," she said. There was little else to add. Fear was often the most effective weapon. "Can I at least get passage to Pentmore?"

The city could be made in one long day's ride, but on foot the journey was dangerous. Hills along the edge of the Hallonath offered plenty of bluffs and box canyons to shelter wandering rejects from the civilized world, and vacant stretches lay afflicted with brigands and highwaymen, roaming tempests of death between fortified settlements. This was a land in which to see and not be seen.

"Of course," the Clanmother said. "We can at least furnish passage. You know that."

Senya looked around the room at the lamplit faces. Eyes averted her gaze. Ashamed glances shifted down and away. "All I know is that the memory of friendship around here isn't what it used to be."

She had been an asset for these people, despite whether they dared admit it. But in the end, it was their sense of safety—barely the illusion of safety in these lingering dark days—that held this group together. If anything threatened that illusion, nothing else would matter.

Finally, she nodded. "Tomorrow morning, then?"

The Clanmother drew in a long, reluctant breath. "Yes," she said with a sadness in her voice. "In the morning."

The room fell quiet among the hiss and pop of sputtering oil lamps. With no business left for her and nothing more to say to any of them, Senya rose and left the Hall without another word.

5

SENYA DISEMBARKED and thanked the cart driver just outside Pentmore's walls. She took a moment to steel herself. A stark grove of limbless poles lined the road, with misshapen dark heads decaying atop a scattered few— remains of criminals awaiting silent judgment from the bleeding flagstone sky. Soft rain fell. Rumbling hooves battered the bare causeway from the south. Senya turned to watch a loose band of armored horsemen pass with their tall pikes aloft, thin unwashed banners undulating in the gray breeze. They dragged along two broken men by the wrists. One prisoner stumbled in a bruised struggle to keep pace, while the second had fallen and clearly died some miles before, if the state of the body was any guide. The bloodied and beaten corpse slid along the stone, an unrecognizable aftermath of flesh and shattered bone. They disappeared through the gates.

For most of her life, Senya had preferred to avoid cities like Pentmore. She was a slight woman, her deep brown skin clearly different enough to raise more than a few suspicious glances whenever she was out among strangers. She wore her black hair chopped short, her cloaks long and deep cowled to hide her flame-colored eyes, trying to hold the outside world at bay. She preferred remote places over cities and towns, places where she could be alone with the animals. Sheep and pigs were better than most people anyway.

Pulling her haversack close, she felt Raedwin's star taker against her side. The weight of it. The weight of him. She'd examined it more than once during the ride. Ancient Cornumbrian script showed the names of several stars on a pivoting framework plate. A straight arm pinned at the center could spin full circle, pointing to a ring of numbers along the outside edge. Trying to use the thing for navigation was pointless, of course. She'd never had much desire to learn any of its methods, so the device was unlikely to help her track down her brother. Not in this world, nor in the Crosslands beyond it.

This whole thing would be a lot easier if she could connect—reach over whatever distance lay between them and sense Raedwin's thoughts. Understand his state of mind. Maybe then she'd be able to better understand what was going on. But these past years had seemed like her brother was intentionally hiding—from the world, from her, and maybe even from himself. Like he wanted to be lost on purpose. Avoiding her help. Or maybe her judgment. She thought she knew him, but sometimes she wasn't so sure. She didn't want his absence to sting, but she couldn't quite help it. Despite all the time and distance between them, it still did.

Why did Raedwin have to drag her into these things? At some point he'd have to figure out how to find his own way out of trouble. They'd grown far too old for games like this.

Tightening her cloak, she strode through the gates. A maze of stone huts and tall wooden buildings lined the cramped cobblestone streets. Scattered residents scurried in the rainfall. A man stood atop a rocky outcrop, playing a mournful tune on a weathered instrument of goatskin bags and hollow tubes. Senya made her way toward the lake.

Cevellica had directed her to a row of aging merchant buildings down near the water, opposite a certain rowdy alehouse. A side alley offered a more direct path. Senya descended past a trio of children grappling with one another. Two of them plunged, slipping in the mud and throwing punches and shouting. The pair leapt up to attack the third, and all three sprinted away.

"Hey, there," came a hoarse voice behind her. Senya turned to find a ragged man sprawled in the trash-strewn corner of a doorway. He was wild and bearded, with steel-gray hair choking away most of his face. "I'll give ya seven Brins bronze for a touch!" The man sat up. Eyes peered like black shinebeetles in a garden of wire brush. "Just a touch. Skin t' skin."

"Not for sale," Senya replied.

"Ach!" the man called. "Nine, then!" He struggled to get up. Senya continued down the alley.

"Ten!" the man shouted behind her. "I'll go as high as 'leven. Haven't 'ad a slice in moons!"

Senya walked on. The man called after her. He stumbled out of the doorway and spilled his useless bulk into the wet alley. Senya came to a corner and descended three stone steps to a small alehouse partly sculpted into the side of the rock hill. A dripping wooden sign pronounced The Jilted Bear in carved letters. Shouting erupted from inside. Then laughter. The sharp sound of tankard against tankard mingled with the sour stench of pipeweed. Rainwater poured from the drain edge of the wooden awning. She faced a heavy oaken door opposite the alehouse.

This was it. Time to believe or to forget the whole thing. There'd be no half measures once inside this door. Senya struggled to find her center, concentrating on Raedwin.

They'd been so close. Her brother had clung to their bond as if it offered some sort of open promise for eventual redemption. She could never allow him to face alone whatever trouble was waiting for him, hidden somewhere out of sight. What if Cevellica had told the truth, and there really was no other way for him to get out of the Crosslands? No other way for him to come home, wherever home may be? What if there was something coming after him? What if she lost him completely? She could disagree with the paths her brother took all she wanted, but that did nothing to remove their consequences.

At least this way she would know.

She knocked sharply on the door. Pulling a short razor-edged knife from the folds of her cloak, she spun the tip inward and gripped it hidden in the cuff of her sleeve, the blade cold against her wrist. Ready.

A heavy iron lock slid open, and the door swung away into shadow. A broad-shouldered man appeared, his head a webwork of scars. A black patch covered his right eye. He had no ear on that same side. The man smiled, showing three missing teeth.

"You must be Senya," he said in a raw voice, but gently enough. "Welcome." He stepped aside and gestured for her to enter.

Six ironbound timber columns braced the towering ceiling. A few high windows allowed slanted slivers of light into the dim and dusty space. Iron braziers spread an uneven glow over crates and piles of canvas sacks, clay vessels, wrapped bundles, and two long rows of raw-cut lumber. The scar-faced man led her to a low-ceilinged room at the rear. He went about lighting a set of brass oil lamps mounted on the wall. A round red carpet lay in the middle, with a series of soft bearskin chairs ringing a low table in the center.

"Have a seat," the man directed. "I need to gather the others." And with that, he disappeared.

Senya's feet moved as if on their own, her mind shifting to a floating awareness, seeing but not fully seeing, her mind awake to details. A strange scent drifted to her, something like burned fats and lavender. Woodsmoke and metal. She noticed several unlit candles forming a wide ring at the rim of the table in the middle of the room. The ceiling creaked overhead with footsteps from more than one direction. Muffled voices followed.

Finally, she sat.

Soon a tall man strode into the room, wearing a long wine-colored robe in the style of the ancient Kalldonians. His head was shaved bare save for a close-cropped strip running front to back over the top, dyed a deep red. A black tattoo of some arcane symbol graced his left eye—the markings and bearings of a sorcerer.

"Welcome, my dear Senya," he greeted. "I am Korsta. We're very glad you have come."

"No wonder I had so much trouble with my lambs," she said, holding her voice steady.

He stopped. "I'm sorry?" Surprise lit his face. "Your lambs?"

"I don't much care for necromancy," she said. "Whatever you did out there. Conjuring up your Dark Arts. So many more of my ewes died than usual, and too many lambs were stillborn. None of it natural."

He moved to sit next to her, offering a mug of warm brew. "I understand how you might think necromancy could be involved in all of that, but any deaths among your sheep would have nothing to do with us. What you describe is not how we do business."

Senya took the mug and held it in her free hand. She did not drink. Instead, she reached forward and set it at the edge of the low table, nudging one of the candles out of alignment.

"I do understand your feeling though," Korsta said. "And I am sorry for your loss. Such things can be most frustrating." He smiled, reaching to correct the misaligned candle. "Nevertheless, death is the most natural event of all."

Cevellica stepped into the room. Her stilted movements were somewhat more fluid and assured than they'd been back at Senya's house. There was nothing airy or intangible about her. No tricks of light and shadow. She was just a little awkward. A second woman followed, remarkably similar, possibly a younger sister.

Ordinarily, all that human eyes could perceive of Vallahnir were glimpses of simple shadows, vague movements of pale form. Some would call them ghosts. Apparitions. Sunlight usually disrupted the illusion, so Vallahnir would be nearly invisible during the day. So said the tales. If these two were indeed Vallahnir, they'd undergone some serious transformation.

"Thank you for coming," Cevellica said as she took a seat facing Senya. The other sat beside her. "It is a true and vital thing for you to be here."

All four sat in silence for a moment. Senya wondered if there was something she was supposed to do or say. She still held the hidden knife, suddenly uncertain how exactly she would use it if it came to that.

"Why did you terrorize my home?" she said abruptly, without exactly meaning to do so. "There was no need to cause all that mayhem. Those people are innocent."

Cevellica opened her mouth, searching for something to say.

Senya kept her eyes steady. "People saw," she said. "*Pale women in gray cloaks, floating among the night mists*. All hovering around my door. How did you expect that to go over?"

Korsta glanced back and forth between them. "I'm sorry," he said slowly. "I think we're starting with the wrong tone here..."

"It doesn't take long for people to turn on the one they think brought wraiths out of the Crosslands to haunt them."

"I would like to apologize," Korsta said, an easy smoothness coming into his voice. "That would be difficult for anyone to go through. But I can assure you that our actions have been misinterpreted. These sightings must have been tricks of the eye. Cevellica came to see you alone. There were no others. And she returned here immediately after. So what you're describing could not have been us."

A pair of grim-faced men strode into the room. Heads and faces shaved clean, they both wore hardened leather breastplates over tattered wool tunics. Mercenaries, if Senya had ever seen any. Joyless and quiet, they watched her with bored indifference as they sat.

Cevellica shifted her rigid body in the chair. She glanced at each of the men before training her gaze on Senya. "The Great Knowing," she said, "always seeks balance. Opposes heat with cold, hard with soft, all in the balance of opposites. Water has fire, life has death, and the men of the black robes... have us."

Senya flinched. *Men of the black robes*. That would be the Brohndai, her father among them. Dark cloaks and black faces, all standing in judgment of him, on a bare windswept hill in the Baelhoarg all those years ago.

"So you..." she said slowly, hesitant, "are truly a Vallahnir..." Senya wasn't sure if she'd meant it as a question or a statement, but it came out as a weakened version of both.

"Was," Cevellica corrected.

"And now?"

"Now..." She smiled and held her arms in a graceful gesture of openness, presenting herself to the room as some kind of evidence. "I am what you see."

Brohndai and Vallahnir were on opposing sides of the Veil, holding all things in balance, but how would the Order of the Way come into play in all this? Real Vallahnir did not walk among the living. That wasn't how it worked. These must be something else. Senya wished her father were with her. He would know.

"We are each expressions of the Knowing," Cevellica continued. "You and me alike. All of us. We are not as different from one another as you may think..."

"Please understand," Korsta broke in, pouring gentleness into his voice. "We mean no harm. No harm to you, your sheep, or your people." His eyes fell to the floor, and his voice grew laden with sadness. "But if they were so quick to turn on you, were they really your people to begin with?"

"Don't," she said sharply. "I'm not in the mood. Those people meant what they did to me, and some backwoods sorcerer does not get to decide otherwise."

Korsta leaned forward and placed his fingertips together, as if pondering. The low light glinted over his bare head. "We are here to help you," he said to Senya. "I do hope you understand that."

Her eyes narrowed. "But I'm not the one who needs help," she said. "Raedwin is."

Korsta laughed and sat back. "Yes, of course. I simply mean that we will guide you on your journey to him. Much like you, all of us wish to bring your brother back to us."

Senya drew an uneasy breath and let it out slowly. "May I ask where he is?"

Korsta's face darkened as he shook his head. "Sadly, your brother is far from here. He is in Kalldonia. But distances do not matter in the Crosslands. You will see him soon."

But she had already seen him, in her vision. The distance hadn't mattered then either—so at least that much rang true.

"As I understand it, Cevellica has explained the situation, and you understand why you are here. But do you have any questions?"

She had plenty of questions, but she already knew some of the answers. Raedwin in trouble again, the same old story. But in trouble from whom? And from what angle? Sorcerers and Vallahnir. Necromancy at a whole new level. She glanced around the room. Raedwin used to scold her for being too much like water—too fluid, too easily directed by others. He had accused her time and again of too easily being swayed by sweet voices, quick smiles, and kind eyes. Settling too easily, and too permanently. For him, he needed to discover for himself. To explore. He wanted to understand. He needed the assurance of fresh evidence. He wanted proof.

And where has that gotten you? she asked in silence.

Senya did her best to believe they indeed wanted to help. Raedwin did have a way of making fast and strong friends wherever he went. Maybe everything was fine. Any time Senya was among strangers, her nerves were set alight, no matter how good and right their intentions. So maybe this all remained okay. Maybe they did speak the truth and all she had to do was listen. Everything so far had mostly tracked with what she knew of her brother, so she would at least remain open to the idea. In all the scrapes he had ever gotten himself into, a way out always presented itself, eventually.

"Okay," she said. "How is this supposed to work?"

Korsta rose and stepped to a narrow shelf along the wall. He retrieved a lightstick and lit its tip from one of the wall lamps. "Your brother depends upon you." Taking the flame to each of the candles on the table, he methodically lit the full circle. "But coming here is only the first step."

He blew out the lightstick and placed it back on the narrow shelf. "We have methods," he said as he returned to his seat. "Ways of stepping from this world into the other. Much like necromancers, but not nearly so crudely."

Like necromancers. A shiver lit down Senya's spine. Raedwin had truly gone to the far edge this time, hadn't he?

"We have prepared a brew for you." He gestured to the steaming mug at the edge of the table. "First, you drink, and then you sleep. The journey you make from here will be through the Crosslands. You will sleep, but it will not be a normal sleep. Your dreams will lead you to wild places, and you must be careful. Such a journey will be dangerous. Easy to become lost along twisted paths in the Crosslands, like our beloved Raedwin has. You will need to remember and stay focused on him, and him alone."

At this Korsta paused. At length he frowned, shaking his head. "Your brother has pushed his practice to an extreme, and time is running out. If he remains much longer, his body will truly die, and there will be no path left for his return."

Pushed to an extreme. Again, that was the brother she knew.

"All of us begged Raedwin not to do what he was trying to do," Korsta assured her. "We tried to convince him his actions were too dangerous, that he could easily become lost."

"And what about your leader?" Senya asked. "This... Crassica?"

Korsta gave a sharp glance at Cevellica before bringing his attention back to Senya with a gentle smile, creasing the black tattoo around his eye. "Sadly, even Crassica herself cannot reach him. Perhaps there was a time in which she could, but now Raedwin's danger has grown too grave. He needs his sister to remind him of reason and to guide him back. Simple as that."

Senya nodded with a sardonic smile. Her brother never engaged in simple things, and there was likely more to this story than what either this conjureman or Cevellica had said so far, whether they were aware of it or not. More remained hidden. Whatever role this Crassica played. Nothing true ever fit a short explanation, especially where Raedwin was concerned.

She reached out and took the mug in her free hand, holding it, studying its weight. "I should warn you," she said, her eyes on Cevellica and Korsta both. "If we do this, I'm likely to see and learn more than you think I will, for better or worse—for any of us."

All things are possible," Korsta acknowledged.

"This may open doors that none of us are ready for."

One of the men across the table let out a coarse laugh. Korsta gave him a sharp glance. "Enough," he said, his voice freighted with authority. He held silent for a long moment. "Nothing in this world is assured," he said at length to Senya. "We of course understand that. But if we align our intentions on the health and safety of Raedwin, we cannot go wrong. None of us."

Senya smiled thinly. "Sure we can," she said quietly.

Raising the mug in a mock toast to the sorcerer and the Vallahnir, Senya took a small swallow of the brew. The liquid was sweet and pungent. She drank more and tried to listen as Korsta explained their objective to help guide her, but his words started to shift and dance. She lost focus. Her eyes grew heavy.

"Soon," he said, his voice growing distant. "You will sleep. Don't be afraid."

"You are coming with," she managed through thick and soupy lips, her voice sounding heavy and slow, outside herself. "Yes?"

"It is like we said," Korsta assured. "We will guide you, but you must focus. Remember your brother. Focus on Raedwin."

Senya drifted. *Don't be afraid. It is like we said.*

But she was afraid. Already this was not exactly like they'd said, not at all what she'd expected. Would they still guide her? Maybe she had to focus better. Had to remember. She remained alone.

Focus.

The two mercenaries stood and stepped toward her. Their image blurred and shifted as they moved, their forms flickering with the lamplight. Her head fell sideways.

"There now," Korsta said. "That's okay. Let it flow." He shifted to Cevellica, his voice suddenly sharp, losing all of its gentle kindness.

"Now," he said. "The table."

Korsta shoved his hands under Senya's limp arms and lifted her roughly from the chair. The knife fell from her sleeved hand and clattered to the floor.

One of the men laughed at the blade as he scooped it up. "Girl came prepared," he growled. "Good for her!"

Together Korsta and Cevellica laid her in the center of the candlelit ring.

Senya tried to focus, tried to think of her brother while everything in her wanted to scream, wanted to struggle and kick. But her body was no longer under her command. So helpless. Lost already. Whatever was in the brew had been especially strong and worked very fast. Korsta stretched her flat.

Her eyes remained open. She could see, and she could feel, but she could not move. She watched the movements of the sorcerer as if she had separated from her body and left her flesh and bone behind. Cevellica and her pale-skinned partner stood by, expressionless and silent.

"Let yourself sleep," Korsta whispered. "Sleep now, and focus on finding your brother. A great journey lies ahead."

The room swam. Senya drifted in and out as Korsta and Cevellica together began to chant a series of guttural words not made for human ears. The sorcerer produced a small clay bowl from somewhere outside the lamplit circle and pulled a thin brush through inky liquid. He marked her forehead. Their chanting shifted into song as he drew symbols on her skin. Senya's mind wandered in and out of sleep as she tried to hold on, beckoned by distant dreams.

"Okay," Korsta said at last as Senya's eyes closed. "She's out. Let's get her tied and wrapped. And tell Karch to bring the cart around."

Wait. Tied and wrapped? And why would they need a cart?

And then everything changed.

At first, a series of strange visions led her through a rough valley with a low rock wall at the top of a long ridge. She crossed over the wall. Grass grew and the sun shone. Then Raedwin was there in the distance, moving through shadowed hills outside some citadel. Partly ruined, but populated. Vaguely familiar. He was clearly searching for something, oblivious to the man following.

Senya called out to him, tried to warn him, but her voice was blocked by hidden barriers. Raedwin remained closed off, like before. Contained. Her words were muffled and distorted. Silenced. And then he was gone.

She journeyed for many miles, calling out for her brother again, but no answer came. None had ever come. Years she had been calling. Maybe a lifetime. Many days passed as she walked. Maybe weeks, or months. Or perhaps only a few minutes. Time became a distant thing.

She went on. She crossed mountains and streams and forests, and she passed into another wide valley. But she never did see a tower, iron or glass or otherwise. She saw no other people. No Korsta, no Cevellica. There was no further sign of her brother, and no answer to her calls.

Fear dripped into her heart, quickening her steps. Fear and confusion, giving way to anger.

At last, a deepening night came that enveloped her beyond imagining. A night without stars, without words, without any sense of life at all. Lightning flashed. Still, she pushed on.

PART TWO

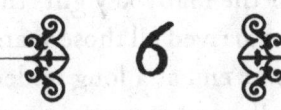

6

RAEDWIN STOOD at the great window atop the Sevenfold Keep's westernmost tower. Latticed panes cut his view of the Kalldonian countryside into fifty separate shapes, each lined with its own sliver of lead. Panning his spyscope to find a smooth space in the sturdy glass, he focused on the citadel far below. Workers hunched over the splayed parts of a disassembled machine like so many larvae attending to the corpse of some colossal iron insect. They struggled and shouted at one another. Pointed and argued. One shook his head and threw up his hands in resignation. Lowering the spyscope with a frown, Raedwin watched without the aid of telescopic glass. Sometimes it was better if the details remained beyond his sight.

He wore his thick black hair cropped short in the style of the old empire, framing his heavy black brows. To some, he seemed young, maybe no more than twenty, but in certain light, his youth disappeared entirely. Shadows revealed furrows and weathered creases along the corners of his penetrating orange eyes.

A sharp knock at the door. "Master Raedwin," a grizzled bald man announced with a bow as he entered. "Her High Honor is able to see you now."

Raedwin turned back to the window. "Can you send word down that they've got the spur wheel positioned wrong? They're making a mess of the whole thing out there."

"Of course." The man straightened. "Right away."

Raedwin set his spyscope gently on a small wooden table. He followed the man down the curving iron stairway that dominated the tower's open core. Crassica herself had designed and built the structure twenty years before, and there was nothing else quite like it in the known world. Rising from a foundation of stone into a sheer pillar of metal and glass, the tower stood on long elegant legs of treated iron, each bolstered with an internal buttress of crossed struts arching overhead. Its audacious engineering had immediately fascinated Raedwin from the first moment he'd laid eyes on it, and Crassica had quickly named the observatory at its peak as Raedwin's private workshop—one of the many key gifts that had helped convince him to stay when he'd first arrived all those years ago.

The staircase came to its end at a long underground hallway. Stout iron pillars braced the walls, and mounted torches augmented natural daylight streaming down through mirror-lined glass. After several turns, Raedwin's escort arrived at a heavy door at the far end of the hall. A delicate bronze mouth gaped at one side. His escort pulled a brass chain beside it.

"Your High Honor," he called into the mouth. "Master Raedwin is here."

"Yes," Crassica's voice echoed. "Do send him in, please."

A series of metallic snaps sounded. The bald man pressed the door inward. Raedwin stepped past and entered alone. The door closed behind him.

Crassica was at her most comfortable underground, and her subterranean chambers maintained a certain graceful elegance. Sophisticated arches carved out of the bedrock swept overhead in long dignified curves. Tall shelves lined the windowless walls on either side, crisscrossed with scroll racks and bookshelves packed with leatherbound volumes. Pointed sunlight fell through two pale slivers of sky cut into the polished stone ceiling. Stately ferns swayed in a gentle artificial breeze, painting a delicate dance of shine and shadow over the room.

Crassica sat at her massive oaken table in a chair built from carved horns of Kalldonian cattle. Her pale white skin stretched taut over bony features, burnished to a glassy sheen. She was almost passable as an ordinary woman, but her individual parts came together in an ill-fitting disjoint, bloodless and hairless, as if split between two worlds—ancient yet also ageless. Many found her blue feline eyes alluring, while others thought she was too pale and strange, her pallid nature much too disturbing. Raedwin thought she was beautiful, in her own weathered way. She was stately. Handsome. Her elegant grace still held a certain allure.

"Good morning, my sweet." Crassica beckoned for him to come sit. Brilliant white cloth robed her long pale form. Reaching for a bulbous ceramic smokevessel on the table beside her, she gave a toothy smile. "You wished to see me? Perhaps to discuss your machine to harness the wind? It appears to be moving along better now…"

"Barely. The men you've allowed me can't figure dawn from dusk out there."

She packed a crystalline nugget into the smokevessel's neck. Lighting a match, she held flame to nugget, melting the delicate crystals into a shimmering bluish liquid. With the chrome mouthpiece to her mouth, she drew in a deep breath, pulling the sweetly cinnamon smoke inward. A watery churn sounded from the vessel's interior.

"They do try one's patience sometimes," she said, releasing tendrils of smoke to the ceiling.

"If I could get better people. The ones I asked for…"

"I am sorry—I truly am," she sighed. "But I cannot spare the men you requested. I believe I explained that." She folded the mouthpiece onto its leather tubing and offered it to him. Raedwin shook his head.

"My sweet," she said gently. "Why do you never partake?"

To those who didn't know better, Brasti Ore wasn't of much interest. Found nowhere else in the known world, it sparkled in full sun but otherwise wasn't much to look at. Structurally it was strangely brittle. To those who fancied gemstones, or silver and gold, it was nothing. But to a sorcerer, Brasti Ore could dance. Vibrations hummed through the muddy stone like an earthbound song. Music orchestrated on the misbegotten limbs of angels.

With the right touch, Brasti Ore could wake the dead.

Several decades ago, Crassica had discovered a way to refine the raw element, rendering it very useful to more than just a few fringe dabblers in the Dark Arts. *Amaris*, she named it—Child of the Moon. To most people, the crystalline salts would give a kind of euphoria, an ecstatic and almost religious furor that would sometimes last for days. But to Crassica, breathing the smoke of liquefied Amaris allowed her to stretch beyond her body. It gave her vision and awareness that nobody else could reach—those of her kind or any other alike. With concentration, she could even embody and control the weaker minds among men.

"You know that concoction is meant for nobody but you," Raedwin said. "So I will continue to politely decline, thank you."

Like anything else, Amaris had a cost. For most people, and occasionally for the unfortunate child, the refined salts held the power to kill if not managed properly—much like the Brasti Ore from which it came. Ecstasies and bliss locked its victims into a dance that never ended easily. Among the people of Katliga, Amaris had proven more popular than Crassica had ever thought possible, and its casualties lay muttering in the gutter, staring openly at the blazing sun.

"I would cradle you from harm," she said to Raedwin. "You know that."

"I do, yes. But even the best of intentions can easily go awry."

Crassica sighed and settled in her chair, as if poured there from some distant cascading stream. "This is indeed the truth," she said quietly. Decades ago, she'd created an underground trade of Amaris, untraceable back to her, linked and controlled by warlords kept on a short leash. Lanius, Crassica's beloved Sword Hand, had long since taken over its distribution, fueling his own strange lusts for money or power or maybe just to watch dozens of lives slowly disintegrate under his touch. All through Kalldonia, and as far north as Corregidon, the salts became known as the *Brasti Blend*, the *Medley*, or, in certain corners, *Brassy*.

"We do not always reach perfection, my sweet," Crassica said at length.

Raedwin tried for a smile. "I need five, that's all. I need smart, and I need strong. Just to make sure they get the cross braces placed correctly."

Crassica shook her head. "I am too shorthanded. You know that. I am truly sorry."

"But we need more water. Especially this summer, when the..."

"I do hear you," she said, stiffening. "And I understand. Your projects are vital for all of us, and of course your needs remain vital to me. But you are asking for my best, and my best are otherwise engaged. Lanius requires their service at the moment."

Raedwin sat back. *Lanius.* Of course. Whatever the Sword Hand wanted, the Sword Hand received. "He needs every one of your best men?"

"My sweet, please do not be cross..."

"This will slow me down. And it'll slow down my research to find a new and better method to refine your ore."

Crassica smiled. Her face lowered and cocked like a protective parent's. "I am sure you will find a way. You always do."

"I still need to visit the mine, of course, to investigate origin paths..."

Crassica shifted, clearly unsettled. "The *mine*? Why would you need to visit the mine?"

"If I'm to find a better way, then I'll need to see the chain. Start with how it's pulled from the earth."

She drew from her smokevessel. "Nonsense." She exhaled, waving her hand at the thought. "The refinement happens here. Your work should happen here. Focus your efforts. You are to stay in the citadel."

He watched his mentor for a long moment. He'd spent so much time under her tutelage in a shared pursuit of knowledge, tinkering with the architecture of life's desire to replicate itself. Much of it happened right here in this very room—Crassica lecturing on and again about how one molded and shaped the world, sculpting existence for the betterment of all. She'd long acknowledged the shaping of actual lives and bodies, but conveniently left out exploring any ramifications of her actions.

Raedwin chose his tone carefully. "Why won't you let me leave?" he asked with a quiet, innocent calm.

Surprise lit her face. "Oh, my sweet," she cried. "Why would you say such a thing?"

"It's been over three years since I've been allowed to roam. This isn't how it used to be."

"But I need you protected. Shielded from harm. You are so much safer here. Outside, the world is..." She paused to consider, her brow knitted. "Filled with chaos. Pain."

"And, don't forget, where one finds all your precious Brasti Ore..."

"We have plenty for you to study. I need you to look at the engineering. The clarification. The purity. In here. Not out there."

"But if I could just..."

"Please," she said, her voice rising. After a moment she smiled again. A new gentleness came into her face. "It is for your safety, my sweet. You must understand, you are very precious to me."

Raedwin gave her nothing but a weak smile in return. He did not say okay, but he knew better than to take it any further.

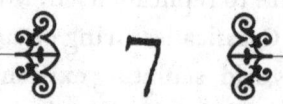

7

RAEDWIN WAITED until well after dark before setting out. Crassica generally spared him the consequences of most transgressions, but if he was caught in direct defiance of her order, she would not be pleased. He left lamps burning in his workshop to show he'd be working well into the night and was not to be disturbed. Slipping quietly down the long iron stair, he took a turn into a little-used side passage connecting to another set of crude stone steps leading down, deep into bedrock.

Raedwin ignored several dark openings descending into darkness on either side and followed the main tunnel eastward before turning sharply north. Ordinarily in a place like this, he could place his hand on bare ground or stone, and the touch would allow him to connect with deep energies held within the earth, to feel their vibrating pathways. He'd be able to reach and find Crassica's mine through veins of bedrock and see what he needed to see. But over the years, Crassica had made such connections impossible. Mostly he'd ignored the cage of unseen force she'd placed over the Keep, meant to enclose and protect. The prohibition merely meant that when he wanted to see more, he just had to work for it.

Fresh night breezes greeted Raedwin as he emerged from the underground passage. A shattered piece of the Keep's wall met the lower courtyards of the citadel just above the dry moat bed. A wide stone bridge arched overhead. Moving southwestward along echoing cobblestone, Raedwin passed a series of haphazard ruined buildings that surrounded the once-glorious Grand Gate at the southernmost edge of the citadel.

Craftsmen and artisans strode among the partly rebuilt ruins. Crassica would have eyes among all of them, so Raedwin stuck to the shadows. Keeping out of sight, he quickly made his way past and turned to the east along the outside edge of the wall. He skirted the crumbled remains of the huge circular southern tower, following a downward slope into a dry rocky streambed.

Raedwin glanced over his shoulder. Nobody wandered the glittering yards behind him. None stood in high tower windows. Nobody took notice of his passing.

"I thought I might find you sneaking around out here," came a voice near the wall behind him.

He spun to find a woman in a long gray cloak emerging from the shadows. Her pale face glowed from deep within her cowl, as if a slice of the moon had descended from her lofted perch to stroll casually among men.

"Sadahlia," he whispered. "What are you doing?"

She stepped toward him. "I came to see what ill-advised behavior you were about to engage in."

"Ill-advised?" He raised an eyebrow. "I'm just coming out to inspect the inflow gates."

"In the middle of the night?"

"It's only late evening."

"Very late. And the wash has been dry for years. The gates are there, serving their purpose. As are the pipes. That you designed. And saw installed."

"All the more reason to take a look."

A wry grin slipped across her face. "You should try for a better story than that."

She was stunning, all the more so in the evening twilight. Much like Raedwin, Sadahlia was an outsider. Though she'd been the first out of the Crosslands to join with Crassica, she remained different. Headstrong. Independent. A vanguard among Crassica's troubled progeny.

He moved to embrace her and held her there in the shadows, her body strikingly warm against his, piercing through cloak and clothing. Always in sync, he and Sadahlia formed a special sort of music together, their notes sourced from somewhere deep in the core of all things that walked the earth and breathed the air of life. Together they felt perfect.

"My love," he whispered. "Why don't you come with me? Let's have nice stroll in the moonlight..."

She laughed and stepped out of his embrace. "We'd be spotted straight

away! Might as well announce to Crassica right now that you and I are...
well..." She smiled at him, her blue catlike eyes sparkling. "No, my dearest.
I came to warn you to be careful. Our Crassica hides some things for
a reason."

"I need to understand the mine so I can better understand the process.
Why all the secrecy?"

"Because you can't fix what you don't understand."

"That makes no sense. She wants me to fix it."

"To fix the refinement process, not the mine."

Raedwin had never quite understood why Crassica was so open about
some things and so adamantly closed about others. Why was he not allowed
to see? "I don't need to know everything," he said. "Just enough."

A sadness came into Sadahlia's smile. "I guess the trick then is to know
how much is enough."

He placed his hands at her waist and pulled her close again. "This is
enough, right here, isn't it? You and I. The two of us, together. Here. In
this place."

"We're hiding in muddy shadows against a ruined fortress wall..."

He grinned. "All I'd ever need."

"And so then what? We hide out here forever? Sneak around in caves
like moles? Never have the freedom to simply be seen?"

"I can talk to her. I told you."

Sadahlia pulled away. "Not about us you can't. You know that. We
belong to her, and that's the way it is. The way it's always been." After a
moment, her eyes locked fully onto on his. "Someday," she said quietly,
"you're going to have to sacrifice something you truly care about in order
to save what you most believe in."

He let out a limp laugh and shrugged. "But not today." He leaned in
to kiss her forehead. "Today is just us."

"Be careful, please. At least give me that."

"I will. I promise."

Sadahlia stepped away. He watched as she moved along the hidden
stretch of wall back toward the Grand Gate and disappeared into shadow.

Raedwin followed the creek bed, soon climbing away from the citadel
through the cover of low hills and bare stony hillocks. Twice he stopped
and listened, watching for anything or anyone following. Satisfied he was
alone and unseen, he broke from the streambed and rose over the open

country to the east. A dark line of forest crouched along far hills, miles distant, rising full and thick into patterns of brooding ridgelines. The moon rose over the stony teeth of mountains beyond.

Raedwin hadn't always needed to sneak around like this. When he'd first arrived at the citadel, he had been filled with curiosity and a thirst for knowledge and understanding. He'd been allowed to explore at will, with so much energy back then, and so many aspirations. He'd found so many things and learned so much. Explorations of thought, of science, of wonder—all of it brought into focus by Crassica in this place, with no boundaries, no limits, and no laws. She had clearly drawn him here for some purpose, although exactly what that purpose was remained a mystery.

For a while, her reasons seemed to be purely physical. She'd enticed him to intimacy, and for a long time he'd rarely left her bed. A consensual, yet strange, situation. Preoccupied with having a child, Crassica had been focused and determined, fully obsessed. But no matter how hard they'd tried, how many midwives or sorcerers she employed or rituals they engaged in together, each pregnancy had ended early. Seven separate times she'd found hope, and seven separate times she could not carry. Death waited for each child, for each attempt, for each new slice of hope.

Raedwin never admitted to Crassica that the whole idea of having a child with her had frightened him. Maybe with another, with Sadahlia especially, it would be an act of love and a beautiful engagement, but with Crassica it struck him as a dangerous gamble. To him, their inability to conceive was the expression of a protective divine providence, a sensible limitation set forth by the Knowing herself. But he never said anything. Standing in the way of Crassica's plans never ended well for anybody.

At first Crassica had become enraged by the miscarriages, blaming her false body, the world, everyone around her, and the Knowing herself in the darkest moments. But she never blamed Raedwin. They had actually grown closer because of it. Even so, over time she'd become silent and contemplative, plotting toward some new hidden course, some secret new potential known only to her. She'd grown distant and removed. The two of them had evolved into something more like professional colleagues than anything resembling lovers. New arrangements made for new goals.

Finally, Raedwin arrived at a low hill. White scars lay across the broad slope. Ancient images of horses stretched well beyond human scale, as if explaining themselves to the sky. Raedwin would never make it all the way to the mine on his own, not without permission and guidance, but he could at least try to see, learn what he could from here, and discover what the earth had to say. He made his way to an exposed slab of granite on the far side, near the top. Hieroglyphics carved by the Old Ones peppered one side of the rock in the slanted moonlight—horses, a calf, a running deer.

Raedwin had never been to Crassica's mine, had never seen it, but he did have a vague sense of where it was. Kneeling to touch the stone, he whispered words and incantations from a time before counted time began, when the Old Ones had peopled these lands with their low domed huts of tanned skin, their cookfires and tribal dogs. He closed his eyes, better to see things beyond seeing, visions locked in the bedrock stratum of the earth. Reaching into the distant mountains, he probed for broken ground. Anguished stripping of rock.

And then there it was. He could sense it, well inside the forest some miles to the southeast—a festering sore, filled with wriggling larvae struggling to devour its nutrients. The ore itself vibrated like a living thing, with the dormant energy of stars, formed in the earth's long beginning. He could understand its shape, its power, the alignment of lodestone to purity. There was truth to be known in that place.

Water was there as well. Foreign to the bedrock, brought by mechanisms of human hands. Aqueducts and troughs, tanks of stone and wood. Massive cisterns set high above the east edge of the quarried gorge waited to spill man-made floods, directed to hammer away earth and stone alike. The work of thousands, accomplished in seconds.

And then something else pulled his gaze. Something drew his vision away, far to the north past land and sea, over mountains and forest. Past Jordinia and the Straits. North of Dunnenwyr. All the way to Brinsfallon.

To a long green shoreline. To Lake Pentmore, and then south along a cartway into a thick dark forest.

To a broken cart.

To Senya.

Raedwin shuddered. He saw his sister there, on the ground, alone among massive twisted trees. Was that the Hallonath? Pale vultures circled. A man crept ever closer, step by silent step.

Senya.

His sister spun and seemed to see him, to call for him, but her voice was lost in the wind. He tried to answer, but his mouth would not move. No words would come.

Why was he seeing her now, after all this time? Had something happened? Was something about to happen?

His past life with Senya had become so distant, so vague. After leaving, he'd roamed the land, wondering who he really was. He'd refused to tell her where he was or where he was going. What he had done to Sidmor back then had left him stumbling and humbled. How could he search for truths and knowledge after that? What did anything mean if it all could abruptly end in quick and brutal death?

When they were young, Raedwin and Senya had mostly kept hidden to protect the family from rumors and cheap talk. They'd become closer in so many ways because of it. Nearly inseparable, but also exhausted and worn down. His sister had stood beside him through it all, through everything, nearly silent, learning right along with him how to express one's true and quiet feelings of love.

But now he'd found this place. Found Crassica. Everything he'd ever wanted or needed was here. The caravans brought food and wares from all over Kalldonia. Water flowed freely through the ruined citadel, and his machines harnessed and stored it. Crassica's library held what might've been the greatest repository of all knowledge in the known world since the Great Fall. The ruined towers still commanded views of all the lands around. Here Raedwin was cloaked in security, hidden away from all the cares of the rest of the world. Free to study and learn. To be whoever he wanted to be.

At first, Crassica's prohibitions had struck him as strange and unnecessary. He'd argued and railed against them, fought the rules, and blatantly disobeyed now and again, but over time those desires had all faded away. He'd gotten distracted by the wonders of the work he was doing, by his life here, alongside Crassica. And Sadahlia. His secret connections with Senya grew fewer and farther between. Over the years, Crassica had gently made it more and more difficult, and Raedwin's efforts to sneak out from under the shell of the Keep grew all the more tiresome. Over time, he'd gotten used to her rules and dropped the effort altogether, without actually realizing. The silence became a normal part of life.

But in the end, he'd neglected to make sure he could reach his sister at all if the need did arise. The realization pummeled his heart. *His own sister.* How could he have been so stupid? So lost? His accident with Sidmor wasn't the end between them—that had only been the start. Raedwin had managed to let it die all by himself.

Raedwin, he heard her call, her voice flickering and broken in the wind. She said something about forces beyond, somewhere in the Crosslands, and something about escape.

Get out of there, she said, clear and sharp. *Come back home.*

And then she was gone. Raedwin stumbled and fell back, the vision suddenly broken either by Senya or by the land itself. He hadn't managed to say anything, not even hello. Unable to tell her how glad he'd been to see her, a refreshing surge he hadn't realized he needed.

Maybe Crassica's long-fingered grip had expanded to reach this far outside the Keep. He stood and stared at the rock for a long time. Scanning the land in all directions for signs of movement or rising dust, he watched for movement. Nothing ahead, nothing behind. The slow swirl of moonlit sky spread above the creased and defaced land. A lone nightbird circled overhead in the moonlight. He turned and hurried back toward the Keep. He'd been gone too long already.

THE WINTER had been good to Brogan. He had a fair amount of smoked fish and venison in storage, with spring already starting to show in the trees. But fresh meat was always a good idea. Typically on his hunts, he stuck close to his lodge on the western fringe of the dreaded Hallonath, avoiding the deeper and darker parts of the strange forest. But today he'd tracked a half-dozen deer eastward all the way to where the Old Kreskill Road veered close to the big bend of the Brundsril. He'd been this deep a few times but did not know this part of the forest well. The Hallonath wasn't a place for the unwary. For anybody who didn't pay proper attention, these woods offered plenty of quick and easy ways to die.

Keeping his eyes on the ground, Brogan searched for new sign. Hunting hadn't been his first life calling, nor his second, but he made up for his lack of experience by being very, very quiet. He could hold his body in steady balance with his surroundings, whatever those surroundings may be, and move nearly in silence. That, and plenty of patience, had brought him enough success to survive out here for years.

Ferns reached into his path, and Brogan brushed the green blades aside. The track had been pretty clear up until this point but had broken up and disappeared. Low branches forced his body to contort in a slow-motion dance with the forest as he crept over the uneven moss-covered ground.

The quiet was the first thing that gave him pause. A muzzled strangeness cloaked everything this morning. No singing toads. No breeze to brush the high branches in the trees. No birdcalls or bugs. Nothing. Brogan kept on. Eventually he'd find something. A rabbit or two, or maybe a tardy squirrel.

As a young man back in Corregidon, Brogan could find nearly anybody who'd wanted to hide—better than most, maybe better than anyone. But he'd left those bloody cobblestone streets a long time ago. He'd escaped to build a new life and then lost all that as well. Now, a little older and a lot more broken, he found himself wandering a bit too far out to find fresh deer or boar, meat that he probably didn't actually need, or maybe to find absolutely nothing at all.

A flash of white gleamed through a gap in the trees ahead. Brogan froze.

He could barely make out a girl lying on the ground some distance away, her body stretched over bare paving stones in the middle of a clearing on the Old Kreskill Road. Not something he expected to find way the hells out here. In the city, a random body in the street would've been a common enough occurrence—Corregidon had plenty of streets and plenty of bodies—but this forest had only one ancient unused road, and no people at all.

Crouching low, Brogan crept a little closer between a pair of massive oaks. He waited and listened. The gnarled trees all stood silent. Black trunks crowded past sight into the misty distance. He moved forward again, inching himself over colossal roots to slip behind another tree.

The girl was alone. Wrapped in dirty binding cloth, with nothing but her face exposed. She looked to be maybe sixteen or seventeen, maybe a touch older.

An image of his own daughter lit through Brogan's mind—her charred body wrapped for burial outside the cave in which she'd died, tiny and waiting, lying next to her dead mother all those years ago. Burned, battered, and alone. His heart skipped. The image cut, keen as ever.

Brogan glanced at the trees and branches overhead. No vultures spiraled the sky, and no flies fussed at the girl's closed eyes. Tiny puffs of breath drifted from her lips. She was definitely still alive.

A rough wooden cart sat askew some distance up the broken road. One axle lay cracked and useless, its wheel shattered. Hay and blankets filled the plankboard base, forming a makeshift bed. Somebody had been carting this girl through the forest under the cover of darkness—never a good sign. Brogan readied his short bow. He'd lived in and around this strange and twisted forest long enough to know that diving straight into a suspect situation wasn't the best idea. Better to wait and see.

A tall pale woman emerged from the underbrush and crouched next to the girl on the ancient causeway. Her milky skin shone in the morning dim under a hooded gray cloak. Reaching with ashen fingers to awkwardly fumble at the girl's wrappings, she tugged at the cloth where a few strips had started to release.

A second pale woman appeared next to the first, with a matching gray cloak. They spoke to one another in a strange hushed tongue that Brogan couldn't quite place. The sound was both familiar and foreign at the same time, like whispers from some forgotten nightmare.

Brogan wanted to back away. This wasn't really his fight. Trouble like this was for heroes in songs or tales in alehouses, the kind of thing for young idealists or old idiots. But the taller of the two ashen women stood and looked directly at him. Her lithe form held an eerie beauty in its movements. Her eyes met his. Skin so white and exquisite. Like an ancient porcelain doll from Brogan's distant childhood.

The second woman turned and stood as well. Together they watched him and waited. Nobody moved. Morning mist drifted through the brooding trees.

The taller woman held up her free palm in a gesture of peace. "Everything is appropriate," she called. "There is nothing to find here." She took a step toward Brogan, an unspoken menace in her fierce blue eyes. "We do not require your help, thank you. We mean no harm."

Brogan wasn't so sure about that. He stood. "How 'bout we ask the girl there if she agrees?"

Both women stepped toward him through the trees. "She is of no importance to you," the leader called. "We are taking her for healing."

"Doesn't look like that from here." Brogan slowly opened the sheath strap for his long knife, holding his bow in one hand.

"Appearances can be... deceptive." The lead woman reached to take the hand of the other. A wry grin crawled across her pure-white face.

A sudden terror stabbed through Brogan—an attack of alarm, an assault of fear, a storming invasion of panic. His body froze, rooting itself to the spot. Dread ripped through him. This was an onslaught beyond a simple threat, a keen blade born of thought and emotion, of smoke and desolation. Founded in the power of death itself, a pure and paralyzing fear assured him with silent confidence that his end had arrived at last.

The two women advanced, hand in hand. Stilted and awkward, they moved as if under some great burden.

The leader held up a pale and bloodless palm. "You must not tell what you have seen here," she called, drawing a fearsome black dagger from her belt.

"I'm… not much of a talker…" Brogan forced each word through a stiff, unyielding jaw. The second woman also drew an ugly long blade.

Brogan staggered backward. His heart hammered. Struggling to breathe, he could barely move, his hands heavy and numb.

A gaunt draft horse emerged from the underbrush up the road. The haggard beast moved with the plodding sound of iron shoes on stone, idly pulling at long grasses on the ground. The remains of a sturdy collar drooped from its neck. Both women turned with a start, confused by the horse's arrival, breaking their paralyzing force.

Brogan rolled across a huge root into a sheltered hollow and immediately nocked an arrow. The smaller woman lunged at him in a blur of gray and steel. Brogan drew and loosed. His arrow flew high into her belly. She let out a shrieking cry but kept coming. Brogan's second arrow slashed open an artery at her neck. The woman crumpled to her knees. With a last lunge forward, she swung her black dagger well shy. Brogan loosed a third, splitting her collarbone. The arrow shaft wobbled. A whimpering, wet gurgle escaped as the woman collapsed.

Brogan readied another. The remaining woman stood near the edge of the causeway, waiting for something. Or for someone. Morning mists drifted and pinched away a shining shaft of sun. A dim haunt fell.

The pale woman studied Brogan and took a step forward before pausing, reluctant to leave the shade of the deepest shadows. Her eyes flared. Brogan's heart pounded, each breath coming white in the cold morning air.

He was in this thing for good now. No turning back, no turning away. He drew, took aim, and let the arrow fly. The woman stumbled, fletching buried in her chest. She charged forward. He sent a second into her shoulder. Yet she came on, diving with her black dagger.

Brogan ducked to the side, knife quickly in hand. The woman tripped on a root and fell. Brogan jumped and landed with his boot on her wrist, sinking his blade into her neck. Her body gave a few spasmodic jerks, and the black dagger fell from limp hands.

Brogan yanked out his knife and swore. Even after all these years, it didn't matter where he went or tried to hide—violence would find him. Street thugs in Corregidon, bands of boneskins or bears in the mountains, and now a pair of strange ashen women in the Hallonath. None of it ever got any easier.

He pulled back the woman's gray hood. Surprisingly beautiful. So young and out of place. No eyebrows, no hair. He lifted one of her lids. Sleek and feline, the brilliant blue iris cradled a slender vertical pupil—eyes clearly made for seeing in the dark. But as he watched, the woman's face suddenly aged and faded. Life slipped from the bloodless flesh. Her skin dried and settled over bony features.

Brogan glanced through the trees, scanning for companions. Things like this never happened in isolation. There had to be others. Something more sinister underneath the sinister thing one could see on the surface.

Early daylight streamed through the misty branches. Nothing moved. Silence fell. He secured his bow over one shoulder. Emerging into the clearing, he headed for the girl. Felt her cheeks. Tawny brown skin warm to the touch. She was alive, but her breathing came slow and ragged, struggling to hold a rhythm.

"Friendly bunch you run with," he muttered.

The girl's black brows curved gracefully over large deep-set eyes. A short lock of curly raven hair escaped from under her wrap. She had been beautiful once but now appeared deflated, lean and nearly lifeless. Caked blood formed a strange arcane symbol on her forehead.

Brogan winced. *Sorcerers.* That was all he needed. He loosened the girl's wrappings. Inside, her hands were bound, arms secured against her chest. But other than her corpselike state, she seemed to be okay.

A man emerged from the trees up the road, a bit behind the horse. His chin and head were both shorn smooth. Boiled leather armor braced his tattered wool garments, and his twisted face held a permanent ugly glare. A mercenary. Probably hired out of Pentmore or the Cellenway frontier, ready to take on anything for the shine of coin or a cask of good ale. He stepped into the clearing toward the horse.

"There you are, you hellscursed waste of..." He trailed off as he caught sight of Brogan next to the girl. "What the...?"

Brogan laid his knife on the ground and rose, palms up. "Easy, friend..."

"Who in hells are you?"

"Nobody special. Just passing by."

"Well, best to keep on passin', then." The mercenary drew a handaxe from his beltloop. He gestured casually. "And I'll thank you to step away from the girl there. She be our parcel to carry and no busywork of forest folk."

Brogan heard himself say no without thinking. The man glanced around the clearing. This lone hunter had to have partners in the shadows, hidden archers waiting for his next move. "Where them others?" he said warily. "Them two white birds?"

Finally noticing both bodies twisted in the underbrush, the mercenary raised his axe and lunged.

Brogan met the attack with a blunt thrust of his empty bow, catching the mercenary's gut. Grabbing his knife, he spun to drive the blade deep between ribs. The man let out a searing cry and several wheezed obscenities before collapsing. He did not move again.

Brogan pulled his knife and wiped off the blade before inspecting the cart. The axle was shot, and one wheel lay in two pieces. He stepped back through the trees to the body of the first woman. Putting a boot on her chest, he yanked out his three arrow shafts. Retrieving the other two as well, he examined each for damage before shoving them back into his quiver. Good arrows took time to make or good money to buy, and Brogan had neither on hand.

He checked the tall creature's cloak and found a small oilskin pouch strapped to a belt. A few quick shifts of the binding and it was free. Surprisingly heavy. He opened it, dumped the contents onto the ground, and nearly lost his breath. Almost two dozen Kalldonian gold pieces gleamed alongside seven silvers, two bronze, and a handful of sheckers. A small fortune, by any measure.

He caught sight of a rolled parchment tucked to the side of her belt, tied with a leather strap. Pulling it free, he opened it. Fire had marred the goatskin along the edges, and several wrinkles blemished the surface. Aged ink showed complex interlocking circles and lines, crafted with perfection beyond the abilities of human hands. What was maybe a moon sat alone at the top, a small circle at the bottom, and a series of fishlike marks in the centers of different sections. And then something with horns. A spiderlike symbol with legs near the middle.

Brogan had seen things like this before, written in necromancers' halls or scrawled on the blood-soaked earth near the scene of some desperate last stand, but never anything as well-crafted and highly honed, nothing as intricate or nuanced, not even back in Corregidon. Like a machine had created it. He rolled the parchment and returned the money to the pouch, shoving both into his belt. He'd figure all of this out later.

The horse had not gone far. Brogan used the remains of the draft

collar as a lead and guided the animal back to the girl. He looked her over again. She seemed free of injuries or broken bones or anything he would aggravate by lifting her. Grabbing a blanket from the cart, he laid it over the horse's back. He hoisted the girl. Lighter than he expected, so thin and fragile. He secured her to the horse as best he could. Without another glance at the clearing, Brogan led the horse into the forest, back the way he'd come.

Near midday, he emerged from the trees to a cleared hill ringed with a rugged wall of spiked poles near the top. Brogan climbed and passed through a narrow gate, locking it behind him. A few paces past a tight grove of trees, he came at last to his small stout lodge. Rainwater dripped quietly from the edges of a thatch roof.

He slid the girl from the horse and brought her inside. The previous night's coals pulsed in the hearth at the far end. Laying the girl gently on a wooden table, he went about lighting a pair of small tallow lamps, set some dry wood on the coals in the hearth, and blew life into the flames.

The girl's breathing remained steady. She was a little older than he'd first thought but couldn't have been more than twenty. Brogan spread a small stack of thick blankets along one wall near the hearth and moved her there, straightening her body for comfort as best he could. Untying her arms and legs, he surveyed her for injuries. Anything that could cause such heavy sleep. He found nothing. He tried to wake her, but nothing would get her to stir. And no matter what herbs and oils he tried, the symbol on her forehead refused to budge. She slept through it all.

Standing back, Brogan was suddenly aware of his own filth, his clothes and skin marred with blood and stench. Mud reached to his knees, and a trail of muck led from the door to where he stood. The reek he must be pushing forth. He pulled his boots off near the door and changed into cleaner trousers as well as a fresh tunic.

Back in Corregidon, he'd spent plenty of nights preying on the weak and powerless at the order of local strongmen, and plenty of days afterward he'd tried to make up for it by defending those same victims, time and again. Penance to pay and forgiveness to seek—a curse or a blessing, or maybe both. Brogan would step in when he saw something wrong, whether he really wanted to or not. He owed it to his daughter. And to his wife. He'd lost both of them up in the high valleys of the Elrune nearly a decade ago, and this helpless woman, barely more than a girl herself, was maybe some answer to a question he'd long forgotten how to ask.

The fire popped. Brogan retrieved the parchment again and sat to examine it more closely. He held it up and ran his fingers along the supple material. Maybe it was a chart of the stars. Or a plan for a kind of mechanism, like gears of a metalsmith's mill. Opposing forces, one resisting the other. The sky against the earth, or water quenching fire. The moon was at one end, opposed by the sun maybe? A tension between the two.

Whatever it meant, Brogan was a hellsmarch from adding it all up. He put the parchment away.

The girl slept by the fire. Afternoon faded to evening, and evening into night. Brogan climbed to his sleep loft and collapsed onto his matted bed. He stared at the low thatch ceiling overhead. Sputtering light from the fire blinked and flashed across the timbers.

His daughter would've been about the same age as this girl by now. Maybe a little younger, but close. Sweet Glenna. What would she have been like, had she lived? Would she have been more like her mother or more like him? Would she have stayed with everybody up in the mountains, or would she have gone back to Corregidon, wanting more city spark out of her life?

Brogan shook away the thought. None of that mattered now. His daughter was gone, and so was Dahlwea. That was that. No use in dwelling. This girl was in her own trouble, whatever it was. All he could do now was see to her and hope for something better to come for her.

After a time, he slept. Dreams of his fallen wife drifted in. Her shape flickered against the edges of sight, her voice calling to him in some unsettled foreign tongue. She was so close. He could almost reach and touch her, still radiant after all these years. She spoke in a song, her voice flowing through the trees as he searched for her. The flames of the fire that killed her had cooled and gone, but something was missing. He searched and became frantic. He caught a glimpse of gray cloak and white skin. He followed. His lost daughter was there somewhere as well, her body blackened and twisted by the same death-bringing fire, wrapped for transport and stretched out in a narrow shaft of moody sunlight on the tilted, fractured ground of the Old Kreskill Road.

9

RAEDWIN KNEW immediately that someone had seen. Three armed men arrived in his tower unannounced and demanded that he come with them. Crassica wished an audience, and he was not to wander the citadel alone.

He thought he'd been so careful. But seeing Senya had left him distracted on his return to the Keep. He'd failed to pay attention to who was watching. Or following.

Senya had known. But how? Raedwin could barely fathom the confusing set of circumstances that must've led to his sister seeking him right then, right there. All these years, and she was still looking out for him. Could it be possible for her to watch his movements from that far away, after all this time, with his own Sight remaining blocked by Crassica?

Get out of there, she had said.

What did that mean? Get out of where? Had she seen the men following? Or had she meant get out of Crassica's citadel? Or out of Kalldonia altogether?

Come back home.

Raedwin's escort marched him through a long colonnaded concourse. Stone pillars lined the center of the cavernous space. Tall alcoves carved into the living bedrock held elegant wooden chairs, six along each wall, twelve chairs for the twelve Sisters of Crassica's Great Gathering, the Acolytes of the Appointed, the Bringers of the Great Dawn. Usually whenever Crassica was trying to impress or intimidate, each chair would be occupied. There would be attendants for each, as well as servants for those attendants.

The room would be full, pulsing with power. Yet today all sat empty, as did Crassica's ornate throne on a short dais at the far end of the hall. No attendants, no servants.

Something about the absences struck Raedwin as odd. This group would not normally miss a disciplinary exhibition like this. Typically, Crassica would splay herself casually across the arms of her throne, a highly controlled display of the blatant reach of her power. Pomp and pageantry, wielded as a weapon. Raedwin had come to know nearly everything one could know about Crassica, yet after all these years, something remained out of sight. Unknowable. Dueling fragments of life and death braided together, with both equally empowered to dominate.

Maybe it hadn't been Senya in the vision. Could he really be sure of what he had seen, or what he had felt? Could this all be some game of Crassica's? Or maybe his sister playing some weird trick? He'd long neglected the places from which he had come and all the people he had left behind.

An image of Sidmor struck him. Together with Senya, happy and alive. The laughter and the love between them.

And that last image. That last day.

Get out of there.

If only he'd been able to shout that same warning back then.

Raedwin hadn't meant to run away, but his flight from Senya all those years ago, in hindsight, did look a lot like abandonment.

The men led him to a side door the color of spent blood. A metallic pop echoed through the chamber, and the door shifted inward. The lead escort pushed it open, gesturing for Raedwin to enter alone.

The side room was tall and graceful, less than half the size of the adjacent great hall. Crassica stood over a table in the far corner of the room. Gray smoke tendrils curled upward from her smokevessel. Amaris shimmered in its tiny bowl. Leaning over the table, she pointed at several parchments laid before her, instructing the captain of the guard in quick, harsh tones. Her plans for dealing with clans roaming the forests east of the citadel. Tensions from forbidden gatherings. Performances of banned rituals.

That would be the Sevenfold's Children. Raedwin had caught a glimpse of the strange creatures years before, a few of them bounding among distant trees. Long athletic bodies and cunning black eyes. Nearly human, they gleamed with a hidden and sinister sophistication beneath their animal nature—a flashing inner force. He'd heard tales of their unpredictability, a quick violence and pack mentality. None of the stories were good.

The captain raised his voice, clearly concerned. "They will come for us, Your Honor," he warned. "Someday. Maybe not now, but soon. Either for us or for the mine. Just like before."

"Nonsense," Crassica insisted. "They are merely wildlings dancing in the forest. They are nothing."

"If they ever organized as a single group..."

"Let Lanius know what is happening. He will sort them properly." Crassica waved him away.

The captain gave a stiff nod and spun on his heel. He left the room. Crassica moved in measured steps and settled into a wide chair facing Raedwin. The door swung closed behind him, its lock slipping into position with an echoing metal snap.

"Were those chaperones really necessary?"

Crassica reached for her smokevessel's mouthpiece and drew in deeply. "You have become... elusive of late," she said with an exhale of smoke. "I simply wish to watch over your safety, as I have said before."

"My safety."

"There are dangers in this world, my sweet, many of which are right outside our very walls. You know this."

"I was never in danger."

She closed her eyes and took in another long pull from the smokevessel, releasing a stream toward the room's lone skylight. "I specifically asked that you not leave the citadel."

"For reasons I still do not understand."

"Do I need to seek your counsel for every decision I make?"

"Where are all your Sisters, by the way? Who would miss this little parade of yours?"

Crassica allowed a sly grin to crawl across her lean face. "Their whereabouts are none of your concern."

He gestured to the door through which the captain of the guard had left the room. "Troubles in the forest?"

The vessel bubbled as Crassica drew sharply from the mouthpiece. "Those in the forest denied my stewardship long ago. They have chosen their own path and remain beyond our abilities to help." She let each word draw out with her exhale. At length, she cocked her head and studied Raedwin. "Did you procure whatever knowledge you sought whilst on your little transgressive walk?"

Raedwin's face twitched. How much did she know? How much of what he had seen was a true vision of his own, and how much of it was... her?

"I did see something..." he said. "That I did not expect..."

A flash went through Crassica's face. A twitch. Immediate. Involuntary. She covered it with a quick smile. "Yes? Unexpected in what way?"

Raedwin thought for a moment how to explain. Visions of a distant forest. The Hallonath. Vultures. Huddled men. *I saw my sister*, he wanted to say. *Something is wrong*.

"I'm not sure," he admitted. "It seemed far away. And maybe from a long time ago..."

Crassica drew again from the smokevessel. She nodded, considering. "The presence of Brasti Ore in the earth can warp one's perceptions..."

The presence of Brasti Ore. "What are you hiding out there?"

"Hiding?"

"What little I saw was... unpleasant."

She held her gaze on him, wordless for a long moment. "You, my sweet, are in the grip of a foolish infatuation. Foolish and misguided."

"I don't understand why wanting to know a little more is such a problem."

Crassica studied him. Her eyes blazed. "While I do admire your quest for knowledge," she said, her voice becoming low and firm, "there are times in which you go too far. You must listen to me. Some things are not for your eyes."

Like Senya.

"What did I see out there?"

"You blunder, my sweet. You get into your head that you always perceive the truth. That you have such keen and magical Sight. But the fact of the matter is you are not in as much command of your vision as you attempt to be. Why must you push? Do I not provide everything you need right here? Do you not have all the tools, the repositories of knowledge, the space to work and think and explore your ideas? Why must you want more and more and more?"

"I need to understand."

"Admirable, to be sure. But not always the best course."

"But if I cannot understand the full picture, then how am I to see the best path forward?"

"The full picture can be dangerous."

"So can ignorance."

"From now on, I think it is best for you to remain in your quarters, or your workshop, unless you have an escort."

"A prisoner in my own tower."

"You are free to move about the citadel as you will, of course. With an escort."

"Is that really a difference?"

"Please. Concentrate on your task at hand. Ore refinement, here within these walls. Calm yourself and understand that I have the best intentions for you. Focus on beauty and purity. Work on your beloved wind machine, if you like. Feel free to start something new if it strikes your fancy. Let me know if you lack anything, and I will have it brought to you."

"Freedom of movement." He let the edge in his voice cut. "Can you bring me that?"

"Is this your comedy again? You know I struggle to understand such things. I only speak for your safety, of course. You know I value you so much, my sweet."

"How long is this arrangement to last?"

"Until you make it clear that you understand."

"I think I'm starting to understand already."

"Good," she said. "See that it continues, and things will go much better for both of us."

10

BROGAN WATCHED over the girl for three days, but nothing changed. He tried giving her water, which she took slowly, but he could not wake her, no matter what he tried. The symbol on her forehead could not be removed.

Maybe he'd missed something out there on the road. A detail left behind. Something else those ashen women carried that would explain all of this. Something in the cart he hadn't seen. A potion maybe. A container or vial with some awakening concoction or special elixir. Or maybe there was a second parchment that gave the key to unlock the girl's mind. There had to be something. He resolved to ride back out to see what he could find.

The day broke clear and hopeful. Brogan fashioned a rope bridle for the horse and a crude saddle of blankets. Making sure the girl was warm and comfortable before leaving, he retraced his path out to the ancient causeway. The cart was there, broken and tilted askew on the overgrown paving stones, along with the corpse of the dead mercenary. Right where he'd left them.

Brogan dismounted. He stepped carefully, watching the surrounding trees for any movement, any sign of fresh danger. He searched the cart's plankboard base, the hay in the bed, and the driver's bench, as well as every crack and crevice in the wood. But he found nothing. He scoured the paving stones underneath and the twisted underbrush to either side. Still nothing. He traced the course of the cart itself to where the wheel had shattered and the base had dragged for several yards. Maybe something had fallen and bounced along the stone, off into the underbrush. But again, nothing. No sign of any containers or vials of any sort. No potion bottles or pouches for salves or ointments. Nothing.

He stood and glanced around. Something was missing. Something off. *Where are the other two bodies?*

He retraced his steps, found the matted and broken ground, the signs of his struggles, but no women. He looked again. The mercenary's body was there, but the two strange women were gone. Not a trace remained. No chalky skin, no gray cloaks, and no cat's eyes. He scanned the trees for any indications or hints, examining the ground for tracks leading away.

Maybe somebody had taken the bodies. Maybe there'd been more than the one mercenary.

Or maybe boneskins had gotten to them.

He hoped to the Knowing that it wasn't the boneskins. A hideous cross between human and animal, with dull yellow eyes and oily raven hair, boneskins were quick and brutal, with boar-like tusks protruding from thick lower jaws. Rough, translucent skin that was as hard as bone, like raw untanned hide, exposed the workings of muscle and sinew underneath. An inborn armor. Or outward horror.

Nobody knew where boneskins came from. Erupting into the world several decades ago, they'd showed an endless hunger for violence and raw flesh. Utterly without fear, they'd ravaged north through Dunnenwyr and split the bloated late Kalldonian Empire right across its middle, breaking civilization itself apart. Terrifying in appearance as they were, their savage barbarity was worse. Shocking stories followed wherever they roamed, accounts of all manner of atrocity, tales of a nameless and ravenous tide slowly eating the world alive. Brogan would never forgive them for what had happened to his wife and daughter.

But boneskins would've left tracks, as would anything else. If the two women had stood up and walked away, he would've been able to see something. If somebody else had come and hauled them off or dragged them somewhere, they would've left marks. Crushed grasses and matted leaves. Boot impressions. Scuffed stone. But he saw nothing. It was as if the two corpses had lain there for a time and then vanished altogether. But where would they have gone?

Brogan froze.

The girl. Back at his lodge. *Alone.*

He sprinted to the horse, mounted, and rode as close to a gallop as he could manage. Bent trees slapped his face. Roots threatened, tangling the ground. But as he arrived home, he found her the same as before. No change, no threats, no intrusions.

He stoked the fire and sat beside her, watching for something. Anything. He stepped outside and checked his perimeter, examined the fence line for any footprints or damage to the wall. Nothing. He set two extra locks on the gate and went back inside.

All of this was new. This defied anything he had ever seen before, even out here in the strange and feared Hallonath. A bundled girl asleep on the ground, narrowly shy of death, with no apparent wounds. Pale-skinned women wielding otherworldly power, with bodies that disappeared once dead. A scourge of silence. This could prove to be a bigger problem than Brogan was capable of handling alone.

But what could he do? He needed to make sure this girl was okay. Regardless of being in league with all kinds of Dark Arts, she clearly needed help. She needed *real* help. Real help from a true healer.

Suddenly the girl drew in a sharp breath. She opened her eyes, which shone a fiery orange—the color of fire and sun, powerful and alive in the lamplight, like nothing Brogan had ever seen before. She blinked.

"Hello there," he offered.

Her strange eyes moved to follow light and dark, shapes of flickering light and shadow, focusing at last on the flame. She blinked at its brightness. Her mouth opened to say something, but no sound came. She lay agape for a few long gasps. Trying to speak, she muttered a few incoherent phrases, almost forming a word or two.

"Aid wind," she sighed. "Raid win."

Brogan brought his ear close. She said something else, something about a path and maybe a wall. Or was it a fall?

"Raid win," she whispered one last time. She closed her eyes, and her breathing settled. She fell back asleep. Brogan waited for something more, but nothing came.

What was a *raid win*? Was that what those freakish ash-cloaked women out there had been trying to do? A *raid win*? Brogan waited for more, but the girl remained still. She did not move again. He settled back and sat on the floor.

The fire cracked and popped in the hearth. He watched the flames and waited for the girl to move or say anything else. When nothing came, he cleaned up the room and climbed the ladder to his sleep loft. Maybe it would make more sense tomorrow.

Brogan woke with a start. His lodge was silent and bare, pitch black but for a thin glow outside the heavy shutters. Morning was close. He sat up. A strange silence gripped the pre-dawn dim. No breeze, no buzz of insects, no morning birdcalls. He rose and climbed down the ladder. His front door stood ajar. Gray light of the coming dawn stretched over the clean dirt floor. He glanced at the makeshift bed in the corner.

The girl was gone.

He bolted outside. Rushing to check the muddied space between his lodge and the spikewood wall, he looked for breaks or openings, searching for any sign. The girl was nowhere in sight.

Making a quick ring of the house, he found nothing. He checked the small grove opposite the garden, the deepest shadows, and still nothing. Only after walking the full perimeter did he find her down the slope near the gate. She was awake, on her knees, slumped against the wall, struggling to undo the locks.

Brogan approached slowly. She brandished a stolen meat knife at him.

"Stay away," she warned.

He held up both palms. "I'm not here to hurt you. I'm trying to help you."

She turned to the locks, keeping the knife trained on him. Her body swayed, unsteady on her knees. Each time she tried to work the mechanism, her balance drifted. She caught herself on the wall with her free hand.

"You've been asleep for quite a while. You're probably a little groggy."

She fumbled with her free hand. "How do I open this thing?"

Brogan took a step closer. "It's cold," he said. "Let's go back inside."

She stiffened, pointing the knife. "You need to back off."

Brogan froze, his palms facing her. The girl took a quick look at the muddy clearing and the small tidy grove. His spikewood wall. "Are we still in Pentmore?"

Brogan almost laughed. "Pentmore?! We're leagues away from Pentmore. This is the Hallonath."

She sighted down the length of the knife. "You lie."

"That's possible, but what would be the point? Look around you. The truth is everywhere."

The girl's shoulders slumped. Her knife arm wavered as she stared at the gate. "Hells," she muttered. Her mouth dropped open. She slid to sit with her back to the wall. "The *Hallonath*? Really?" She let the knife settle into her lap.

"I'm sorry," Brogan said gently. "I didn't mean to frighten you." He explained as quickly as he could how he'd found her—the pale women, the mercenary, the missing bodies. The girl's mouth remained open as she listened, without words or sound. Finally, she frowned and shook her head.

"The Hallonath," she whispered.

"I brought you back to keep you safe from whatever was going on out there."

Her eyes narrowed. "Who are you?"

"My name is Brogan. This is my home."

"So you're not with them?"

"I don't even know who they were. I was hoping you could tell me."

She shook her head again. She opened her mouth to say something but remained quiet for a long moment. "They were supposed to help me find my brother," she said. "But..." She trailed off and did not continue.

"I tried to wake you, but nothing worked. You've been here for four days."

She closed her eyes and let her head fall back against the wood. "Four days," she whispered.

"But the ones who were carting you through the forest, they're gone. You're safe now."

The girl let out a choking laugh. "Safe?" She raised her head, blazing eyes vigilant and suspicious. "You really believe that?"

Brogan took a quick look around him. His walls had served him well enough for years, but they suddenly did seem a little meager.

"I don't know who you are," the girl said. "And I don't know where we are. I don't know..." Her voice faded. "I don't really know much of anything."

"They were hauling you somewhere. Do you know where? Or why?"

She stared at the ground near his feet. Didn't answer.

"I'm only trying to make sure you're okay."

"How are you supposed to do that? You don't know what you're up against."

Brogan opened his mouth, finding himself at a loss. "You mentioned your brother," he said. "Maybe I can help you find him?"

She let her head fall back against the wall again. She stammered and started a word or two but fell quiet.

"I need to make sure you're safe," he said. "Then I'll leave you alone."

She laughed, brief and dark, with a skeptical exhaustion that only comes from years of experience. "Four days asleep," she said. "And dragged all the way out to the Hallonath."

Brogan fumbled for words. "I don't know any more than you do about what is happening," he said. "But I can help you. Get you back to wherever you need to be."

The girl watched him, her face flat and resigned. "They told me my brother is stranded inside the Crosslands," she managed at last. "So how are you supposed to get me back there?"

Brogan nearly laughed again. *The Crosslands*? Was she serious? Nobody was stranded inside the Crosslands. Nobody could be stuck in a mythical place that existed only in stories.

The girl shivered in the morning cold.

"How about you come back inside," he said gently. "Let's at least get you warm. They may be coming back for you, and we should figure out what we're going to do about it."

"We," she said, almost a question, but not quite.

"I'm just trying to help."

Her body shuddered as she moved to stand. "Okay... you can help me back inside." Her legs quivered and nearly collapsed before she caught herself against the wall. She pointed the knife blade at Brogan. "But I'm keeping this."

HER HIGH HONOR Crassica the White loved her library. She loved the promise and opportunity it offered, portals into the past, complicated and divergent views, arguments as well as answers. The stored knowledge held in her library's vast collection had given the Sisters of her Great Gathering many of the skills they needed to walk among the living. Yet more knowledge remained to be unlocked.

She made her way down one of the darker and more forgotten wings. Lanius walked beside her. He was a wiry man, built of unyielding sinew and focused strength. Her favorite living weapon.

Twice the height of most underground chambers beneath the Sevenfold Keep, these rooms reached all the way to the surface. Slender shafts beamed down from three overhead windows to splash sunlight along the floor. A narrow iron catwalk lined the double-height stacks, providing a network of access to the highest reaches along each wing.

"I've given the Chief of the Keep the task of watching him," Lanius said as they walked. "Kraegha will be properly thorough."

As the Sword Hand of the Master, Crassica's Chief Protector, wielder of weapons of faith and the cleaner of various messes, Lanius had never liked her library. That much was obvious. To him, this place was far too focused on idle thinking and not enough on action.

Holding a bright oil lamp, Crassica searched the volumes. "Do not overstep," she warned. "Our Raedwin only needs a little guidance toward the proper path."

The last time Lanius had been in a proper library was probably back in Kalldon, over two years ago. Crassica had sent him there to remove a certain irritating local landlord. Her reasons had been complicated and admittedly petty, but Lanius had not cared either way. He never cared. Lanius simply listened to whatever task she presented and then completed it quickly and efficiently. Caring only got in the way. One of the many reasons she cherished his service and loyalty. A sword did not care about reasons for the work at hand. A dagger never sought to understand its purpose. These were merely tools. And Lanius was the most keenly honed and highly refined tool in Crassica's vast arsenal.

"Shall I have him grabbed if he goes wandering again?" he asked. "Or lingers a little too long at the stables?"

"He is not a child," she said. "He will obey gentle reminders. Do not worry yourself overmuch."

She passed scores of leatherbound spines. Not even the librarian himself knew what these particular volumes held. This was Crassica's own private corner. Most were ancient texts filled with theories and practices, many copied from even older scrolls, a few of them holding truly breathtaking power.

After a time, she glanced over at Lanius. His long hair, nearly pure white, cradled his pale face and piercing dark eyes. "How go our efforts in the forest?" she asked.

Lanius shrugged with a frown. "The Children have vanished back into the trees, as we expected. I have men pursuing."

Crassica nodded, turning back to the shelves.

"We lost more this time," he added. "Their tactics are improving."

"Then we must improve our own as well."

She stopped, scanning for the book she needed. Newly acquired, the volume had been gathered from a deal she had made with a powerful occultist in Darizi. It contained certain knowledge passed down from long ago, from a time before the Old Ones articulated their methods of binding life with death, their careful ways of shaping a fresh new birth out of the stingy clutches of the Everlife itself.

Men and women were all born, lived for a time, and then died. Each was an expression of the eternal Knowing herself. One life folded into another and repeated itself, for all time to come, each living thing an immortal continuance of the original. Such everlasting, unending beauty.

"The single power greater than control is that of creation," she said to Lanius, pulling their talk away from the Sevenfold's Children. "The forming of life. The power of making. Birth is the one thing that really matters. Everything else is secondary."

The realization of this truth had come to Crassica quite a long while ago, back in the Crosslands, well before her counterfeit life in this body began. A mother's own grandmother reflected in her daughter's face. An expression, the shape of the mouth, a living piece of the one who had come before. Each parent beautifully realized through the child before them.

"The passing of generations gives life permanence," she said to Lanius.

But not for Crassica. This line did not exist for her. She would never continue. She could have no children. She was an Angel of the Evening, a lamplight guide of the moon. Formed in the Crosslands between the living and the dead, she was allowed nothing more than to be one of the countless, faceless escorts for the newly lost. Death had been her sole purpose, the core of her former existence, the fabric of her former being.

Of course that had meant that Crassica could never bring anything new into this world. She could never hold what one living thing gave to another, the nurturing path of creation. She would never experience birth. She would never truly matter. And this, Crassica could never accept. Even back then, in her original state locked within the Crosslands, she had recognized a bigger purpose for herself, a wider journey at hand. Confinement was never going to work, her whole existence eternally suppressed into a mundane sea of sameness, fated and bound to stand among the innumerable legion and be nothing more than a spectator to life's grand game. Was she to remain forever in the endless non-plane of the Crosslands, the numberless, flaccid in-between, neither completely dead nor truly alive?

Crassica's answer, of course, was a definite no.

First, she had found methods and practices to form herself into a physical body. She breathed. She spoke. But the simple crafting of a body to allow herself to walk among the living—a great victory to be sure—was not enough. Crassica needed more. She wanted life. True life. Her ambition would not diminish. She needed what she needed, regardless of the risk or effort required.

Many years ago, she had attempted to have a child to prove her living stature. She had tried many ways over many years, serving her self-made body through plenty of men—strong and weak, young and old, vibrant as well as anemic—but all had failed. None had proven worthy. In the long years of vain attempts, she'd nearly abandoned hope. Her less-than-human womb seemed destined forever to remain empty and barren.

So she shifted focus. She would not be denied. For decades she searched for a way to craft children by other untested methods. Throughout generations, she spent her time in study and effort, striving to unlock the code of life. She learned so much in those early days. The results had given rise to several lovely and frightening creatures, many to the corrupt delight of the late Kalldonian Empire's bloodthirsty leaders. But they were never her children. They were a fallacy, hardly more than a series of grand mistakes. Abominations, all of them. They would never be her children. They would never be a reflection of her soul. They would never carry her essence into the future, into their own descendants. Too foreign they were. Too disconnected from her hope for a long and fluid lineage.

Raedwin's arrival then was like a great gift delivered from the Knowing herself. Blood of humanity fused with the immortal Brohndai. She surmised his qualities immediately, so poorly hidden by the lad's futile attempts to remain anonymous, qualities that could prove to be exactly what she needed. She lured him to her bed with the best of her subtleties, and they had spent the next few years together. But Raedwin, in the end, had failed—the same as all the others. Only in the last year or so could Crassica finally admit it. Even with Raedwin she had failed to foster a proper bloodline.

She stopped along the stacks, pulled a worn leatherbound book from the shelf, and held it under the lamp.

"Here we are," she said to Lanius, or maybe to nobody. In her hand was the core of her fresh new hope. After everything, after all the failures, this volume offered something different.

"We will get what we came for at last," she said.

The rituals in these pages held a novel solution for her long-suffering aspirations—procedures and formulas that would guide her complicated path forward. A way to infuse her soul into the womb of another—not to craft a child of her own, as she had failed to do so many times for long anguished years, but for Crassica herself to be born anew.

She had studied the text time and again when the book had first arrived, but of course she needed more than simple study—she needed to fully absorb and memorize every nuance of the script in order to ensure success. For this idea to work, she needed the truths of these rituals to be assimilated deep into her core, deeper than thought itself.

Her dawn had arrived at last. The true way to fulfill her dream of life. Breeding remained the key, breeding and blood. "Raedwin does not yet realize the importance of his presence here," she said to Lanius.

What Crassica had needed all along had been right in front of her eyes for years—just not in the way she had previously thought. She needed the blood of an immortal, much like her own, to use as the vessel for her own true, human birth.

"Twins," she said, "carry the same blood as one another. And where one twin goes, so comes the other."

12

SENYA SAT on her makeshift bed near the hearth, working herself further awake. She wasn't quite sure what to make of what she'd seen in the darkness. Seven towers and a Vallahnir queen. Crassica. *The headmost*, as Cevellica had said—one Vallahnir describing another. The Clanmother had been right after all. A whole coven of Vallahnir. But how they had bodies and walked among the living, she could not fathom. Senya had seen shades of thirteen in all, including Crassica, Cevellica, and her companion, all strolling around. Talking. Alive.

She struggled to understand the other things she'd witnessed as well. Raedwin and the strange man following him. Was that a dream inside the nightmare, or something real and true? So difficult to discern. In any case, her calls and cries had all been lost on the wind.

Clearly Cevellica and Korsta had lured her, but in doing so, they'd given her something in the exchange. Something unexpected. But what it was exactly, she couldn't quite tell. Not yet. She remembered the men tying her feet and hands in the Pentmore warehouse. They'd lifted her as she'd lost consciousness. If she concentrated and really tried to see, maybe there had been a cart.

Why was there a cart?

Raedwin had been with the Vallahnir, but something else had happened there. Something recent. A break that Senya could only sense. The images had all been vague and cloudy. Rushed, like they'd made a mistake in allowing her access. They'd exposed her to something, and they knew it. But she had no idea why. Or what any of it meant exactly.

She listened as Brogan explained yet again how he'd found her. And found Cevellica as well, along with the second Vallahnir. Probably one of those men from the warehouse. She studied Brogan as he spoke, watching his quiet sadness. His face was hard, marked by the varied scars of time and violence, yet he had kind and gentle eyes. Close-cropped graying hair. Plenty dirty. His skin had probably been light once, but now was mostly sun lined, tan and broken. He seemed good-natured enough, holding back a dormant fury buried beneath the surface. This man had seen more than a few hard years.

Senya shifted and lay back down with her eyes to the rafters. Still so dazed. A voice in the back of her head tried to convince her that all of this was just another part of her journey, a test of some kind. She remained in the Pentmore warehouse. They were with her, somewhere. There was no man named Brogan, no lodge in the Hallonath, no fire on the hearth. All of this had to be false. A Crosslands trick.

She shook away the thought. *Focus. Don't let them pull you back in.* But her eyes fell closed anyway.

Brogan reached out and shook her shoulder, his coarse hand real and true. "Hey," he said. "Don't drift off again. No more sleeping. Not yet."

She forced her eyes open. She knew in her heart that this was real—all of it, the good as well as the bad. Brogan had seen Cevellica and her pale twin trying to cart Senya somewhere through the forest. They'd lied to her. They were never supposed to move her anywhere. Not her body.

But if this really was the Hallonath, then why bring her all the way out here? So far from Pentmore. What was their plan? Had they been trying to drag her all the way to Kalldonia? Was that even possible? She blinked and sat up, leaning on one elbow.

"Was there a sorcerer with them? Bald, with a stripe of red hair?"

Brogan shook his head. "No sorcerer. But there was this..." He reached to a shelf near the fire. Grabbing a leather pouch, he pulled out a small rolled parchment and handed it to her. "Maybe this means something to you? I can't make any sense out of it..."

She took the parchment and held it up to the lamplight. Thin lines crafted with a deft and sure hand, almost machined with precision. Whether it was old or new, she could not tell. She had never seen anything like it before, but the markings did strike her as somehow familiar. The shape of the moon was clear, as were the fish, with some kind of creatures in the top circle. Strange stars for an uncertain sky. It almost looked like a chopped-up version of the Everliving Tree, showing the flow of light and darkness from being to nonbeing, death into life and back into death again. She rotated it and put the moon at the bottom—darkness and death, which meant the top showed the sun—light and life. Two parts of the Great Circle. Branches of the Unseen Oak reaching up into brightness, existence, and vibrancy, while its roots dug down into absence and loss—the Everlife and the Underworld. And where they met in the middle, where they overlapped, lay the Crosslands.

Maybe it marked a location? But if that was the case, what direction did it give? Vallahnir wouldn't need a map of the Crosslands. None of it made any sense.

"I don't know," she said quietly. "This is…" She shook her head as she trailed off. She handed the parchment back to him. "I don't know what it is."

Brogan looked over the markings once more and returned the parchment to the oilskin pouch.

"My name is Senya, by the way," she said. "For what that's worth."

Already her journey had been so bizarre and pointless, longer than it should've been but also very short. Maybe the parchment was supposed to show her something, but what it was, she had no idea.

But she knew somebody who would.

"I need to leave," she said abruptly.

"No, you don't," Brogan objected. "You can stay as long as you like…"

"I don't think so."

"I don't have much, but we've got food and water here. Shelter. A good fire. You need to get your strength back…"

"No," she cut him off. "I need to leave. Now." Her voice was gentle but steady. She did her best to explain what had happened before he found her—Cevellica's visit, the Pentmore warehouse, the strange brew that had knocked her out.

"They lied to me about whatever they're doing," she said. "I'm out here for no good reason. They came at you with blades drawn and tried to kill you for no good reason. None of this adds up, and none of it is likely to be good."

Brogan offered a flurry of strategies and tactics, their best options for defending his lodge if they came for her. "We can line the spikewood with torches," he said. "Light watchfires in a ring. I've got an extra few knives and a really good axe…"

"Brogan."

"I know this isn't the best place to make secure, but we could probably…"

"They're Vallahnir, Brogan."

Brogan burst out with a nervous laugh. "*Vallahnir*? Is that some kind of joke? If it is, it's not very funny…"

"You came across two in the forest. The same two I met in Pentmore."

Brogan shook his head but said nothing. She watched him think it through, wrestle with how it could not be possible. She had thought the same thing, back in Pentmore. But now that she'd seen their shades in the Crosslands, she understood. These few had found a way to become solid and real, a way to hold shape and form in the daylight as well as shadow, living on both sides of the Veil.

"Gray Ladies of the Gates," Brogan muttered aloud. "Right here in the Hallonath…"

So different from any story he would've heard, so different from any nightmare tale he would remember from childhood. More strange and subtle. Less noble.

"I need to leave," she repeated.

"You're in no shape to travel," he objected. "It's not safe. Did I mention you're in the Hallonath? Have you heard of this place? Not so fun if you're not exceptionally well prepared. And it's not only the forest you need to worry about… there's plenty of danger in just about every direction you could go from here."

"I need to get to Faeroen." She pointed to the parchment in the oilskin pouch. "My father needs to see that."

"Your father? On Faeroen *Island*?" Confusion flickered across his face. "But Faeroen's where the…"

"My father is a Brohndai," she finished the thought for him, watching him struggle further, more at a loss for words, trying to piece together what he was seeing. Brohndai were not born, they did not love, they did not hate, and they did not die. And they definitely did not have children.

Brogan sat back and shook his head, rendered fully speechless. Senya typically saw this very same reaction any time she told someone the truth. Nobody could ever quite fathom it. Brohndai were the last of the everliving embodiments of the Knowing's eternal presence upon the earth—immortal shepherds of life, teachers of the Wisdom, spirit guides in the Eternal Way of the Knowing. For centuries beyond memory, Brohndai had lived all across the known lands, mostly in scattered monasteries where they offered healing and guidance to any who sought it, until the Kalldonian

Empire banished their ancient practices well over a hundred years ago. It turned out that several dozen immortal men teaching a balanced and independent self-reliance didn't fit well with the empire's need for control, hierarchy, and dominance.

After their banishment, the Brohndai had all fled across the North Sea to Faeroen Island, a hidden bastion of myth and legend, where they'd remained out of sight and out of mind ever since, drifting into the past.

"A Brohndai..." Brogan murmured. "So you're..."

"I am half Brohndai, yes," she answered, knowing the question already. "It's a long, old story, but I was born, the same as you, and I will die in the end, the same as anyone."

He offered a kind smile. "Just not today."

She nodded with a smile of her own. "With any luck, yes. Not today." She pointed at the parchment. "But my father will know what to make of that, and of all these Vallahnir walking around. Whatever is happening here. If not him, then one of the Elders. Somebody."

"On Faeroen Island."

"Yes," she said.

Brogan cocked his head, taking this in. "Do you know how far away that is?"

"I understand why this is confusing," she said. "I'm confused myself, if I'm honest. And for you—first a pair of living Vallahnir show up, and now the daughter of a Brohndai—it would be a lot for anybody. But I can't see how Raedwin is wrapped up in whatever this is. I can't connect with him like I used to. And I can't decipher that parchment. Something is happening to him, and now to me. So I need to talk to my father. And the Elders. They need to see this."

Brogan stared at the floor, shaking his head slowly. After a long moment, he spoke with a sigh. "There are only two ways back to civilization from here. North, through the forest to Wayburn, or west, through the boneskin lands."

Boneskins. Senya shuddered. She'd seen a few of the frightening malformed creatures in the past, and the thought still haunted her.

"I can help you get to Wayburn," he continued. "They've kept a stone bridge secure over the Brundsril for decades. They hold it against roving bands or boneskins and whatever nightmares wander out of the deeper forest."

"Just point me the direction," she said. "I can manage from there."

"This is the Hallonath. Nothing is easy out here."

"I wasn't looking for easy. But I do need to go."

"I understand. Let me at least help you get to Wayburn."

"No." Her voice came out heavy and more abrupt than she'd intended.

"It's a long day's ride, and you've just woken up. You need strength. You're in no shape for a journey like that on your own."

"You've been kind enough already. I can't let you put yourself out there for me."

"I go twice a year to trade, and I've been due for a visit anyway. They'll offer help from there, if they can. They're good people. You'll need a ship to get to Faeroen. And to get a ship, you have to get to Corregidon. Wayburn will help get you on your way."

Senya still did not know what to make of any of this, but Brogan obviously knew this land and had good intentions at the very least. He would likely prove to be a good ally in getting through whatever she faced ahead. If she was honest with herself, the thought of help felt quite a bit better than venturing into the Hallonath alone, boneskins or none. She'd need every ally she could find from here on out.

"An awful lot of trouble might be following me," she warned finally. "With or without boneskins at our heel."

Brogan offered a worn and broken smile. "Trouble's come my way before, and it'll come again. Doesn't much matter what I do to keep out of its way."

She gave him the best smile she could muster as well, with all her fear and worry cutting right through it. "Okay," she said at last. "I guess I could use your help getting to Wayburn. Thank you. I'll see what they can do from there. Then you won't need to trouble with me any further."

RAEDWIN HAD known from the start that Crassica was different. She was certainly ethereal and otherworldly, and her colorless skin gave him plenty of suspicions, but he tried to avoid thinking about it. He'd been with her for seven full weeks before he realized the truth.

"In the Crosslands," she had told him. "Vallahnir are one and we are all, none distinct from one another. We are everywhere, but we are nothing. Which, of course, I could never abide."

Astonished into silence, Raedwin had given no real reaction. Crassica had gone on to explain that Vallahnir had no true identity in the Crosslands beyond a vague shape and form. They were as numerous as the trees, but as singular as a mountain. Their movements were beyond measure but held no individual choice. None were independent.

"But here," she said, "in this body I have crafted for myself, I am *Her High Honor* Crassica the White. I am master of this house and queen of my lands."

She'd led him up a long narrow stair into the Sevenfold Keep's easternmost tower to witness some vague event she'd refused to explain. As they emerged onto the crumbling top floor, low mists and fog swirled over the entire citadel below, wrapping everything in a thickness that was both comforting and deeply unnatural.

Crassica told Raedwin to wait. The blinding haze slipped through gaps in the ruined walls, shrouding what few stones remained. Then, without warning, the mist retreated, pulling back into the cloudless Kalldonian sky. Before them stood a woman, as if formed from the gathered tendrils of the mist itself. A flowing gray cloak hung from her slender form, the material glinting in the murky light.

"What do you see?" Crassica asked Raedwin. "Tell me. Describe her."

The woman looked older than the crumbled stone of the ruined tower, yet her face was that of a young girl. Sapphire feline eyes. Raedwin opened his mouth to speak but could find no words. This was a ghost made flesh, a spirit of childhood stories.

The Vallahnir stepped forward and nearly fell before catching herself, like a young child first learning how to stand upright. Words came in a choking, guttural shout, forced and wielded without control or nuance. Like wounds torn in the fabric of a separate, more primeval existence.

Crassica replied to her, much in the same strange language, but with a more defined aspect to her voice, more control over the sounds.

"Language takes time," she said to Raedwin. "Our new Sister has yet to achieve command of such things."

"How?" Raedwin stammered. "I don't..."

"It is important not to obsess over origins. The beginnings do not define the ends."

Crassica helped the Vallahnir to sit on a stone bench along one side. The mist had gone, revealing a view of the cliffs below and the ruined village beyond. In the distance far to the east lay the dark line of forest at the edge of the mountains. Crassica spoke to the Vallahnir again and directed her to lie back on the bench. She stroked her forehead.

"Is she alive?" Raedwin asked.

"Tell me what you see."

"I see a ghost. A woman. I don't know."

"Touch her. Tell me."

"Does she even know we're here?" Raedwin knelt next to the Vallahnir lying on the bench. The woman held a stately elegance. "She's a... Vallahnir... just from...?"

"You still have not touched her."

Raedwin laid the tips of his fingers on the Vallahnir's shoulder. Warm. Hot to the touch. She gave a start and turned. Her striking blue eyes were crisp and knowing but focused beyond him, onto nothing.

"She is familiarizing herself to this body," Crassica said, moving to a large stone chair. She sat. "It can seem much like a strange sort of cage at first."

Raedwin watched the pale woman, this living Vallahnir, this dream made flesh. So beautiful, so fragile, so frightening. She stirred and uttered a series of words in a harsh, throaty growl. Crassica stood and stepped to her and laid a hand on her shoulder, answering in the same partial language. The Vallahnir drew in a long gasp and then was quiet.

"She says her chest moves by itself," Crassica said to Raedwin. "She breathes, and she finds it strange. I told her this is normal. This is how life works." She smiled at Raedwin. "There is no need for breathing where we come from."

"If she's alive, can she be killed?"

"Of course she can be killed. This is also how life works. We can all be killed. In the end, the details are a little more complicated, but this life my precious Sister has now achieved can indeed be taken from her, the same as from any living being. But as masters of the Crosslands, we have certain ways of controlling what happens immediately after."

"She's incredible. She's beautiful."

"Indeed she is. But I am glad to hear you say so. I cannot parade my dear Vallahnir around the countryside to gather opinions just yet, as people outside this citadel would struggle to find sense in such things."

"Why is she here?"

"Why should she not be here? This one is not the first, nor will she be the last."

"There are others?"

"I was the first to achieve a living form, and there have been seven so far who have joined me. The first is brilliant and beautiful but rather fragile. So very human in that way. Sadahlia, she is called. I will introduce you to her someday. She is here in this very Keep. Perhaps you have seen her. Since Sadahlia, the others who have come are gifted with more powerful bodies but less articulate minds. They move about in this world with much more freedom, each in her own way, but are less intriguing in conversation."

"But why are they coming here? Are you drawing them here?"

Crassica smiled again. "We are all drawn here, my sweet. You, as well as the rest of us." She stood, stretching long on her thin legs. "But come. Enough for now. She grows tired, as do I. She must rest." Placing a hand on

Raedwin's shoulder, Crassica gestured toward the stone stairwell leading down. "There is far more to show you. So much for you to learn."

And learn he did. Raedwin had been so new to this place back then. He'd spent hours exploring all through the Valle d'Brasti and its Sevenfold Keep in those early days, loved mapping the cavernous hallways in his mind, mastering the shape of all the deep vaults. From the beginning he'd found himself making easy decisions—take the door to the right, and right again, and then take the middle passage with the stairway leading down. Each turn had led him into a new passage or stairway, through an opening into yet more hidden chambers. Each choice had been a simple gut response, with no concern for getting lost or strolling past the burn time of his torch. There had been no rush and no place for him to be. No one would call for him to mind the burners or stoke the Kenson or match the wellmark notions. Not tonight. Not anymore. Nobody would ask him to scrape the residue from the simmer kettle. Here he was his own man at last. The ancient fortress and bustling citadel of Her High Honor Crassica the White had finally given Raedwin the opportunity to search and learn. Here he could examine and research at his own will. This was a place of knowledge and discovery, of reach and grasp. A place like no other he had ever seen.

One particular hallway's ceiling reached overhead in highly crafted arches, different from all the others. Strange purple light bathed pillars along both walls. Hidden machinery gave the space a slight breeze, humming quietly as if the halls themselves were part of some vast living thing. A red glow pulsed from an open doorway at the far end. Music drifted as well, notes merging together in harmonies and cadences, melodies and countermelodies wrapping and braiding into a sumptuous fabric beyond simple sound and beauty—as if the song itself were dancing.

All those years ago, a doorway of light and music, opening to a world he never could have imagined.

The room's long thin tapestries of red silk gently swayed with an artificial breeze. Low lamps lined the walls, giving warm scintillating light of natural flame. A woman was there, seated at the short end of a polished black instrument. Her elegant pale fingers worked keys and levers, coaxing the music into a gliding sparkle. A deep crimson hood partially hid the player's face in shadow. Lamplight gleamed on her smooth white skin as the song came to a velvet end.

"You play beautifully," Raedwin said, his voice coming out all thin and paltry.

The woman turned to him and smiled. She was stunning beneath the hood of her silken gown. "Thank you," she said. "I don't know why Crassica keeps such a beautiful thing hidden all the way down here." She ran her slender fingers along its polished surface. "Such a lovely instrument." She glanced at him. "Are you going to stand in the doorway all night? Or would you like to come in and sit down?"

He moved to take a seat on a long high-backed couch gracing the opposite wall.

"You're Raedwin," she announced, as if that explained something. "Crassica has told us many things about you."

He shook his head and let out a brief laugh, suddenly examining the fabric as if he were in the market for a soft-woven bloodred couch. Had Crassica huddled all her Vallahnir Sisters together to share sultry stories of their intimacies with one another? "I don't know what you've heard," he said. "I'm a simple fisherman's son from Vesterlag."

The player rose, an easy smile brightening her face. "There's no need to lie." Her voice came low and vibrating. "Not here. Not with me. I know who you are." She moved toward him. The tips of her fingers slid along the polished instrument. "You are the sole living son of a Brohndai. You represent Crassica's hope for renewal, her beloved bridge between humankind and the Everlife."

Raedwin shook his head and let out a laugh. "Crassica's a little crazy with all that stuff."

The player joined him on the couch. "There is a fine line between insanity and genius, I've found." She reached out to touch him with a fluid and graceful motion, her skin hot against his. "We are each given a role. Some choose to play along, and some do not. Some play well, while others stumble and forget their lines and are given boos and hisses by the surly audience. Some play by their scripts while some choose to step onto a different stage altogether, weaving an improvised drama of their own choosing."

"Like you?"

"Like all of us here, I suppose, even you."

"Your speech," he said. "It's… so clear. Crisp and articulate. The others of your kind I've seen, they don't…" And he trailed off, uncertain how to finish. "Except for Crassica."

"You'll find Crassica the exception for many things," the player explained. "Not the least of which is speech. My other Sisters are all quite new to this place. They're barely children in this world. Mastering speech takes time for us, the same as for anybody else. I've simply been at it longer."

"How much longer?"

She removed her hood. The fluttering lamplight glinted over her perfectly hairless head. "Over sixty-five years I've walked among the living." She smiled again. "Almost as long as you."

Turning to a tray of crystal glasses and a pitcher on a side table, the player poured two drinks. She handed one to him and raised hers for a toast. "To our petty little dramas," she said. "Life is such a small and useless thing after all. And to *Her High Honor* Crassica, our potentially insane mentor, for believing in quite the opposite, and for bringing all of us misfits together, whatever her reasons may be."

He held the glass to the light and examined the shimmering liquid.

"Just drink," she said. "Let a lady have her toast."

He sniffed at the edge of the glass. She laughed, a sound of pure brightness. "Don't you trust me?"

Raedwin shrugged. "I'll admit, I would like to know you a little better…"

They toasted then, and drank. The cool liquid was bright and delicious with a flash to its taste like nothing Raedwin had ever experienced before. Sliding sharp and easy down his throat, the drink warmed him from within.

"Trust," the player said, "is such a beautiful thing."

Trust was indeed a beautiful thing. But he found himself thinking of Crassica as he drank. He'd become her lover, and she likely held some claim over him. But they'd never spoken about it outright. Trust was one thing, but truth was something else entirely. Talking to this woman was probably against the rules, whatever rules there were. At least it felt like it.

"I don't think I caught your name…" he said at length.

The player laughed again, and the room swayed and took on a dance of its own. Somewhere in the distance, perhaps through an open shaft at the end of a long stone hallway, someone slid an elegant bow across taut strings, drawing music into the air from the wellspring of life's first light in the darkness of the Crosslands.

"You, my dear," she said, pulling him close, "may call me Sadahlia."

They sat for hours talking, leaning into one another in their small pool of brightness. The lamplight caressed her smooth pale skin. As they spoke, their words braided together as if from two pieces of the same mind, light given to darkness, their living bodies becoming simple reflections of sky and lake, of stars and water. Hadn't they always known one another? Somehow then, even as he remained pledged to Crassica, Raedwin knew that from this moment on, he would never be quite the same again. A song from somewhere in the faint distance lighted their tiny room with the flourishing sound of dreams being born.

14

SENYA WAS the first to notice the crows. Wide black wings circled across a heavy overcast sky, dipping down through uncertain fog and returning again to their high circling pattern. Brogan's plan was to take the bony draft horse at first light and ride hard to Wayburn together. Senya had managed to scavenge a pair of small leather trousers from his stores, as well as a wool tunic with a hooded cloak for warmth. He'd given her a stout crossbow to sling over a shoulder, along with what few bolts he could muster. But they'd only made it as far as Brogan's door before stopping.

"Do you smell smoke?" she asked.

A buzz hummed through Senya, like millions of insect wings coming from somewhere close, just out of sight. She could almost see Cevellica's flickering gray robes between the ranks of dark trees at the bottom of the hill. The Vallahnir's whispers. Calling to her without sound or thought.

"There." He pointed. "What is that?"

Someone had arranged stones in a ring near the gate. Long branches lay across in a starlike pattern, with blackened remains of oil pitch fires smoldering at each joint. Senya went to the ring and crouched to examine. Arcane symbols marred the largest stones, a few she almost recognized. Her brother had dabbled with plenty of fledgling Dark Arts, and in his wake, she'd picked up more signs than she liked to admit. Peculiar languages. Curious markings of necromancy. All sorts of ancillary sorcery. He'd shown her certain characters scrawled on calfskin that would light on fire if he spoke a certain word. Others that caused objects to shimmer and liquify or disappear for a heartbeat.

101

"It's a Warding of Blocking, I think. Meant to contain us."

Brogan glanced at nearby trees and branches. "You know about that kind of stuff?" His voice was terse and tense.

"A little bit." Senya placed a hand onto each bare branch and spoke quiet counter-phrases woven out of the air and mist, fused with the tarnished earth. Simple words that blocked most rudimentary incantations.

Brogan scanned the spikewood wall. "Good to know."

Senya rose to kick the branches apart, spreading the star pattern into a disconnected, incoherent pile. She shoved the stones out of arrangement. "That'll at least break the Warding."

A sliver of red flashed as a man emerged from behind Brogan's lodge, inside the spikewood wall. Korsta, from the warehouse in Pentmore.

"You," Senya whispered.

White skin shone under his shoulder armor, which reached high and stiff around his neck and chest. Articulated scars formed arcane symbols intertwined with black inscriptions over his bare torso and upper arms, continuing onto leather bracers at his wrists. A thick Kalldonian battle apron girdled his waist, and he had an iron-tipped warstaff strapped to his back. The sorcerer stepped forward with easy confidence.

"Senya, my dear," he called. "You appear to have fallen from the kindness of our care into the hands of this..." He turned to Brogan as if considering how to articulate his grave distaste. "Woodsman."

Senya bristled. "You lied to me," she shouted. "You need to explain very quickly exactly what is going on. Why am I out here? Where are your two *Vallahnir*?" She nearly spit out the word. "Where is my brother?"

Korsta bowed with arms wide. "In due time, all will be known to you. But first, you must return to your proper path..."

Brogan took a step forward. "She's not going anywhere with you. Not now, not ever."

Korsta's brow furrowed. A twisted grin slid across his weathered, tattooed face. He shook his head. "The woodsman speaks, but his words carry little weight..."

"We've broken your Warding," Senya said. "You have no hold over us."

"You may destroy the Symbol, my dear Senya, but you cannot destroy the Blocking so easily. It is time to stop playing like a child."

Anger rose in her. Amber light flickered at the limits of her vision, with a sharp, churning edge. Unfamiliar. New. She became a quiet island in a forest of noise, with a fresh sense of undiscovered strength.

"Why was I taken out of Pentmore?" she demanded.

"You are bound to us through your own action, your own choice, your own truth."

"I'm bound to nothing if it's all based on lies."

Korsta reached for his warstaff. "Truth and lies are relative things."

Heavy smoke began to billow from behind Brogan's lodge, as well as all along the far side of the spikewood wall. Flames broke out and flared, clearly lit before Brogan and Senya had come outside. The bony horse was nowhere in sight.

Brogan drew his shortsword and strode toward the sorcerer, passing the blade back and forth between thick hands. Korsta took a step backward. He muttered quick incantations, wielding some sort of conjured defense, before shouting an order to the trees.

Senya saw the arrow before it nailed Brogan. A small bug-like blur from somewhere in the branches above, holding in a frozen instant between space and menace far faster than any possible reaction. It slammed into his shoulder. A second slashed across his leg. A third pierced his lower ribs. He cried out as he fell.

"Wait!" Senya shouted. "Leave him alone, and we can talk!"

An empty breeze pushed through the air. Flames surged. Korsta lunged at Brogan, his warstaff flying. He tried to pin the smaller, wounded man. Brogan rolled to regain his footing, but Korsta smothered him. Senya bent to load the crossbow as they struggled. Two more arrows flew, seeking Brogan's exposed back, but they found only bare ground.

Senya aimed. The crossbow sprang almost without her realizing it. The bolt pierced deep into Korsta's side. He screamed, losing his grip on the warstaff. Recovering his shortsword, Brogan followed with a blow that cleaved the sorcerer's skull.

Light flashed between the flames and the spikewood wall, revealing a muddy webwork of boot tracks and footprints. The Blocking was gone.

The clearing fell quiet. Nothing but the crackle of fire echoed. Flames grew quickly, engulfing the far side of the wall as well as the entire rear of Brogan's lodge.

"Whoever is up there!" Senya shouted to the trees. "You have to stop all this nonsense and show yourselves! You don't have to do it this way!" She needed to talk. She wanted answers.

Fire climbed the edges of Brogan's thatch roof. A pinch-faced mercenary leaned from his perch in the branches of a tall oak.

Brogan let fly with an arrow. The shot went wide, but the mercenary lost purchase as he ducked. He slipped and fell to the ground. Quickly recovering, he stood, wavering on an injured leg. The mercenary limped forward, drawing a long straight blade.

A second archer slid into view, and Brogan loosed. This time his arrow was dead on. The man's face showed shock and panic as his body fell backward against the limb that held him. Twisting away and jerking, he lost his grip on the branch and spun before crashing to the ground in a distorted heap, his neck broken.

The limping mercenary rushed at Brogan.

"Stop!" Senya shouted. "If you're here for me, you need to back off!" But the mercenary dove past her and slashed at Brogan, who braced with his bow to fend off the attack.

Senya lunged and cracked the man's skull with the empty crossbow. A spasm rocked his body. She hit him again. And then again. Her blood raged, battling against the primordial prohibition that prevented any Brohndai hand from striking against the living. But her human nature ruled as well—now bolstered by something new, a fresh and vaguely sinister tinge. Brogan rose and hacked with his shortsword. The mercenary toppled over, lifeless. Brogan stood and panted with exhaustion. Senya lowered her weapon, shaking as she stared at the body. Pooling blood leaked into muddy leaves.

Brogan's eyes swept the clearing. "You see any others?" Smoke billowed and drifted across the clearing as the fire wreaked havoc.

Senya shook her head, eyes on the dead mercenary. "I don't know," she managed.

How had it come to this so fast? Battle lines drawn, with no sense of purpose. So useless. So pointless, all of it. Nothing gained, nothing earned. Still as lost as before, and now Brogan's home was gone.

He wiped his blade and slid it into his hip scabbard. Together they tried to quell the fire, but with only one able body and nothing with which to carry water, they could do little but watch it burn. Flames ripped over the thatch, through the timber frame, and up into the nearby tree, fueled by oils and dry brush piled against the lodge and wall alike. A burning branch fell, shattering part of the remaining structure. Brogan crumpled to one knee. His breathing came tight and labored.

Senya turned to him. An arrow to his shoulder, one in his side, and a slash along his leg. Fire raged over the hilltop. Plus the horse was gone. She had a lot of work to do if they hoped to get to Wayburn alive.

Through all the years of her childhood, Senya had absorbed as much as she could from her father. Wherever they roamed, he would discretely travel to neighboring villages, advising and administering remedies to the sick and injured in secret. She had watched and remembered, learning all the modes of the human body, ways to correct the wrongs and urge broken flesh to mend itself.

Ignoring the smoke and fire devouring Brogan's home, she tore several strips of cloth from one of the dead mercenaries. Hurrying back to Brogan, she crouched to examine the arrow in his shoulder. The barbs had not penetrated far enough to make purchase. She pulled it free.

Brogan swore. "Can you at least..." He wheezed sharply through his teeth. "Warn me when you're gonna do that?"

For Senya, the problem with being a good healer was that it kept her much closer to pain and cruelty than she'd ever found comfortable. A constant witness to the brutal results of violence. She wrapped the wound.

"Didn't have to be this way," she said quietly, mostly to herself.

"Mercenaries like these can't be reasoned with," Brogan assured her. "They've got a job to do, simple as that. And so this thing ends in one of two ways—either with you in chains being dragged away by them or with us getting in a bit of a fight, with you here and free. Everything burns either way. Doesn't matter what you'd offer."

But it had to matter. There had to be some way for a choice to have been made without all this death and with Brogan uninjured. No fire, no lives lost. Maybe she could've refused their drink in the warehouse back in Pentmore. She could've posed a few more questions. She could've gotten up and left, given this whole thing a little more thought, or maybe gone to look for Raedwin herself. She could've tried a lot harder to put eyes on him and connect with him to find out for sure whether anything they'd told her was the actual truth. But she had done none of those things. And so here she was.

She had to get to Faeroen. She had to let her father and the rest of the Brohndai know what was happening.

Senya bound the shaft in Brogan's side. Her movements were not gentle, but they were effective. He winced through shallow gasps. With a curse, he reached to yank out the remaining shaft.

She grabbed his wrist. "Wait," she scolded. "I can't stop your bleeding right now if you take that out. You need to rest."

"We need to get out of here."

"Not yet." She eyed the hillside. "We need somewhere safe. Somewhere hidden while I fix you up."

"I can walk," Brogan insisted. He pointed at the base of the hill beyond the edge of his walls. "Down there. A little cave. Has some water."

Senya helped him stand and led the way through the gate and down the slope away from the burning lodge.

If her mother had been with her back in Pentmore, she would've known better. Her mother had always been able to read people and know their true intentions. She would've never allowed Senya to fall into this mess. Her mother would've been smarter. More vigilant. More adept at picking her way forward. Her father knew the human body, but her mother had known the minds of men.

Some distance into the trees, well past the edge of the burning spike-wood wall, they came to a large boulder extending from the slope, forming a shallow protected cave with a small natural spring deeper in. Senya directed Brogan to lie down. "I need to gather some wood."

"I can help you," he offered.

"Just lie down. I'll be right back."

Nearby trees had plenty of dry moss hanging low, filled with crisp withered twigs. Excellent tinder. She found several thick dry branches as well—bare and easy to break. Returning to the shallow cave, she lit a fire near the mouth of the overhang. With a few fist-sized rocks at the center, she laid a handful of the larger branches over the top, as well as a small log. As the flames devoured the moss and twigs, she rose to grab a waterskin and offered Brogan a drink.

He let out an exhausted laugh. "Last night I thought you were the one who needed a good healer. I guess now it's my turn."

"Hush. You need to rest," she said. "I am sorry, for whatever it's worth. I'm sorry for all of this."

Brogan grunted and waved her off. He drank again. "Did you burn down my house and put these arrows in me?"

She sat back against the side of the cave, putting her feet toward the fire. "I'm sorry I got you into... whatever this is. Whatever they're..." She trailed off and she shook her head again. Where to start? She was sorry for so much. Sorry for all this nonsense, for the lies, for letting herself be dragged out here in the first place. She was sorry for him being pulled into her plight without his consent, without his need, without him knowing what he was getting into. And for not being able to understand any of it herself.

"It's okay," he assured. "I was ripe for a good shake-up."

Senya bent forward to stoke the small fire, shoving its pulsing coals together, building heat. The smoke stayed low and nearly invisible outside the cave mouth. Satisfied, she rose. "I need to grab a few more things," she said and left without allowing argument.

She climbed back up the slope. The fire at Brogan's lodge had diminished, burning inward rather than spreading. The roof and walls had already collapsed. A pile of logs on the ground remained aflame, lessening with the lack of fuel. The hilltop glade lay otherwise quiet. Senya made a quick scan with everything her senses could muster, but she saw and heard nothing. A slight breeze sifted through the branches. No buzz like before, no sense of Cevellica or any other Vallahnir anywhere nearby. Even so, she moved quickly.

The gash on Brogan's leg would need sewing, and sewing meant a clean needle and thread. Arrow fletching typically had long catgut strands to bind feather to shaft, which would serve her well for thread. And the mercenaries had shot plenty of arrows. She found two. Moving through the smoke to the archer's body near the scalded tree, she removed his leather tunic. Bundling the arrows with the tunic, she rose and scanned the scene again.

A glint of brass on the body of Korsta caught her eye. Stepping closer, she saw the golden sheen of a metal plate shoved into the dead man's belt.

Its curved edge appeared from under his crumpled battle apron. Intricate rings and delicate arms. Engraved markings.

Raedwin's star taker.

She'd thought it lost in that warehouse back in Pentmore, but Korsta had clearly brought it with him. Why would he do that? Would they be using it as some sort of guide for wayfinding out here in the forest? Strange, if that were the case. They could've simply followed the Old Kreskill Road, or used landmarks for north or south or whatever one uses for such navigation.

How far had they been planning to travel with her tied up and comatose?

Shaking off the thought, she retrieved the star taker and rolled it in the tunic with the arrows. There wasn't time to ponder all the possibilities right now. Rising, she descended the hill back toward the cave.

Good needles came from hawthorn trees, which would be shorter compared to all the towering oaks and firs around. Probably too early in the year to find them by their bright snowy flowers, so she would likely smell them first. Strangely sweet and musky. It took some time, but eventually she found exactly what she needed near where water from the cave's spring fed a marshy sump. She snapped off one of the long smooth thorns and stripped it clean. Holding it in her teeth, she grabbed two more for backup.

Returning the cave, she set her findings beside the fire. A stone divot in the floor gave enough space to create a small basin. Making something of a loose waterskin from the dead archer's tunic, Senya scooped water from the spring and got the divot filled. Using a pair of stout green twigs, she poked into the center of the fire, retrieved a few of the hottest stones, and dropped them in the water. Steam rose. Soon the water bubbled and popped in a raging boil, filling the shallow cave with haze.

Senya wiped the hawthorn needle and dropped it in. Grabbing Brogan's knife, she went about unlacing the thread binding the arrow fletching.

"What are you doing?" he asked, watching her.

She cleaned the resin from the thread, pulling to straighten it. "I've picked up a few things about healing over the years," she said. "Mostly from my father."

Once clean, she laid the thread in the boiling water.

"Okay, let's see this leg." She peeled the layers of cloth away to expose the cut across his thigh. The gash sighed open. Blood trickled over his skin.

It was not deep and looked clean. So far, so good. But she needed to close it. She dropped a cloth rag into the basin.

Using one of the twigs, she retrieved the thread and secured it to the end of the needle. With speed and deftness, she sent five quick loops through Brogan's skin to close the wound. He winced at the sting of each.

"You've done this before," he said through clenched teeth.

"My brother used to get into scrapes all the time," she said flatly. "But I'm not as good as I used to be." She reached over to the fire and poked to settle the new branches. She added more wood and pushed the tip of Brogan's long knife into the heat of the embers. Turning back to him, she tore the cloth away from where the arrow remained stuck in his side. Leaning close, she touched the wound with her fingertips. Fresh blood pooled.

"Okay," she said after a moment. "Here we go."

Brogan reached out to grip a stone as Senya pulled on the shaft. It moved slowly and wetly. His head flew back, grinding hard into the dirt. He swore and hissed. Blood trickled from the wound. Senya reached to the fire and grabbed the knife. She held it in one hand and pulled the arrow shaft with the other, scorching the edges of the wound. Brogan cried out and swore again. Skin smoked as Senya guided the barbed arrowhead. The air stank of burnt flesh and dirty blood.

And then it was free. She tossed it onto the fire. Using the knife's hot tip, she scorched the skin to stem any remaining blood flow from the ragged wound. She grabbed the hot cloth from the water and wiped it all clean as best she could.

"Only a little longer," she said. "That was the bad one."

She unbound the wound in his shoulder. The damage there was minimal. She cauterized, cleaned, and packed it with cloth. Tearing long strips from an extra bit of the mercenary's clothing, she bound both wounds tightly.

Brogan lay back, exhausted. "Good to have you around."

"Quiet," she ordered. "Just rest." She pushed the fire together again. Flames rose. After a time, she sat back. Brogan rested beside her. Their immediate danger was likely past, but the Hallonath was notorious for bringing deadly surprises to anybody who wasn't careful.

"How far is it to Wayburn?" she asked.

"Maybe thirty miles?" he said. "It's a bit of a walk on this leg, but we can make it."

She nodded, considering everything that had put them here and their uncertain way forward. "Those Vallahnir hold the key to my brother," she said. "I believe that, whatever it is. No matter what they told me or what they're trying to do out here."

"Sure," Brogan cautiously agreed. "Yet they don't strike me as the most trustworthy folk to have dealings with. Might prove difficult to pull anything like the truth out of them, if you happen to get in a position to try."

She managed a weak smile. "I don't know exactly how to say it, but thank you for helping me. For what you did. For everything you're still doing."

The fire popped. A small stream of sparks rose, and a stray one floated across the boulder overhang before blinking out. They spoke no more, and the day moved into afternoon, then slipped into evening. Senya gathered fresh wood and laid it beside the fire. Brogan closed his eyes and slept.

15

SADAHLIA'S DRESSMAKER stood behind her in the looking glass. Stretching a strip of fine, bright cloth across her upper back, the dressmaker noted the color and lay of the fabric. She dropped the strip to Sadahlia's waist. Slender fingers marked the position. These same fingers had crafted most of her garments over the last two decades—so many costumes, so many tiny exhibitions, so many small parades boasting elegance and grace in this contrived court of Her High Honor Crassica the White.

This latest was to be a formal yet revealing affair. Crassica needed to entice one of Kalldon's nascent warlords at an upcoming feast to honor the power-hungry beast of a man, and she had insisted that Sadahlia be as sultry as possible, without appearing aggressively so.

The dressmaker stretched the cloth strip across her hips, muttering to herself while considering placement and position.

Sadahlia gazed into the looking glass. She sought to find some respondent life there, some evidence of a true spark to render reality to this existence, beyond her self-crafted facade. There were rules here. Always had been. But what of her need for Raedwin? What of her love? This was no transgression against the Knowing. This was no fault of theirs. Her desire for him had crystallized through no action of her own. So why should she suffer for it? Why should he?

"There is no balance here," she whispered aloud. "There is only struggle."

The dressmaker glanced at her and smiled. "I am sorry, my lady," she said quietly. She knelt and examined various hemlines and falls of cloth.

111

She stood and draped fabric over Sadahlia's shoulders, holding several marking pins in her puckered lips. Drawing the sheet square, she adjusted its fall. Her skilled hands gathered the cloth at the waist and tried different positions of fold and flow. Points of potential joining. She muttered to herself as she considered angles and shape.

Sadahlia let out a sigh. How long could this flawed and foolish dance continue? What was the use of beauty when one's entire existence was false? She could feel, and she could believe, so maybe that did mean she was truly alive, despite the fact her body was not. In the end, was she really all that different from Raedwin's Brohndai father in the Far North? He had succumbed to his own desires as well, with consequences rippling through the entire fabric of the Knowing. The father had begat the son, and then the son had brought those same yearnings home to Sadahlia—fostering a confusion within her that neither could ever have possibly imagined.

Crassica appeared in the doorway, her milky shape rippling in the looking glass. She drifted into the room. The dressmaker followed Sadahlia's eyes and straightened.

"Your High Honor," the dressmaker humbly greeted, bobbing a short but proper curtsy. "A pleasure."

Crassica gave a thin tight smile. She turned and gestured toward the door.

The dressmaker dipped her chin in deference. She laid the cloth on a side table and placed the marking pins in a small ceramic dish. She bowed to Sadahlia. "My lady," she said and left the room.

Crassica closed the door behind the dressmaker. She regarded Sadahlia. Her razor smile held firm as she came closer. "I trust you remain enthusiastic about the entertainment of our young friend from Kalldon."

"*Enthusiastic* is a strong word."

Crassica's jaw clenched as her upper lip curled. "Oh, my delicious Sadahlia. Why do you mock? You sound like our sweet Raedwin. You of all our precious Sisters should know the larger picture."

"Oh, I know the picture. We are all just players in your grand production. Of course I understand."

"The crafting of your presence here has a role, the same as any other. You would be wise to remember that."

"I remember clearly," Sadahlia said sharply. "But do you? I was with you before all this began. Do you remember? I see what you want me to see, but we should both try to understand where all this might end. You as well as I. After everything, are we all just a handful of misguided deviants, or are we trying to truly be something more? Something new. I'm not sure I remember the call anymore."

Crassica came to Sadahlia and reached up to brush her cheek. "These insects among whom we weave our tale need not be overly troubled by our passing. Why not spread enjoyment rather than fear? Why not allow some play rather than simply dominating them all?"

"For you, there doesn't seem to be much difference."

Crassica shrugged. She picked up one of the dressmaker's marking pins. "You should be aware, by the way, I have ordered our dear Raedwin confined to his places of study. Or those in which he is working or procuring materials."

Sadahlia displayed nonchalance with a weary sigh. "What's he done this time?"

Crassica waved a casual hand. "Oh, it is nothing to really be concerned about. I am allowing him to move about the Keep however he needs to achieve his ends, but he is strictly to remain within the citadel, returning to his tower each night. At least for now."

"Is this some sort of punishment?" Sadahlia spoke slowly, keeping her voice steady.

"Not yet, no. I merely need him to be more careful where he goes, that is all. And who he sees."

Sadahlia watched her. "Who has he seen?"

Crassica placed the marking pin carefully back in its dish. "It is not who he has seen just yet. It is who or what he may meet or see in the future." She smiled at Sadahlia. "So you will understand that I need all of my Sisters to stay away from him."

She forced a smile. "Why would I go near him? You know he annoys me."

"There is no reason to let it upset you," Crassica assured. "I have already spoken to the others. This should not impact anything nor harm the brilliance of his work. Chief Kraegha will be tracking his movements, so we can be assured of his continued safety."

"His safety." Sadahlia stiffened. "That is nice word for it." She allowed herself a frown, as if pondering Crassica's order. When finally she spoke, she let her words out slowly, under control. "It does strike one as a little harsh, though, I will admit."

Crassica tilted her head. "Really? What makes you say that?"

Sadahlia turned fully to her, studying the aging Vallahnir's face. There was a time long ago in which she'd deeply respected her mentor, maybe even loved her, but over so many years, she'd been witness to so many strange and dubious efforts, and their separation had completed itself years ago. It had simply taken a while to realize.

"We can't escape the Knowing, no matter how much we might try," Sadahlia said gently. "Her fabric is woven through the tapestry of all things, and outside the Knowing there is nothing. There is only being and non-being. There are no other ways."

Crassica stepped toward her, coming uncomfortably close.

"So we both need to remember," Sadahlia continued, "not what you want, nor what I want, but that all of our desires are useless next to the eternal threads of the Knowing. And the Knowing herself does see what you are doing. She is always watching."

Crassica reached up and slid her fingers under Sadahlia's chin, pushing her face slightly upward. The exposed lines of her neck pulsed with living blood coursing through her pale body. "We are shapers of our own world now," she whispered. "Beyond the reach of your precious Knowing. We are the writers of rules here. Arbiters of our own justice. You, my dear Sadahlia, need to understand that, most of all."

Sadahlia pushed a smile through Crassica's grip. "Oh, I understand," she said between her teeth. "More than you'll probably ever realize."

§ 16 §

BROGAN'S SLEEP was plagued with nightmares. Dreams of running through a dim and confusing forest. Massive wildfires raged on either side, trees swaying in the twisting inferno. On the far side of a deep black chasm, his lost bride reclined next to their daughter on a quiet grassy slope, wearing a light dress the color of an evening sun. His heart ached. He cried out to them from the edge of the fire. His wife smiled and hailed in a language he could not understand. Her voice fell silent in the drifting air, forfeit to the abyss between them.

You, at least, can be free, she whispered, the sound close to his ear. Her breath hot against his skin. *Go, and save yourself. There is no hope for us.*

He woke to the sound of drums thudding a steady pulse into the earth. Then nothing. Rising onto one elbow, he listened. The small sheltered cave lay silent and alive. Waiting.

"Bad dream?" Senya asked from near the fire.

Brogan nodded. "Yeah." He sat up.

"About a daughter you lost."

He turned to her, brow furrowed. "How did you know?"

She turned to the fire. Poked the coals with a stick. "I have that effect on people sometimes. Especially if the daughter is gone."

For a time, they both watched the flames in silence. A coyote cried some distance away, its otherworldly wail echoing through the trees. "We got out of Corregidon with a few other families," Brogan said as the sound died away. "Went to live up in the mountain valleys of the Elrune.

Pastured a few cows and planted some mountain wheat and berries, even built a little brewery. Life was almost good."

"You don't have to tell me. I'm sorry—I shouldn't have…"

"No, it's fine. I just…" Brogan's mind moved to memories that had never found words before, broken pieces of his past that couldn't easily be worked back together. "I've never told anybody," he said. "Been out here on my own since they…" His words floated loosely, addressing the night, the forest, and Senya maybe only as an afterthought.

"We were almost happy. Until the boneskins came."

Senya let out a quiet gasp. "Oh, gods…"

"Half the people with us were simple farmers and sustainers, not fighters. They'd never hit anybody with anything more than a fist. We tried to get out, but the boneskins kept coming. They hunted us down like the whole thing was some kind of game. Burned through and ravaged everything that moved. Didn't slow down until they hit snow. And then feasted on the dead. After a while, we ran out of room and got ourselves pinned down in some caves with no water, no food, and no hope to speak of. And Dahlwea, my wife…" He trailed off, his voice failing at the forming of her name.

Brogan regained himself. "Dahlwea wanted me to end it for her. She thought there was no way to stop them. They'd rape her and our daughter both, and then kill me, in that order. She wanted at least to control her own death and to take our little Glenna with her."

The weight of distant defeat curved his shoulders low. The fire cracked and pulsed, devouring the fresh dry wood.

"She said it'd be better to burn than be ripped apart by animals."

Senya studied him. At length, she reached out and placed a hand on his arm. A simple human touch, after so many years without. They sat like that for a long silent moment.

"All I had left was to fight," he said. "Fought my wife, fought myself, and fought those godscursed boneskins, all on my own. But Dahlwea, she couldn't take the chance of watching me die right in front of her, so she lit a pyre. Took Glenna's life first, and then her own. The cave was already a furnace by the time I got back. Blood covered the stone. Both of them were already gone."

Brogan leaned back and stretched his legs in front of him. He shook his head, eyes holding on the flames. "I never got why they came after us so hard. We were nothing special. We'd never been anything special." He gave Senya the best smile he could muster.

"I've not had a great history at keeping people safe, but I'll do what I can to help you," he said. "That much I promise. Regardless of whether I turn out to be useless again in the end."

Tiny sparks rose from the fire and floated upward into blackness. Birds cried from the branches in answer to the deep calling grunts of toads in the marsh. It was almost pretty, almost the sort of scene Brogan would wish for if he ever wished for things. But wishing served no purpose. There was what happened and what did not happen. The rest was all vapors and uselessness.

"Hold still," Senya warned. Dawn peeked through the trees, red under a slate-gray sky, their second morning in the shelter. Carefully she peeled away the bandage on his leg and examined the wound. She pressed near the edges with her fingers. "Does that hurt?"

"No more than it does all the time."

She poured water into a small metal pot, placing it at the edge of the coals.

"Hey, where'd you find my one good pot?"

Senya crushed a few small leaves and dropped them into the simmering water. "About the only thing left up there we could still use."

She examined his leg wound again and then unwrapped his shoulder and side. She bent and scrutinized each wound closely. Turning away, she crushed a few smaller leaves in the pot with a blunt stick, like a makeshift mortar and pestle. She dropped in some needles and short wide grasses, grinding them all together.

"I have to ask," Brogan said. "I shouldn't, I know. I have no right to ask, and you don't have to answer. It's none of my business really. But I have to ask…"

Senya grabbed a longer, thinner stick and poked the fire to push a few fresh coals next to the pot. She continued to grind the mixture into a wet paste.

"Vallahnir aren't real…" he continued. "They don't walk around. And no Brohndai in all history has ever had a child. Never heard of either thing. Ever. Not in any tale in any alehouse anywhere…"

She glanced at him. "So how is it that a Brohndai has a daughter?"

"Sorry. I guess you probably get that a lot."

"Only every time." She ground the mixture, and then with a rag she pulled the pot from the fire and set it near Brogan's leg. "I have brother as well. A twin."

"There are two of you?"

Laying the rag carefully next to the pot, she tested the mixture's temperature with her fingers. Satisfied, she scooped and spread a thin layer over the laceration in Brogan's leg.

"My father was once the Faramund of Yesteralen," Senya explained as she worked. "Which meant he was an envoy of the High Council of the Order. Even after the Banishment, he continued to serve all the various temples of the Way as best he could, mostly in secret. And my mother was a devoted pilgrim of the Way, paying homage at all those same temples. Both of them traveled under the blind eye of the empire. She was from the Baelhoarg, the ancient home of the Brohndai, but they actually met in Jordinia. They shared stories of home and made one another laugh. They learned from each other, inspired respect, and started to feel things."

Senya gently pulled a strip of fresh clean cloth around Brogan's leg, wrapping twice and tightening, then tying it off. "Which, of course, was against the Way. Such emotional attachments are not allowed."

She moved to begin spreading the paste into Brogan's side, her touch light and comforting. "The Council did not agree with my father taking up intimate relations with a woman, and they got a whole lot more agitated when they found she was pregnant. So they cast him out. They stripped him of his authority and titles, his position in the Order. All of it."

Brogan opened his mouth, but any attempt at words all seemed flat and strange. He said nothing. Senya wrapped his side with new bandages, drawing them tight and true.

"So now my father has become true flesh of the living world," she said. "He is now mortal and has started to age, the same as the rest of us. Some day he too will die, like you, and like me." She placed a hand on his chest. "Can you turn a little? I need to do your shoulder."

He obliged, feeling as though he should say something—something reassuring or helpful and kind—but his mind fell to nothing but platitudes and false hope.

"For all time and memory," Senya continued as she worked the paste into his shoulder wound. "The Brohndai passed through this world and lived among the people but were never really of the people. Brohndai did not fall in love, not with any one individual, not ever. To some, my father and mother were unnatural. They were a disgrace. An atrocity. At best, nothing more than a cursed accident." She fell quiet as she wrapped his shoulder.

"I doubt any of this was an accident," Brogan said to the fire.

"I can't imagine what they looked like back then, down in Jordinia. A tall black-cloaked ghost of the Baelhoarg together with a tiny woman of the North."

Finished, Senya stepped away and knelt by the fire. She pushed a small crushed bundle of mosses and strange twigs to the edge of the coals, sending up a shower of sparks.

"Misfits are often the best match," Brogan said quietly.

The bundle crackled, and smoke curled from its twisted center. The air filled with a pungent sweetness. The throbbing pain in Brogan's leg and shoulder ebbed, releasing its grip. His body eased and relaxed. Firelight danced across the stone ceiling.

"They fled by ship," Senya said after a time. "Got caught in a storm from the Knowing's own nightmares. My mother went into labor, rather inconveniently, and so I was born at sea, in that storm. Within sight of Vesterlag's port. My brother, Raedwin, arrived two long hours later, on the wood-plank floor of a dirty dock warehouse.

"Right from the beginning, life with an outcast Brohndai brought constant scrutiny and finger-pointing to our little family. Suspicion and blame everywhere we went. No chance for us to live around other children. No chance at all. But there we were. And so we tried. Did what we could. My father remained never far away but always in the shadows. Giving protection when he was able, advice and healing when he was not. Such was the bargain my parents struck. Until some years ago the Order demanded that he return to Faeroen and give up his wanderings once and for all. He's not been allowed to leave the island since."

At length, Senya gave Brogan a small, tired smile. "And so here we are."

She reached out with a long stick to tighten the coals and then placed two fresh chunks of wood crosswise. Stepping away, she went to sit with her back against the cave wall.

Brogan watched her. "And that's it?"

"What more did you want?"

"Where's your mother?"

Senya watched the fire. "My mother is gone," she said. "Passed into the Everlife years ago."

"She must have died young."

"No, not at all. She lived to be pretty old. She was a strong woman."

Brogan struggled to find words, confused. "But how…"

"I've got the gift of a lingering long life, courtesy of my once-immortal father," she said slowly. "I'm not as young as I look."

"You're what… nineteen? Maybe twenty if you push it…"

Senya turned to him. "I have already seen my seventy-second summer."

Brogan's mouth fell open. "Wait," he said dumbly. His words fell out before he could temper their coarseness. "You're fucking *seventy-two* years old?"

She smiled for real at his shock. "I have the blood of a Brohndai… so I'm blessed—or cursed, as the case may be."

All this time, the slight young woman next to Brogan was actually older than any person he'd ever met in his life—as old as grandmothers of kings, grandfathers of patriarchs—nearly as old as the most ancient village elder in all of Brinsfallon.

"Seventy-two," he muttered to himself, shaking his head.

His gaze fell to the fire. Whatever was in the smoking bundle at its edge did lift his spirits and ease his mind, but all of this would take a little more than a few herbs to get used to. Brogan's lids grew heavy.

"Seventy-two," he whispered. "Hells…"

Senya poked at the fresh wood. A shower of sparks rose and bounced across the boulder ceiling, becoming lost in the gnarled tree limbs hanging outside the cave. Soon, Brogan closed his eyes and fell asleep again.

🔆 17 🔆

CRASSICA DID her best to ignore Lanius's probing questions. She preferred to let him sort the details out on his own. "I do not know how many of the Sevenfold's Children there are out in the forest," she repeated. "Nor how powerful they could be if they all joined together as an organized force." She did not much care about either. The first of the Sevenfold's Children had long ago bred their own children, and generations had followed those. She had not taken the time to track them all. "There is little chance of them all banding together anyway," she added. "We have taken many pains over the years to make sure that could never happen."

"Viewing the Children as nothing but an abomination is not wise," Lanius said. "There are other methods of control."

"Which I have tried. You forget, it has been many, many years. How far from the mine are they? Do they threaten our guards?"

"Not yet. But this is one attack. There will be more to come."

"I am sure training and weapons will outplay numbers if it comes to that. I need you to see this resistance quelled. Right now, I have other matters in need of attention."

She studied the series of parchment maps on the table again. Some were ancient and some much newer, all drafted with a deft and knowledgeable hand. The North was somewhat familiar to her, yet many of its workings remained a mystery. Brinsfallon's fertile lands reached over great distances, braced by Stronaway and Cellenway, with the Elban and Brundsril rivers snaking across its heart. She already had plenty of eyes in Corregidon, and more than a few in Donasberth and Pentmore. Her ample coin could buy others, if needed. But Brinsfallon was not Kalldonia. She could not see those lands as well as she would like.

Lanius followed her gaze. He let out a noise of curiosity. "Has something gone wrong with your… project?"

"Nothing you need concern yourself with just yet."

Crassica ran her fingers over the maps. The idea had been simple—from Pentmore, one traveled southward along the Old Kreskill Road through the Breach to Ryngsvoy, and then only the Straights remained. Once in Toncana, Senya would be within much easier reach. Nothing left to stand in Crassica's way.

And yet the plan remained in stasis. Delayed.

What had she missed? Someone or something had pushed life from two of her Sisters, causing great effort to effect their return to the field of play. More delays. Crassica had nearly felt each arrowhead penetrate from here. The dreaded forest of the Hallonath should be a place of great strength for the Vallahnir, not a weakness. If her Sisters could not find a way to restore Senya to their path, Crassica would have to find another way.

But maybe the answer lay in a different direction altogether.

"Speaking of this… preoccupation," Lanius said, an uncharacteristic hesitation entering his voice. "You ordered Raedwin to be tracked and watched at all times, but I'm not sure the effort is being properly carried out."

"This remains his home. Do not overcomplicate."

"He is being allowed to move about nearly at will. What does tracking his movements accomplish?"

"He is not a prisoner. I simply need to know where he is. And what he does."

"He's already lost Chief Kraegha's trackers several times. And once lost, who is to say where he goes? And what he does?"

"Our Raedwin has heard the message, and he will comply. He remains in our service. For now, we do nothing but observe."

"I cannot ensure he is properly followed if Kraegha's people do not do their jobs."

At last, Crassica turned to him. She did appreciate his zeal for a properly executed task, but sometimes his attention to details remained below her level of interest. "Let it go for now," she said gently. "It is best if Raedwin remains complicit, happy, and here. Concentrate on the Children and your task in the forest. As long as Raedwin is not running off to join them, it will all be fine."

"There's more than his work going on with him—that much I can guarantee you."

"He is a curious child. Discovery is like a drug. We can afford to let him have a taste here and there to keep his interest sated."

"And when he bites off more than a taste?"

Crassica assured him with a smile. "I still need him for a little while longer. My focus remains in the North. Soon all will be made right again, after this... distraction... is remedied."

Lanius nodded agreement. As always, he would do as she asked. He glanced at the maps. "Is the twin back in hand, then?"

"She will be," Crassica replied with an easy confidence. "Soon enough."

18

RAEDWIN WAS awakened by a quiet knock at the door and saw stars glittering outside the wall of windows. He sat up and rubbed his eyes. He'd fallen asleep at his desk again. Had the sound of the knock been real, or had it come from some fleeting dream?

Another followed, soft and indefinite. He rose. Sliding the iron bolt, he opened the door.

A cloaked figure stood silhouetted against dim torchlight. Sadahlia's eyes gleamed from the shadows beneath the hood.

"What are you doing?" he whispered. "You're not supposed to be up here..."

"I need to see you." She pushed past him into the room.

"You're crazy. They'll catch you." Raedwin glanced at the dark stairs behind. Quiet and empty. No movement, no sign of watchers. He swung the door closed and latched the bolt.

"I slipped past as they shifted patrols," she said.

"Why are you here? I thought we agreed..."

"I needed to see you."

He moved to embrace her. "I'm not complaining. It's just dangerous."

She stepped away and sat in a chair next to the edge of his worktable. Her back rigid, hands on her thighs, she stared at a blank spot on the far wall. She slid her palms forward to her knees and back again.

"I saw you dead," she said.

"You what?"

"It was a vision. Or a dream. Sometimes I have trouble with the difference."

"You saw me dead?"

Her eyes focused on the wall. "It was an image of long ago, or of a day yet to come. I can't tell. Men carried you, rushing through a burning building. Friends of yours. They were good to you."

Raedwin lit another tallow candle and then an extra oil lamp in a small alcove near his writing desk. A warm glow filled the room.

"Roof timbers fell in flame all around. Your sister was in the shadows, crying." Sadahlia turned to him, her eyes glistening. "And yet more tears came from your false Vallahnir courtesan…"

"Don't say that. There is nothing false here. Please don't say that. You are my love."

"I saw it. It was a vision. You were dead."

"Only a bad dream."

"Vallahnir do not easily dream. For us, the images come from a place of sight born in the Crosslands—a place of meaning and truth."

He dragged a chair next to her and sat. "You're not a Vallahnir anymore, not really." He reached for her. "You are Sadahlia. You are here with me. I am not dead."

"They are coming for us. Not tonight, and maybe not tomorrow, but they will. Someday. And maybe soon. They will come for you, and they will burn your house around you, and your unholy pleasuregirl will weep until there is no salt left in the world."

He pulled her to him and spoke into her pressed cheek. "Please do not say that. We are here. Right now we are here. Let's not scar our time together with words like that."

"But it's true," she insisted. "Crassica dresses me and paints me and parades me through these halls as if I'm some fancy toy, some plaything she gets to display to those she wants to control. She is my madam. I have become her trophy girl meant for show."

"Nobody controls you."

"Why do you think she needs so much of her precious Amaris? Did you think that's just for fun?"

Raedwin knew the refined crystals of Brasti Ore helped support Crassica's perceptions, deepened her energies and resolve, and maybe allowed her greater insight in ways he'd rather not think about. But control over others? That was too much. Or at least more than he wanted to admit.

"And you and I sneak away into the bowels of the earth like rats," Sadahlia said. "Giving payment in useless secrets and silly promises."

"Please do not talk like that."

"I am nothing more than a whore for the pleasure of her manipulations."

"You are the pleasure of my heart. You are my world. I love you. That is all you need. I love you, and we pay one another with promises we will keep, not with useless secrets."

She moved away from him and regarded his face, her eyes searching his. "Tell me why you stayed here," she said. "Years ago, in the beginning, you were so curious and engaged with your work, but then you became hesitant and suspicious of this place, and especially of her. But you stayed. Why?"

"I don't know. I was fascinated. There was so much to learn. The library. The knowledge and discovery…"

"Even then. After the tower and the library, you weren't yet sure."

"It took time."

"Is that all?"

"And you."

"Exactly." Her voice quieted, heavy with a grave weight. "And now our fates are sealed."

"I'm not sure I know what you mean."

"From the moment we met, the two of us have been owned by her. Separately, and together."

"She doesn't own you. And she sure as all four hells doesn't own me."

"Doesn't she?" Sadahlia cocked her head. "Look at you. Confined to your workshop. Tracked everywhere you go. Watched, like a prisoner."

Raedwin shook his head. "That's temporary. I wasn't careful enough…"

"We were both brought here, both invited by her. Decades apart, but the seductions were complete. For both of us. And now we're left here waiting, wondering what our master has in store—for both of us."

"Seduction is one thing. Ownership is something else."

"I am no longer allowed to speak to you. Did you know that? None of us are. Not in private, not in the open, not alone, and not in a crowd. Not in a ceremony. Never."

"She doesn't know anything about us."

"I will not be treated like this. I am not hers to control."

"I'm not either. We belong only to ourselves."

She gave him an exhausted smile, like a mother to a child. "All the pieces on the gameboard are at the whims of the player," she said quietly. "The Peasant never knows its position against the Knight. Or the Queen."

"Let's leave, then. Get off the gameboard. Let's get out of here."

Sadahlia let out a long and tired sigh. "I have trouble moving quickly over distance—you know that. Travel takes a level of training and focus that I never pursued. The others are much better than I am."

When Sadahlia had first crossed over to this living plane, she'd said it felt like stepping through a heavy curtain onto a fully lit stage. Confusing as well as alluring. Her performance in this life had been a stumbling and awkward affair until a rhythm could be found. Breathing, walking, and speaking—even bleeding—had all been new adventures to master.

"I would be a burden to you," she said.

"I will carry that burden. Anywhere."

He knew they could do it. They really could. Between the two of them, their knowledge of the Keep would allow them to escape unseen. They could make their way north. Together.

"My sister lives outside Pentmore," he said. "It's far from anywhere. She knows this world, and she would understand. I've been thinking about her a lot lately. She would take us in. She would help."

An opaque sadness flashed over Sadahlia's face. "Crassica would end me if she caught us trying to flee." She sat back down next to him and let her head rest against his shoulder. "I don't know what she would do to you."

"We'll live with Senya in Brinsfallon and raise some goats," he said. "Or maybe move to the Baelhoarg. Crassica would never find us in the Baelhoarg."

Sadahlia laughed, the bright sound ringing through the dim. "Can you imagine me in the Baelhoarg? We are not so easily hidden. Not outside these walls."

"Senya and I lived our whole lives that way. We'll figure it out."

Sadahlia smiled. Her cheek twitched, holding back a bitter sadness long held in check. "No, my love," she said. "Not yet. It's better to stay here. Keep hidden and listen. Find out what she's up to exactly."

Raedwin considered this. Maybe she was right. Maybe it was better to stay here. But in spite of all that, they were both still running blind, one step behind, seeing less and less as everything unfolded around them.

Some time ago, Sadahlia had told him the story of her emergence into this world. She'd explained how it had taken long years of study and practice, with repeated mistakes and successes. It was similar to Raedwin building his sophisticated machines with wings of wood and bronze to catch the wind, enacting his will over the land. They were the same, in a way. Wasn't he looking for his own living rhythms, just like her? They still had so much to learn from one another.

"I wish Crassica would tell me the truth," he said.

Sadahlia pulled his face to hers, watching him with her glittering feline eyes. "Even if she did, you shouldn't trust it. There's something hidden underneath everything she says."

He opened his mouth to answer, to say that of course he never really trusted Crassica, but he knew that wasn't the truth. From the very beginning, he'd been a little naive with her. His machines and experiments were for learning and for advancing the knowledge of humankind, for the good of all, and he had thought he was trying to find strengths in engineering, better mobility and cleaner water. But maybe he'd been trying to master himself all along.

Crassica over and again proclaimed the ideals of knowledge and learning. Of building. She had long told him that with enough study, some day they might possibly cure humanity of all disease. But Sadahlia had warned him that such talk was all a show. *She has plots and schemes, one on top of another,* she had said. *Ways of manipulating everyone around her to whatever ends she likes. Never mind the problems they cause.*

Always a plan. Hidden moves. Raedwin could usually sort out what each thing Crassica did was about, how it worked, and where each little endgame landed. Until now. He sometimes didn't approve, and often disagreed, but at least he usually knew. But Crassica's latest efforts were more opaque than anything she had ever done. He'd failed to find her cause this time.

Sadahlia let her hands fall away. "Do you remember your vision of the mine?"

The question caught him off guard. Strangely out of place. "The one from the hills outside the walls? I barely saw anything."

"Did you see any of the workers?"

He tried to remember. He hadn't given it much thought since the vision had shifted so fast when he'd been pulled away to Senya. More emotion than actual sight, muddled and confused. "It felt like hunger," he said. "Not something engineered or planned. More like an injury—like a gash in the earth. A wound."

Sadahlia nodded, considering. "You've heard of the Sevenfold's Children, yes? In the forests east of here."

Of course he'd heard of them. He'd even seen them. "Why?"

"You think she's ever told you the truth about them?"

"I've heard the stories..." Recent talk of breaking borders and attacking boundaries. All of it sounded more sinister than Crassica let on.

"Stories are one thing. The truth is something else." Sadahlia reached out to hold his hand, fixing on his eyes for a long moment. "You think you know who and what they are. And you think you understand what is going on out there at the mine. Crassica's Brasti Ore—her *Amaris*—and what it does. But how much of that knowledge came from her, filtered and focused into what she wants you to think?"

She looked down at their hands together, her grip tightening as she considered her next words, weighing their consequences. A sentry called out the turn of the hour far below the workshop.

"I have to go," she said at last. "The next time we meet, I will take you. There is more to all of this, and it's time you fully understood."

$$ \text{❧ } 19 \text{ ❦} $$

SENYA WATCHED Brogan gather his things and strap a sword to his hip. Three full days had passed since the attack, and he claimed to be strong enough to make it to Wayburn. Senya wasn't so sure about that, but she agreed it was best to get moving. She took the crossbow and gave a silent wish that she would not need to use it again.

They moved quickly, keeping to the cover of dense trees. Brogan explained that Wayburn lay to the north, and if they aimed generally northeast, they'd come eventually to the Old Kreskill Road, which would point the rest of the way from there. Hesitant mists held low to the ground. As they crested a small rise, their way forward disappeared into a thick blanket of impenetrable fog.

Brogan paused in silence for a long moment, then led Senya with caution into the hushed vale. The mist soon pinched away most of the morning light, shrouding the trees with a faint gloom. The forest fell silent. After a time, they came to a place where the land choked at a narrow point, and they forced their way forward. Boulders the size of small houses lined a wide rocky space. They slowed.

Two pale figures emerged from a murky haze at the far side of the clearing, their lean bodies erect and poised. Hoods pulled low, gleaming blue eyes peered into the world from the earth's earliest primal breath. Flickers of light from among shadows. In another time and place they would almost be beautiful.

Cevellica stared without emotion, devoid of either sympathy or malice.

Puncture marks scarred both of the Vallahnir's cloaks, bloodstained holes in the thin gray cloth where Brogan's arrows had penetrated days before. The mist lay thick and gray, offering no hint of the sun.

Senya stepped into the clearing. Vibrations ran through the earth at her feet as she gathered force from the grasses and ferns, all the trees surrounding the glade. Voices swirled in her head. Incantations from the fabric of all living things. All of it new. Foreign, even. Seeing Cevellica again awakened a strange new level of senses, brought to life from deep within her Brohndai blood, sparked by the arcane rituals they'd enacted upon her back in Pentmore.

"I would ask you about my brother," she called. "But I know that whatever answer you gave would still be some kind of lie."

A bared-toothed grin opened beneath Cevellica's gray hood. She pointed at Brogan. "This one," she hissed, "has caused much trouble."

"Yep," he answered. "And here's a little more." Without pause, he nocked an arrow and shot the quiet nameless Vallahnir through the face. Her head flew back, the arrow perforating false skin and bone, illusory tissue of her self-made body. She let out a short cry and wavered on her feet. Brogan sent another shaft into her chest. The Vallahnir collapsed.

Cevellica pivoted her focus to him. Senya watched in horror as Brogan's footing wavered. Cevellica was doing something to him, something Senya could almost see—a swirling barbed pain as Brogan stumbled and went down to one knee. Cevellica stepped toward him slowly, a sinister casualness in her approach. She smiled again. Brogan wheezed and gasped, his hands splayed on the ground.

"We never meant you harm," she assured, her voice smooth and inviting. "And yet you did not listen. Sending arrows, without words or waiting." She stepped closer. Brogan choked into silence. "So we shall take you now, on this day, in advance of your appointed time."

Senya raised the crossbow and loosed the bolt. It flew low and nailed Cevellica in the thigh. The Vallahnir's eyes flashed with an inhuman savagery as she stepped back, snarling in pain.

A sudden terror knifed through Senya as well then, a primal fear pouring forth with a sharp light, the spearpoint tip aimed into her heart—focused and fierce, bent on a white-hot control. Whispers came. Voices jeering in a throaty tongue. Volatile panic coursed through her body and set the forest on fire. Everything slowed. All light went dim. Nothing remained but an overwhelming desire for Cevellica to go away. To back off and be gone. All breath left her. She fell to her knees, unable to move.

Volcanic chants built in Senya's mind, churning, until a frustrated cry erupted from her mouth involuntarily, coming from deep beneath her toes, forming words from somewhere else entirely. Her scream ripped through the clearing as she slammed a fist to the ground.

A shockwave ring split the air—tearing Cevellica's gripping force away.

Brogan rolled to his back. He gulped the damp air, suddenly free.

Cevellica stepped away and drew a fearsome black blade. "Old Powers are not for this place! A new age has come!"

Senya stood. Her voice continued on its own, whispering an ancient song with lyrics narrowly beyond recognition, from the earth and the living forest alike. The song surged through the air, penetrating all manner of skin and bone from both within and beyond her, from a time long since lost but also from an age yet to come.

Brogan came to his feet and drew his sword. A pained recognition flashed across Cevellica's face as she flung coarse words from her own brutal language. She lunged with her blade high. Brogan jumped to block her path, and together they fell to the ground in a blur of clothing and a quick flash of steel. The Vallahnir let out a shriek. Brogan's blade cut deeply across her side. He spun and drove the point through her ribs. The Vallahnir struggled with her final remaining breath and then lay still.

Senya fell quiet and stared at the bodies of the two Vallahnir, by all appearances nothing more than two awkward corpses on the ground. Death to life and back to death again. What strange hidden sorcery had Crassica discovered to allow these few to build bodies like this? Such cursed and twisted necromancy, fused with all levels of the Dark Arts.

Brogan rose and came to stand beside her. "So what now?" he said. "I got this far once already."

Senya gathered her words for a long moment before answering, drawing from nearly forgotten memories of stories alongside her father in the firelight. "Creatures of the Crosslands cannot be killed with knives or arrows alone," she said quietly, almost a whisper. "At least not permanently. From this sort of thing, they are able to return, given a little time and effort. So we have to force them back into the Crosslands for good. We need to finish them."

"That sounds good. But how?"

"Severance and fire." She turned to him. "We have to separate heads from bodies. And then we burn it all to nothing."

Although not human exactly, the faces of the Vallahnir remained too near the real thing for the task to be easy. Senya looked away as flames caressed their pale features. Though everything they had told her was a lie, these elegant women still held some connection to her brother. And that connection was now gone. As far as Senya knew, these two had been the last of anybody in Brinsfallon who knew anything about Raedwin's whereabouts.

She had seen thirteen Vallahnir in her vision, but was that all? Or did Crassica have an untold host hidden somewhere? The old tales told of no limit, no number. Vallahnir slipped in and out of the world as if from a dream, and they simply took you with them if they wished.

Where had these thirteen come from? And most importantly, was Raedwin with them?

All Senya's remaining hope now rested in the Brohndai Elders of Faeroen and any sense they could make of what was going on, along with whatever help they might be able to provide. The same Elders of the Order's High Council who had once cast out her father and mother both, for nothing more than the blatant crime of falling in love. The same Elders of the Order who had condemned them to fend for themselves, with two tiny children, out on their own in the deadly Baelhoarg cold.

The fire grew to a roaring blaze and devoured the bodies quickly. Skulls crumbled to ash as the flesh burned away, so unlike the bones of the living. Swiftly returned to dust. As the fire died, Senya and Brogan spread the remains across the clearing to complete the banishment.

Whatever the Elders had to say, Senya would not surrender. She would not let this fail. She would not allow herself to be controlled by any fate other than her own. She stepped away from the flames and the remains of the two distorted Vallahnir, the corrupt providence they'd aimed to hold over her, and together with Brogan continued on their uncertain way toward Wayburn.

PART THREE

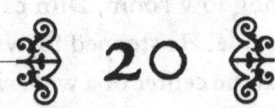

20

RAEDWIN STROLLED through the sunlit courtyard of the lower citadel. Colorful carts displayed various wares, while smoke drifted from a compact cookpot nearby, spreading aromas of stewing vegetables and pork. Faint music jangled from a performance on a wide platform. Most of the residents and all the servants would be here today, along with a few ragged and tattered locals from the countryside. Everybody came for the caravan.

Raedwin wound his way through the small loose crowd. He'd doubled back and slipped his trackers in one of the more confusing corridors beneath the Keep, but just to make sure, he ducked out of sight at the rear of a tall plankboard cart. Sadahlia was there, on the other side, moving past a makeshift array of multicolored silks and fabrics. She glanced at Raedwin and caught him watching. Her glittering eyes shone. She slipped behind a display of handwrought jewelry.

He moved to follow, keeping an eye on the walled edge of the courtyard as well as the gateway through which he'd entered. No sign of anyone tracking him.

On the other side of the caravan, Sadahlia pulled a long slip of red silk through her elegant hands. She turned away and moved on. Each cart she passed took her closer to a particular area of neglect and disrepair in the walls below the Keep, closer to cracks and fissures that allowed passage to deep and hidden pathways disconnected from the rest of the citadel. With skillful subtlety, she ducked through a split in the stone foundation and disappeared.

Raedwin took a different route to a separate portion of broken wall. None took notice. No eyes tracked him. He slipped into shadows unseen, and the caravan sounds died away behind him. Moving through the musty ruins, he came to the top of a stone stairway leading down. He lit a torch and held the flame aloft before descending to an underground hallway. Water dripped down one wall. He pressed on into the heaving darkness.

The hem of a cloak disappeared through a doorway ahead. Raedwin followed and entered a long low room. Dim candlelight pulsed from a second opening on the far side. He stepped forward with steady care.

Sadahlia stood naked in the center of a wide ring of candles. Her white skin smoldered in the scintillating glow. She grinned at him. Raedwin dropped his torch to the floor and slid off his leather satchel. Wordless, he stepped through the ring of candles and kissed her.

With a body somewhere between substance and illusion, fused from elements of both life and death, Sadahlia wasn't exactly human—in truth, not actually alive. But what did *alive* really mean? She held more life and love in her than plenty of the people Raedwin had known over the years—plenty who lived and died all over this world. She'd built herself an existence full of joy and sadness and laughter and shame, all of these things and more. Sadahlia had a surprisingly adept understanding of humor, one of the most difficult human dances to fake. She'd brought Raedwin so many things he'd only dreamed about before coming here. Crassica herself hadn't reached these heights.

They made love standing against the ancient broken wall, bearing down on masoned stonework built long before either of their lives had begun on this earth. *Made* love, as if together they'd created the idea of it in this very moment, crafted it out of a shared desperation coursing through their bodies with the unbreakable union of life penetrating death, entwined together as one. She moaned and let out a cry. He gripped her muscled back as if clinging to the glittering shell of his own misspoken life, pressing their bodies against the cold embrace of stone. He shuddered, his hand splayed against the hewn wall.

Finished, they stood motionless. The sound of each breath scattered through the echoing darkness while the torch guttered on the stone floor. She sighed quietly. "Each time we are together," she whispered, "I understand life a little bit better. I can feel it a little more completely."

Raedwin shifted to the side, rolling his back to the wall next to her. "I'm so tired of sneaking around like this," he said. "Hiding down here in the dark all the time."

"She's a jealous creature, our Crassica. And she fixates on you."

"But why?" He watched the candlelight bathe her pure skin. "I wasn't the first she lured here. Probably won't be the last."

Sadahlia gathered her clothing from the corner and began to dress. "You hold a special place of esteem in her eyes, for whatever reason. Still to this day."

Raedwin pulled on his trousers and set his clothing right. "Her own projects occupy her well enough, I'm sure. We are not on her mind."

"You are," Sadahlia said. A sharpness flickered in her eyes and then dissipated. "You shared her bed for years. She does not forget. Ever."

Raedwin shook his head but did not answer. They did have to hide—he knew it as well as anybody. No matter what they wanted, nor how hard they tried, this was the way things had to be. He did not understand Crassica's motivations, could not see her next move, and really didn't understand why she insisted they remain connected. There was something in her endless talk of blood and progeny, something she'd found in the library, her hope for the future—but what it was exactly, he had no idea.

Sadahlia slipped on her gray cloak and drew it closed. She extinguished the candles and placed them in a small hidden nook. Raedwin pulled her close and embraced her, pressing his body against hers. The heat of her skin surprised him, even now.

"I want to show you to the world," he whispered. "I want to declare your beauty from the towers and proclaim you from the mountains."

"You mustn't forget, my treasure," she warned. "The world might not like what it sees in return."

She bent to retrieve his burning torch from the floor. "I have a love for your living soul, the same as Crassica. I want to share. I want to experience all of it, the same as her. But you should know that our kind cannot carry children. No matter how alive we Vallahnir bring our bodies to be or how much we can experience, no matter how much I may love you, it cannot be done." She gave him a slow, sad smile. "I'm sorry if you had some other dreams for the two of us in mind, but I will never be a mother."

Raedwin shook his head. "That's never crossed my mind," he said, despite whether somewhere on some quiet night maybe it had. "The child of a half-blood Brohndai and a wayward Vallahnir? I can't imagine what that might be like."

Sadahlia sighed. "I can," she said quietly. "Life and death fused together into a brave new tomorrow." She smiled and nodded. "That would truly be something to see." She stepped out of the room and leaned into the corridor, glancing both directions.

"Okay," she said over her shoulder. "Let's go. They'll be waiting."

An oil lamp flickered in the center of the room. Shivering light wandered across facets of the small dirty space, the raw bedrock ceiling barely higher than their heads. The far wall was almost completely collapsed. Three men stood around the lamp, two of whom Raedwin had known for years—Kraegha, the Chief of the Keep, and Devron, the blacksmith. The third introduced himself as Solinius, the lead stablehand. After a few brief words of welcome and assurances that nobody had been followed, Kraegha glanced at each of them. His square jaw was sunbaked and creased, his ropy black hair falling across his shoulders.

"All right," he said. "This is everybody. Let's keep it quick." He trained his gaze on Raedwin. "I understand several days ago you had a vision of the mine. While you were outside the walls."

"Wasn't much of anything. It was confusing and brief. I got pulled away before I could make sense of anything."

"That's by design."

"But it wasn't Crassica… I got pulled away by…" Words failed him. How to describe it? Raedwin glanced at Sadahlia. She held her eyes steady on him, gently urging him forward. "Something else," he said finally.

"Her ways are meant to confuse," Devron interjected. "To misdirect. To drive attention elsewhere." He was a stout, thick-shouldered man, with hair cropped nearly to his skin. Various minor burns marked his hands, creased with forge soot. "The mine is not what you think."

"I'm not sure what I think. She won't let me near it."

"And why is that?"

"I still don't like this," Solinius broke in quietly. His face was stern and stale, watching Raedwin with quiet judgment. He had a thin unassuming nature that made him nearly disappear from the room. "This isn't Raedwin's fight. He shouldn't be here."

"It's not a fight," Kraegha countered, giving Solinius a sharp glance. "Not yet." He turned to Raedwin. "Tell me," he said. "What do you know of the Jehndai?"

"The what?" He'd never heard the word before.

"You know them as the Sevenfold's Children, out in the forest east of here. Their true name is the *Jehndai*. What do you know of them?"

Raedwin glanced at each of the men in turn, all loyal servants of Crassica, as far as he knew. Sadahlia had explained they held some sort of interest in how Crassica managed her world, especially the Brasti Ore. But what would the Sevenfold's Children have to do with Brasti Ore?

"From what I've seen, they're not people at all," he said. "More like upright gazelles. Unpredictable, they say. Quick to violence. Dangerous."

"That's what Crassica wants you to think," Kraegha cautioned. "They are a true people, with a tragic history. And she controls them. Or tries to. Uses them as slaves to rip her precious ore out of the ground."

Raedwin shook his head. "No, she uses men from Katliga or some such place to work the mine. I've seen them pass through here. And she pays them well, as far as I've known."

Kraegha laughed, a sad kindness in his eyes. "Crassica never pays for anything she doesn't have to."

"You know that raw Brasti Ore can kill," Devron said. "Burns the skin at a touch. And so it always comes to you tempered by oils, suspended in vats. But for the workers at the mine, it's deadly. So she can't use just anybody."

"And the Jehndai don't matter," Kraegha added. "Not to her."

Raedwin found himself standing in disbelief. He'd heard nothing of this. The mine was small and only produced enough ore for Crassica to refine the crystals she needed for herself. Why would such a workforce be necessary? Why go to such lengths? And why would she lie to him about it?

"Those who manage to slip out of her grasp continue to live under her yoke by proxy," Kraegha said. "Hiding like animals deep in the forest."

"Crassica tries to make them think they're free to live as they wish out there among the trees," Devron said. "But whenever she needs more workers, she sends a culling run of kidnappers. She takes the strongest she can find and slaps them all in chains. Puts them to work at the mine."

Raedwin shook his head again. None of what these men said matched what he'd known of Crassica. She was strange, sure. Ambitious to a fault. Strong-headed and single-minded. She operated the Keep like a dictatorship, but if any of what they said was true, Raedwin would've seen something. Heard something. He was around her too much to have missed it.

"You've heard of the fighting? That's a desperate people struggling to gain their own freedom—not the simple annoyance she wants you to believe."

Could she have been doing all of this without him knowing? For all these years?

"She hides more than you think," Sadahlia said gently. "Most of the dirty work is done by others. Mostly by Lanius."

Lanius. Of course. That would explain the means, but not the ends.

"He's operating a side scheme to sell Amaris in Katliga and Kalldon," Devron explained. "With her approval, of course. They've been shipping it north. We suspect that Lanius leads the corruption at the center of the mine's new expansion."

"She had honor once," Kraegha said. "And she's been the source of plenty of good things in the past, but now her honor is all but gone. She has ambition, which is useful and good when good is its aim, but now the fire of her ambition burns everyone around her."

"If we let her continue to expand," Devron said slowly. "We enable a tyrant."

Raedwin's eyes remained on the floor. His head swayed from side to side, almost on its own. "Even after everything," he said, nearly inaudibly, "I thought she was better than this."

"Yes, she is," Kraegha agreed. "Or at least she was."

"You see a reflection of yourself in her," Sadahlia said gently. "You're too close, my love. You see her pride in you, which is what she wants you to see."

"The time has come to force a change," Kraegha said.

Raedwin turned to him. "You're talking about sedition."

"Are we? Is sedition possible if she is not our queen? Would you have her as your true sovereign, given the choice?"

Of course he would not. But shouldn't there be alternatives to all of this?

"The more you help her, the more she becomes the oppressor." Kraegha took a small step forward. "She's built lives for all of us, and we are grateful for that. But there are limits. She wants too much. We don't want her destroyed—we just want sensible barriers."

"She doesn't *need* Amaris to live," Devron said. "She desires power. More control. More reach. Is that what she *needs*? Does she need forced labor to satisfy a desire that worms through everything she does and explodes in size year after year? Think. Why has she asked you to better refine the ore? Is there something wrong with it? Is there a problem you can see?"

"It's because she's fading," Kraegha said. "And she knows it. Her body fails her, and she denies it. She has too much need for control. More and more and more."

"She has become a colossus," Solinius said sharply. "And we are left as mice beneath her feet. She crushes those in the forest—the Jehndai, the Sevenfold's Children—without any regard to consequences. So who's to say when she'll decide to step on us as well?"

Kraegha watched Raedwin, probing for answers to his judgment, for some discernible sign of which way he would fall. Raedwin stood in silence, struck dumb by the onslaught from men he'd long trusted and respected, a barrage of honesty that felt like weapons.

"This isn't her destiny, nor is it ours," Kraegha assured him. "She only holds power because we give it to her. Us. Those in this room and everybody in this Keep. And it starts at the mines. It starts with the ore, and it ends in her smokevessel."

Raedwin nodded slowly, letting his gaze fall back to the floor. "And yet she wants more."

"Always more," Devron agreed. "And where does it end? How far do we let this go?"

Raedwin drew in a long breath and let it out slowly. "Okay," he said. "What would you have me do?"

"Nothing, for a time. But be ready," Kraegha said. "This is a delicate thing. Crassica cannot know of this, under any circumstances. We are not looking to bring her down—we only seek to alter and contain her wild ambition. End her reliance on this brutal slavery first, and then maybe her need for the ore altogether."

"Eventually what we'll need from you is to come with us to the mine," Devron added. "Show us how to end it, for good. And if not for good, then at least for years to come."

"There are no oaths here, other than to keep these thoughts in secret," Kraegha said. "We do what we do because we believe a better way is possible, and nothing more. Our word does not hold us. The truth does."

Sadahlia watched Raedwin as he took all of this in. At length, she reached out and held his hand in hers. He turned to her. That face. His wellspring of love.

"You're asking for chaos," he said to Kraegha. "Where does all of this lead?"

"When the time comes," Kraegha said, "you will know. All we ask is that you be ready."

"Ready for what, exactly? Do any of you know? Crassica does not play games with her enemies. If she finds out, it's over. For all of us. I can try to be as ready as I'm able for whatever it is you're talking about, but that time isn't right now. It can't be right now. I don't know what else to tell you."

Solinius let out a scoffing hiss. "I told you he wasn't ready."

Kraegha shot him a reproving look. "He's been with Crassica for seven years. He's plenty ready."

Raedwin shook his head, exasperated. This all came across like some low-level attack for crimes he hadn't yet committed. Crimes hidden within riddles and wrapped beneath hints and whispers.

"How am I supposed to care about something I can't even see?" he said at last.

Sadahlia pulled him closer. "You do care," she whispered. "You always have and always will. You don't know it yet, but when you see, it'll become clear. When the time comes, you will know."

21

CRASSICA HAD known the strange creature's real name once, but whatever it was, she had long since forgotten. She had taught him several names of people and places and things over the years, names with purpose and meaning, but his own name was not among them. Why would he need such a thing when he had Crassica's nurturing presence to sustain him? For many decades, the men of western Stronaway had called him the Hermit of Montcarsel whenever they spoke of him, which was very seldom, and that was enough name for him.

Almost more boar than man, the Hermit of Montcarsel held only a passing pretense of real humanity. Scars ran the length of both cheekbones. Tufts of hair jutted from random creases and lined the ridges of both ears, while his teeth and nails were too long to be human and too short to be anything else. A thick scablike crust mottled his gray skin. Occasionally the judging eyes of men stared at his ruined tower from far below, hunters in the forest lancing their suspicious gazes at the Hermit's haunted solitude, their small piercing eyes filled with short sight and small ideas. But he had not talked with another living soul in decades, and he paid the annoyance of hunters little mind.

Decades ago, when Crassica had first gone to visit the tower of Montcarsel herself, she'd had to explain the importance of the Hermit's home and how this place contained a delicate portal to the hidden paths of the newly dead. A door for her and her kind. She had thanked him for allowing her to come and intrude on his secret space, and she'd implored him to please stay and look after it for her. She'd asked that he keep his house in order and not concern himself with the thoughts or gazes of useless men. He must ignore such things. Simply maintain Montcarsel as a place of passage and be completely loyal only to her.

The Hermit had been more than willing to oblige. He knew that Crassica cared for him, and that meant something. Even here, she had reached through the passageways of the Crosslands and offered the gentle caress of her long and loving embrace. The power of Amaris flowed as her eyes watched through his, her whispers soft against his contorted neck.

Crassica had explained so many things to the Hermit in those early days. She had told of the Vallahnir and the Brohndai and the balance they brought to the world, of her own emergence from the bland and colorless Crosslands to walk as a named and vital person among the living, and of her desire to remain here. She explained how the Knowing brought forth light and dark, fire and water, stone and air, as well as life and death itself. True beauty lay in the perfect union of opposites, of spirit and life, light and darkness, man and woman. The Vallahnir and Brohndai themselves were merely two sides of the same expression—both articulations of the Knowing's desire for balance.

Her Hermit had listened, and he had believed. She had told him that the full comprehension of the Knowing could not be held on a slender weighted scale of skin and bone, of nothing more than delicate living flesh. One must choose sides. One needed to be with or against, to be either the flame or the quenching, the water or the stone. Either believe in the inconsistencies of truth or trust in nothing but lies.

The Hermit was an attentive student. Crassica had shown him so many things in so many ways. She had opened his malformed eyes and misshapen ears to allow him to see again, albeit with both his eyes now belonging only to her. Her student did not fully grasp what made one thing connect with another, or what made one thing miss while another hit and stuck with an eternal resilience, but she knew he loved her. He believed, and he trusted. He knew his place in this world, the ways in which he was to listen, the ways in which he was to watch, to gather, and to hold. He would serve as her eyes and ears in this place for as long as she would have him, which had already been a very long time.

And now he stood atop the crumbling roofless tower of Montcarsel and waited as she had asked. Its uneven fractured walls jutted from the southern fringes of the Domnall like a shattered and abandoned tooth left to rot in the wet and surly forest. The ruins had lain mostly empty for decades, save for the Hermit's quiet, enduring presence. The slow grip of the forest had risen to reclaim its own, slowly devouring the sad remains of a once-proud structure.

From where he stood, the Hermit should've held a commanding view of the Domnall climbing to the east until it surrendered against the massive glaciated peaks of the Iron Wall. To the west the forest could normally be seen, diminishing down into the vales and glades of the distant Hogshallon and Elban rivers. But just now an unnatural fog swirled over the tower, wrapping the stones in a close heaviness both primordial and newly born. The Hermit's eyes could vaguely make out the long line of the distant horizon. The blinding haze spilled into the open space until the remaining walls became shrouded and lost. The strange mist blanketed the tower and brought the space in tight and dense, as if the rest of the world no longer existed.

And then the mist retreated as quickly as it had come, revealing four women standing in its place—passengers freshly arrived through the tower's transcendent portal. Gray cloaks hung from their tall slender forms, ageless beyond the crumbled stone of the ruined tower itself. Their pale white faces and feline blue eyes appeared young and fresh, indeed quite beautiful. They stood and waited as the last fingers of mist drew away.

With Amaris surging through her, Crassica spoke, and the Hermit's voice welcomed the four Vallahnir to Montcarsel. She turned him away to descend a rough set of stairs thrust through the ancient bedrock. The Vallahnir followed in silence, moving with some effort as they operated their displaced bodies with a quiet strain. Crassica's Hermit led them to a series of rooms set against the tower's ruined courtyard.

The interior chambers were lined with warmth and comfort, brought to life by the Hermit's own disfigured hands. Wooden planks and thick carpets graced the floors. Bearskin tapestries lined three walls and held the cold of the stone at bay. A fire roared in a hearth at the far end.

The Hermit made his way to a set of wooden chests and opened a hidden compartment. Sliding a secret panel aside, he drew out a long brass key and then replaced the panel and closed the chest. Taking a torch from its wall mount, the Hermit led the Vallahnir down a series of steps into the bedrock vaults below the ruins. Soon they arrived at a cavernous underground chamber with a massive iron door at the far end, its hinges stiff with time and rust. Ancient markings crawled over the smooth surface.

Each of the Vallahnir placed a hand on the door, fingertips touching, and with low voices began to chant in a tongue seldom heard among the living, sounds from deep within the Crosslands. The Hermit pushed his key into a dusty slot, rotating it sideways. A dull red glow emerged, bleeding color over the face of the door. Thin streams of energy penetrated through time and rust alike as the bolts slid clear. The four Vallahnir stepped into a dim chamber.

Riches beyond count lay in front of them, pieces of gold along with scattered gemstones, fixed ornaments, and goblets. Bracelets sat next to amulets and scepters, with more than one jewel-studded crown. The room was not large, but it stretched to the edge of the torchlight. Stone shelves lined each wall with stacks of coinage filling each shelf, arranged and delineated into careful rows—Kalldonian along one section, with Brinsfallon to the right alongside those from the Baelhoarg. Carefully organized adornments, bracers, and cuff clips all sat against the back wall.

For decades Crassica had used the Hermit to slowly amass the wealth of this room, a safe and protected harbor in Brinsfallon's abandoned eastern frontier. She had culled from warlords and highwaymen, from conquered fortifications and abandoned strongholds. From usury and sweeteners sent by criminals who used others' fear of Crassica's support of them to their own devious ends. And for all of those decades, the Hermit had quietly collected and held, watching over it all.

One of the Vallahnir moved forward. She pulled an oilskin pouch from her cloak and filled it with a careful mixture of bronze, silver, and gold pieces. The other three did the same. Together they now held a nondescript sum of wealth beyond what most men could conceive of in any one place since the violent fall of the late empire.

The four turned and left the chamber. Closing and sealing the great doors behind them, the Hermit led them back up the stone stairs. Their breathing came labored and strained, nubile young bodies moving in a weak and ancient way, like escaped apparitions from some degenerate infirmary. The Hermit stopped and watched as the four exited through a side corridor to the stables. With his careful assistance, they chose four sturdy horses, animals that he himself had nurtured and held in constant good health at Crassica's careful direction.

The four pale rumors of mist surveyed their new surroundings and conversed in hushed tones with one another as they carefully mounted and rode out onto the forest floor. The girl they sought was somewhere far to the south, in a distant forest known by the people of this world as the Hallonath. The girl and her brutal companion had destroyed two of Crassica's beloved Sisters already. The girl, and time, were both slipping from their grasp.

Gathering strength of men and arms in Pentmore, the four Vallahnir would go to the girl and retrieve her. They would pull her afresh into their pale embrace and drive her westward to Corregidon. There, the spiders in the net would bring her home to Crassica at last.

One by one, the Vallahnir urged their horses westward. A stony path led out of the forest, down into the peopled farmland beyond. The four rode stiffly into the misty shadows under the trees, by all appearances four grim specters of the living dead.

22

SENYA FOLLOWED Brogan northeast through the forest. Gaps in the trees offered wide views to the west as they made their way along a tall rocky ridge. Brogan's wounded leg set their pace. The Brundsril's silver ribbon meandered through the green valleys of Cellenway in the distance. Somewhere out there was Corregidon, maybe fifty or sixty leagues away. And beyond the city, the sea. From there, Faeroen Island would be several days' sail north. The Order of the Brohndai, and her father's help. So many leagues away, and so far yet to go.

They dropped eastward over the ridge, deeper into the Hallonath. Spring-fed undergrowth filled a marsh at the base of a long rock face. A dense grove of trees crowded where the murky water funneled through gaps, cascading into the fog-filled valley below. They sloshed through leafy greenery as the morning sun slanted through branches.

"Wait," Senya said as she veered from the path next to a massive oak growing alongside a pool, its sturdy roots gripping the broad bank. She stepped calf-deep into the water and knelt.

Brogan stopped. "What are you doing?"

Senya plunged her hands into the water and closed her eyes. "I need to try to see..."

The water was cool against her skin. She slowed her breathing and calmed herself, reaching southward with her purpose focused. Raedwin was there somewhere, far beyond the southern mountains and the Dunnenwyr shore. The dry grasslands of Kalldonia. He had to be there.

But all she could see was blockage. A blindness in the middle of her vision. Raedwin remained hidden from her, the same as before.

Senya broke off the attempt and stood. Stepping up the bank, she rejoined Brogan. "Okay," she said. "Let's go."

"What was that?"

"Sometimes I can connect with my brother. Water helps."

"Connect. What does that mean?"

"See him. Feel him. Talk to him."

"And he sees you too?"

"Sometimes..."

"Can anybody else see you?"

She gave Brogan a smile, trying her best to reassure without words. "We used to do it all the time when we were kids."

"I thought he was lost, down in Kalldonia. How can you just...?"

"It didn't work. Something is blocking him, and I can't see. I can't tell where he is exactly." She gestured ahead. "So let's just keep going."

Brogan seemed to know better than to push. He led on. After a time, their path dropped rapidly to meet the tight valley where the Kalldonians had forced their ancient causeway through the western fringes of the Hallonath. At long last, they stepped from the trees onto the Old Kreskill Road's patchwork of skewed and broken paving stones.

Senya sensed the body before she saw it. Human remains beside the causeway ahead, stretched into a malformed distortion in the underbrush. Flies buzzed, flitting and fussing over the decaying remains. There was no head. Most of the flesh from the legs and buttocks had been carved away. Entrails hung in tattered ribbons from spiny branches, the simple residue of a hunted carcass left to rot.

They stopped, suddenly wary. The land all around lay quiet and settled. The body had probably been here for several days at least, playing host to a miniature invasion of scavengers, mites, and larvae. Wolves and birds had come and gone some time ago. Little remained to tell man from woman, but one thing was certain—this was not a simple death.

"Looks like boneskin work," Brogan said quietly.

Wayburn and its people were stout and disciplined fighters and knew these woods well. From what Brogan had said, they would never let somebody wander out this far on their own. Maybe this was an isolated incident. Maybe boneskins had caught somebody alone and unarmed. But Senya knew that was unlikely. Not out here.

"Probably hunted down for sport, tortured and killed, and then just…" Brogan took a long time before finishing. "Eaten."

Senya glanced at the forest for eyes of watchers or any sign of movement. Boneskins could be anywhere. Their soiled ragged garments often matched the color of the forest. They could be completely invisible when they wanted.

"I thought going through Wayburn meant avoiding the boneskins."

Brogan didn't answer. He rose and guided her into the forest away from the road, northward through a gap between two massive boulders. Keeping well clear of the causeway, they moved quickly in silence. Cresting a last low rise, they finally descended a rocky slope to the river's edge. Whitewater crashed through bouldered breaks and settled into deep green pools, rolling languidly through a short, stout gorge. Huge trees hung over the ravine, reaching for light. Contorted roots clung to the stony edge.

Taking the lead downstream along a series of sandy beaches, Brogan climbed slowly over stretches of fallen timber. Senya kept close, the crossbow ready. The river fell twice in cascading submissions from one lazy dark pool to the next. At the second whitewater surge, piles of storm-broken logs forced them to climb up nearly to the gorge's rim. They kept as close to the edge as they could, the thudding river helping bury any sound of their passage.

They crept for a mile or more before coming to the lip of a broad pool where the river bent against a mossy cliff on the far side. A wide stone bridge reached across the gorge. The stone walls and slate roofs of Wayburn stood on the far side. A wisp of smoke drifted into the trees. Five birchbark canoes sat tethered on the near shore below.

Strangely deserted, the settlement's sturdy stone gatehouse crouched in silent sentry of the river crossing. Its single ironbound oak door lay open, cracked and hammered to pieces. Nobody stood guard at the bridge. No faces lined the wall.

A voice shouted somewhere across the gorge, followed by another voice, and then laughter. There was something off in the sound. Too rough, too wild. More shouts came from beyond.

And then Senya saw.

Several ragged boneskins ran wild in a flat expanse near the Wayburn walls, their raven hair loose and knotted, caked with mud or dried blood. Maybe both. They kicked a human head across the muddied grass between them. Parts flew. Blood-crusted hair and flesh. The face spun and landed, its desolate eye sockets vacant and dry. Probably a former resident, cut to pieces and rendered a simple game thrown about by animals.

Brogan stepped back and ducked with Senya into the shadowed cover of trees and underbrush. With a last glance at the devastation of what used to be Wayburn, he led her through the forest back the way they'd come.

"How many, you think?" Senya whispered as they settled into deeper cover.

"Plenty to give us a very bad day," Brogan answered. "They've taken the whole place over. Wayburn's gone."

They weighed their options. Without help, the best they could do was run. But where? Try to stumble their way back to the smoldering ruin of Brogan's home? They'd be worse off there, with no shelter and even less protection. Pentmore was the closest city, north out of the Hallonath along the road, but the river would be difficult to cross at best. They could fashion a raft of sorts, but that would take time, and spending the night in the Hallonath with boneskins all around did not appeal to either of them, nor did walking all the way to Pentmore out in the open. And once there, they'd be no closer to the sea.

They quickly decided to make for the unguarded canoes they'd seen on the nearside beach. Stealth and silence would be their best chance now.

"If we're lucky," Brogan said in a low, uneasy voice, "we'll just float all the way to Corregidon."

Indeed, a forest full of boneskins was far more than she wanted to bravely face alone. And neither did he, most likely. "Sorry," she said quietly. "Looks like you're stuck with me for a little bit longer."

"It's what I do," he whispered with a slow-forming grin. "I get stuck with people."

She smiled. "Thank you," she said quietly.

"Besides, I know a sailor or two in the city," he added with a nod. "Might get you all the way to Faeroen after all, you keep treatin' me this good."

Brogan chose a route back upriver to find a way down to the water. No sign of pursuit showed, and no sound followed. Senya caught a glimpse through the trees of dark figures moving, stalking upriver. She loaded the crossbow and followed as he descended out of sight through a gap to the rocky shoreline below.

He froze and waved her back. A boneskin woman draped in filthy rags and pelts stood watching from the far rim. Short, blunt tusks jutted upward from a heavy jaw, bone and sinew showing pale through her hardened skin. She peered at them through dull yellow eyes. Raising a curved knife, she released a bellowing wail.

Senya dropped to one knee and aimed the crossbow, bringing her off hand across to steady. A long shot for a crossbow. Loosed, the bolt passed harmlessly through the boneskin's hanging pelts.

The creature smiled with a grotesque mismatch of teeth and screamed again, words and pronouncements in the twisted language of their kind. Calls to others. The alarm raised.

Brogan swore. He slid the recurve bow from his shoulder, nocked an arrow, aimed, and let fly. The creature's scream choked into a savage halt. She collapsed. Loose chunks of her crude clothing spun limply down to splash in the water below.

Senya reloaded the crossbow. Brogan led her downstream less carefully now, more focused on speed than stealth or safety. Twice he slipped and smashed his leg against rock. A sharp grimace flashed over his face. They kept on. Shouts flew back and forth across the water.

At last, they reached the beach upriver from the boats. They took the open ground at a run, feet plunging softly in the wet sand. Senya kept an ear out for calls erupting from behind. Soon they rounded a wide bend, and she caught sight of the boats.

Three half-breed boneskins stood waiting with dark, menacing stares. Nearly human, but not exactly so, these were the degenerate residue of ravage and rape, of decades spent marauding and coupling with crushed societies in the wake of the boneskin horde. One stood leaning on a brutal war axe, while the two behind held long rusted blades in each hand. The stone bridge stood empty overhead. Nobody ran along the ravine's rim. They seemed to be alone.

The boneskin with the axe gave a wicked grin. Tusks so stunted they barely showed. "Lookie," he called. "Midwintie fest we get! Cha ya! No' even season!"

Brogan went on. Senya followed.

"Tellya wha," the leader called. "We take girl, an' you go pass! You can keep you face!" He laughed. The other two shared in the jest, exposing shattered grins of sharp, uneven teeth.

As they closed in, Senya raised the crossbow and shot over Brogan's shoulder. At this range, the bolt blew clean through the front boneskin's neck. The creature raised his hands to stem the discharge of blood with surprise in his eyes, voiceless as he fell. The other two leapt forward.

Brogan crouched and loosed, but his arrow flew wide. The boneskin was on him before he could react. Brogan held the attack at bay as one blade slashed the sand. He grabbed a wrist, struggling.

The other came at Senya. With a shout, she raised her empty crossbow to fend off the whirling assault. They wrestled and fell, locked hand in hand. Reeking breath blasted her face. Hair thick with filth and decay. The boneskin's long rusted blade flashed. She managed to roll the creature underneath her, pinning his neck with the crossbow body. Laying all her weight onto its narrow steel edge, Senya used the bow cut off the boneskin's air. He struggled and hissed. She heaved onto the metal, pressing the creature while she managed to pull a knife from the boneskin's own boot scabbard. Driving it down, she pierced through the creature's chest.

Brogan flipped and slammed a knee into his attacker's midsection. They rolled. Brogan twisted free and drew his shortsword. The boneskin grinned as he rose from the sand and pushed matted hair from his face. "You eyes we eat last," he growled. "So till end, can see!"

Brogan said nothing. He was not a large man, but he was very quick. The boneskin showed a brief expression of shock as the blink of Brogan's shortsword shattered his left forearm. Blood sprayed. Brogan slashed across the creature's neck. The boneskin buckled to the ground.

Shouts came from upstream. Others crept into view.

"Get to the boats!" Brogan cried. Grabbing his bow and glancing back, he punched four arrows into the sand and nocked a fifth. The boneskins upstream ducked behind cover.

Senya rose on unsteady legs and trudged the last several yards to the canoes. Brogan loosed his arrow, catching a charging boneskin in the gut. Yet the creature came on, all flailing mismatched wool and screams. Brogan loosed another. A shaft to the chest, and he stumbled. Sand flew. Still the boneskin rose and crawled slowly on.

Cutting the first canoe free, Senya started dragging it toward the water. Another boneskin emerged from cover upriver. Brogan sent an arrow into the edge of a tree trunk, and the blotchy muscle-bound face ducked away. With the canoe's bow afloat, Senya pulled the war axe from under a grisly body nearby and punched gaping holes into the bottoms of the remaining four boats.

An arrow flew by from across the river. She glanced up. A tusked face ducked behind a tree. Arrows were such a rarity with this kind, aimed with little skill. They'd probably found it while raiding Wayburn's weapon cache.

"Brogan!" she called, climbing into the canoe. "Let's go!"

Pursuit emerged from cover upstream, emboldened for a last-ditch attempt at a charge. Another shaft hit the water. Brogan grabbed his remaining arrows from the sand and ran. The motley group gave noisy chase down the beach. Brogan stopped and dropped one with an arrow before whirling to toss his bow into the canoe. With a surging push, he lunged aboard. The canoe slipped into the current as stones hurled by boneskins along the far shore hit the water on either side. Another arrow splashed harmlessly away.

They pulled the stiff wooden paddles with all the strength they had. The canoe gathered speed. Those on shore reached the downstream edge of the beach, blocked by the cliff that held the bridge. With inhuman screams, a few scrambled upward through the rocks to the lip of the gorge and gave chase through the trees. A huge boneskin threw himself from the bridge's stone railing just as the canoe passed underneath. His body missed the boat and plunged, frothing, into the swirling river. Furs and wool cloak became an oily black churn. Frantic arms pulled desperately toward the surface of the icy water. His face burst out and gasped for breath. Then he sank and was gone.

Brogan and Senya heaved on their paddles, pushing the canoe faster into the current. Both shorelines eased closer as the river sped them forward. Soon the shouts died away behind.

They paddled for hours, keeping vigilant against any pursuit. Dark trees huddled along both banks in a silent riot of black and green, a tangle of brambles and mosses amid thick black trunks. The Brundsril flowed flat and smooth as the gorge slowly widened. After a time, the rock walls fell away. The trees opened into clumps and breaks of grassland hills, and soon the river's shore abandoned its thick burly oaks altogether. Both riverbanks spread into a barren and forgotten countryside stretching into distant sallow fields warted by a few scattered groves. They had left the Hallonath at last.

Brogan urged to press on through the night. They rested when the river's current rushed and paddled when the water opened into slow, glassy pools. Starlight blinked on the black surface. Late in the night, clouds closed across the sky, and a soft rain brought near-blindness to the water. Vague shapes of varied blackness marked the rocky edges of the river. Brogan kept the canoe in the center as they floated on into darkness.

23

RAEDWIN SAT BACK, and the new chair's iron mesh groaned with his weight. Mounted close to the floor of a wide basin in the center of a high conical room, the chair was designed to recline its occupant deeply, almost supine. Relaxed. A tranquil repose for whatever mysterious event would follow. Almost cradle-like in effect, the chair faced away from two others identical to it—the three set in a star pattern with backs nearly touching. Despite its strange skeletal look, Raedwin found the chair to be surprisingly comfortable.

Constructed in a dusty unused chamber next to Crassica's own rooms, this whole project was one of the Vallahnir master's more confusing and mystifying ventures. Raedwin's tasks had been narrow and limited—design the three chairs, direct piping to bring an unnamed liquid in and out of the basin, and craft proper air flow. Long iron columns braced the living bedrock walls, rising from the central basin and narrowing to a glass dome high above—a nearly spot-on replica of the windowed wall of his own workshop. The glass was positioned to address the full moon at a particular time and month. Open fireplaces waited cold and dead at each of the three corners of the room. A dance of elements, all orchestrated at Crassica's careful and specific direction.

Raedwin had asked over and again what this chamber was intended to do. He'd argued for more details about its purpose and function so he could better help with its design, but so far Crassica had remained evasive. "This body of mine grows old," she would vaguely say and leave it at that.

Or she'd mutter something like, "Transference is a delicate process," and say no more. Between her smokevessel and her various machines, Crassica had her own manufactured way of living, so maybe this room really was something simpler than he thought, something new to harvest energy from the moonlight. For three people. At the same time.

The meeting with Kraegha, Devron, and Solinius in the tunnels under the Keep continued to haunt him. In helping Crassica with projects like this, what more was he also doing? What hidden scheme of hers was he supporting? Was this chamber part of some broader plan? He'd started questioning every move she had him make, but still, Kraegha had told him to wait. Watch and learn. Be ready. So for now, Raedwin would continue to do his duty until he better understood the bigger picture.

A powerful hum pulsed through the air, the smooth whir of metal on metal, with a hidden rush of steam. A large protective egg-shaped cage emerged from a portal halfway up one of the walls, sliding downward along a metal track between iron columns. The cage held a lavish padded iron chair, which in turn held a lounging Crassica.

Raedwin stood. He had not expected a visit today. The apparatus came to a soft rest on the floor. Crassica pulled her tall angular frame to full height and opened the chair's shell. Retrieving her smokevessel from the cage, she stepped out and moved along the edge of the central basin to a set of steps carved into the side. She descended slowly to the middle step and sat, placing her smokevessel beside her.

"The chairs look effective," she said. She filled the vessel's tiny bowl before lighting the crushed crystals. She allowed smoke to obscure her face as she drew from the mouthpiece. Her long fingers stroked the vessel's smooth ceramic belly. "How do they feel?"

"They're fine," he said. "Comfortable enough." He had already explained all this, but he knew his role in this dance. Crassica didn't really care about the answer. He was to sit and listen and be obedient while she droned on about life and beauty and existence, offering forth a series of wandering thoughts that would all go nowhere. He knew his role, but the dance itself was quickly growing old. Especially now.

Crassica held her eyes on Raedwin for a long minute. Outside, a shifting cloud obscured the slanted sunlight through the overhead glass. The room brightened again as it passed. "You do still believe in what I have built here, yes?" she said. "The grace and beauty that I seek? These are not personal things. They are for the good of humankind. To make life easier. To smooth the paths of the living."

Raedwin smiled, studying his hairless pale mentor. "Controlling a life isn't the same as being alive," he said. "And taking a life will never be the same as having one—no matter how many you might own."

Crassica leaned against the stone steps. "I do not wish to argue with you today," she said slowly, as if allowing some last bit of herself to escape. "I actually came here... to speak about your sister..."

For this, Raedwin had no words. Crassica had so rarely talked directly about Senya. The unexpected mention struck him as very strange. Almost sinister.

"Unfortunately," she continued, rolling each syllable out of her mouth in careful succession. "There has been an... incident." She pulled from the smokevessel and let out a slow exhale. Smoke tendrils climbed toward the ceiling. "Our dear Senya has been waylaid by bandits and highwaymen in the Hallonath while on her journey here, to us."

Raedwin's mouth fell open. *Here?* Why would Senya be coming here? Was this what he had seen in the vision? Men coming for her in the forest? Was this what she had been trying to warn him about? What Sadahlia had warned him about? As far as he knew, Senya enjoyed a small quiet life on a farm somewhere outside Pentmore. He had seen her. She never went anywhere and would not exactly jump at the chance to journey across two continents to a place like the Valle d'Brasti. And she would never allow herself to be waylaid by highwaymen and bandits out in the Hallonath, of all places. Not on her own anyway.

He barely listened as Crassica went on to explain something about the Old Kreskill Road and the loss of good Vallahnir, plus a few trusted associates. None of it sank in exactly.

Devron and Kraegha had been right all along. Nothing Crassica did was ever real and true. She held something underneath, some deeper stratagem that she would never allow him to see. And now she'd dragged Senya in as well. He sat back down, nearly collapsing on the edge of the metal chair.

"Why are you doing this?" he finally managed, his voice thin and quiet in the strange dry room.

"I was simply hoping to illuminate possible motives." Crassica closed her eyes and drew in another long pull from the bubbling smokevessel. "You have the blood of the Brohndai, and you hold something of the Old

Sight, connected with your father and sister both. I would like to know what you see."

"This is going too far."

"Do you see her making her way north to your father on Faeroen Island perhaps? Maybe a cleansing bath in the Mirrorwater itself?"

Raedwin doubted Senya would be trying to go anywhere other than home, wherever home might be. He said nothing.

Crassica smoked. The vessel churned. "Well," she said, with a fresh coy edge to her voice. "We shall have to find her that much faster, then, won't we?"

A side door swung open. A tall man with long powerful legs strode into the room unannounced. He marched along the edge of the basin toward Crassica. Oily hair fell in dark ropes streaked with gray, framing his sunbaked face. A weighty beard cradled his chin. He wore what would have passed for elegant sailing dress in some spent foregone existence, with tall leather boots. A woolen vest hugged his linen tunic under a thick oilskin jerkin. His salt-crusted cloak billowed from under a fur collar.

"Ahh, my dear Delsorka," Crassica called with a toothy smile. "Welcome."

The man crouched to one knee and bowed his head as he reached the steps. "Your High Honor," he said. "You require my service?"

"I do indeed. Please stand, thank you. Have you met Raedwin of the Baelhoarg, our good son from the North?"

Delsorka strode down the steps and removed a heavy glove. He extended his hand in greeting. "I do not believe I have. A pleasure. Well met. I've spent a fair amount of time in the North myself, at least in the port cities…"

Raedwin stood to shake the man's hand. A thick scar ran across his weathered face from the left side of his chin upward into his hairline above the ear. Another twisted scar seethed on his forehead. His hard piercing eyes were countered by a wide and generous smile.

"Raedwin is very important to me," Crassica said, still seated on the steps. "Very special. And of course, his sister as well."

Raedwin wanted to shout to this stranger that Crassica had never met his sister, so Senya could not possibly be that important to her. All of this was part of some larger lie that he was not yet able to see. But he said nothing.

"And you, my dear Delsorka," Crassica continued, "are an important man with many important tasks, so I will not bore you with piles of inconsequential conversation. Let us drive to the heart of the matter. Raedwin's sister has been taken. We are uncertain by whom. We do not know where she is being led, nor to what ends, but suffice it to say that our dear Senya was abducted in the forests of southeastern Brinsfallon while she was making her way here. I have already sent four trusted emissaries in pursuit, but I cannot be certain of her whereabouts. And so what I need now is a presence in Corregidon to assist her if she arrives there."

"By presence, you mean a force of arms."

"To be reckoned with, for sure. But not in the open. Connect with our friends for assistance. They will be expecting you. All manner of diligence must be paid to the clandestine quality of what I ask. Which is why you stand here now. The tip of our well-honed spear."

Delsorka bowed slightly. "You are very kind to say so."

"Crassica," Raedwin broke in, his voice coming in a low growl. "Leave Senya alone, or you'll need to reckon with me."

"I have studied the maps," she said to Delsorka. "I need you to sail north to Donasberth and establish your men there, as well as in Corregidon itself. Brinsfallon is a strong and prosperous land, as you know, but it is not a place I can easily see. And if you are able to get people into Cairn and Posselhead, all the better. I would like to watch for the sister of our fiery friend Raedwin here. Help her if you can. Bring her to us if that is her wish."

Crassica turned to Raedwin, and her face softened. She smiled. "Look closely, my dear Delsorka, and remember what you see. They are twins, Raedwin and Senya. The sister is slighter, and far more elegant than the brother, but you can guess that she appears much like this one who stands before you."

"Your *High Honor*," Raedwin said sharply. "Think closely on what you are doing..."

Delsorka began to circle, taking him in. Raedwin knew what he was seeing—a dark-skinned man with a particular set to his cheekbones, the structure of his nose. Eyebrows and mouth. His black hair. Neckline and shoulder. The loose, balanced way in which he tried to stand. Exposed.

"She will have fiery orange eyes connected to all things aflame upon the earth," Crassica said. "Earthen brown skin. Ageless beauty."

Delsorka continued to study. To most people, Raedwin seemed almost of two worlds, a man made of light and shade crafted by revelation and concealment intertwined together. He often looked as though he were only nineteen or twenty, but in certain light, his youth disappeared, and his swarthy skin showed weathered creases of age along the corners of his eyes.

"Crassica," Raedwin warned. "Listen to me. Leave Senya alone."

"Oh, she is not to be harmed, of course, my sweet. She is to be helped on her way, ultimately to be reunited with her beloved brother. So our friend Delsorka must sail up there, find her, and sail on back. Easy as anything."

Delsorka stopped, glanced at Crassica and back at Raedwin. "I'm no kidnapper. I've smuggled just about anything a sailor can haul in this world, all around both continents and all islands between, but rarely was my quarry involuntary. Everyone has standards." He nodded to Raedwin. "So I can assure you that your sister will be safe from harm."

Raedwin stood in silence, quietly livid. This was all wrong. Until this moment, everything he'd done had felt like his own choice, like a whim that could help or harm, but with the consequences on himself and nobody else. He would live or die with whatever came, but the damage would remain limited. Until this moment.

Delsorka turned to Crassica. "But I need to let you know, Your High Honor," he said, his voice drawn and lean, "a venture like this will cost."

"Oh, I know." Crassica took in a long draw from the smokevessel and blew out. "Believe me, I know." She grinned and glanced at Raedwin. "All things of consequence have their cost."

24

A LIGHT RAIN fell over the gray waters of the Brundsril. Brogan and Senya made brief camp without incident before continuing on at first light. It wasn't until the river opened its fertile valley westward into rolling heathered moorland that the rain fully cleared. Huddled groups of proud trees reached to one another in low bushy lengths amid residue of hedgerows where long-vanished farmers had once tended this lonely land.

The sky opened into an afternoon of hazy joyless sun. They pushed on. Hours passed. The weather settled into an unbroken granite gray. More rain threatened but did not come. After a time, a stone farmhouse peered from a distant hill as they drifted around a wide slow bend in the river. Vacant windows stared like indifferent black eyes. Smoke curled from the stack. They passed the remains of a marble dock along the riverbank. Stone pillars with wide steps. Kalldonian design, likely built in the waning days of the emaciated empire and left to disintegrate when their lofty civilized influence vanished.

Reeds parted on the shore. A boy stood there. He watched Brogan as they drifted past. Man and boy stared at one another in a silent survey of potential threats. Deciding plausible strengths of force. Who raises the alarm to whom? Brogan reached for his bow and nocked an arrow, laying the weapon across his knees.

We have come to this, he thought. A simple boy now a potential threat of untold gravity, and himself a passing assassin aboard a floating journey of unknown depth or distance. The reeds flickered, and the boy was gone.

They drifted and waited. The shoreline gave no more sign of movement. No alarm raised. Brogan returned the arrow to his quiver and set his bow aside. He pulled his paddle through the water. The boat surged forward.

The river bent again as the day grew late. Shadows stretched high into the trees along the riverbank, the upper canopy glowing orange with a bloody sunset. The distant west slipped from blue into purple, fading to a dim slate gray. They slowed pace. Brogan chose a long sandy shore on the downstream side of a tall series of boulders. Watchtower sentinels in the gloom. They paddled hard into the bank and alighted to heave the canoe fully out of the water.

"Tonight, we should have a fire," Senya said. "I need to clean your wounds again."

Brogan headed into the forest to gather firewood while Senya worked to get a small blaze going. When he returned, she tended to his wounds and then took the first watch. Brogan lay back and stared at the reaching black branches overhead, their naked yearning for the open night sky. Senya sat near the fire. A wide coruscating bend of the river glittered in the moonlight behind her.

In dreams, Brogan struggled with a strange long boat, a flimsy canoe with tall masts and broad sails. His wife was there. And a baby. Something lurked in the water below, its sinister teeth biting at the hull. He awoke with a start, his breathing harsh and heavy. The sun pierced the crest of the distant Iron Wall, sending speckled pins of light through shifting treetops.

"Another nightmare?" Senya said.

Brogan rose to a seated position on his blanket. He hadn't realized he'd fallen asleep. Two small fish pegged to narrow sticks leaned over the fire, roasting quietly.

"What happened to my watch?" he said. "It's almost morning."

"Don't worry about it. I'll be fine."

"Don't you need to rest?"

"I've been asleep long enough. My eyes need to stay open."

"But you've got to sleep at some point…"

Senya did not answer for a long moment. "They've done something to me," she said at last. "Something has changed. I'm not tired. Not yet."

Brogan watched the flames reflected in her blaze-orange eyes. The fire cracked and sent out a small spark. "You tried that thing again, didn't you? With your brother..."

She nodded in silence.

"And still nothing."

She nodded again.

The glittering shine of a tear slipped down her cheek. Abruptly she wiped it away and stood. "There's fish here for you," she said. "Probably good for you to sleep some more, if you can." And she stepped away into shadows.

They left when the land was yet gray and dim in the long hour before sunrise. The Brundsril was beginning its sweep back to the west after a brief northward push. They paddled for a short time before a strange sound came to them on the breeze—something there and then gone. Brogan cocked his head in the stern of the canoe to listen as best he could. An unmistakable distant din. Warhorses and steel. Signaling to Senya as the sound came again, he pointed frantically to the southern shore. A deep rumble rose from the folded ground to the north. They paddled hard for the cover of brush and trees, settling the canoe in a tight hidden eddy obscured by shadows and overhanging branches.

A vanguard of grim bearded men appeared along the northern shore, marching astride armored horses with their breaths showing white in the cool air. Twenty in the forward phalanx. Dented brutal shield works hung to the side of breast collars. Shining pikes swayed high and sparkling in the misty light as they rode westward along the tall bank. Several ranks of foot soldiers followed. First came those with some semblance of armor, however mismatched and ancient. Some carried swords, while others held scarred and notched war axes to match their scarred and notched faces. Long braided hair ran down armored backs. Ragged wine-colored cloaks attempted to lend unity to the loose-fitting multitude.

Next came the forced joiners. Men without armor and probably without honor, without a past and promised an unproven future. Perhaps as many as a hundred bent and broken souls struggled to hold pace. Some marched bearing swords, and some carried pickaxes and wood mauls. Yet others went forth with only homespun alterations of spade handles or garden instruments studded with iron nails or heavy chains—serfs or bondsmen from the southern frontier, some likely abducted from whatever unlucky village, rounded up and forced onward.

Draft horses followed the joiners and dragged three small high-wheeled carts over the muddy roadless ground along the riverbank. Dozens of wounded men rode slipshod in the heaving carts, wrapped and bleeding, some moaning openly. A select few of the brawniest joiners shouldered the back edges of the carts to help shove over the roughest spots of the track. A pocket of stern horsemen followed at the rear, solidly clad in shining plate metal and formidable visored helms. They kept their long whips ready at hand with a merciless eye on the unfortunates in front of them.

Finally came four sturdy horses, almost as an afterthought to the motley array, separated from the rest of the group by a slight but defined distance. Atop each horse rode a thin woman. Their pale ghostly faces were obscured under low gray hoods. A glint of sapphire eyes. Brogan's breath caught as one pivoted to peer directly at their hiding place among the bushes and reeds but then eased as she looked away.

And then they were gone. The army disappeared through a distant crease in the land as the river took a lazy bend away.

Brogan swore. "Now there're four? How'd they get back to us? What about the heads and the fire and the whole..."

"Those four are new," Senya said sharply. "Not the ones from before."

"Hells." Brogan spat. "How many are there out here?"

Senya shook her head. She gave no answer.

This was not very reassuring. If the Vallahnir could replenish their numbers after what he and Senya had already been through, the road ahead just got a whole lot more dangerous.

"I don't know how they got here," Senya said at length. "But it doesn't really matter. What matters is why they're here. What they're doing. And what they want."

Brogan thought over their course, the collection of armaments, and guessed at their purpose. "They're going the wrong way," he said after a moment.

She turned to him. "How do you mean?"

"An army like that, probably out of Pentmore, gets pulled together once a year or so to go after bandits and boneskins. Maybe more often these days. Whipped up to purge the frontier and make a show of strength. But if they're here to do that, then Wayburn is behind us. They should be circling to push upriver, not down. And they wouldn't have four Vallahnir driving their rear."

For a long moment, Senya watched the empty space where the army had disappeared. "They aren't here for the boneskins," she said at last. "They're looking for me."

"The whole army?"

"Just the Vallahnir. I'm sure the army will take whatever boneskins they find along the way, and maybe they're chasing some right now, but I doubt any of the leaders know what they're really looking for. Only those four do."

"Hells," Brogan muttered. "And now they're in front of us."

"We may have to leave the river. We're too exposed out here."

Brogan shook his head and spat again. "You know..." he said slowly. "Back when I was in Corregidon, with some of the stranger things we'd be asked to do, like when we had to find some weird artifact or nab a conjureman or warlord... there would be a hint of something bigger behind it—or someone. We called it *the Pale*. We got paid extra not to ask questions whenever the Pale was involved, but people would whisper. The Pale was a boss above the other bosses, one you'd never dare try to cross. Dark Arts were involved. Or necromancy. Some kind of sorcery. That's all we knew." He turned to Senya. "You think that was this... Crassica? Even back then?"

"I don't know. Maybe."

"Hells."

They did not speak for a long time. At length they decided to keep to the river for now, with an extra vigilant eye out for anybody along the shore. Brogan released his grip on the covering brush, and Senya pushed the canoe back into the river current. They set their paddles on their laps and let the current carry them forward slowly, not eager to gather too much speed and risk overtaking the disappeared soldiery.

25

RAEDWIN WAITED for Sadahlia at the peak of the crumbling north tower for hours. He paced nervously. Timing was essential to pull this off between guard changes. Picking up a loose stone, he spun it in his hand, caressing the rough dryness before idly dropping it. Moonlight glistened over slate rooftops below. A nightbird soared, its wings stretching wide across the unbroken face of the starlit sky. At last, Sadahlia emerged from among the tower's remaining fingers of stone. She stopped and glanced behind her. After a moment, she came to him.

"More watchmen than I expected," she said.

"Did anybody see you?"

"I know this place better than they do."

There had been two guards outside his own door and another at the end of the hall. Two more in the courtyard. All armed. None had been easy to evade. Crassica's latest orders were making a difficult thing all that much harder.

He took her hand. "I was afraid you wouldn't make it."

"My love. I will always make it."

Love. A word to end all words. Or a word to begin them.

"Something is going on," he said quietly. "Something big. I don't understand it."

Sadahlia's brow twitched as she sought to read his face in the moonlight. "What happened?"

"Come. I have to show you." Raedwin went to the waist-high remains of wall at the southern edge of the tower. Far below, a handful of people walked the open spaces, with a scattering of torchbearers along the walls. An occasional servant scurried across the courtyard.

"Crassica is suddenly talking about Senya again," he said. "Trying to get her to come here..."

"Your sister is coming here?"

"Crassica says something happened to her in the Hallonath, of all places." He led Sadahlia westward through a massive breach in the tower's side out onto what remained of the north wall, continuing down into a wide crack that gave access to the wall's interior passage. "And now she's sending some sailor up there to get her. Somebody named Delsorka..."

Sadahlia stopped short with a quiet gasp. "Oh, gods," she muttered.

"Who is Delsorka?"

"He is a man who is very good at what he does. If Delsorka is involved, then somebody somewhere is probably going to die."

Raedwin swore under his breath. He led on in silence, descending ever deeper underground. These were not so much passageways as a series of accidental openings, shifts from one ruined space to another—nothing that would ever be patrolled by Crassica's guards.

"I need to do something..." he said as they walked. "Only I don't know what..."

"It's not time yet."

Once underground, they soon arrived at the long marble-floored hallway leading to Crassica's residence. Raedwin's timing had worked—no guard at the moment. They slipped into a side passage connecting to the newly appointed chamber with the three strange iron chairs. Raedwin's latest project.

Sadahlia stepped past him into the room. "What... is this?" she whispered.

"I was hoping you could tell me. Have you ever seen anything like it? Crassica gives instructions but won't explain why. Or what it's for."

Sadahlia reached out to touch an edge of one of the chairs. "Three of them. Linked. And what are those pipes?"

"Something she's building with that sorcerer of hers, Ghellan..."

"And three fireplaces. With a glass window to the sky..." She turned to him. "Who are the chairs for?"

He shook his head. "No idea. But I don't like it."

"Do you think this is for Senya?"

"I didn't before. But now... I don't know. What could she do with Senya here? None of it makes any sense."

Sadahlia slowly circled the three chairs, examining them.

Raedwin watched her. "I need you to tell me what you know," he said at length.

"I'm in the dark, the same as you."

"I can't stand by while... whatever she is doing. We can't wait any longer."

Sadahlia shook her head. Her eyes darted around the room. "I only know what happened before," she said. "I don't understand what Crassica is doing now, especially not with Senya..."

"Well, tell me what happened before. Maybe there are clues for whatever this is..."

Her face fell motionless. Impassive. "Once you see, things will be different..."

"Things are different right now."

"There won't be any going back."

"Look at us. Look at this room. What's there to go back to? I need to know. I'm building these mystery cage chairs for some secret ritual, and now she's talking about my sister. All of it's concealed. Everything's in shrouds. There's already no going back."

Sadahlia took in a breath and let it out slowly before speaking again. "There is a place, here in the Keep..." She trailed off, her face twitching at the side of her mouth. She blinked. Gripping her hands together, she fidgeted with each of her fingers as her mouth opened and then closed again.

"Tell me..." he said gently.

"I don't know if you're ready..."

"I need to know."

"You need to understand that the things Crassica did here happened a long time ago. I did not realize what she was still doing until only recently. Otherwise I wouldn't have kept it hidden from you..."

"Kept what hidden?"

"She has wanted children from the beginning, as you well know, and wants to become truly born herself. But there are others... other things she has done... I don't know if any of it has to do with Senya... In truth, I don't think so..."

"Tell me."

"It wouldn't make sense if she was..."

"Sadahlia, please."

She opened her mouth to speak again but seemed to reconsider. Shook her head instead.

"I want you to show me."

"It'll only make you angry."

"I'm angry already."

Sadahlia stepped up from the depression holding the chairs, her body proud and regal in the moonlight streaming through the overhead glass. "Not this kind of angry." She reached out to take his hand. "But come. Let's go see."

Together they moved quickly through the empty halls. Ducking into shadow as the returning guard passed by, they soon slipped into a passage leading down. Sadahlia grabbed a torch from a wall mount and descended into darkness. Raedwin grabbed his own and followed. Once beyond the possibility of earshot, she spoke slowly, considering each word with care.

"After Crassica abandoned the idea of motherhood, she took to the crafting of creatures, searching for something like a child of her own. She tried everything—all levels of the Dark Arts. Spirit conjuring. Necromancy and vivisection, animancy, all of it—along with a few of her own new methods mixed in. Anything to help her mimic the act of creation."

Maybe somehow Raedwin had known this, maybe he hadn't. Maybe some things had always been clear, tucked in the back of his mind, hidden from scrutiny. Blocked by denial.

"And the emperors of Kalldon paid her enormously to create an unbreakable army. She gladly obliged. It gave her wealth and opportunity. She crafted new and unique creatures with powerful bodies and quick reflexes—an army to conquer and devour. But none of it went the way any of them expected. The empire was never very good at being careful, and the creatures were too smart for easy training. Too many escaped. Others murdered their handlers. They remained a lot closer to their animal cousins than any shared human ancestry. So the empire created a prison to shape them. A twisted nursery, savage and cruel. The guards spoke only the languages of Dahlphroaig and Rosswyld in order to fuse a natural hatred into their new pets, while feeding them human flesh to focus their purpose."

Raedwin's mouth fell open. He had no words for this. He'd long known the empire to be brutal, but this was something else entirely. All of it under Crassica's guidance.

Sadahlia led on. "The empire's plan was to release them on the frontier of Rosswyld," she said. "Putting their enemies to a grisly fate. They planned to build a wall and seal away the whole peninsula east of the forests, but a wall takes too much time and can't be built in the middle of a war. So Dunnenwyr just... fell apart. So much quicker than the empire ever thought possible. And their new pet army turned out far too clever and wild to control—with the pack mentality of wolves. They didn't much want to stay contained in Rosswyld, so they fled into the forest. North into the mountains. Some raped and ate their way through the burning chaos, eliminating whatever hope might have remained for a peaceful return to Kalldonian life."

"*Dunnenwyr the Damned*," Raedwin nearly whispered.

Sadahlia led him deeper into the disused tunnels, farther than they'd ever ventured together before. Water dripped from hidden fissures. The air grew thick and musty, alive with molds and sodden whispers.

"Nobody knew what to make of these creatures," she continued. "Nobody had ever seen anything like them before. All bone and blood. Killing machines left imperfect, unfinished. With no name to speak of. Almost immediately, they became known as the *boneskins*."

Raedwin stared at her back. "The boneskins came from Crassica?"

Sadahlia stopped. "I know it's hard to imagine, but it's the truth."

He had no words. If Crassica had really created the boneskins, then what other level of deviant manipulation was she capable of? Had he himself been helping to craft new horrors all these years? Was he doing so now?

Holding the torch aloft, Sadahlia continued down a long circling set of stairs drilled deeper into the bedrock. The air shifted and warmed, moving against Raedwin's skin as if the ground itself were breathing.

"They were never intended to reproduce," she said. "But as with a lot of things Crassica touches, the truth took its own path. Some gathered in groups and marched through the Kreskill Breach into the Hallonath, and some charged into the Brinsfallon frontier. None ever came back to Kalldonia. In these lands, they're all but forgotten."

Raedwin's jaw clenched. "And then after that?"

"After that, Crassica cut ties with the failing empire. She moved her knowledge, her history, and all her loyal followers out of their gaze, to here—the Valle d'Brasti."

After a time, the stairs ended. The passage opened into a vast vaulted chamber, shrouded in fleeting shadows. Sadahlia stepped forward, raising her torch.

"But the lives she crafted here were supposed to be kinder and gentler. More human. Holding special promise for renewal and rebirth." She spoke quietly now, as if unwilling to disturb tortured spirits of the dead. "Here, she was supposed to have learned from her mistakes."

A wide pit dominated the middle of the cavernous room. Empty torch mounts lined all sides. Three expired braziers hung on each of seven columns surrounding the central depression. A place once meant for brightness, now vacant and lost in the depths of memory.

"The Sevenfold's Children," she said. "The Jehndai... came from this room."

Raedwin held his own torch aloft. The room opened into greater brightness. He approached the edge of the pit. A lone set of steps led down through a wide notch to his right. A series of heavy cages cluttered the bottom, set at odd angles to one another. The joints had long since shattered, their doors thrown aside.

The room spoke mostly for itself. It was a larger crude, disused version of the room he'd been building near Crassica's chambers. Each cage housed a small cot or a bed of some kind, disintegrated patches of fabric and wool stuffed with decaying horsehair. An overhead iron grid held dead and dusty candles beside dark lantern mounts. Empty oil lamps hung beneath tarnished metal aprons.

"Stories tell of a fight—maybe battle is a better word—that started right here in this room," Sadahlia said. "The Jehndai subdued their guardians and broke free. Every last one. And now the forest holds them. Generations along."

Raedwin stepped deeper into the chamber. Several rusted instruments lay on a dusty shelf nearby. A set of small thin blades, toothed with corrosion. Metal clamps and grippers of some kind. A bone chisel. He could almost hear the cries under Crassica's knife. He could imagine the clang of iron chains, cage doors thundering among shouted orders to secure arms and legs while she carved their living flesh.

"The Jehndai were not the first," Sadahlia said. "And now... I'm afraid they won't be the last."

This was a room made for pain—a place built to force the world to bend and twist, to become a thing warped and artificial, crafted of suffering and desolation.

"And now she's bringing Senya here…" he whispered.

Whatever Crassica did, she thrust her control into every detail. An abandoned pit deep in the bedrock could now just as easily be a ritual chamber with three strange metal mesh chairs, positioned to address the full moon.

The room suddenly felt pinched and choked, the ceiling too low, the air too thick and warm, too wet and close. A broken space, strewn with anguish and torture.

For so long, Raedwin had wanted to believe in Crassica, to trust in the good nature of his mentor, and to deny that she would've ever participated in anything like this, but part of him realized he'd probably known all along that these kinds of secrets lingered underneath. He'd been in denial all these years. The glory of her good, built on the blood of others. A vast emptiness woven from gossamer nonsense.

"We are the progeny of this place," he said at length. "Our ignorance. Turning a blind eye. We are all to blame for this, for what happened here. For what's still happening." He strode back toward her. "It's time. We have to leave. We have to get out of the citadel. Get away from Crassica. We have to get to Senya and warn her."

Sadahlia stood for a long moment. "Okay," she said finally, her voice resolute. "But we cannot just leave, not like that. Crassica would never allow it."

"We'll go north. I have to find Senya…"

"No. Think, my love."

He wanted all of this to be easy. Clear. Now that he'd made a decision, Raedwin wanted to be done with all of it—especially if his sister was in trouble. But Sadahlia was right, of course. Crassica would never allow them to simply leave. They'd have to fight their way out. Nothing would ever be easy.

He froze. "Her Amaris," he said quietly.

Sadahlia nodded. "First, we have to deal with Crassica's mine. We have to block access. Otherwise she'll just pull me back in. Probably you as well."

Raedwin's eyes dropped to the rubble-strewn floor. To attack the mine, they'd need horses and weapons. Good fighters. But how many? Who would join them? And how many of Crassica's men would they be up against?

"Kraegha and Devron already have a plan," Sadahlia assured him. "They have people in place. They've been scouting. Planning for months. It's almost ready..."

Raedwin turned to her. "That's why you took me to see them."

"You are important," she said. "To all of us."

"And they've already planned an assault?"

"Opportunities come and go. We've been waiting for the right one..."

Raedwin stepped to her and pulled her to him. "This is the one," he whispered. "Our time is now."

"I will be a danger to you," she warned. "I am sorry."

"I'm a danger to you as well. Don't be sorry."

"I will be slow."

"And I will be fast. Together, we're perfect."

"We cannot go together. That would draw too much attention."

"Let me work with Kraegha and Devron. We will meet somewhere, later—after the mine is destroyed. We'll stay hidden and make for Brinsfallon. We'll need a ship. That'd be the fastest way..."

"A ship will be difficult, my love. I cannot remain at sea, not for long. This body will not do well over water."

"By carriage, then. We'll make for Darizi and find disguises as roving merchants. Or the wilderness. Yes! We'll live off the land. Follow the edge of the mountains. Stick to the forests and foothills and sneak through to Lothania. Nobody there will care. And then by carriage to Toncana."

Sadahlia smiled. "A true adventure. And where should we meet? Do you know of a place?"

"I'll have to think on it."

She frowned and cocked her head. "What do I bring? Oddly, all these long years and I do not know how to travel."

"Bring yourself. I will handle the rest."

"I'll need a weapon."

"Yes. That's a good idea," he said. "A dagger would be the simplest and easiest. Do you know how to use one?"

"Well enough, yes. And maybe a bow?"

"Also good."

"We will be free together, under the open sky," she said. "Summer is coming. At night it'll be warm and we can sleep outside. We will watch the stars together."

"The library has plenty of maps. I'll find a place. I will make my way to you after the mine is finished and Crassica has no more Amaris to use against us."

Sadahlia shook her head. "Over seventy years I have walked this earth, and I've never slept outside under the stars."

"Well, my love," Raedwin said, pulling her close, "get ready to really live."

26

THE TALL three-masted *Siege Runner* sailed a steady clip along the north-western tip of Lophlyn. She was a grand thing, with crisp sails and a polished hull, a warship down to her bones. Her new design was long and narrow, and she sailed a strong clean line. And if the wind failed, she had an experimental double-rowed bench to provide for more hands at the oars than any other vessel in the known world.

Delsorka's journey so far had been smooth, helped along by clear weather and steady winds, yet something still bothered him. He'd had trouble sleeping the past two nights, which was a rarity for him at sea. Something nagged at him even more than this half-green crew he'd been handed, more than the rushed preparations and the curious nature of their task. Crassica had all but shoved a sorcerer on board, which bothered him more than anything. Some old man named Ghellan. That one had given Delsorka extra pause from the very beginning when the pale old Vallahnir had first made mention of his coming along. Delsorka never really liked sorcerers or necromancers, or any kind of conjurer really—especially at sea. He didn't like to tempt fate on his boats, and sorcerers tempted everything. This last hasty move by Crassica was something completely new, and he didn't like it one bit.

Stepping out of his cabin, Delsorka greeted the armed sentry. Moving quickly through the lower deck, he bounded up into the fresh night air to take in the set and trim of the sails, the state of the weather and the steadiness of the breeze. He considered the likelihood of a clear morning to come. Ordinarily this would give him confidence. But this trip remained under a burden of questions and hesitations—things any sailing captain knew to be particularly destructive if left unchecked.

He went to the taffrail. Three birds flew low and black along the waves, no doubt using the light of the moon to aid in their hunting. Rigging creaked overhead. Stretched cordage moaned as the *Runner* heaved over another swell. One of the topsails flapped for a few seconds and then caught as the trimmers adjusted to shifts in the breeze.

Delsorka strode the quarterdeck, thumbing the twisted scar above his eyebrow. Ordering him so far north for a look and listen, or just a simple grab and go, was among one of old Crassica's stranger requests. Take Senya by whatever means and bring her back. Simple and straight. Not so much *help her if you can*, like she'd said at first. Her tune had changed as soon as Raedwin had left the room, of course—a clear sign there was more to this whole story than she'd given Delsorka. Grab Senya and bring her back, whether she wanted to come or not. *Extreme prejudice.* No more *if that is her wish.* No questions asked, and no answers given.

So. More of a kidnapping than a rescue. If anybody else was with her, Crassica explained, Delsorka was to be rid of them. Bring nobody else along and allow nobody to follow. Not exactly his favorite type of job, but he'd do what he was asked. For what Crassica paid, he didn't have to like it.

The old crone had surprising reach, deep into Brinsfallon. A living, breathing Vallahnir could strike utter fear into the hearts of almost anybody, and Crassica was awfully adept at using that fear. Her underground network in the North stretched all the way from Corregidon to Pentmore and from Posselhead to Cairn. Plenty of obedient muscle to do all the dirty work, and plenty of coin to hold everything in place before and after. Delsorka himself had run a fair share of refined Amaris up this coast, for her and Lanius both. Pound for pound, the money a tiny bag of that stuff fetched in Corregidon made it more valuable than anything else he'd ever seen.

But what did Crassica want with this Senya girl? Something had the old woman stirred up, for sure. Clearly, Senya wasn't trying to make her way to Kalldonia on her own. And her brother, Raedwin, hadn't been too enthusiastic. Not at all. Probably knew more than he let on as well.

Secrets bothered Delsorka. He preferred to know why he was doing what he did. Regardless of whether the assigned task was dark and brutal, he wanted to know the reason. Money, power, whatever it was. He didn't love some of the things he was asked to do, but life hadn't given him a wealth of occupational choices. He at least wanted the opportunity to weigh his moral misgivings about working for certain nefarious causes. Secrets denied him that choice.

"Maddon," he called. "See that the top foresheet is made. We need that sail to pull all she can."

"Aye," came the return call.

They'd been on a nearly due-north heading since leaving the Gulf of Dunnen and rounding the Tooth with a strong southerly at their back. Boasting three masts and wide square sails, the *Runner* ran very nicely downwind. It was one of the many things Delsorka loved about this ship. She was responsive, she was strong, and she was very fast.

Yet this crew worried him. Many of Delsorka's regular gang of scoundrels and outcasts had wandered too far afield to be ready in time to sail, so Crassica had kindly finished out his ship's complement with some of her own people. As fresh and loyal as they might be to Crassica, Delsorka had no history with them, no background. More than a handful had never been at sea. Not the ideal way to begin a journey.

A sailor approached. "We've made the Blastonbrees, sir. I was told to let you know."

Delsorka thanked him. The Blastonbree Islands. A treacherous archipelago chock-full of pirates and marauders, studded with notorious reefs that could split a ship like the *Runner* wide open from stem to stern if they weren't especially careful.

"Maddon," Delsorka called. "When you're ready, bring her northeast by north, and let her skirt the break until we're past the eastern peninsula. And get extra eyes aloft. I don't want any Grillhaven Ghosts sneaking up on us in the night."

"Aye. You got it." The younger man barked a quick succession of orders, and the deck came alive with activity. The ship surged to starboard. Delsorka strode the darkened deck and made his way forward to the bow. He looked out over the moonlit swells. The dark hulk of South Blastonbree Island loomed low on the horizon ahead. Ordinarily they would come well away and hug the northern Lophlyn coast, but Crassica wanted them north in a hurry. So a hurry meant close calls and cut corners wherever Delsorka could judge them to be safe. And sometimes even when he couldn't.

He turned and went below. Rows of hammocks swung from the timbers, creaking with the roll of the ship. Simms, among others, had saved several pulls of rumwater and had used them all at once in celebration of a birthday. Simms led the heaviest sleepers in a loud and grating snore.

A sliver of light peered up from the hold as Delsorka stepped past the hatch.

Odd, he thought. No reason for light to be burning down there at this hour. Dangerous, in fact. He slid down the ladder and strode among the stores to a series of compartments near the stern. Light shone along cracks in the flat wall planks. The captain swung the door open.

Ghellan stood with a start, stumbling and nearly falling as the ship lurched over a swell. Clearly not accustomed to the sea. The old man's bald head was tattooed with intricate inscriptions running from his forehead down around both eyes. He wore inscribed leather armor over a wool jerkin. Twin braids dangled from his chin. A pair of bright tallow lamps swung from hooks on the rafters. Wooden decking lay at the sorcerer's feet, fashioned into a sturdy square with several archaic markings burned into its surface.

"Ghellan," Delsorka said. "What in hells is all this?"

"I am crafting what we of the Arts call a birdcage."

"A birdcage."

"It is to silence our prize once she is on board."

"First off, I need to know about anything and everything that happens on board this ship. Are we clear on that? I find you sneaking around with an open flame again, you'll find yourself swimming home."

Ghellan bowed low and offered the palms of both hands. "I do apologize. Necessity dictated secrecy. I did not think to bring you in on my particular actions. But of course, that was wrong. It will not happen again."

"You've got an open brazier flame. Everything around you is dry old wood. That's not the best combination."

"I can assure you of the utmost care taken," Ghellan said in a creamy voice.

"It's a stretch we'll find this girl, let alone get her on board. But if we do, why would she need to be silenced? Why's she so important?"

The sorcerer stiffened. He opened his mouth and seemed to consider his words before speaking. "She is a child of the Elders, my dear captain," he said at length. "A daughter of a Brohndai, and born of the water. She is much more powerful than most can ascertain, perhaps more powerful than she realizes herself. She lures people and creatures, often in ways that are hidden to those being drawn. At sea, she could prove to be very dangerous. Perhaps she could bring forth things we cannot fathom, even accidentally."

Delsorka shook his head. "Funny how old Crassica didn't mention that part." He examined the plankboard base carefully laid out on the floor. "So this thing here, this is supposed to help?"

"Indeed." Ghellan reached into a nearby brazier and pulled a glowing iron from its coals. He crouched on the loose platform. "I will embed a powerful enclosure to encapsulate her here, separating the rhythms of her deeper powers from the water, rendering them useless." He pressed the iron into the wood, continuing a wide star-shaped burn he'd already begun. "This will keep her from connecting beyond the walls of this room. Effectively, it will silence her."

The bald sorcerer started to sing. He passed his hands over the markings in the wood, eyes closed in concentration. The shape and form of the song pulled at Delsorka's ears with words from the sea joined with earth and sky as well as the brazier's flickering flame. Guttural sounds from the ancient language of spirits and deft magicians, of necromancy and the damned.

"All right," Delsorka said as soon as Ghellan had finished. "Make sure you let me know what you're planning from now on. Always. Every time."

"Yes, my dear captain," Ghellan said with a dip of his chin. "I will certainly do so."

Delsorka shook his head, not quite sure he believed that. Turning to leave, he stopped and glanced back at the sorcerer. "You know, I've found that toys and gadgets like this rarely act in the way intended. Especially when they get too complicated. Better to keep a well-honed blade at your hip and make sure you know how to use it."

Ghellan smiled thinly. "Of course, captain."

27

BEFORE TONIGHT, Lanius had never been directed to track one of their own. Before Raedwin, his target had typically been some outlier in Kalldon or some idiot from Katliga or Darizi who'd slighted Crassica. Occasionally he'd grab and stash or correct some delinquent debtor who required insight into the error of his negligent ways. Usually a well-played threat would be enough to get Crassica's point across. Occasionally Lanius had to take a life, quick and ugly. Silent moves under the cover of darkness. But he'd never had to track somebody like Raedwin, not inside the Keep itself. He'd never had the benefit of stalking his prey in a place that he knew better than the back of his own bloodstained hand.

Lanius glanced over his shoulder. The hallway was clear. He ducked into a shadowy alcove and flipped a mechanism hidden in the stonework. A heavy latch creaked quietly. Several counterweights slid, and a section of the wall swung away. He stepped through. The hidden doorway closed in silence behind him.

He stood at the far end of a rarely used extension of the library. The familiar stench of stagnation and mold greeted his nose—the slow decay of vellum and parchment. He crept toward the central room along a dusty stack of shelves filled with forgotten scrolls and ancient leatherbound volumes. Keeping to the shadows in a position to observe, he waited. Crassica had been clear—under no circumstances was he to allow Raedwin to discover him. He was to simply watch and to find out whatever Raedwin did when he managed to escape his trackers.

His target sat at a scribe's desk under a narrow pool of light cast by three oil lamps. An open scroll lay in front of him, along with two parchment scraps. Raedwin bent into the lamplight and studied the scroll. Too far away for Lanius to discern, it looked to maybe be a guide for one of his complicated instruments. Or instructions. Maybe a map.

Raedwin dipped his quill into thick black ink and drew a long curved line on one of the scraps. He glanced at the larger scroll and then back to the line he'd drawn. He made shapes and crosshatches and a few more gestures with the quill and then penned words alongside. He made a note in each margin.

Simple following was never Lanius's favorite. He much preferred a dance with keen blades and skill, with lives on the line. Stepping and weaving, steel clashing against steel, ability against mastery, weapon and flesh alike. The beginnings of such dances held certain tests—thrusts and parries, pokes and slaps—the dipping of one's toes into the pool of death. Where are each of our weaknesses? What shall we exploit in one another? Who is faster, stronger? Who shall prove smarter? Plain following and watching was too simple. Flaccid. This sort of thing struck him as a waste of his innumerable talents.

The librarian emerged from shadows on the far side of the room and shuffled to an empty scribe's desk. He opened a heavy book and proceeded to study its pages.

Raedwin made a second copy of his small parchment, set down the quill, and spent a moment examining his work. He laid a felt sheet on the copies and pressed them dry. Sliding the ring holder over the scroll, he stood and walked to the librarian's desk. They shared a word. Raedwin set the scroll on the desk and headed out of the library.

Only after he'd gone did Lanius step from the shadows. He approached the librarian and pointed at the scroll. "Don't put that away," he said. "I'll be back to have a look."

The librarian glanced up, eager to chastise the rude speech of this abrupt encounter. But recognition flashed across his face, and he thought better of it. One tried not to question Lanius, the Sword Hand of the master—not unless one wished for trouble, perhaps even to die. The Sword Hand did as he wanted, and the rest of the world suffered the consequences. The librarian clearly hated these facts, wished for further words, but Lanius did not wait for an answer. He was already gone.

Once outside in the bolstered torchlight of the Keep's courtyard, Lanius kept to the shadows along the walls. A handful of servants hurried about their normal evening business. Scanning the scene, he caught a glimpse of Raedwin ducking into the doorway of the smithy.

Clever, thought Lanius. The smithy had two back doors, one at ground level and the other on the second floor, which opened onto an elevated walkway to the building behind. The blacksmith rarely cared who used his rooms for passage, or why. Lanius hurried to the far corner and slipped through a gap into the alley behind. Raedwin emerged on the second floor and spun to vault over the rail. He swung to hang below the walkway before dropping easily to the ground.

Lanius froze. He slipped into hiding behind a corner of stone. Raedwin strode toward him along the passage and glanced back over his shoulder. Without warning, he stopped, kicked open a wooden pit cover at his feet, and quickly descended a set of hidden stairs. The wooden cover slid closed over his head.

Even more clever, thought Lanius. *The guy is quick.* First go vertical to the second floor and then in as little as five or six steps be back underground. No wonder old Crassica had so much trouble keeping track. Lanius strode crossways to the bakehouse next to the great hall and flew down the stairs to the lower storerooms. He ignored inquisitive looks and whispered questions as he stepped behind sacks of grain to a slender wooden door in the back. He produced a long key and slid it into the oiled lock. The mechanism made barely a noise as he opened it to admit his narrow body.

Striding down a dark passage that fed several storerooms along the service house corridor, Lanius paused at a junction of passages. Muffled footsteps came from the hall to his left. He followed and descended a short stone stair. Whispered voices echoed ahead. Lanius continued into another chamber. Light flickered from a doorway at the far end.

"Yes, I know," said a woman, quietly. The voice was vaguely familiar.

Lanius crept closer, keeping to the shadows.

"And you'll need to keep to this ravine here once you're past the walls." Raedwin's voice.

Lanius moved into a vantage that allowed a view into the torchlit room. Raedwin was there, crouching over one of the freshly drawn scraps he'd brought from the library, pointing down at different places on the parchment as he spoke. Kneeling opposite him, with her gray hood pulled low over her beautiful white face, was the first of Crassica's Great Gathering of Vallahnir, the one known as Sadahlia.

Now isn't that interesting, Lanius thought. *The head of the Vals creeping around in the underpassages with the master's little golden boy*. He was sure Crassica would find this particular detail most interesting and would reward him plenty to hear all about it.

Raedwin ran his finger down the center of the parchment. "And then you just follow the river," he said quietly. "All the way to this abandoned farmhouse."

Sadahlia stared at the parchment in silence. "Okay," she said at last.

"It's far away from any village or settlement. It's a shell of a building, but there's a cellar. Nobody will possibly know."

"Underground?" She laughed. "We'll feel right at home."

"There's a flat hill nearby, with a ring of stones. Nothing else around."

"I like it. So when do we go?"

"Night after next. Crassica will be away for a few more days. Nobody will notice. If you can time it right, you could leave well before sundown. After we finish, I'll meet you there."

Sadahlia examined the map sprawled between them. She whispered something that didn't reach Lanius's ears. Raedwin rolled toward her out of his crouch and pulled her face to his. They kissed. Stretched out to lie together on the stone. Embracing and holding one another, they whispered secrets that none but the two of them could hear.

Well, now, that, Lanius thought, *is even more interesting*. He remained motionless in the shadows until the weight of their breathing filled the damp moldy air. He crept back down the corridor and made his way to the surface, emerging into the moonlit courtyard.

Lanius returned to the library. The librarian shuffled along the catwalk at the far end of the room, searching for something in the stacks. Lanius strode to the scribe's desk. Mismatched parchments cluttered the surface next to a ledger book. A quill pen with a clay bottle of black ink. A neat stack of blotting felt in a short nook. He slid the parchments aside and glanced at the set of side shelves. Raedwin's scroll was nowhere to be found.

The librarian appeared, stepping between Lanius and the desk to push the larger man aside. "You cannot parade into Her High Honor's library and begin flinging things around," he scolded. "No matter who you are."

"Where's the scroll?"

"There is a process and a method to this place." The librarian stiffly stepped to a side table and reached out to retrieve the scroll in question. "This library has thousands of volumes." He handed it to Lanius. "You cannot seek ownership over things that do not belong to you. Without process, there is chaos."

Lanius gave a thin mirthless smile. "And chaos reigns supreme in my world." He held up the scroll. "Thank you."

Upon examination, he found the scroll revealed a wealth of hints and clues, as well as a few solid truths. It was indeed a map, drawn from the period of the late empire, showing lands north of the citadel, tracts of ownership and placement of villages all labeled by a deft and long-dead hand. Countryside lanes wove a patchwork of connection between settlements and arrow-straight Kalldonian causeways.

Raedwin said something about a farmhouse. A few hours north of here. Alongside a river. Lanius scanned the scroll. *Can't be the Dophini. Too far north... but maybe...*

He ran his eyes along an unnamed tributary that flowed out of the forest east of the citadel and bent to flow north, joining the Dophini. Three different settlements dotted the edge of the water, robust villages from the time of the empire but now mostly vacant and battered wastes. The second among them he knew to be inhabited. And then there, almost hidden, alone on an abandoned rise outside the third ruined and deserted village, sat a tiny pinprick on the map marking the crumbled remains of a fortified Kalldonian farmhouse.

28

RAEDWIN TOOK final stock. Water bag, flint, and steel. The map he'd drawn to find the farmhouse. His mind's eye could see Sadahlia alone in the darkening folds of land north of the citadel, making her way alone, hidden and hurried but exposed to the elements, exposed to danger. He longed to follow. To be with her. But he had work to do first. The mine had to be knocked out, or none of this would turn out well. He could see Crassica away in Kalldon. Her keen senses, sharp eyes, and fluid sense of the world. He shook his head, banishing both images. Kraegha had already pulled the guard. It was time to go.

Gathering the remaining items for his journey, Raedwin slung the haversack over his shoulder, bedroll secured to the top. With a quick farewell to his beloved workshop of the last seven years, he left the room and descended the long iron stairs in seething torchlight. He slipped unseen into the kitchen storeroom.

With breakfast still hours away, no workers had yet arrived. Raedwin quickly filled an empty wine skin and grabbed some apples, dried fish, smoked saltpork, and a roll of bread. Wrapping each with care, he slid them into his haversack along with a large wedge of cheese. Sneaking out the same way he'd entered, he pulled the cowl of his cloak low over his face and kept to the shadows.

Built in the Old Kalldonian style like the rest of the crumbling fortress it served, the stables sat in the low southwestern corner of the lower citadel. Thick walls of quarried stone lined with brick supported rough timbers and a gabled slate roof. Raedwin slid open the greased iron latch of the bay door and stepped inside. Several muzzles poked over stall doors and voiced their curiosity in nickers and low snorts. He lifted a saddle and hackamore from the tack room and walked midway down the line. Whispering softly to a chestnut mare, he ran his hand down her nose. Once inside the stall, he slipped the hackamore on her muzzle and tossed a blanket over her back. He heaved the saddle into place and secured it.

"Glad to see you're finally listening," came a voice from outside the stall. Raedwin turned to find Solinius approaching in silhouette against the light.

"I'm glad you finally trusted me," Raedwin answered with a nod. He strapped a long stout knife to his belt.

Solinius handed him a shortsword in a sturdy scabbard, which he buckled at his waist, along with a small dagger in a boot sheath. Raedwin led his horse from the stall out the open bay doors.

A man waited in shadows, already mounted on a tall horse, tail swishing against flies.

"Kraegha," Raedwin acknowledged. He mounted and stepped his horse alongside.

The Chief of the Keep's bright eyes squinted against the rising moon. "Best that you keep that cowl drawn low," he said. "Hide those fire-glow eyes of yours. You're not exactly difficult to recognize out here. Even in the dark."

Kraegha circled his horse and headed away from the stable. Raedwin followed. Keeping to the shadowed gullies and creases in the earth, they crossed the rawboned lands east of the citadel, a broad country of stony grasses. Patches of fertile ground lined flush creek sides. Once thick with herds of Kalldonian buffalo, the land lay empty for miles. War and blight had forced most livestock southward into the more civilized and defensible havens below the Mondini River. Now almost nothing roamed these hills.

Some distance from the walls, they passed the rocky prominence where Raedwin had last connected with Senya. He called for a halt. "I need to try one quick thing, just for a minute."

Dismounting, he stepped to the familiar exposed stones carved in ancient picture languages of the Old Ones. He went down to one knee. The morning's first light broke over the distant mountains. Placing both bare palms on the rock and earth, he closed his eyes.

The connection snapped open, quick and bright like a window to the morning sun. Senya was there, clear as anything, floating on some distant river in a birchbark canoe. A strange man sat in the bow.

Pulsing strength emanated from his sister, something new, a power Raedwin had never experienced before—a clarity of bond, the depth of her associations coming from somewhere beyond the water. All of it new, everything different.

Outside the reach of Crassica's blocking at last, he felt his voice ring clear and true.

Senya, he called to her.

29

SHE NEARLY fell out of the boat. Raedwin's voice came so crisp and lucid, hit so unexpectedly, Senya briefly lost her sense of balance. Her paddle fell against the edge of the canoe.

Senya, Raedwin said again. Simple and true, as if they were just waking up across the room from one another as children.

Morning mist still rose from the quiet gray river. Senya pulled her paddle from the water and set it carefully in the boat. Brogan took no notice. He pushed on. Leaning forward, Senya placed both hands over the side and trailed her fingers in the water.

It took you long enough, she called to her brother.

Sorry, I've been... And he trailed off, as if considering how to explain. *Held up*, he finished at length.

By Crassica.

How did you know?

She's doing something. I've been trying to reach you. To warn you, or at least to find out where you are and figure out what's going on.

She's trying to lure you here. Did you know that? She's sent people after you. I don't know why she's doing it.

Where are you?

I'm in Kalldonia. But do not come here. I'm leaving this place.

Something is happening that is bigger than both of us. We need Father's help. I'm going to Faeroen. Crassica is doing more than you think.

So I'm learning.

She is very dangerous. You have to be careful.

I'll be fine. You're the one in danger. They're coming for you. More Vallahnir. I don't know how many. I wanted to warn you. I don't know where you are right now, but you need to get somewhere safe.

She's already come for me. She's already sent Vallahnir. We already dealt with them.

Raedwin paused. *We?*

I have help. A friend. A good man.

She's not going to stop.

I know.

Raedwin fell silent. She could sense the energy of his regret. *I'm sorry,* he said.

You should be.

I've gotten out now. Things are happening. I'm with others. We're going to cut off her power and destroy her ways of controlling all this. So for now, stay safe. If you're going to Faeroen, then stay there. Do not come down here, whatever you do. Stay out of Kalldonia.

You're getting deeper into trouble, aren't you?

I'm going to end this.

Why did you start it in the first place?

I'm sorry. I really am.

With a Vallahnir, no less. Even for you, this is beyond... And she paused, uncertain how to continue, unsure if she wanted to. The river flowed cold against her fingers. She let out a long sigh. Now was not the time.

They aren't all like Crassica, he said.

How do you know?

There is one. Down here. She is different. Here name is Sadahlia, and she's coming with me. You will meet her.

Crassica is not finished with you.

We're out now. We'll cut her off soon enough. And then we will join you.

Raedwin, she urged. *Will you please, if you ever listen to me once in your life, listen now?*

I'm listening.

Be careful.

I will.

I'm serious.

I know. And I'm listening. I will be careful. And Sen... He trailed off. His image shimmered as he lost focus for a moment. *I want you to know...* But he did not finish.

What?

Just that I'm sorry. I'm sorry for what I did. For what I've done. For what's happening to you. For leaving... He remained quiet for a long moment, gazing through the immeasurable distance between them.

And... for what happened, he said finally. *Back then.*

That was a long time ago.

Still.

Thank you. Thank you for saying that. But we can talk all that through some other time.

I'm sorry I turned my back on my family. It will never happen again.

Just be careful. Stay out of her way. And stay safe.

I will. You too. Stay safe yourself. You don't know what's coming for you.

But she did know. She knew more than any of them realized. *I'm not afraid of what's coming,* she said. *I've seen them already. They woke up something dangerous in me, dear brother. They don't realize. They don't know. Whoever thinks to harm you is the one who needs to be afraid, not the other way around. So let them come. I'll be ready.*

And then everything went white.

"Are you okay?" Brogan's face came into focus, silhouetted against the sky behind him. Senya lay back on the riverbank, her clothing wet. Rivulets slid off and pooled against her body. Her feet in water. The canoe's bow was hastily shoved into the bank, untethered.

"You fell in," he said.

"The river?"

"You bent over, with your hands in the water. You were rocking back and forth. I yelled at you, but it was like you weren't even there. And then you started to shake, leaned over too far, and went in."

She sat up. "Sorry about that."

"Are you okay?"

"I'm fine. I just..."

"Was that it? The connection thing? Was that your brother?"

"Yes," she said. "He called to me, out of the blue. I couldn't believe it." A cool breeze cut across the riverbank. Senya shivered. Brogan hurriedly unrolled a blanket and covered her shoulders.

"He's gotten out," she said. "Escaped somehow, and he's leaving. Says he's coming here, or will be. But he's down in Kalldonia. And he's still in trouble, no matter what he tried to tell me. He says he's going to cut off Crassica, but I don't think it's going to be all that easy, whatever he's trying."

Senya shivered again and pulled the blanket tight around her shoulders. She turned to Brogan. "This doesn't change anything," she said. "I still need to get to Faeroen, fast. Raedwin is heading for some new disaster. We have some time, but he's not nearly as safe as he thinks he is. I can feel it."

30

GRASS GREW tall over the hills, dotted by groves of reaching oaks and the occasional ancient stone house. Some distance south of the Valle d'Brasti, Raedwin and Kraegha joined a rough cartway climbing due east, tearing across stony and embittered ground like some ancient knife scar line.

Soon they entered the shaded arms of the forest. Towering oaks stood apart from one another, allowing the burgeoning sun to reach deep into the trees. After a time, Kraegha left the cartway to follow a wide wash upward into trackless land. The hills on either side grew steep and tall and became more like walls than hills. At a bend in the wash, with a prominent granite boulder jutting from the left side of the shallow canyon, he reined his horse to a stop.

"We walk from here," he said. "And we stay out of sight."

Securing their horses to nearby trees, Kraegha led Raedwin up through a gap in the wall. After a few steep lunges, they gained the lip of the canyon. Crouching low, Kraegha motioned for Raedwin to do the same. They moved from tree to tree, continuing eastward, taking care to remain hidden behind earth mounds and boulders.

The mine announced itself before they actually saw anything. A steady drumbeat of hammers on stone. Hundreds of them. And then shouting and screams. As it came into sight, the mine opened before them like a gaping wound split deep into the earth. Much of the narrow valley had been completely stripped away, all the soil and ground blasted and scoured to expose veins of bedrock bones. The uneven stepped walls teemed with workers scrambling on long crude ladders set against the rock. Pale fur covered their long lean bodies wherever they were not covered in mud. Slender ears tapered to tufts of black hair at the tips, positioned at the back of their heads. Wide black eyes.

Jehndai, all of them. The Sevenfold's Children. Just like Kraegha and Devron had said in the secret meeting deep beneath the Keep. Bound together by iron chains at their necks, they struggled to lift heavy baskets of raw rock, handing them overhead to waiting hands above. At the rim, they unloaded each basket into heavy wheeled carts and then lowered the empties back down with rope. Hundreds labored all through the unnatural gorge, chipping at stone and soil alike with crude hammers and pikes. The only humans Raedwin could see were the well-fed and well-armed men standing at protected watchpoints, whips and crossbows at the ready, lending a sharp sense of fear and vague order to the crawling chaos.

"Devron's longbowmen are already in place among the trees," Kraegha whispered. "Ready for the signal."

Raedwin noticed long aqueducts running from somewhere higher in the mountains to a series of wide stone tanks above the mine on the far side of the narrow valley. A prominent sluicegate waited on the downhill side. "How many?"

"Enough to get us started. First we'll take the outer guard, and then however many we can get before we start breaking chains. And then, together with the Jehndai, we'll have the numbers."

Raedwin shook his head. "That won't be enough."

"Surprise can work wonders in places like this."

"The Jehndai will run as soon as they're free. They'll leave us here to deal with very armed and heavily armored killers. That's your plan?"

"They won't run."

"How do you know?"

"It's not escape they want. It's vengeance."

"And then what?"

Kraegha grinned. "That's where you come in. You know more about raw Brasti Ore than anybody."

"Not more than Crassica."

"It explodes if struck hard enough, yes? I've seen it happen."

"It's actually the gas it puts off that explodes. And the dust. The solid ore itself will only burn your skin."

"So how do we spark an explosion?"

Raedwin pointed to a series of stout buildings along one edge of the gorge. "They probably store loose ore in there. That's where it's most dangerous. If you can pile all of it down at the low end of the gorge and get well enough away, a few fire arrows ought to be all you need."

"So it blows up, chokes the end of the ravine with rock and rubble. That won't do much to destroy the operation..."

"Then you blow the water tanks."

Kraegha surveyed the scene, thinking it over. "Dam the gorge, and then flood the whole valley," he whispered. A grin slid across his face. "Hadn't thought of that. Years'll pass before anybody can pull ore from this place again."

"It's still a crap plan," Raedwin muttered. "I don't like your numbers game."

"If the numbers are right, it's not a game. The point is to destroy the mine, not to kill everybody. Or get everybody killed. This needs to be an uprising by the Jehndai, not us. We are not actually here. The blood of Crassica's men won't be on our hands, not directly. We'll go back to the Keep after this. We'll offer our proper outrage and condolences. There's more work yet for us to do."

"I'm never going back there," Raedwin said, his voice low. "This is it for me."

A cry went out from a tower nearby. Another repeated the call. In a near panic, several Jehndai workers along the bottom of the ravine rushed to the ladders and began to climb, struggling to coordinate the chains linking one neck to another. Those below nearly lifted the ones above as they climbed. One worker slipped, his flailing hands grasping for muddy rungs and finding nothing but air. For a brief moment he was suspended in space, loose of the ladder and the broken earth alike. Then he fell. His neck jerked taut on the chain. The Jehndai's body spasmed for a moment and then hung lifeless. He was left to dangle alongside the others as they hurried to haul their collective chain up the terraced side of the mine.

A few had not made it onto the ladders yet. Several struggled to at least gain the first few rungs, each glancing furtively at the massive water tank above.

"Oh, gods," Raedwin muttered.

The sluicegate opened with a metallic boom. Water poured forth, ripping down the far side of the ravine in a massive flood, tearing earth and rock away in a furious scouring purge, along with any of the Jehndai unfortunate enough to have been left on the floor of the mine. Hammered with a deadly onslaught of water, the unfortunates were driven under by the frothing boulder-filled wall, leaving nothing behind but freshly exposed veins of ore.

And then it was done. The sluicegate closed, and the water slowed to a sliding wetness. A new cry went out, and the workers descended without sound back down the ladders, each picking up where they'd left off, hammering away at the earth. Only when the dangling, broken body of the fallen was brought to the ground did guards climb down and see to its removal—along with the unlucky few who'd drowned in the flood. For expedience, they separated heads from bodies to quickly release the iron chain. Ordering the others back to work, they hauled the headless dead away.

"New plan," Raedwin said after a time. He pointed to the main gate with the central guardhouse. "I march in there like I'm sent by Crassica herself. Yell about this and that. Throw a tantrum. I'll gather a group in tight to me, especially the Minemaster. Easy targets."

Kraegha nodded. "You draw all kinds of attention," he said. "Everybody takes notice. They'll wonder what is going on, and you'll demand long explanations of every piece of the operation..."

"While you and Devron and Solinius quietly get rid of the perimeter guards."

"And work our way inward from there."

"The archers take out the bunched-up group, all at once. And I stand and hope they don't kill us all before we get the upper hand."

"I'll be with you."

Raedwin shook his head. "No, you can't. None of you are allowed to be here. I'm the only one they can see. The rest of you are going back to the Keep so you can't be tied to this. Me, I *want* her to know I'm here."

Raedwin returned to his horse and rode toward the mine's main entrance via the cartway. He stopped near the guardhouse. Dismounting, he strode forward. Nothing had really prepared him for this, but the image of the falling Jehndai flashed in his mind over and again. The neck breaking, body dangling, the indifferent removal. Rage boiled in him, and he let it flow. Better to let the truth out. Don't act. Be the strength.

"Hey!" he barked at the Minemaster. "Are you in charge here?"

A sinister grin slid across the older man's face. Narrow, deep-set eyes and a close-cropped beard. Vainly kept, neatly tailored. "At last," the Minemaster called. "Crassica sends her favorite pet! To what do we owe the pleasure? Must be something special indeed!" He glanced at the men around him as they gathered close, sensing some mild, fun spectacle.

"Does Crassica know what you're doing out here?" Raedwin nearly shouted.

The man squinted as if considering. "She was here herself..." He trailed off as he turned to the guard next to him. "Just a couple of weeks ago, wasn't it?"

Raedwin pointed at the Jehndai slaves. "These are people," he hissed. "Not animals."

The Minemaster spat with a laugh. "That so?"

Raedwin caught sight of motion in the distance. Devron led a pair of bowmen to subdue first one and then a second pair of outer guards in silence. Solinius appeared along the far lip of the mine, stepping deftly past each of the subdued guards. A knife-wielding man crept beside him, both of their faces masked.

"Her High Honor," the Minemaster continued. "Is juicing up for some extra big... project, as I understand it. Is that why you're here?"

"How many lives is all of this worth?"

The Minemaster's face darkened, his patience waning. "How many lives are you worth, Master Raedwin? You sit in your tower and think the things you do are worth so much more than what we do out here. You stay clean and nice up there because you can't see us. Doesn't make you any less dirty."

The Jehndai continued to dig and scrape the earth, oblivious to the swift assault happening out of sight above the rim. As the sentries disappeared, Solinius began to unlock chains, unburdening one worker after another.

"This is one long unbroken thread, from us to you," the Minemaster continued, his voice rising. "The things you tinker with, the fancy toys you make for Crassica, all of that starts right here. It starts with us and ends with you."

Jumping into the attack was not part of Raedwin's plan, but sometimes plans changed. Everything was different now. This Minemaster and his crude men were from the world before Raedwin's eyes had opened, all of them steeped in the lies of the life he thought he'd been leading for years. The Minemaster was right—Raedwin had enjoyed status and position, the luxury of pursuing idle fancies, and all of it had been built on this, on the pain and the devastation of these people, the strange effluent of Crassica's horrific ambitions. And now all of it, all the lies, the misdirection and hidden ambition, all of it focused on this one man.

"So, then," Raedwin said, "it shall end here with me as well."

At no point in his long life had Raedwin been properly trained in the arts of killing, in the position of body and placement of weight for a balanced thrust, but he had been in plenty of street fights. He knew how to carry himself. With a smooth movement, he pulled a long knife from his belt and lunged forward to drive it into the Minemaster's chest. But in the blinking realization that Crassica's beloved pet was not actually here to discuss methods of the mine or to inspect its processes or really to have any words at all, the Minemaster shifted just enough to cause Raedwin's blade to blunt against bone, deflecting the force away to a slash across skin.

The Minemaster screamed alarm.

Raedwin lunged and stabbed again, opening a long gash across the man's forearm. The other guards sprang forward. Two pulled swords while a third loaded a crossbow. Raedwin lunged again, but the Minemaster had drawn, and met his blade.

"Get this lunatic off me!" the Minemaster cried to the others. But as he shouted, arrows flew in from the trees and pierced the chests of three separate guards in succession. The Minemaster stepped back, holding Raedwin's assault at bay until two quick arrows dropped him, and a third pinned him to the ground.

Several newly freed Jehndai ran along the open rim of the mine to tackle one of the remaining guards, ripping at eyes and tearing at flesh. The guard screamed in pain and terror. Two guards near Raedwin fled. Devron's men dispatched two more, while Kraegha eliminated a third. The last guard standing disappeared under a frothing boil of Jehndai fury as they methodically tore him apart.

Whole groups of chains were loosed and cast aside. Some embraced the men who freed them, while others stood in dumb silence, not yet quite believing what was happening. A few grabbed loose lengths of chain and began to beat the bodies of their dead captors, tearing and mutilating flesh as they screamed in fury.

Kraegha came to Raedwin and gripped his shoulder, his grim face almost smiling. "Thank you," he said. "We can take it from here. You've got a long ride ahead of you. She'll be waiting. Go."

Raedwin nodded, his body floating with adrenaline. He could barely take in what he'd seen here. Subjugation, freedom, and now destruction. He turned away and stumbled for a few steps before gaining fresh control over his body.

Mounting his horse again, he descended the way he had come, down the cartway through the trees toward the bouldered shoulder of the valley. He was well over the top and more than three miles away when a deep and thunderous boom shook the ground underneath him. He thought he could hear a long, glorious cheer riding toward him on the breeze.

31

ONLY A MILE or so past where the Brundsril met its tributary out of the Sontrath, the smell of death hit Brogan first. Fresh blood and woodsmoke, mixed with burning human remains. The first body they saw lay face down in the water, nudged against a boulder along the northern shore. Hair drifted with the current in long loose tendrils, oily mud matting the back of the dead man's head. A grove of bone-white arrow shafts stood tall and proud in his torn back. Probably shot trying to escape. A lone boneskin reclined dead on the riverbank nearby, staring at the grayness of the clouded sky, his chest a bloody gape of shattered bone and ruptured organs. One hand gripped the sandy earth like some final vain attempt to embrace the sentient world.

Brogan and Senya drifted through the scarred scene without speaking, their paddles held motionless. A scattering of massive trees leaned over the slow churn of the water. Bodies stretched all along the shore—twisted, mangled corpses on top of one another, some with horrific wounds and others with no visible wounds at all. The open ground beaten and matted. Black birds circled above, their dark wings rising aloft before falling again to join the feast below. A great smoking heap sat on a narrow strip of beach. Broken shield works, helmets, and lances. Desperate attempts at defensive structures were shoved askew on high embankments.

At first the scattered corpses appeared random and arbitrary, slapped together from some mixed party of blood and mud, but the battle's fuller story soon became apparent. The army they'd seen earlier had clearly overrun a huge band of boneskins along the water, slamming into their desperate and failed attempt to cross. Probably lost nearly a third of their men right here. With bloodlust and fury on them in pursuit of the fleeing boneskins, they hadn't taken time to bury the dead.

Then Brogan saw the Vallahnir.

Four pale riders waited ahead, high on the looming riverbank. A breeze drifted their gray cloaks.

He pulled hard on his paddle, surging the canoe back against the current. Without a word, Senya quietly slipped overboard and went underwater. Brogan nearly shouted but swore in silence to himself. He kept on, paddling hard to follow the undulating shape of Senya through the few long strokes to the southern bank. She emerged dripping under the cover of brush behind a large bundle of oak roots. Brogan all but shoved the canoe into the bushes.

"What the hells," he hissed at her. She motioned for him to be quiet.

Hidden by bushes, they sat and watched the Vallahnir together. Senya shivered. The four riders took no notice, discussing something with one another as they shifted nervously along the tall bank. After a moment, they urged their horses forward in a switchbacking descent. Stopping short at the water's edge, their mounts flailed and cried at the confusing commands from untrained riders.

"We have to leave the river," Senya whispered. "We go overland from here."

"They'll swim those horses right across," Brogan objected. "We need to find a good place to dig in for a fight. If it's just the four of them..."

"They won't cross without boats," Senya said, eyes holding on the Vallahnir. "The river's too deep."

"They can't swim?"

"Earth and fire are their elements, not water."

One of the Vallahnir scrambled along the ground, either having dismounted or having been thrown. Brogan watched as she heaved inhuman curses at the seething current.

Senya hugged herself, her body still shivering. "They know I'm here," she said quietly. "They sense that I'm nearby, but the river frustrates them. We're too close. Too exposed." She scrambled through the brush up the bank beside the oak. "Let's go."

They covered the first mile at a dead run. The river might be a barrier, but even barriers had crossings. They pushed on as the sky above broke into patches of blue. After a time, Brogan slowed to a stop.

"There's no ford or ferry before Corregidon," he said, gathering his breath. "We should be okay for now if they can't cross any other way. It'll take too long to build boats to carry horses—if whatever's left of that army remains somewhere nearby."

Senya shook her head. "They, or somebody they control, will meet us somewhere ahead, we can be sure. We'd better not slow down until I can get out to sea."

"Okay." Brogan glanced around, gathering his thoughts. The Cellenway Moors were a lawless, unaided land, stretching rough and desolate for many miles. But more than a few hardy shepherds worked these hills. Stone homes huddled in small defensible groups, some more armed and wary than others. They could prove helpful or harmful, with equal measure of risk in both.

"We'll head west," he said. "Try to catch a cartway. Find ourselves a ride."

They roamed for a time upcountry through a gray boulder-studded land. The day diminished to a smoldering igneous band along the distant horizon. Arriving at a rocky notch in a long backbone ridge, they stopped. A cluster of buildings stood on a low prominence far to the northwest. Smoke trailed from a lone chimney. Dust rose over a nearby field. They stood and waited. No clear sign of movement, but the farm was nicely kept and well attended.

"This'll work," Senya said at length.

"Be careful. Anyone out here could just as well fill us full of arrows or come out hacking with axes," Brogan warned. "Or worse."

"They won't harm us." She stepped forward and led the way along a rising ridge beside a wide peat dig. Dark earth sat stacked in tall square mounds. No movement from the houses or the barn. Two shepherd dogs emerged and came toward them, baying and howling with risen hackles. The dogs lunged forward with each explosive bark.

"How about," Brogan said quietly, "we wait right here..."

But Senya strode forward. The dogs barked ever more sharply. They edged at her, teeth snapping as she approached. With an outstretched hand, she slowed. She sang softly, her quiet tones floating on the breeze. The dogs settled to a whimper. Their ears sat back and tails wagged nervously. Tongues fell from open mouths. Senya crouched low, and the dogs began to lick her hand as she sang.

Seven large men approached, armed with axes and shining hatchets. Three had long stout knives strapped to their legs. One shouted to the dogs. Senya stood. Brogan raised an arm in greeting. "Sorry to intrude," he called.

The men ordered the dogs to them. Senya backed away and waited next to Brogan. The dogs settled, tails wagging.

"Fine day for a wander," the lead man called. "You folks lost?" He had a thick unkempt beard on his weathered ruddy face.

"We're making our way to Corregidon," Brogan answered.

"Hells, on foot? You've any idea how far that is?" The men spread along the contour of the low rise. All seven had long thick hair pulled back, tucked away for work. They stood with axes and hatchets and all accoutrements of farmland defense at the casual ready.

Brogan gestured behind them over his shoulder. "Came up from the river. Had some trouble with our boat."

"Trouble with your boat."

"Figured we'd try walking."

"And where you from, before the river?"

"Upstream," Senya said. The two dogs shifted, suddenly restless.

"We'd like to find passage," Brogan added. "Maybe a wagon or cart or carriage. Anything heading west."

The man's beard opened into a wide grin. "Tired of walkin' already? You ain't even started."

"We can pay."

The man's face brightened, and his eyebrows rose. "Yeah? And coin is ever so valuable out here, a hellsmarch from nowhere."

"I can give you nine Bronze now and a Kalldonian silver once we make it to Corregidon. If you have a cart and can get us there quickly."

The man nodded. He considered this as he surveyed their strengths and weaknesses. He let his gaze lie on Brogan's shortsword and stout recurve bow. His assessment would've shown seven against two, and one only a delicate young woman. "You know," the man said. "There's no law out here. Nobody to come help you if things go sour. We operate all on our own in these parts against men or boneskins or whatever else happens by. So I'm a bit curious why you think we won't just cut you down and take your money and this girl here for our pleasure and not have to make that long cold trip to Corregidon at all."

Brogan's hand slipped instinctively to the hilt of his sword. He took quick account of all seven men. Axes and hatchets suddenly not so casual, all of them much more ready to swing than gave him comfort. One gripped a mean cudgel that Brogan had not seen as they'd first approached.

"I'm also a fair bit curious," he replied. "With no law out here, and nobody to come help you... why you think we won't just slaughter the lot of you, sit down at the table for a nice lamb stew, have a long rest, and take your cart whenever we hellscursed please—and not have to pay you a single shecker."

Senya took a step forward. Both dogs began to whimper. "You don't know who we are or what we can do," she added. Her voice carried a new weight, ringing steady and piercing the wet morning. "So you'd be wise to be more careful with your tone." One of the dogs let out a whine, building into a sharp yelp.

The lead man glanced at the whimpering dogs and turned to her, taking new account. "Fair enough," he called. He gave a genuine smile. "Just thought I'd ask. We've got strange gray-cloaked wraiths wandering the moors these past few days, so we're all a bit touchy. Turns out we do happen to have a nearly full load of wool that could find its way to market, with proper motivation. Make it twelve and two, and we can leave this very evening."

Brogan watched the man's eyes, holding steady in a checked silent conference across the misty space between them. They said nothing. Nobody moved. The dogs settled again.

"Okay," he said finally. "If we can leave right now, you have a deal."

The man smiled again. "Only take but a minute. I'll get to hitching them horses." He strode forward and held out his hand. "Name's Carthy, by the way."

32

RAEDWIN URGED the mare to the fastest pace he dared. Following the fringes of the forest northward from the mine for several miles, he at last angled back to the west and regained his bearings near the Valle d'Brasti. The small river he sought ran east of the citadel. Keeping under cover of shadowed gullies and deep draws and dales, he followed its long curve to the northwest. The sky darkened and the moon rose. He rode for a time and soon left the river along a vague trail northward. Passing over the remains of an ancient road, he came to a ruined hilltop fort that marked his turn again to the east. A line of narrow trees bordered a grass-filled path up to the ruins of an abandoned farmhouse.

He drew the horse to a stop and waited. Listened. The night gave him little more than the cold glow of the moon. A curious silence. Shadows lay sharp and clear over the land. Toothy stone debris beckoned from a distant hill, marking what remained of the house. Something moved among the trees, or maybe only his imagination. A breeze brushed his face. Raedwin urged the horse forward along the overgrown path.

The ancient structure's crumbled bones stood defiant in the moonlight as he approached. Something of a gatehouse and a fragmented low wall defined themselves against the ragged sky. The thought of Sadahlia waiting alone caused him to bring the horse to a trot up the line of trees.

At the shoulder of the hill, the ground gave way to a cluster of what used to be the residence, a sheep corral, and something of a livestock pen. Dry southern breezes circled through the fingers of stone, whistling quietly against the remains of a chimney. Movement flickered in the corner of his eye. He spun, but nothing was there except tricky shadows and the inconstant glare of the moon. He rode on.

Pulling his horse to a stop, Raedwin dismounted. The breeze fell quiet. Even the crickets held their sound.

And then he saw her. Sadahlia stood amid the wreckage of the home, the moonlight brightening the air around her while leaving the scattered stonework in the dark. A beacon of hope among ruins.

He went to her and held her. They stood and said little. Words of love whispered so close to one another that none but a single ear could take them in. They descended into the black opening of a cellar against the remains of the destroyed home's back wall. Low lamplight glowed where she had crafted a makeshift bedchamber some time before. Soft boughs under plush blue blankets. Linen pillows stuffed with down. A small but sturdy oil lamp.

They embraced again. He kissed her, soft and unhurried. She pulled away, holding his face in her hands as she looked into his eyes.

"Is it done?" she asked.

"The mine is done and gone. It'll be years before anything can be pulled from that place again."

"And she can't replace the Amaris she has in the Keep?"

"She'll have no more ore and no more crystals. She'll fade soon enough."

Sadahlia turned away, her face darkening. "I thought I would feel more of a change," she said. "Like her grip would weaken already. Something. But I haven't felt anything."

"It's probably the distance. We are here now. We made it. We are out. She can't get to you anymore."

Sadahlia smiled weakly, her hope clearly wrapped in a cautious sense of not being able to know for sure. He pulled her to him, placing his forehead against hers.

"Be here with me," he whispered. "We've made it. We are here now. Together."

Her tension loosened in his grasp.

"Together," she repeated.

They swayed as one then, shifting from side to side, beginning a silent dance to unspoken music that only their bodies knew, close and alive in one corner of the cramped room. Plays of light and focus, their vision blurred in the guttering lamplight. Then they were naked together on the makeshift bed, moving and coursing through one another with the kind of powerful need driven by release from incarceration.

Later, while sprawled across the landscape of fur blankets and linen sheets, they spoke quietly of the path ahead, placing each word carefully into the fragile space between them, as if anything misspoken could cause their whole world to crumble. The wilderness and the trials they would face. First, a long and difficult path through the forest to Lothania, and from there maybe an easier road to Toncana. But then an onerous crossing to Ryngsvoy remained. After that, nothing but road agents and boneskins for leagues.

"I will never make it to Faeroen," Sadahlia said. "You know that, right?"

"There's no need to go that far," he assured. "Once in Brinsfallon, Senya can come to us. We just need to get to Corregidon or Posselhead. Maybe Pentmore."

They spoke no more of the future. He tried to think of a time before Sadahlia, an image of his former self before this place, before Crassica. His life as a child with Senya. As a young man. All of it so distant now, so vague. Everything he'd ever wanted or needed was right here. They were together now, cloaked in safety, hidden away from all the cares of the living world.

After a time, she slept. The milky expanse of her body rose and fell beside him. Raedwin wondered at her sleeping like he wondered at so many other things so many times before. Where had all this begun exactly? The rest of the world was so far away now, so unnecessary. He could barely remember the beginning. First, there had been nothing, and now there was only her, held close to him, right at the edge of shadow. The lamplight caressed her smooth pale skin, the curve of her body underneath simple blue blankets. He knew then, as he had known before, that after this, he would never really be the same again.

Raedwin woke to a sound. The chamber was cool, the lamp doused and dark. How much time had passed? Sadahlia had gone from the room. He rose and went outside.

Crushed grass lay pinned askew by the passage of booted feet. Maybe he and Sadahlia were not alone in considering this place to be hidden from prying eyes. A piece of clothing stared at him from the matted ground near the far wall. He approached to find one of their blankets from earlier laid carefully in the bosom of gap-toothed walls. One corner flipped and twisted in the dark. He crouched to examine it. Clearly Sadahlia's. The slanted moonlight showed a careless boot print marring one edge.

A twig broke. Raedwin spun to catch sight of a figure ducking behind a stone outcrop.

Something wasn't right. Sadahlia had walked among the living long enough to know all about the nuanced surprises that men and women gifted to one another, but this was not like one of her sly games. Not here. Not now. He stood and stepped toward the fleeting shadow. Footsteps and a whisper came from behind.

Too fast, he thought. He froze.

Somebody else is here.

"Sadahlia," he called quietly. He passed the edge of the disintegrated walls. A breeze picked up, bringing the smell of grasses and dry juniper. He called her name again.

A dark shape separated itself from the stone remains of the sheep corral some distance down the slope. The glint of steel. A second shape moved in the trees along the path to the road. A third detached from shadows at the side of the house. Raedwin reached for what would have been his short sword if he'd had forethought enough to keep himself armed. But his sword was with the haversack in the makeshift bedchamber, underground. Behind him. He glanced at the path and realized his horse was gone.

"Sadahlia!" he shouted. "Talk to me!"

No answer came. A figure strolled past the treelined path below, pushing Sadahlia in front of him. Her mouth was bound in black wrap, as were her hands. Stumbling and naked. Her pale skin shone in the moonlight.

"Sadahlia!" Raedwin cried. The figure shoved her forward. "Where are you taking her?" Raedwin rushed and jumped through the stone remains as torchlight erupted behind him. Another lit to his right, casting harsh light on a man's brutal face.

Raedwin raced down the grassy slope toward Sadahlia and the strange figure leading her away. Torches followed. Men shouted to one another, and the whole slope became a swirl of confusing activity. The ground shifted. Raedwin struggled to make sense of what was happening. Sprinting down the slope in the dark away from the remains of the farmhouse, he stumbled and fell. Rising again, he lunged forward. The figure shoved Sadahlia toward a dark grove of black-barked trees reaching up from a creek bed. Shouts chased from behind. A spark of steel on flint in the trees ahead of her. A torch caught. Light flourished before her in the thicket. Raedwin stumbled and fell again.

Somebody landed with him, reeking of garlic and body sweat. Old leather. A hairy forearm caught him across the jaw and pulled him backward and then quickly gripped his arms.

Raedwin struggled to shove a bare hand into the earth. He tried in a last desperation to reach for Senya and call out with no real sense of what he'd be able to say even if they could connect—maybe just to warn her or to plea for distant help. But the man pinned his arms uselessly behind him, lifting him almost effortlessly from the ground.

Torchlight from the woods showed a figure strolling casually toward him through the grass. Narrow nose and deep-set dark eyes. Long white hair drifted thinly in the breeze without weight, as if all the world were underwater.

Realization hit Raedwin like no knife blade devised by hand or forge. *Lanius*.

These were no highwaymen, no random bandits taking up residence in this remote farmhouse. All these men belonged to Crassica.

Lanius held the torch aloft as he stepped closer, his face creasing into a malignant smile. "Why, Raedwin," he called softly. "How very naughty you have been, our little wayward friend. Up to such mischief. And now here you are, caught outside without your fancy clothes…"

Raedwin's heart sank. The mine had not been enough. Destroying the ore, the crystals, the shipments to feed Crassica's power—none of it was enough. He'd been too slow, or too late. Or maybe Lanius had known all along. Now, all was lost. Wherever Lanius passed, behind whatever the Sword Hand ever did, the wrath of all four hells usually followed.

PART FOUR

33

THE TOWN of Donasberth huddled along a short stony beach between two rocky bluffs at the far north of its namesake bay. Several structures rose from the shoreline and climbed in succession, giving the place the impression of a massive stone amphitheater.

"Ready to come about," Delsorka called. "And furl the mains as she settles. We'll let the tops bring her in."

"Aye, sir," came the return call. Several orders echoed in succession across the deck as the *Siege Runner* spun to starboard along the sprawling port. A breeze brought the scent of sheep and woolen mills, of fish oils mixing with salted sea air.

"Let's heave-to when we draw close to the stonework," Delsorka ordered. "No need to rush things. Don't arouse any suspicion if we don't have to."

A low jetty with ramparts braced the mouth of a small waterway at the west end of the beach, creating a well-protected port. The remaining sails brought the *Runner* gently alongside before her hands pulled in the last of the canvas, all sails furled and wrapped against the weather. The ship drifted to a near stop.

"All right," Delsorka called. "Raise flags and let 'em know we've got a full belly. Get the launch in the water to run out a kedge line. Pull up to the outer dock." He turned to Ghellan. "You stay below," he told the sorcerer. "Can't have it known we've got your kind on board. Whatever you do come nightfall is your own business, but if word gets out that you're here, I will not be pleased."

"You needn't worry, my dear captain." Ghellan gave a bow. "You will find I have the utmost discretion in my ways." With a nod, he disappeared below.

Several men gathered along the wooden dock that braced the seaside edge. Pale northern skin almost blue in the bright flat day. Blond hair hung in ropy braids over high cheekbones, brilliant eyes reflecting the sea and cloud-strewn sky alike. Thick wool-lined oilskin cloaks held the salt spray at bay.

The *Runner's* launch rowed to the dock, and the men passed over the kedge line. Those ashore secured the line to a heavy post. On board, sailors shouldered the capstan with some effort, and the ship groaned as she slowly drifted to the dock.

Captain Delsorka stepped away from the work at hand and went to the starboard bow. He'd long admired and respected Donasberth, a place he'd known since childhood. Lively, energetic, and dirty, much like its people. Much like him. Crassica's network took a light-handed approach here, operating more by fear and reputation than actual strength in numbers. Money drove most of it. Money, and a good keen sense of who was loyal and who was not.

After he closed out his official arrival duties and lingered in the taverns long enough to settle potential talk, Delsorka would head inland to Corregidon. He'd leave the *Runner* here. Quicker and more efficient that way. With any luck, maybe Konn's web of eyes and ears would have heard something about their charge or seen something worth knowing. In any event, there would be news of some kind—that much was always true.

✥ 34 ✥

BROGAN AND SENYA reached Corregidon that evening. Rolling in from the southeast, they joined a steady flow of merchants and travelers sauntering their heavy-laden way toward the gates along the Great Brinsfallon Way. Tents and pole shacks clustered both sides of the road. Smoke trails rose from cookfires and iron smelters, with the reek of downwind tanneries drifting on the back breeze.

Carthy brought the cart to a stop some distance from the gate, and they settled up. Brogan and Senya both wished him well on his return path, gathered their things, and headed for the gate.

Corregidon. The Great City of the North, the pride of Brinsfallon. A city well designed against invasion, and Brogan's old home. He led Senya through a wide cobblestone portal onto the sturdy plankboard drawbridge over the moat. Black teeth of an iron portcullis hung overhead. Heavily armed sentries sat bored and surly as they sharpened war axes on the stone wall of the gatehouse.

"Never thought I'd find myself back here," Brogan muttered as they entered the city.

Shadowy cobbled streets offered a tangled mazework that confused any clear path to the critical bridges over the river. Tall structures rose and stacked upon one another, angling into the street as if years on they might pinch away the sky altogether. People mingled among horses and small live-stock in the swarming alleys near the gates. Alms seekers crouched under protective eaves. Noisy tradesmen and merchants lined the narrowing streets alongside meat vendors bristling with mantles of swarming flies.

He could feel Dahlwea at every corner, a spice hanging in the air, even after all the lost years behind him. He couldn't place whether it was good or bad or a matter of the past holding such strong sway that the whole city remained forever marked.

He headed toward the river in the slanted evening light, mostly avoiding the main streets. Senya pulled her hood close and kept her head down against prying stares and catcalls. They crossed over a broad stone bridge brimming with traffic to an island in the center of the city. Empty ship masts towered over both riverbanks. Narrow buildings and military barracks choked most of the inner island away from view. A set of white sails filled as one ship drifted from the skeletal forest out into the river's main current.

Stepping off the High Street at the northern bridgehead, Brogan took a path down a narrow passage along the water. Dark timber-frame buildings frowned overhead. Hanging laundry wafted in the air while sewage collected in gutters below.

Brogan stopped. The same thick alehouse door was there, black and shadowy as always. The same murmurs of music and low rumbling voices. He and Dahlwea had first discovered one another inside this very same door. Gentle, timid sweeps, two quiet eddies in a violent punctured world. His young love, his young bride. They'd laced their half-spent lives with one another over these same dark cobblestones. Ghosted images now a hazed-over memory of music and mead, love and brutality. The hardened grip of thirsty youth. It all lingered. The memory of her, in there still. Probably would be until the day he died.

A new wooden sign overhead pronounced *The Swan* in freshly carved letters. A new sign for new owners. A new life. He gathered himself and turned to Senya.

"All right," he warned in a low voice. "I used to work these streets. This place is full of thieves and thugs. So pay attention and don't upset anybody. Try to blend in."

Senya stared at him. "I don't exactly blend."

Brogan had been thinking of this little problem since they'd come across the Vallahnir back at the river. He'd tried to ignore it, hoping it would all work itself out, but now with the prospect of facing his old network, he saw holes in any hope for making it through unseen. Senya was used to keeping herself small and inconspicuous, and her cloak did most of the job, but there was no hiding those Brohndai eyes.

"Well," he said at last. "We'll do the best we can."

As they entered, the sunken room heaved with a boiling energy. White-washed vaulted ceilings arched over a motley crowd of revelers. Music jangled from a stage in the far corner, barely audible over the shouting din. Disheveled stumblers propped themselves against the bar while the better-dressed merchants huddled in high booths along the back walls. Bristling mercenaries swayed with their tankards in hand, armed and sullen at the edges of the lowered main floor.

Brogan stepped down into the room. He led Senya through the shoving mass toward the bar. Clusters of rough bearded men hurled suspicious glances at the newcomers, whispering to one another. Eyes followed Senya with lewd looks—part desire, part watchful caution.

Sliding onto an empty stool at the near end of the bar, Senya kept her head down and pulled her hood close. Brogan sat next to her with his shoulders low, offering no challenges to the room. He glanced around, scanning faces to find anybody he might know from the old days, any connection with sailors in the usual network.

A man beside Brogan bent his twisted knot of a face toward Senya. With a lustful stare, he muttered drunkenly to himself as he drew near. "That's some specimen you got there," he said to Brogan in a low growl, reeking of ale and rotting fish.

Brogan clenched his jaw. He said nothing.

"Seen me plenty a pleasuregirl, but this here's som'n new..." He leaned closer, bending forward to get a look at her hooded face. "How much you want for 'er?"

"Not for sale."

He turned to Brogan, his voice sharper. "Everything's for sale, friend. And if your little tramp there is too small to defend herself, well, then, you and I get to name a price, don't we? That's the way it works in this world."

"Not with me, it doesn't."

The man's knotted face twisted into a darker frown. "Look," he scolded. "You can't come prancin' in here wavin' your special little trinket around like a bragging bitch and then complain when somebody makes an offer."

"She's not my trinket."

The man barked out a laugh. He stepped away from the bar and slapped Brogan on the back. "Well, then. Maybe I make her mine."

Brogan shifted, barring the man's path with his leg. "We're simple travelers. Tired from the road. We don't want trouble, and neither do you."

The man scoffed and pushed past. He pushed into Senya, grinning a nearly toothless smile. He gave a low snorting chuckle, almost more boar-like than human. "I dunno," he growled. "Maybe I do want a little trouble. Maybe just the right kind of trouble…"

Brogan rose to his feet. The man shoved a finger into his chest. "Sit down, tough guy," he snarled. "Draw a blade if you think you can do something. But look around. This is *my* room. I've got seven people within arm's reach. A handful more over in them booths. How many you got backin' you up? You don't like it? You're in the wrong alehouse."

No eyes were on them. Nobody took notice. No way for Brogan to tell whether this guy spoke any semblance of truth.

The man turned back to Senya. He reached out and slipped her hood back, brushing his hand against her cheek.

Senya gripped Brogan's wrist on the bar top. Her fingers dug into him. She closed her eyes and huddled forward, as if about to be sick. A tremor went through her body.

Don't touch me.

The voice was Senya's but came like a whisper from inside Brogan's own head. Or from the room itself. Her mouth hadn't moved.

The man jerked back, his arm convulsing. Flailing. "What the…" he managed before his jaw snapped shut. He bolted upright. His body went rigid and shook with impotent rage, fierce and strangely silent. His eyes rolled back into his head.

Senya did not move. Her face stayed low, eyes closed. Her hand dug into Brogan's wrist, skin strikingly hot.

The man struggled to let out a cry, to breathe or shout. Anything. White froth seethed from his mouth. His face crashed onto the bar top.

Still Senya did not move. Heat radiated from her body.

"Senya," Brogan said. "What the hells…"

The man's wheezing came hard and ragged with a spitting hiss, and then pinched off altogether. He crumpled to the floor. Confusion and fear ran over his twisted purpling face. He went limp. A single tear rolled down Senya's cheek.

"Senya!" Brogan shouted. "What is happening?"

She gave a start, as if abruptly noticing him. The man on the floor gasped, released from the hidden grip. He hissed and swore, jumping to his feet. "Hellscursed..." He rubbed his throat as he stepped away. "Sorcerous bitch..." He took another step back, eyes wide with fear and fury both. He disappeared into the crowd.

Senya wiped the tear from her cheek. She let go of Brogan's wrist. Music played on in the back of the bar.

"What," Brogan asked, his voice low, "was *that?*" He scanned the room for any sign of response or gestures of affinity with the man. None came.

Senya pulled her hood back up, tugging it low over her face. "I don't know..." she whispered. "I just..." She turned, and her piercing eyes met his. "It's never happened before..."

Brogan said nothing. He cast his gaze over the room again, assessing retaliation, watching for anything. Scuffles like this often ended quickly but didn't often stay ended. Wary faces focused on Senya, watching this strange brown girl with such unexpected, outsized abilities. Clearly more than she appeared to be.

A man emerged from the crowd next to the bar. His fair hair was roped thick and long, blending with a heavy yellow beard. More than a few brawls had marked and pocked his skin, but his deep-set dark eyes shone with a bright, lively spirit. He stepped toward Brogan.

"Well, well," the man called. "Shit straight into the creek! If it isn't Brogan Broadhand, starting scuffles alongside a lady at the bar, just like old times. Back to rue the day he ever left us."

Brogan couldn't help but smile. "Freógan," he greeted. "How've you been?" He reached out a hand in greeting. An easy laugh came unbidden, a weight lifted. "Gods, it's good to see you." He glanced at Senya. "We... could actually use your help..."

"This way."

Freógan led them through the thickening crowd toward the rear of the alehouse. Brogan glanced over his shoulder, watching faces in the low light of the room, scanning for any followers, any pursuit. None came.

Freógan slid into a booth bordered by a pair of heavy curtains. He gestured for Brogan and Senya to follow. "Come, sit." An oil lamp guttered in the center of the table. Once settled, Freógan drew the curtains closed behind them, shutting away the teeming bar.

"I see you're still loitering right about where I left you," Brogan said with a grin.

"Not wise to wander far from the feeder trough, my brother. Especially while we're landbound."

This gave Brogan pause. "Landbound? What happened?"

Freógan winced and shook his head. "Long story."

Brogan nodded and left it at that. Everybody in Corregidon had a long story hidden somewhere. "Freógan here is first mate on a ship called the *Summerhawk*," he said to Senya. "One of very few actually reliable smuggler crews Corregidon has on offer."

Freógan smiled and let out a quick, chopped laugh. He glanced at Senya. "Not exactly a high bar."

"One step ahead of the gallows, though."

"So far."

"And how's our lovely captain?"

"She's good." Freógan studied Brogan's face for a long awkward moment. He cocked his head. "But I'm not sure she'd be all that happy to see you, truth be told."

"What'd I do this time?"

"You left. Stole her sister. Didn't say goodbye. Never came back. Take your pick."

Brogan bobbed his head in acknowledgment. All of these were true. "I need to see her."

The sailor's eyes narrowed slightly. "You need a ship, don't you." His voice became heavy, without the friendly lightness of a moment before. He glanced back and forth between Brogan and Senya for a long silent second, as if testing. "Okay," he said finally. Reaching underneath the table, he operated some sort of hidden lever. "Captain's in the middle of something right now, but she ought to be wrapping up shortly."

The back of the booth swung open on hidden springs, revealing a dark passage.

"Right through here," he said. And with that, he disappeared.

Brogan found himself standing next to Senya in a cramped antechamber behind the booth. Swinging the hidden door shut, Freógan led them down a dimly lit narrow passage into a carpeted room flickering with lamplight. Plush stalls lined both sides, scattered with men and women lounging on wide flat pillows and silk blankets. A pungent haze lay over the air. A woman perched on a tall stool in the far corner sang a mournful strain, her sonorous voice filling the room with a rich, lacy melody. Cloaked figures gathered around low smoking vessels with mouthpiece tubes snaked to their lips. Passing the mouthpieces to one another, they inhaled long strains of rich smoke before lying back with eyes closed in bliss. One of the stalls held three naked bodies writhing behind shrouded draperies.

"What do you care?" a woman cried nearby.

The voice lanced through Brogan. His chest tightened. He would've recognized the sound of that voice anywhere. So familiar, and yet so lost.

"How's that affect the deal?"

Brogan turned. The woman faced away from him, her unruly hair a wild bundle of red tangles shoved into a leather band in a lazy attempt to tame it. The same as Dahlwea used to do. A man sat beside her, head and shoulders in the shadows. Across the small table sat a second man. This one's face was a patchwork of old scars, his hair and beard both cropped short and tight. A gold ring glinted from one ear.

"Everything affects a deal, Kaetas," the scar-faced man snapped. "You know that as well as anybody." He leaned forward onto the table. "Who's the third? She as pretty as the last one?"

"It's a cart run," Kaetas answered. "Quick and easy ride."

The man let out a clipped laugh. "Maybe, maybe not. If my guys have to fight off every hard dick from here to Cairn, then we're gonna have problems."

They sat for a silent moment. "Two silvers," the man said at length. "And we've got a deal."

"Hells," Kaetas cried. "This is supposed to be a favor! We could do this over in Brawltown if I wanted to get mugged."

"I'm in no mood, Kaetas," the man sneered. "Leaving my pleasuregirl in my warm bed makes me cranky. And you're running out of favors after that last stunt you pulled."

"We'll give you one silver and nine Bronze."

The man shrugged casually. "You know..." A lewd grin creased his face. "If you share a taste of this girl you're hauling... Maybe I could knock the price down a little..."

Kaetas tensed. "If you touch her," she said slowly, "you won't be a man for long after."

"Oh, relax, love." He smiled, sitting back. "Just shovin' you around. Only joking. All part of the fun." He laughed and stood. "Nine Brins bronze and a shiny Kalldon silver." He held out a hand. "Looks like you got yourself a working wagon."

Kaetas stood and took the man's hand. Without warning, she yanked him toward her and whispered something in his ear. After a moment she released.

The man took a step back. He frowned and shook his head. "Why you gotta be like that?" he muttered. He turned to leave, glancing at the bearded man beside Brogan. "Freógan," he said with a gesture and left the room.

Kaetas spun. "Fre, I thought I told you to wait in the..." She froze as she caught sight of Brogan.

His breath seized. That face. So like Dahlwea's. He hadn't thought he'd see that face ever again in this living world. Not here, not in the Hallonath, and maybe nowhere outside his own nightmares. Even with their differences, he'd forgotten how much alike they'd looked.

"Well, hells heaped upon hells," she said with an easy and friendly grin. Her brown eyes wide, she took a step back. "It's a godscursed ghost."

Years of sun and salty air had tarnished her nose and cheeks to a crusted bronze. She appeared older. Closer to her sister. Like the past decade was simply gone. Erased, just like that. Brogan hadn't expected it to hurt this much to see her again. Maybe that was why he'd avoided facing this meeting for years.

He gave a tiny formal bow. "Captain Kaetas," he said.

One eyebrow raised sharply. "Really? All ceremonial now, *my good sir*? Is that how we play this? Like we're godscursed strangers?"

"Been a long time."

She gave a stiff nod and a stiffer smile. "Too long," she said, her voice flat.

He stood rooted and dumb, the sound of the room falling away as he stared. All the things he'd lost. The years, the lives, the blood. Like looking into a new window with old eyes. None of it felt good.

"This is Senya," he said with a gesture and a weak smile. Pivoting back to Kaetas, he made an effort to hold her gaze. "And this," he said, "is Captain Kaetas of the *Summerhawk*."

"Well met," Kaetas said to Senya. True warmth in her voice.

The thick-shouldered man next to Kaetas stood and stepped forward. His ropy dark hair and long beard were both braided into stiff plaits hanging over a studded leather breastplate. He wore loose trousers tucked into tall leather boots. The dim light showed a grim and solid face beaten and scarred by decades at sea. He held out a hand in greeting.

"Oh," Kaetas said with a start. "Sorry. This is Brunby, ship's bosun. Brun, this is Senya, as you heard." She paused and let her head fall back slightly. "And this...." She breathed in, releasing a tentative sigh. "This is Brogan. My dead sister's husband. Back from the dead himself."

⚜ 35 ⚜

KAETAS INVITED them to sit. Senya watched the captain as she talked with Brogan, catching up quickly on lost time. She thought the woman quite beautiful, in a weathered sort of way. Sun-bronzed skin under a pile of tousled, unruly red hair. Like a thing untamed.

The room buzzed around her. Swirling emotions spiked and washed over Senya in silent waves from the room's smoky stalls. Ordinarily it was only Raedwin she could perceive and connect with, but that veil was lifting. Now she could sense almost every person in the room. A dream here, the touch of a hand on a leg there. Words whispered into a breath-close ear, all fueled by some strange drug called Medley, burning in tiny bowls. Senya struggled to will herself to ground, to remain steady and present, to be fully here at the table. To focus on Brogan explaining their need for passage.

"And," he added after a long pause, "we're not looking to attract any... undue attention."

Kaetas let out a burst of laughter. She gestured toward the empty passage and the scene he'd mentioned they'd left behind in the alehouse. "You're off to a good start at that, then."

Senya shifted in her seat. She could not explain what had happened back there, at least nothing she understood. A volatile fear had overcome her, coursed through her body and set the room on fire. Everything had slowed. All the light had gone dim. An overwhelming desire for that man to just go away. To back off and be gone. That was it.

But was that it? Indeed, something different was happening to her, something new and alive. She didn't want to think about it, didn't want to acknowledge it, and definitely didn't want to talk about it. She wanted to put it all away and deny that maybe the Vallahnir had indeed unleashed something dark and frightening inside her, all of it clearly out of her control.

"Wasn't sure you'd still be around," Brogan said to Kaetas. "But I'm glad you are."

"I'm a sailor, Brogan. If you wait long enough, I'm always still around." She took a long drink from her tankard and set it back on the table. "Can I ask you something?"

"Do I have to answer?"

"What happened up there in the mountains?"

Brogan opened his mouth to speak. He shook his head and said nothing. Senya could feel his struggle.

"She was my sister," Kaetas said quietly. "I'd like to know. I deserve to know. Up on the Elrune together, hells and gone from the civilized world, and then a terse little note that the whole valley'd been overrun by boneskins. *Dahlwea's dead. So is Glenna. I'm going south. Don't try to find me.*"

Brogan's eyes fell to the table.

"Doubt I'll ever forget that note," she said.

His lips moved over his teeth as his head drifted from side to side.

"And then the years went by."

He nodded. "They do that." His voice came dry and cracked.

"And now here you are. Showing up out of the blue with a cute little Brondy girl, looking to sail to Faeroen Island, of all places."

Little Brondy girl. Senya smiled with a slight cock to her head, pleasantly taken aback by someone saying aloud what most people only whispered under their breath, out of earshot.

Kaetas smiled as well. "You always were picky about your crew, but I'll admit—this is a new one." She reached out and took Senya's hand.

A shock hit with the touch. A flash of sea air and salt spray, the sway of rigid wood underfoot. Crisp memories of distant port cities. Dark alehouses and bright mornings. A naked woman in a warm bed. Senya could not help but look away, slipping her hand loose.

"You're mixed in with an odd stew, Brogan my brother," the captain said to Brogan, "but I do like this one. She's good in the bones. I can feel it."

Brogan didn't move. The oil lamp guttered on the table. A cry rang out from the far stall. Pleasure or pain, or maybe a mixture of both.

"So. Faeroen," Kaetas said after a minute. "The Island of Mist and Smoke. Ice and Steam. Home to the Vaunted Order of the Way of the Knowing, and the Brohndai Wardens of the Mirrorwater."

"My father lives there," Senya broke in.

Kaetas trained her gaze on Senya, considering this. *Of course he does* left unspoken. "From what I've heard," she said at length. "Faeroen can't be found by any normal navigation. They say you need some sorcerous connection. You don't find the Misty Isle on your own—they say the Misty Isle finds you."

"If you can get us close, I can find the port."

Kaetas smiled, holding her glittering dark eyes on Senya. Proud, almost motherly, though in truth actually far younger than Senya herself. "What's the cargo?"

Senya glanced at Brogan. "Just me."

Brogan shook his head. "The two of us. No cargo."

"No," Senya said gently. "You can't. You got us here safely. That's plenty." She hadn't allowed herself to believe he would stick with her past Corregidon. What reason would he have? Plenty more trouble to be found ahead. She would be dangerous to both of them, destructive to anybody around her. Brogan had already helped her more than enough, and the least she could do was try to keep him out of it.

"They burned down my house," he said. "Shot me full of arrows. Ambushed us, nearly twice." The hint of a grin tugged at the corner of his mouth. "At this point, it's personal."

"You've risked enough already..."

"You'll need more than a handful of Brohndai priests on some icy rock in the middle of the North Sea to get you through this. No Brondy will be able to raise a hand against any man or woman who gets in your way, you know that. It's right there in the codex or whatever. Maybe they'd do all right against a Vallahnir or any of the Knowing's little undead nightmares, but not against the living. Not against mercenaries."

He reached out and gripped her shoulder. Like a father. Or a brother. Maybe some kind of martial mentor. "I already told you," he said more gently. "I'm coming with you, if you'll have me. There are more fights to come. Even with a few scrapes and holes in me, I can hold my own."

He turned to Kaetas. "We can give you three Kalldonian silver now. Maybe more when we reach Faeroen."

Kaetas waved the thought away. "You know I can't make you pay for a trip like this…" Her voice was tender, nearly a whisper. "You're family."

"I don't want to take advantage…"

"Of course you do. That's why you're here." A broad smile came over her face. "But that's the hard part, isn't it? Since you're in a hurry, I can only assume there's someone close behind. And knowing you like I do, brother Brogan, it might be several someones. Or maybe a some*thing*. Either way doesn't bode well for an easy little jaunt up and around the Horn, does it?"

"And we need absolute secrecy," Senya added. "Until we're at sea."

Kaetas let her head fall back. "There's always one more thing, isn't there?" She sat up, glanced at Senya and then at Brogan, raising an eyebrow. "Might take some of that money after all, if you're not careful. When can you be ready to leave?"

"Immediately," Brogan said. "Or sooner."

"You do not mince, do you? Some things never change." She reached and lifted her tankard, taking a long lazy drink. "But here's the thing." She set it back down. "The *Hawk*'s not ready to go anywhere just yet. Might take a couple of days to muster. Tie up a few loose ends…" Her eyes narrowed, and she cocked her head. A sparkle came into her eye as if a new idea had only now occurred to her.

"Although…" she said, watching Brogan, a sly, coy edge coming into her voice. "Since you offered to pay… Maybe do us a little favor first instead? Would help us get to sea quite a bit faster…"

"Sure," Brogan said with a tentative edge to his voice. "But nothing out of your mouth is ever quite as simple as it sounds."

"Just a little help tending to a minor detail. We can actually make it to our ship's launch from here, all underground, without being seen. As long as you don't mind getting a little wet. And a little dirty. And enduring the occasional odd smell."

Kaetas stood. "Follow me." She led them across the room to where the singer sat in the corner. Lifting a lamp from the wall, she crouched and slid a thick carpet aside to reveal a trapdoor in the floor, which opened to set of rough stone stairs. Leaning over to kiss the singer on the cheek, Kaetas turned and descended into darkness without another word.

36

DELSORKA WAITED in the shadows with his back to the wood-plank wall. A lone Vallahnir stepped forward. She said nothing. The heavy door swung closed behind her. Her blue eyes glowed in the darkness.

In front of Delsorka at a bare table in the center of the room sat Kaevah Konn. Light spilled over the man's face as he leaned forward under a hazy lamp dangling from a rafter. His was not so much a face as a series of brutal accidents. Cheekbones all rawness and scarred flesh folded back onto itself as if formed from workable dough prematurely baked into a half-finished state. It was a perjury of a face, an insult to the ideals of eyes and nose and mouth. Anemic skin creased into scars that tucked down into other scars that twisted and tucked again, wrapping back into un-flayed flesh. Dim lamplight darkened the heavy folds.

Delsorka remained in the shadows. That sorcerer back on the *Runner* already came across as an overreach. Maybe Crassica was losing faith or didn't see that Delsorka could get the job done without all the supervision. She had usually trusted him to do what he was asked, to go to whatever lengths the particulars of a job required. For whatever reason, this Senya girl was extra important. So Delsorka would watch and listen and take extra precautions of his own.

Konn's cheeks creased as his malformed mouth thinned and slid lengthwise, snaking up at the sides—his version of a smile. "So," he said. "You have come at last. Where are the others? There are three more of you, correct?"

The Vallahnir stiffened. "Four have been sent, yes," she said, her voice something of a hissing whisper. "The others are elsewhere."

Konn's face knuckled into a grin. "Did you enjoy your journey?"

"We pushed the lamb to the fold."

"The Brondy girl, I know. I do get told some things, and I can pick up quite a bit more on my own. Do you know who I am?"

"You are called Kaevah Konn. Master puppet of City Corregidon."

Delsorka cleared his throat. "People usually say the puppet *master* of Corregidon," he advised. "Otherwise, there can be consequences." He had known Konn for nearly a decade and found him to be one of Corregidon's most efficient and enduring professional criminals. He loved working with Kaevah Konn.

"Yes," the Vallahnir said sharply to Delsorka. "Consequences." She held her cold pale eyes on him for a long moment. "We are here to ensure that *master puppet* does the job assigned to him. Properly this time."

"*Properly* this time?" Konn's face twisted in mock surprise. He sat back out of the light. "Let me see if I understand. Crassica first lines up some frontier outfit up in Pentmore to try to grab your girl—an outfit that's got nothing to do with me—and these amateurs figure it's a good idea to go tramping through the Hallonath like it's some royal garden holiday. They get two of your Sisters and their whole crew killed, and the girl gets away. Then Crassica sends you lot to rustle up a whole godscursed army to traipse across the countryside, making a show of pushing her into the open. But still no girl. Am I right so far? And only when she makes it all the way to Corregidon do you finally come to the professionals. And you complain to me about *properly*?"

The Vallahnir stepped forward, a looming yet weightless presence over the table between them. "You would be wise," she said, letting the last word slip to a knifepoint edge, "to remember your place. And your tone. The master is not pleased. And you will not enjoy if she continues to be so."

A visible shiver went through Konn. That was new. Delsorka had never seen this scar-faced lord of the streets given pause by anybody, ever. But he quickly recovered himself and gave his misshapen grin again. "All I'm saying is that you could've skipped all that uselessness and come to me first. Then it would've been handled. *Properly*." He leaned toward her. "Where are your other three?"

"They are sent... to observe."

"They'll find no more information in this city than what you'll get right here in this room. That's how this place works. Better if you know that right now."

"Such is why I am here. Let us not waste more time."

Konn idly played with a five-sided throwing weapon on the table in front of him. "You need to tell the others to be more cautious, by the way. There are eyes in this city besides mine, eyes that can work against you the same as mine can work for you. You're not exactly hidden, you know. Pretty easy to spot when the sun is out. Especially four of you all huddled together. On horseback. Pale and beautiful and all in gray, moving like you're a thousand years old—which I guess maybe you are, plus a few. We heard of your arrival before you came within sight of the city. You really should be more careful."

"We are not in need of your advice."

Crassica used such different tactics in all her various venues—an enticing and seductive lure up close at home in the Valle d'Brasti and a devastating fear from the shadows here in Corregidon. Both masterful, both very effective.

"Okay. Fair enough." Konn shifted back into shadow. "So. To business, then. Just happens that your little target arrived earlier today. Nearly killed a man in an alehouse down in Docktown. Quick as that. All but choked him dead without lifting a hand. *Hello, I'm new here. How do you do? Now I shall crush your throat.*"

The Vallahnir stretched to a fuller height and drew in a long rasping breath.

"But now she's disappeared. Gone silent. She never came out of that alehouse. Slipped into a backdoor smoke den, and from there, only the Knowing can see. That particular room has a passage that leads down to the undercity tunnels. Could've gotten anywhere from there."

"And the other? The killing man?"

Kaevah Konn spun the star-shaped weapon on the table. He picked it up and pivoted it on edge. "You know, I've been quite generous already here. Barely been a minute and you already know most everything you need. *Hi, how are you? How you been? How's that shiny old bird Crassica?* Friendly idle chat." The sound of his voice came thick and wet. "You've been given information that should by rights be compensated for."

The Vallahnir reached into the folds of her road-soiled cloak and produced a small pouch. Her pale fingers brought out two Kalldonian silver coins. She laid one on the table and held a second in her smooth palm.

Konn reached for the coin on the table and pulled it toward him. He left it lying outside the lamplit circle.

"Your target and her burly scrappy partner met a man in the alehouse," he said. "Name of Freógan. First Mate on a Kortain freighter called the *Summerhawk*. Nice lean little caravel. They meet in that alehouse, and then all three disappear. I'd say that's your ticket. The *Summerhawk* awaits. She's docked riverside downstream from the island, held up by some disagreement among sailors." His face slipped into the lamplight. "So you've got until they set sail to do whatever dirty work you like."

The Vallahnir laid the second coin on the table. "For this," she said, her soft voice almost a song—the same enticing seduction that Delsorka had witnessed from Crassica so many times. "We may need the assistance of your people." She laid three more silver pieces on the table.

Kaevah Konn leaned forward and examined the coins. He glanced up at the Vallahnir. "You want her dead, then?"

The tall gray figure stood in silence. Delsorka nearly laughed. Always a dance in rooms like this, no matter where you were, and Konn was especially good at it. The Vallahnir reached into the pouch and laid two Kalldonian gold pieces on the table alongside the silvers. Well over twice of what she'd already handed over.

Konn's marbled face almost brightened, if it could really do such a thing. What would've passed for eyebrows raised as he smiled again.

"Well, then," he said at last. "Alive it is."

❧ 37 ❧

FREÓGAN ROWED the ship's launch under an archway out to the open river. Evening sky stretched to the last remains of daylight in the western hills. A breeze brought rumors of the distant sea, while shouts from dockworkers and shipwrights echoed with faint strains of music lilting into the air from somewhere upriver. So many things the same since Brogan had last shadowed these very waterways.

Freógan rowed downstream toward a lone sailing ship standing black against the darkening stone embankment. The ship's bow bent to almost vertical. Her plankboard hull curved in a long elegant arc all the way to her prominent stern. She had two masts—a small mizzen at her quarterdeck and a thick main forward of her middle. Both stood stark and naked. Twin yardarms tilted steeply from the deck, reaching high and steep into the twilight.

"Is she under repair?" Senya asked. "Shouldn't those yards be squared up?"

The captain smiled. "You know your ships," she said in a hushed voice. "That's a Kortain rig. Triangular sail, not square. Lets her sail closer to the wind than any ship in this port, which fits for rounding the Horn." She gazed up at the dark masts and the angled yards. "She's Cornumbrian designed, out of Kortuga, originally. Descended from shipwrights that built an empire, if you know your history. There's not many of her kind this far north."

Freógan steered to a low wooden dock and brought the boat alongside.

A massive chain ran through a gap in the ship's bowsprit to an oversized ring in the wall. An iron padlock dangled from one end, securing chain to stone.

"Around here, they're all longships or square rigs," Kaetas explained in a whisper. "Nobody cares about upwind speed in the North. Only the size of the hull. Can't say the *Hawk* can compete there. She runs light and lean. But she can get in and out of places nobody else can, that's for certain. Also comes in handy when trying to sneak around in the middle of the night."

Kaetas jumped to the dock and motioned for Brogan to follow. They nearly stumbled over a snoring man sprawled face down next to one of the pylons.

Brunby, Kaetas's thick-shouldered bosun, appeared from the shadows. He wielded a thick blunt stick and bent to say something quietly in the captain's ear.

Kaetas turned to Brogan. "All right," she said. "Here's where you get to earn your way."

He glanced at the sprawled and snoring man, and then at the fat padlock. "You're not serious."

"Nobody was better at picking a Corregidon Keepsafe back in the day. You still got it?"

"Your ship's *impounded*? Hells, Kaet. You could've mentioned that part."

Her face pinched. She shook her head. "Just a disagreement over a debt, wrapped inside a little mistake. Can you do it?"

Brogan glanced at the lock. "Who'd you forget to pay off this time?"

"Not important. How does it look?"

"It's been years, Kaet. I can't even..." He trailed off and shook his head. For as long as Brogan could remember, Kaetas invariably had her own special way with the bait-and-switch. Get you to agree to one thing and turn it to something different halfway through. He'd forgotten how frustrating she could be.

Brunby helped Senya climb onto the dock behind him as Brogan stepped to the chain. Freógan remained in the boat.

The lock was solid and well oiled. Probably spent a long time out on docks much like this, holding delinquent assets or securing seized contraband. It appeared to be a basic warded lock, with a few strange upgrades that Brogan didn't quite recognize. A combination pin roller. Northern design. Likely made by the smiths of Stronhaven, the best in the world.

"You must've really pissed somebody off," he muttered to Kaetas.

"It's complicated. Here." She handed him a set of thin metal lockpicks and a ring of ward skeletons. "Any of this help?"

"No wonder you agreed so easily."

Kaetas glanced over her shoulder at the gangway up to the rim of the embankment. "Not a great spot for so much talking. Can you free her?"

Brogan examined the lock and shook his head. "Can't remember the last time I tackled one of these." He flipped through the ring of skeletons in his hand. "Are these even from this series? How long's she been impounded?"

"Still a lot of talking."

He shook his head again and went to work. Typically, a warded lock like this just needed the right skeleton and a little bit of trial and error, but he hadn't done this in years. A strange faceplate mounted next to the hole looked more like an old Cornumbrian tumbler. He tried the first few skeletons on the ring, but nothing fit. On the seventh try, the key rotated cleanly and the shackle swung free. He almost laughed. The tumbler was just a ruse. Brogan eased the lock out and set the chain to rest on the dock.

He handed the lock to Kaetas. "You could've done that yourself."

Kaetas took the lock with a grin. "What fun would that have been?" She dropped it into the river. Brunby quietly pulled the chain free while Kaetas flipped the mooring lines over the pylons. She whispered something to Freógan in the launch.

Brunby climbed aboard the ship and lowered a rope ladder over the side. Kaetas secured it and motioned for Senya to climb. "If you please," she said with a smile. "The lady with the keen eye for boats may board first."

The ladder sighed and clapped against the hull as she climbed. At the top, Senya swung a leg over and boarded easily. Brogan followed. Brunby waited on deck, helping both aboard. Soon Kaetas joined them. Freógan rowed the launch toward the stern for hoisting.

Kaetas gave a smile to her new passengers and welcomed them aboard. "As soon as Fre secures the launch," she said to Brunby, "let's run a fore and main, nothing more than what the three of us can handle on our own." She glanced up at the sky to get a sense of the breeze. "We should be able to follow the current with this ebb for a while, and maybe a breeze'll pick up. I'd love to make Donasberth by midnight, if we can."

"Aye aye."

"Privos ought to have gotten word by now. He'll have the rest of the crew with him somewhere dockside. They'll be waiting. But waiting, of course, means drinking. So we need to get everybody aboard before they're too drunk to remember they're sailors. If they aren't already."

❧ 38 ❧

DELSORKA HEADED for the docks along the river's edge. The Rusty Anchor was the first alehouse in a long line, so he'd try there first. Find out what he could about this *Summerhawk* and her crew. Kaevah Konn had a good network and controlled most of Corregidon, but he was no sailor. He might miss something. And Delsorka didn't like to miss anything.

Swinging open the heavy wooden door, he was hit by a wave of warmth and human reek. A blend of roasting pig, boiled leeks, and beer. Delsorka grinned. He loved a good alehouse.

He stepped through the din of the crowd. Laughter and shouts, the clack of tankards. Music flowed, coaxed from a whimpering instrument made of several pipes stitched into tanned skins of some bloated northern beast.

"Blander," Delsorka said to the bartender when the man leaned his way, sliding a coin across the bar top. "Know anything about a Cornumbrian caravel called the *Summerhawk*? Moored riverside downstream of Docktown?"

The bartender shook his head and shrugged. "Heard of her, I think. Not sure where she's set exactly."

"Any word of a girl they've got aboard? Fiery eyes, like a little Brondy? Probably hard to miss."

"Heard me plenty, but nothing about a Brondy girl. That'd stick out."

Delsorka thanked him and left the coin on the bar. He glanced around. Sailors and shipwrights, off-shift dockers and wharfies, along with a few merchants—the usual working crowd. Nothing out of place.

He walked out. Tried the Rolling Wheel next. Then the Barrister's Blood. Three in, three out. Nothing unusual. Nothing heard, nothing seen.

Other than what Konn's people had reported, there was little evidence that Senya had ever actually made it to Corregidon. If she was around, she'd gone quiet. But if she'd made connection with the *Summerhawk* and was provisioning to get underway, if they were looking to gather crew, looking for anything, this would be the place to find it. Crews liked to stick together. And if they were in Corregidon, they'd be somewhere in these alehouses and taverns. This was the place where Corregidon made all its waterborne deals.

If, that was, they were still in Corregidon.

Delsorka shook his head. What had gone wrong up there in the Hallon-ath? Who had Crassica tried to send first? And more so, how could Delsorka make sure nothing went wrong here? All of this hinted at something deeper going on. What exactly was the old crone up to?

Delsorka moved along the line and tried the Shield & Sword, a quieter fare for the older crowd. Less fighting, fewer pleasuregirls, and more straight drink. As he entered, music from a bow dragged across taut gut strings drifted through the room, lightening the moody smoky air. He'd known the bartender, Brokker Vey, for decades, though years would go by between encounters. Vey was one of the few men in the world Delsorka could truly call an old friend. He stepped up to the bar, ordered a bitter ale, and took a seat.

"Are we down or up?" Vey asked as he pulled the pint.

"Hard to say," Delsorka answered slowly. He placed a tiny stack of three coins on the bar top in front of him. "Trying to find word on a ship and her crew, but nothing's turning up in the usual places."

"Yeah? What's the ship?"

"The *Summerhawk*. You know her?"

Vey set the tankard in front of Delsorka and took the coins. "The *Hawk*? Sure. Half the crew was in here earlier tonight, matter of fact. Having a great time, same as usual. Then something happened. Was a little strange. They caught word of something or other, started whispering all tight among themselves. Then they all got up together and rushed out."

Delsorka stared at the untouched pint in front of him, knowing the answer to his question before he asked. "When was this?"

Vey shrugged. "I dunno. Three or four hours ago? Somebody said something about getting out to Donny at a lickety clip. Can't remember exactly. Headed out right after that. Paid their tab proper though, with a good tip. So that was nice."

Delsorka did not move. He was not a man to believe much in the meddling of the Knowing and never really went in for the notion of an ever-living presence taking an interest in the workings of humankind, her hand becoming active in moving pieces around on the gameboard of his life. But times like this, it just felt like she was out to get him.

"Ah, hells," he muttered. He stood and stared at his untouched tankard for a long moment. "I do not like to be rushed." He thanked Vey for the information and raised his tankard for a toast. "But I also hate to waste." Draining it in one long go, he set the empty tankard on the polished bar top, turned, and headed right back out the door.

"And this boat is where now?" the gray-cloaked Vallahnir whispered.

Delsorka had followed Konn as he climbed with the Vallahnir to a formidable granite vantage high above the northwestern edge of the city. He stepped to the crumbling remains of an unused rampart. "She's riding the current downriver to Donasberth." He pointed out the distant ribbon of the Brundsril, shining against the last vestige of twilight. "Right about there, I'd make her. But she'll have to wait for the next ebb to get all the way out to sea. She has no setup for rowers like the *Siege Runner* does, so that'll take until tomorrow evening at least. Maybe longer."

The Vallahnir drew in a sharp breath. "Your people are in place," she said to Konn, almost a veiled threat. "In this...Donasberth?"

"They're ready well enough," Konn assured. "Your girl will be taken tonight."

She turned to Delsorka. "And you shall carry her over the waters to Crassica?"

A flicker of anger lit through him. He knew what his job was. He didn't need this minor Vallahnir lieutenant's advice, her opinion, or her direction. "Yes," he said tersely. "Crassica herself explained it, thanks. So we can take it from here. As far as I know, your part is done. You flushed her down the river, and we thank you again for that, but you're now free to go climb back into whatever portal brought you here. We'll handle the rest."

The Vallahnir made no move to answer. The city flickered below as the world darkened around them. "Understand, Captain Delsorka," she said at length. "You are to do as you are told, and nothing more. Do not think to reach beyond your station. Do not propose to tell us what to do."

Delsorka opened his mouth to have a few more words, but Konn stepped in. "Look," he said warily. "One thing at a time. First off, let's make sure we've got your little prize in hand before we go and figure out what to do with her. No need to worry about who's in charge just yet."

The Vallahnir glanced back and forth between both men. Her lovely blue eyes were cold in the fading light. "There will be plenty reward for both of you if you get her to Katliga unharmed," she said. "And ensure the others cannot be allowed to give chase."

The folds of Konn's destroyed face twisted into something like a wry grin. "I thought the others didn't matter."

"The others may live or die—that does not matter to us. Only that their ship does not reach Kalldonia."

Kaevah Konn snorted, a kind of stunted laugh. "You are full of levels, aren't you? Always the next job waiting." He turned back to the dying light over the city. "Well, with the coin you're able to throw around, they probably won't even know we were there until Delsorka's ship is already good and gone."

39

CRASSICA CAME to Raedwin in dreams and nightmares alike, drifting in and out of view. She spoke in the throaty, grating language of the Crosslands—nonsense words for a confused mind. She smiled, but her face was filled with hatred and blame. Then the shape shifted. Her image shrank and became almost girlish, skin darkened to that of Raedwin's own sister, smooth and young once again.

Senya.

He struggled to call to her. Where had she been? Senya smiled and stepped away. Raedwin tried to shout and warn her, to tell her again not to come here, no matter what happened to him, but no words would form. *Get to Faeroen and stay there* became nothing more than a mumble. He tried to scream, but his mouth refused to open. His lips were sewn closed, forced shut and silenced by some unseen hand.

He awoke with a start on the bare floor of his tower workshop, back in the Sevenfold Keep. Stars filled the latticed windows, mocking him with the open sky outside. The room had been cleared of all his tools and papers, anything he could've called his own. They'd added a small straw bed beside a tiny table. A single chair and a bedpan.

He sat up. Pain shot across his bruised ribs, sending a shudder over his swollen head. He blinked. Vague images flashed in his memory. The abandoned farmhouse. His brief time with Sadahlia. Their struggle. A beating.

Lanius had found them. He had known exactly where they would be, and when. The thugs had hauled Sadahlia away separately, with no chance to exchange words, no chance at a touch. Maybe she was somewhere here in the Keep as well.

He stood and limped across the bare room and tried the door.

Locked. Barred from the outside. *Of course.*

He called for guards. For anybody. He cried out, a lone voice in a silent perch of shining glass and polished metal. No answer came. Somewhere a breeze whimpered through iron.

He went to the window, unsteady on bruised legs. Torchlight flickered at several guard stations along the walls. Parts of his abandoned windmill lay splayed across the ground far below, left there either because the workers had no idea how to continue without him or because Crassica wanted to taunt him with visions of his former self. His projects. All the dreams this place once held.

Crassica was probably down there somewhere, watching. Was this a victory for her? Was this the last piece of some grand plan finally coming to fruition? The prodigal servant brought to heel at last.

But where had they taken Sadahlia?

He called again at the door. Still no answer. None of his captors showed a face, and nobody gave audience to his pleas.

Raedwin went to sit on the edge of the bed. He wished he had access to his tools. Space to work. With enough time and materials, maybe he could find a way to banish Crassica back to the Crosslands on his own. He could find something to break her ability to draw power from whatever Amaris she had left, disrupt her rituals and incantations, shatter her methods of binding body to life. But he had no tools, and there was no time to experiment even if he did. Attempting a move like that would bring a whole host of hidden dangers anyway. Problems with indiscriminate effects. Issues provoked by imprecision or bad aim. There'd be no real way to ensure that whatever he tried would target Crassica and her loyal Vallahnir but leave Sadahlia untouched, wherever she was. No way to focus. Whatever he would be able to derive, it would likely cause the end of all of them.

There had to be some method of undoing, some process for unravelling all the things Crassica had put in place. A way to use her power against her. Transform her smokevessel into an artifice of ambush. Maybe a device founded in the fabric of life could bring death to those who didn't belong here. Something with copper and amber. Maybe eels. Raedwin had barely dabbled in alchemy, but maybe that ancient practice held a hidden method that could bring an end to Crassica's false masquerade among the living. There had to be a way to dissolve the particles of her form down to its most base and harmless elements. Purify the impure. If smoking Amaris brought her a power that connected to the Everlife, then maybe he could find its opposite somehow—saltpeter and ash, or maybe a sulfur mixture—something to send her back to the Crosslands with a permanence that she could never undo.

His work had gotten so physical of late, guided deftly away from the mystical by Crassica's own encouragement. He'd left behind the spiritual aspects of matter—water and fire, earth and air. He should've paid closer attention. Instead, he'd drifted off into engineering. Into machines. Crafting devices that clearly pleased Crassica and most surely would never be able to harm her.

He glanced around at the empty room. Not much to work with.

Water and fire, earth and air.

Suddenly, the genius of this particular tower struck him hard. Built of nothing but iron and glass, this was more than a feat of engineering, more than a test to see what Crassica could do with new alloys of steel or achievements of lofty weight distributions. This was a tower made solely of elements wrought by human hands, nothing that occurred in nature. With no stone, no wood, no water—this tower offered nothing to allow somebody like Raedwin to connect to anything or anyone outside himself. Here he could stand at the vastness of the window and be enticed by all the world outside and yet not truly see. His body could not leave this place, and neither could his mind.

This was a room designed as a prison from the very beginning.

"Well," he said aloud to nobody. "Welcome home, I guess."

❧ 40 ❧

"THANKS FOR helping bust my girl out, by the way," Kaetas said to Brogan as they stood at the taffrail. "A little bit like old times there for a minute." The *Summerhawk* lay at anchor some distance off the quay in Donasberth Bay. What little remained of the evening light had long since slipped to full darkness, with a gray glow in the distant west defining the long bent edge of the visible sea.

Brogan glanced at her, wondering whether she was serious. "Any pickpocket in Corregidon could've done the same for a bronze," he said. "Or a handful of shecks."

"Yeah, well, I don't trust just any pickpocket in Corregidon, do I?" She turned her gaze back to the water. "Wouldn't be family."

Brogan stared at the city in silence. The night gave no movement to the air, not the slightest breath. *Wouldn't be family*. They'd missed the ebb tide, and the new flood had already begun. Kaetas had sent for her crew, and by tomorrow afternoon they hoped for a little wind so they could float the evening ebb and finally push out to sea.

Brogan watched the *Hawk*'s launch heave toward the quay, the first of many crossings to gather crew. Maybe he should've never left Corregidon all those years ago. Maybe there had been other, better paths for him back then, and better paths now—better than the ones he'd chosen. Life in the city had been rough and hard and full of violence, but maybe if he'd stayed, Dahlwea would still be alive. Maybe they could've made it out some other way.

But everything carried risk, no matter what direction he tried. That much was always clear. Dahlwea could not be regained, not in this life, and maybe not in the next.

"I miss her," Kaetas said, facing away from him, almost as if she were speaking to the bay or the sea birds, or maybe to nobody at all.

"Yeah," he said. "Me too."

They stood at the rail for a long time, watching the birds ply the water, spreading white and reaching as they cried out to one another.

"I blamed you for a long time," Kaetas said at length. "A really long time."

"You and me both."

"But not anymore. And you shouldn't either. I know with more certainty than just about anything in this world that you did everything you could, come hells and beyond, to keep Dahlwea safe. But the bones landed as they did, and the things that happened, happened." She gazed out at the water. "And now here we are."

"Here we are."

Shouts rose from along the quay as dockhands struggled to haul crates up from the hold of a longship.

"Maybe we can do for Senya what we couldn't do for Dahlwea back then."

Brogan nodded. "Yeah," he said. "Maybe something like that."

"Here we are, you and I, doing the same dance, over and again." She gave him a smile that barely held back the weight of the past. "We'll get it right eventually."

The moon rose nearly full and glittered sharply blue on the dark water. Freógan paced the quarterdeck. Brogan had gone a while ago to sit amidships with his back to the bulwarks. Senya held out Raedwin's brass star taker to Kaetas.

"I'd like you to have this," she said after a moment. "It doesn't belong stuffed in my haversack or on a dusty shelf in Raedwin's workshop somewhere. It really belongs here. On a ship."

Kaetas reached to take the device. "Do you know what this is?"

"Can't say I'm all that well-versed in gadgets focused on the heavens," Senya admitted. "Or instruments designed for their study. I do know it's called a star taker. For navigation, I think. Maybe other things?"

"It's an astrolabe, yes." Kaetas held it, dangling from its ring. "And a pretty nice one."

"I'd like you to have it."

"No." Kaetas shook her head. "Senya, I can't accept this…"

"Sure you can. I'm giving it to you."

"But it's your brother's…"

"Call it payment on his behalf, for dragging us all out here."

Kaetas laughed, the sound crackling bright and pure.

"I'm not sure what he ever used it for, to be honest," Senya said. "He played around with it quite a lot when we were much younger, telling me where we were or what time it was, that sort of thing. Nothing very useful."

Holding the central bar, Kaetas explained how it showed the horizon, dividing the skies above from the unseen below. The inner circle indicated particular stars. The central pivot pin on the intricate face showed one's location. The center of the universe. "In truth, it's a whole map of the heavens right here in the palm of your hand," she said. "This ring it hangs from is called the Throne. And this outer edge holding it all together is called the Mother. When I was younger, I thought every astrolabe belonged to a proper queen."

"Raedwin can come get it back himself if he really wants it," Senya said. "Maybe it'll help us find Faeroen Island, once we get close."

The captain ran her fingers along the shine of intricate engravings in the brass. "It does belong on a ship. That is true…"

A shout rose from the dark water below, a coded greeting as the *Hawk*'s launch neared the ship. Freógan called a reply from the quarterdeck. Brunby strode to the starboard bulwarks and dropped the ladder over the side.

Silence returned for a moment to the *Summerhawk*. The slapping creak of the ladder broke the quiet as the first load of sailors climbed aboard, the least drunken of the lot, those tasked with the overnight watch.

"Thank you," Kaetas said at length. "I promise I'll take good care of it."

Empty of her passengers, the launch circled away, her oarsman pulling hard in the water. The bow creased the stillness and sent quivering breaks through the reflected torchlight on her return journey to gather the remaining crew.

Senya lay in a deep bunk along the side of her cabin under a row of paned windows. How long had she been asleep? Her dream just now had turned dark, twisting itself into a nightmarish vision. Three shadows climbing aboard the *Summerhawk* without a sound. Knives in teeth, blackened with pitch against the moonlight.

So much blood and sweat spent to get this far, and yet the long sail north still to come. She loved the sea, and being near the ocean was a comfort for her, a source of joy even in its moody grayness, but no matter what she'd tried, she'd not been able to pull any further strength to connect with Raedwin—not while on the river back in Corregidon, and not here, awaiting the tides in Donasberth Bay.

A wave of exhaustion washed over her. Safely on the water for the first time in so long she couldn't quite remember, she needed all the rest she could get. There would be gambles and dangers to come, especially on an uncharted path with unknown consequences. But she was willing to do whatever it took, for however long. She was not afraid of those who were after her, and she was not afraid of what waited for her ahead.

Deck boards creaked outside her cabin—different from the mere drift of the ship.

That wasn't a dream. It was a vision. Something moved. Someone trying to remain silent.

Senya rose and crept to the door, slipping the catch to swing it open. Shadows swept across her vision.

A forearm slammed her backward. A hand gripped her mouth closed, someone all in black, shoving her onto the bunk. A second moved toward her. Black pitch covered both faces. Uncorking a tiny glass vial, the shadow upended its contents over a small cloth.

Senya struggled, trying to kick something, trying to cry out, wrestling to unpin her hands and make whatever noise she could. But she found nothing but air and bed linens. The cloth gripped her nose and mouth.

"Hush," a man's voice whispered in the darkness. "Quiet now. Just sleep. We're not here to hurt you."

Senya held her breath, continuing to struggle, but finally couldn't help but gasp. She breathed again. Her body went limp. The hand held the cloth firm to her mouth, but after a time let it drop to the floor. Arms reached under her and lifted her body from the bunk. The room swam and swung to the side. Moving from the cabin to the passage, the shadows returned to escape the same way in which they had come.

And then everything went dark.

❧ 41 ❧

SADAHLIA WINCED at the dragging of chains over wood outside her carriage door. Blades of light stabbed at the edges of drawn curtains. They'd stopped again. How many times had it been? She rose from the plush bench and stood listening as her captors undid a series of onerous locks.

The ride had been strange and long. The carriage itself was quite comfortable, one of Crassica's best, but with her hands bound, Sadahlia had found it difficult to find any real comfort. She'd drifted in and out of waking. Her memory was disjointed and broken. Men had argued briefly before a pair of rough hands offered her food. Fresh tears had flowed from her eyes, even after no more could possibly come. She hoped, ached with hope, that Raedwin was alive and being treated well—or at least better than her. Maybe he'd gotten away.

The carriage door flew open. Sunlight flooded the cramped space, and Sadahlia blinked. Still naked and exposed, she was too exhausted to care much anymore. A man offered escort out of her wheeled prison into clay buildings and street noise. A city, then. Katliga, or maybe Darizi. Maybe Kalldon itself. Two men led her through a gap in a stone wall down a series of clammy steps into dank chambers below the street.

During the journey, Sadahlia had pondered several times whether she would be able to separate from her living body and surrender her spirit back into the Crosslands. To drift away and be finished. Disappear. If she could let herself die, she should be able to travel unbound through the Crosslands. Maybe then she could find a way to rebuild her body with swiftness and cunning, better learn the movements of this world, and find herself born anew in another place alongside Raedwin, hidden and alive together.

But she would need Crassica for all that. The architect of her entry into this world. Sadahlia barely remembered the process. Seven decades had already passed, and her spirit was now encased. Like all living things, she could not simply release. Too skillfully had Crassica guided her into this flesh, and Sadahlia's entry back into the Crosslands would require a true death. Any return from there to the living would take much, much more. Unable to consult with Crassica on exactly how such a thing could be done, she would be on her own. Years would likely pass before she'd be able to find her way back to Raedwin, if she could ever rediscover the path at all. Certain rules remained, even with a Vallahnir.

In the end, such yearnings were idle fancy. The men who had taken and bound her would never allow her to escape, especially into death and the Crosslands.

As they descended, the walls bled with a moldy blackness that spoke of water nearby. They passed through several tunnels. Sadahlia walked with her head high and said nothing. The men offered no words, no encouragement, no gentleness of any kind. Soon they came to a wide cistern with torches mounted to the walls. A broad walkway circled the edge. Firelight glimmered on the surface of a shining black pool several feet below. An iron cage the size of a small room dangled over the water, suspended by massive chains from the ceiling.

There, beside a makeshift wooden bridge leading in a long arc over the cistern, stood Lanius. He grinned as the men ushered Sadahlia to him.

"Welcome, your worship," he called. "Do you like your new home? I do apologize for the delay in getting you here. Considerable effort was required to construct this place properly. It is not so easy to find a way to cradle a wayward Vallahnir with iron and water and stone all at the same time. But of course we needed all three elements, didn't we?" He gestured with a thin powerful hand. "Come," he whispered. "Let me show you."

He led her to the foot of the wooden bridge. She refused to follow. The men behind gripped her shoulders and forced her forward. Lanius guided her across the bridge and into the cage. A plush bed lay in the center of the suspended cell, with a simple writing desk alongside. Lanius unbound her hands and stepped away.

"The master is most displeased at your betrayals," he said. "She does not wish to see you, and she cannot have you in the Keep. But she has never minded making a little coin on the side. I'll admit I do have a fancy for such things myself. Which brings you here." He surveyed the iron room. "A place of exaltation, fit for Crosslands royalty."

Lanius bent close to take in the details of her bruised face. "I do hope your new bedchamber meets with your approval. For the right price, we can provide the local gentry with a little spectacle. Let the world see your naked truth. A tidy little display, available to anyone who wants to pay for a look."

With that, he stepped out and swung the heavy cage closed. He clasped the lock and gripped the ring of keys in his hand.

"You like to forget who you are?" he said, with a sharpness in his wiry voice. "You like to forget who made you and where you come from?" A thin smile crawled across his pale face. "Well, that's a shame. Because you will have quite a long while to think about these things. Here, in this place, you will remember exactly who—and what—you are. You shall be reminded of these things every day. For a long, long time to come."

42

HEAVY FOG filled Donasberth Bay. Brogan stood with Kaetas in the bow of the *Summerhawk*, and the slate sky stretched from land to sea and back to land again in one long unbroken sheet. Three corpses lay against the starboard bulwarks. Several crewmembers spread lengths of spent sailcloth next to them.

"Grabbed her without a sound," Kaetas said. "Knocked her out with a mixture of poppymilk and belladonna, maybe mixed with something else, I don't know. Very well-made stuff."

At first light, the captain had ordered the anchor weighed and the *Summerhawk* to get well offshore for better security. They'd anchored again in deeper water abreast the Brundsril's main current, making it much more treacherous for anybody to row out and try to sneak aboard again.

The crew clothed the murdered sailors in their rusted mail shirts and heavy leather boots with a shortsword in hand on each breast, leather helms on their heads. They wrapped each body tightly and added ballast stones out of the keel for weight. Brunby sang through it all, giving ancient blessings and rites of passing for a safe journey through the Crosslands. Kaetas offered a word on sacrifice and life, thanking the sailors for their service. The crew hoisted and slid the wrapped corpses down a long plank overboard into the waiting waters of the bay. A moment of silence passed with the quiet sound of water against the hull.

Kaetas had already sent most of the crew ashore to look for information, to find anything on whoever had taken Senya and where they'd gone.

Somebody along the docks reported seeing someone of Senya's description being carried by two men in the early dawn, apparently hauled aboard a tall three-master from Kalldonia called the *Siege Runner*. Captain named Delsorka. The ship had left almost immediately. She'd put out an impressive double course of oars and rowed out to sea against the early flood tide. Rumors held that a powerful sorcerer was on board, or something worse. But with no clear sense of where they'd gone, Kaetas and her crew remained stuck.

"I don't take kindly to ladies being kidnapped," she said to Brogan. "I cannot let that shit pass. Not on my watch, and especially not on my boat." A fresh spark came into her eye. "So I'm with you on this one, wherever it leads, and wherever we need to go. To the end. Call it revenge or whatever you like. It's personal now for me. There's definitely more trouble to be had, and I'd like a piece of it."

"Well, thank you," Brogan said. "For whatever that's worth. I think she'd appreciate it, and I sure as all four hells certainly do."

A thought suddenly occurred to him, and he nearly laughed. Silently kicking himself for letting hours pass before thinking of it, he freed the oilskin pouch from his belt and pulled out the parchment he'd found on the Vallahnir back in the Hallonath, all those days ago. Part of the reason they were making for Faeroen in the first place.

"Maybe," he said, "we could start by trying to figure out what this is?"

Kaetas made sure nobody followed through the twisting streets of Donasberth. Rounding the base of a low rock hill, she climbed a narrow labyrinth of cobblestone alleys. Scattered residents scurried in the light rainfall.

"I still can't believe you didn't show it to me before," she scolded. Again.

Brogan didn't bother to answer. He'd already explained himself three times, and now Kaetas was just talking to herself. He'd forgotten about the parchment, simple as that. It had been meaningless to him and Senya both, and somebody on Faeroen was supposed to maybe know what it was. Senya's father or some other Brohndai scholar. It hadn't occurred to him that they could try to decipher it themselves and use it to find out where she'd been taken.

Climbing the final three steps, Kaetas rounded a corner and came to a set of wooden door pillars bracing a tall stone building. A dripping sign overhead showed a crude hammer and anvil. Not where Brogan would've expected to find a local master of the Dark Arts.

"Are you sure he'll know what it is?"

"If anybody anywhere can figure that thing out," Kaetas said, "it's Drogaen."

Entering quietly, they stepped downward into a surprisingly cavernous space. Fire blazed from a heavy work furnace. A heavyset bald man hammered away at a flat chunk of red iron near the mouth. An assortment of metal tools sat on a wooden table, and several instruments lined the walls.

A second man emerged from a back room carrying an armload of firewood. He was tall, with a bony face all out of proportion. His round eyes sat too far apart from one another under a brow too heavy for such a small forehead. A wiry tuft of black hair stood erect on his otherwise gleaming pate. He smiled as he caught sight of them.

"Captain Kaetas!" he called. "What a pleasant surprise. How excellent to see you!" He set the wood on the rack next to the furnace.

Kaetas smiled. "Drogaen," she greeted. "How've you been?"

The man stepped forward. "Up, down, all around, same as always."

The smith at the furnace hammered away, taking no notice of them.

Kaetas made a glance at the tools, the worktable, the furnace. "A smithy? Really? Took me a while to find you."

A frown furrowed Drogaen's face. "My last workshop..." He trailed off and waved away the thought, as if the rest of the sentence was too bitter for words.

"The fire? I heard about that."

He shook his head. "Turns out some experiments with alchemy can deal a dangerous hand indeed. But come." He gestured to a set of narrow wooden stairs that lined the back wall to a room at the rear. "Let's go up so we can talk."

Nestled at the top of the stairs, Drogaen's home was simple and spacious. Generous light streamed through a set of wide round windows facing the sea. Shelves lined two sides of the room, densely packed from floor to ceiling with well-kept leatherbound books, split at intervals by scroll racks. Clearly an organized house of letters. Each item had its place, every object accounted for and positioned just so, with deliberate intention to every arrangement.

Drogaen gestured for his guests to sit. His dark eyes glittered with energy that defied the ponderous, restrained motion of his body. Brogan brought out the parchment and laid it on the table. "A friend and I found it with a group of necromancers out in the Hallonath."

"We need to know what it is," Kaetas added. "Or at least how to read it."

"Ah!" Drogaen exclaimed, leaning forward. His fingertips brushed the small symbols—the fish, the horned head, the strange spider-like figures. "Markings of the Old Ones. These are older than language. Very ancient. They require very few rules for the passing of information—ideal for creating meaning between planes... Like between the living and the dead, for example..." He looked hard at Kaetas. His eyes narrowed. "What exactly are you up to?"

"Don't worry about it." She tapped the parchment. "Focus."

Drogaen shook his head. He rose and stepped away from the table to a heavy scribe's desk next to the scroll racks. His long fingers retrieved a quill and a bottle of ink along with a thin translucent sheet of fine stretched vellum. He returned to the table.

Laying the thin vellum over the parchment, Drogaen dipped the quill into the ink and began to make loose, quick markings on it, tracing the thicker lines but ignoring the circles, star figures, and symbols. He traced inward along some of the tiniest of lines at key points. When finished, he sat back and slid the vellum off the parchment, rotating it to Brogan and Kaetas.

"What do you see here?"

His drawing was indefinite and meaningless, almost like two wriggling animals, or two warriors engaged in swordplay, their capes billowing. Or maybe two misshapen vultures arguing over a scrap of prey. The top shape the aggressor, as if wielding some burly weapon, while the bottom shape held up an arm in paltry defense.

"Well, hells," Kaetas said quietly. "It's a map."

Drogaen nodded. "Indeed it is."

Brogan glanced between them, confused. "How is that a map?"

"The northern and southern continents are there," Kaetas explained. "Brinsfallon, Dunnenwyr, and the Baelhoarg in the North. Kalldonia and Cornumbria in the South..."

"Yes," Drogaen agreed. "And the symbols indicate whatever is most commonly found in the places they mark. Cows signify grasslands or

open range. The Northern Snow Deer shows plains and steppes. The fish denote waters and the sea."

He rose from his chair. "However, the symbols do not provide the primary meaning." He moved slowly and deliberately to his shelves and began to examine the spines of certain volumes. His lips moved, fingers running along titles. Soon he selected a book and drew it from the shelf. Returning to the table, he set the book down and opened it, thumbing the thick parchment pages.

"The circles and stars inscribed upon your parchment are not new," he said. "They are old beyond old and represent certain resonant tunings, energies that spill from this world over to the next and back again." He came to a particular page and held it open, spinning it to face them.

The page was dense with words, scribed in a deft and flowing hand. But unmistakably in the center of the page sat the circle and star patterns

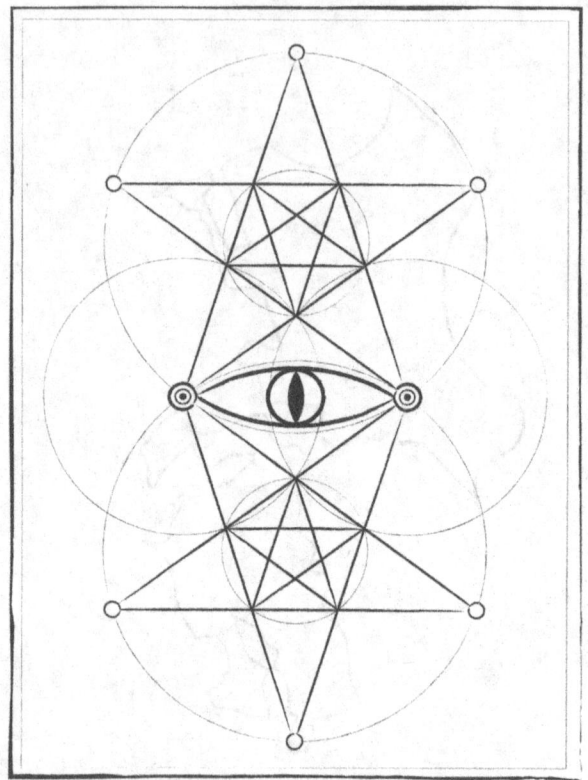

from Brogan's parchment, clean and unencumbered with any of the heavier tracings or underlying symbols.

"This is the Eye of the Knowing," Drogaen explained. "It's a portrayal of her Mode of Balance—all things in existence holding opposites inside their very core, contrary forces that interconnect and complement one another. Only together are they complete. Only a union of balanced opposition can bring forth the possibility of all life."

Drogaen gazed at the book in front of him and at each of them at the table. "There can be no south without its sister north, for example. No darkness of night without the light of day. No inside without defining what is outside. And no life without death."

He slid his fingers across the book. "But as one can pass from north to south, and from outside to in, one can also pass from light to dark and back again. And from life into death as well. Most find this last passing to be permanent, of course, but the Vallahnir of the Crosslands exist in that very overlap, in the place through which the living and the dead cross over."

Drogaen moved his attention to Brogan's parchment. "Now here, we see the Eye of the Knowing overlaid onto a map of the north and south lands." He touched a long bony finger to the point of each star, where several lines passed through one another. "At each of these places where the energies converge is a portal into and out of the Crosslands—doors that allow passage by those who are tuned to the deeper harmonies of the Way."

His eyes narrowed as he examined the parchment. "Each aligns with the stars above as well, and they are marked by temples built by ancient clerics and early priests, long before the empire. Most of these places have been forgotten and left to decay, and some have been nearly lost to corrosion and degradation. But all are accounted for on this map." His fingers traced each spot in turn as he spoke. "Here, in the inner circle of the North lie Yesteralen, Vasselroy, Storlavet, Blochsnil, and so on, all places strong with Brohndai energies. The core circle in the South has Darizi, Katliga, and Kalldon, as well as many ruins along the shore and beyond, all permeated with Vallahnir influence. Opposition provides balance. In the North, the portals strong with the Vallahnir lie at Svetlann, Trundsven, Montcarsel, and Vesterlag. Of these, all lay in ruins and are seldom visited. Most are nearly lost to the eyes of men."

Drogaen paused, holding his hands on the parchment. "The Brohndai, of course, long held all of these places in check and maintained a balance between the living and the Vallahnir. But with the rise of the Empire and the banishment of the Brohndai from all but a few forgotten corners, the strength of these temples has long since diminished and fallen away. The balance has declined, and many are now in disarray. Those of us who are watching can certainly perceive it.

"So your parchment then tells us what? It shows the lands of the North and the South, and appears to offer guidance to the bearer as to how to orient oneself to these places in relation to the portals. And yet there is more than that. Certain portals have been emphasized with stronger markings, circled with rings. Faeroen Island at the top of the map is accentuated and circled, which of course is the home of the Brohndai in exile. At the far southern edge, the Blackmere in opposing balance. And in the North, Montcarsel is marked with some importance."

Drogaen's hand slid to the lower portion, to the large black dot with its thick double rings at the edge of the inner star. "But here, this is clearly the focus... marked in the same way as Montcarsel, but with emphasis. If I am not mistaken, this is the citadel of the Valle d'Brasti in the northeast of Kalldonia. A very ancient place indeed."

Drogaen's hand fell away from the parchment as he sat back. He considered something for a long time before he spoke again.

"The Valle d'Brasti began countless centuries ago," he said at length, "when a wandering group of Old Ones found their tired horses licking stones along the bluffs and realized the whole prominence was riddled with salt. Early chieftains and warlords soon took hold and dug deep mines, many of which remain to this day. Ample limestone supplied the construction of seven stout towers for protection, which became the famed Sevenfold Keep. Wealth and power built on a honeycomb of hidden tunnels. Over many generations, much darkness and torment has come to that place. A long history of fire and sword, of broken memories and an unsettled past. In the end, however, the same tunnels on which it was built proved to be its end—too many holes in the otherwise impregnable Keep. Too many easy breaches. Assassins and marauders plagued from underneath, long before the earliest days of the empire.

"This place has long been deeply shrouded," Drogaen said. "It has birthed many strange and dark things over recent memory." His voice drifted off with these last words, eyes still on the parchment. Sea air swirled outside the windows. "That place," he whispered. "That is the place."

After a moment he reached out and pointed to the double-circled corner of the inner southern star. "From what I can tell, the intention of this parchment is to guide its bearer there, to the Valle d'Brasti." His voice slowed, taking on a new gravity. "To help whoever held it—someone versed in the languages of the Crosslands, perhaps—to find their way back home."

❧ 43 ❧

SENYA WAS a slight woman, smaller than Delsorka would've imagined. She had not yet been awake when Konn's men had brought her aboard and laid her gently in the hammock. The drugs they'd used were very successful, but their effects tended to linger a little too long. A day and a half passed before she started to open her eyes.

Delsorka found her strikingly beautiful, no matter how much she tried to hide it with her heavy cloak drawn close and her hood pulled low over her face. Those eyes. Orange as furnace coals. Some things could not easily be hidden.

"Hello, Senya." He gave a courtly bow of his head. "I'm Captain Delsorka." He held out a hand. "It's a pleasure to finally meet you."

Ignoring his hand, she lay staring at him, quietly blinking.

He gave her a waterskin, which she took and drank from greedily.

"Welcome aboard the *Siege Runner*," he said. "No rules out of the ordinary apply, just the usual. When you're on board, I'm in charge. Captain, judge, jury, executioner. God of All Things. No more, no less. But of course that's just the official line. Never really works exactly like that. I've got to keep everybody happy the same as anybody else."

She shifted in the hammock. "You kidnapped me," she said, her voice cracking with sleep.

"I'm taking you to see your brother."

Her eyes narrowed. Still a little groggy. She watched him for a long silent moment. "You kidnap people all the time, don't you?"

261

Delsorka stiffened. "I don't much like that word."

"You do it for *her*."

The girl's sleep was fading awfully fast. "Crassica?" He allowed himself a brief nod. "She often gives a compelling argument, I'll admit. And an awful lot of coin."

Her eyes burned into him. Something more was in that gaze—he could feel it. The ship's timbers groaned as men heaved their oars overhead.

She closed her eyes and started to sing. The sound came light and easy to Delsorka's ears in smooth, woven notes. Like old friends inviting him to play. The strains rose and moved, the melody ringing a wide and distant echo beyond the cramped cell, with all levels of hope and sadness joining in.

She stopped. Brow furrowed, she cocked her head and looked at him strangely, and then at the overhead beams, the bulkheads and the narrow planks forming each wall. "What is this room? What have you done to it?"

Delsorka glanced around him. Thankfully, a series of small incense lamps obscured some of the more sinister markings, but nothing could hide the pattern of animal bones lashed to the lintel above the door. A few of the strange runes remained visible, as did the vial of goat's blood in the corner. "Ghellan calls it a birdcage," he said. "It's for your safety."

"My safety."

"There are plenty of hard, ugly men aboard this ship, and I can't quite control everybody all the time. Not on a boat this big. Down here in the hold, you'll be safe. That much I know."

She stiffened in the hammock, a fresh clarity coming into her eyes. "I'm going to ask you this one time," she said, her voice pointed and low. "I need you to listen. Are you listening?"

This gave Delsorka pause. All remnants of grogginess had fully left her voice. A strange and fresh strength replaced it.

"Do not lie to me," she said—a command, not a request. "That is all I ask."

"Well..." He cleared his throat. "I admit that maybe this is a little less comfortable than a regular cabin, but it's definitely safe..."

"Do not lie to me, Captain Delsorka. Let us tell the truth at least to one another. I am not in this room because it is safe for me. Maybe it's safe for you, but definitely not for me. I am a prisoner."

"I'm taking you to see your brother. That is the truth."

"But that is not your purpose."

"You want to see him, do you not? There is truth in that at least."

"Where is he?"

"He's down in Kalldonia. Safe with friends, last I saw."

"With *friends*?"

"With Crassica. He wanted to come find you himself, but he was… detained by work."

"I told you not to…"

"It's not a lie. I saw him. He was with Crassica. Apparently he's with her all the time. That's what they told me, and it was true, as far as I could tell. Your brother is quite a fixture down there. Something of a leader, from the look of it all. Crassica herself seemed pretty close to him, maybe even a lover. I'm not really sure."

The ship heaved and groaned underneath. Senya studied his face. "There's no point in listening to you, is there?"

"It's the truth."

"Does it matter? They told me he was in trouble. They said he was locked in the Crosslands. But all of that was a lie. Everything a lie. Why would you be any different?"

Delsorka almost laughed but culled it quickly. *The Crosslands?* Where had that story come from? "I don't know anything about that," he said. "Raedwin wasn't in the Crosslands when I saw him. He was up and around just fine."

"What about the others I was with? The boat you *kidnapped* me from?"

Delsorka winced again at the word. "I understand there was a little trouble when Konn's men went to retrieve you, but that's nothing you need worry about."

"How many?"

Delsorka shook his head. "Unfortunate things can happen in my line of business."

"The captain? Brogan?"

"I don't know names, but unless they were on watch, I would assume both are fine. However, they will not be allowed to follow. That much is clear."

She stared at him, still reading, still assessing. "Why is there a necromancer on board?"

Delsorka could not hide the quick shock that ran through him. *Hells. Who is this girl?* He'd made sure Ghellan hadn't shown his face since Senya had been brought aboard. How could she tell? Pinching his face, he cocked his head.

"Ghellan? I'm not sure I would go so far as to call him a necromancer exactly…"

"I would."

Delsorka opened his mouth for a moment but found himself unable to find easy words. "Okay," he said at last. "Fair enough." He hadn't wanted that old conjureman on board to begin with and didn't have a good honest answer as to why he was here, even for himself. "Crassica requires some things of us," he said, choosing words carefully. "No matter where, or who, we are."

"But at sea?"

His face twitched. *Exactly my point.* He offered another, more conclusive smile. "We do things a little differently on board the *Runner*, and sometimes we're a little unorthodox." He tried to give her his most reassuring face in an attempt to switch the subject away from things he'd rather not discuss. "But don't worry about all that. Just rest. You've had a bit of a journey. I will allow no harm or pain to come to you—that much I can promise, no matter my charge. I will make this voyage as comfortable as I can."

He gave her a decisive nod. Confident assurance. "Let's go see your brother, shall we?" He stood and stepped toward the door. "Together."

"They'll come after me, you know."

"Will they?"

"Nobody likes a kidnapper."

"I really wish you would stop using that word."

"They've probably already set sail. What time is it?"

"In that little boat of theirs? Good luck with that. Konn will take care of any attempts at pursuit, trust me. That's what he's best at. And this ship is an awful lot faster than that one. So we're pretty okay at the moment."

"Who is Konn?"

"Don't worry about it. You worry about staying comfortable, right here in this lovely cabin we've prepared for you. And get your rest. Only the Knowing can say what's ahead for you."

He did his best to offer kind wishes for the voyage as he backed out of the cabin. Swinging the door shut, Delsorka slid a key into the heavy oiled lock and spun the mechanism. The sound of thick bolts sliding into place echoed through the ship's hold. Ghellan rushed forward from where he'd been hiding among the shadows. Laying hands on the cell door, he began to recite guttural words from some ancient tongue, words that wrapped the air and singed the ear.

"What's that noise?" Senya called out. Ghellan ignored her. He ran his hands along the door planks and sang a short chant before stepping back. Delsorka said nothing.

"Hello?" called Senya. "Was that singing?"

Delsorka stepped to the door. "It's nothing," he assured her through the planks. "I'll send down some food and drink." Shooing Ghellan away and motioning him to the upper decks, he wished Senya well before following.

"What's that burning smell?" Senya called from her cabin.

Delsorka paused but did not answer. The ship's timbers groaned as the *Siege Runner* made her way quickly south.

🙰 44 🙰

RAEDWIN SAT on the edge of the bed and waited. He waited for word, for food, or for any kind of response from the world below the tower. He sat in the chair at the table. He walked from one wall to the window, felt his feet on the tile, then the rug, then the tile again. He pressed his palm against the iron walls and then sat on the bed again. After a time, the sound of soft footsteps echoed up the long stairs outside his door. A key slipped neatly into the lock on his door. The latch drew.

He readied himself. Raedwin knew this Keep, knew its tunnels and secret passageways. He'd only need to get down from this tower, and the rest would take care of itself. He grabbed the chair and put his back to the wall beside the door. He lifted the chair overhead as the door began to open.

"Careful," came a deep whispered voice. "I am a friend."

Raedwin froze. He held the chair aloft, ready to strike. But regardless of whether he got past this man, who knew what guards Crassica had posted at the base of the tower? On the stairs? In the halls? The door remained slightly ajar.

"Speak your name," he countered. "I doubt I have any friends left around here..."

"But you do," came the whispered voice. "Those who know the ill wishes of the Honored One and disagree with her intentions." Two gnarled hands emerged from the doorway, palms up, showing themselves in sur-render. "May I enter? I mean you no harm..."

Raedwin moved to the side, away from the door, and lowered the chair. "Slowly…" he warned.

A man shuffled into the room. He was short and portly, with thick workmanlike arms and long thinning hair clinging to a balding pate. Large friendly eyes. His jowls fell softly in an aging sag from his cheeks.

The man kept his hands up. "Hello, I am Manka." He glanced at the open doorway. "I only dare spare a moment. We know the master has imprisoned you, and we do not wish it so."

Raedwin set the chair on the ground. "Have we met before?"

Manka's pale skin flushed. "Of course. But within a team of workers. It is no bother. We are together in this." Manka leaned forward, his whispers coming more urgently. "There has been a purge. Crassica is in a rage. Something about destruction of her mine? Kraegha has been executed. Devron and Solinius as well, along with several others."

So they found everything. Raedwin's hope drained. Kraegha and Devron had been so careful to remain hidden, wanting little more than to clip Crassica's wings, to blunt her access to power before they tried to find a new balance alongside her. A hope he had never quite shared.

"Why am I still alive?" he asked.

"Crassica treasures you. She always has. You are a prize of some kind, although we have not yet deciphered her true intention. However, it does appear your imprisonment is tied to the master's First Vallahnir, the one called Sadahlia."

Raedwin's heart leapt. "Yes," he cried. "Is she alive? Where is she? Is she here? What has happened?"

Manka held up a hand, urging quiet. "I have heard rumors and stories, and little of reliable value, but it appears they have taken her to Katliga. She is held in such a way that will not allow her to end her own life and be re-formed in the Crosslands. Crassica refuses to let the two of you find a way to meet again."

Raedwin put out a hand to steady himself on the edge of the bed. He sat.

Of course. The Crosslands.

Meeting in the Crosslands had not occurred to him. He had not thought of killing himself and had not considered Sadahlia doing so either. The simplicity of it so cold, so clear, so true.

"Where is she in Katliga?"

Manka sighed. "She is held... underground. Beneath a house of..." His voice trailed off. "She is held in an iron cage over water. Men pay for a glimpse. To view the legend of a living ghost."

"A carnival sideshow."

"We have offered money for her release."

"And?"

Manka shook his head. "It is doubtful her release is a question of money. There is likely nothing that will get Crassica to let Sadahlia free."

Raedwin's mind fumbled at solutions and ideas to spark some new route or a fresh path, but nothing came.

Katliga. Unable to end her life and begin anew. And he, stuck here, unable to get to her. The depths to which they had fallen, and the lengths to which Crassica would go to keep them there.

"Is Crassica still getting ore somehow?"

"We do not know," Manka said. "A few strange carts arrived from Katliga, but I cannot surmise the storage of such things."

As strong as ever. What had they missed?

"I have to get out of here."

"We are putting together a plan. There will be four knocks here at your door. And then a fifth. Wait for them. This will come in a few days' time. Maybe less."

"And Sadahlia has to rot in that hole while we wait."

"Soon after the knocks, this door will open. It will remain open. You are to wait for a moment, and then you are to walk out."

"How do I know I can trust you?"

"Trust nobody, not even me. Keep your eyes on everything and everyone."

"She'll know somebody helped me."

"She will not know who, nor how many. There are plenty of us, and we are careful."

"Kraegha and Devron were careful too."

"There are many of us reaching for change," Manka said, clearly understanding the gravity. "Our eyes have opened to both Crassica's past and our future. It is time for all of this to end."

"Okay," Raedwin said. "Four knocks, the door opens, and I walk out."

"I will give you a set of code words," Manka replied. "Use them when you reach our people in Katliga. Do you know this part of the Keep?"

"Like I built it myself."

"Make your way into the southeast tunnels, to the great pit. You will find a passage in the far wall. A set of stairs to the surface. From there you will emerge in the village east of the bluffs. A horse will be waiting. There will be no people. Only the horse."

"Can you find me some weapons?"

"I am sure we can find a shortsword. And perhaps a hunting bow."

"The sword ought to do."

"Remember the words you are given. We have people who can help. In Kalldon, as well as here." He rose and gripped Raedwin's arm. "May the Knowing guide you."

"Thanks," Raedwin said. "But I doubt the Knowing gives two shecks about what happens to me."

45

MOST MEN were afraid of her. They would not descend beneath the streets of Katliga to view this caged siren of legend and song, this manifestation of the beauty and clarity of death itself. But others were brave enough, and those came gladly. They paid with bags of coin for a glimpse, their fat teeth shining through open grins. Lanius watched from the shadows as tongues slid over wet lips, men ogling from the ample platform beside the cistern. Those who came seemed to possess nothing resembling fear or an understanding that fear even existed. Nor had they any care of how others lived or died. They simply had far too much coin, and Lanius was happy to take it from them in exchange for a chance to watch this embodied revenant of the Crosslands sleep. Or sit. Or do nothing at all. And then they returned to watch again.

Lanius had made careful assurance that no connection would be made between this place and Crassica, no throughline to the Valle d'Brasti or to himself. He'd manipulated everything through a complex network of middlemen, as was his typical clandestine practice. By crafting a story of this caged creature being captured in an Oscilianne Islands raid, he knew there would be no trace. None of the pirates or brigands from Ocennas would be able to say otherwise. And so the wealthy men of Katliga, bored of whatever vices they'd used to spice their empty lives so far, came and paid well for the chance to descend through secret rooms into the sewer dark. They paid to follow underground canals and passageways fit more for sludge and excrement than for human traffic. They paid to pretend their lives were dangerous.

With no semblance of privacy, Sadahlia lay exposed. The patrons watched her stare blankly at the walls or lie prone on the iron floor of the cage. They stood and they stared at her sleeping body on the silken bedding. Her white skin glowed in the low lamplight, the bruises of her treatment visible on her nearly human flesh. The woman lying before them came straight from their own nightmares, from fables and childhood stories woven by firelight.

Some wanted to be with her. Others wanted to own her. They would offer vast sums of money for the chance to abuse her body, but all were denied. To attempt such a thing would mean immediate execution by armed attendants. Lanius made sure that part was clear. None would be allowed to approach, and none could touch her. Some would touch themselves instead, while others would do nothing but stand and stare. They would whisper to one another or mutter quietly, and then they would depart. After a time, some would come back for a second viewing, while others grew bored and lost interest, moving on to whatever new and titillating sin they could find elsewhere.

The truth, in the end, was far less interesting than the legends.

✦ 46 ✦

THE THIRD morning out of Donasberth brought all the savagery of the unbound sea down upon the *Siege Runner*. Frigid swells heaped upon one another, their wavetops disintegrating into long tendrils of windblown drizzle. The ship dodged and parried the blows, but still she took several massive hits across her bow. Men in the rigging hauled sails in as a towering wall of water collided with her port side. The ship heaved wildly to starboard, and several sailors slid across her deck, crashing against the bulwarks. As the *Runner* righted herself, Delsorka yelled for a heavy safety line to be run fore and aft, stretching taut from the mainmast to the quarterdeck.

"Anybody who's out here needs to be secured to that line," he shouted into the din. "And get everything else strapped down!"

The crew slid hatch covers into place, securing them with sliding brass locks. Another wave crashed across the deck. Stretching oilcloth sheets over open vents, they rode like this for some hours, pinned against the sudden gale. A series of three soaring waves caught the *Runner* at a particularly bad angle, crashing flat against her starboard side and twice shoving her nearly sideways into the sea.

Sunlight faded into a gray and surly evening. Delsorka lurched across the rolling deck to steady himself against the quarterdeck steps. He quick tied a short cord to the safety line running from bulkhead to mast, securing the other end around his waist. Steel-gray water with a frothy white spray greeted his survey of the deck. The bow crashed headlong into another massive wall of water, spreading white churn over the planks.

Shouts erupted behind him. Delsorka turned to see Senya emerge from below. She walked barefoot along the glistening deck, wrapped in a night cloak.

Delsorka stood agape. *How in hells did she get out of Ghellan's birdcage?*

She stepped slowly forward into the jaws of the storm, as if floating above the seething deck. Her eyes focused on the distant clouds, seeing nothing in front of her, nothing of the ship itself, either unable or unwilling to hear the shouts behind her. Another wave crashed over the bow. The ship surged.

Delsorka steadied himself against the ladder before stumbling forward. *Gods take that conjureman,* he cursed silently at Ghellan. *And his useless box of nonsense.*

Senya had already made it to the figurehead at the bow. She put one arm around the carved wooden shoulder of the stem and climbed onto the thick support at the base of the sprit. Pulling her cloak tight, she stood there in a sideways embrace with the ship, the full fury of the open sea bearing down upon her. Delsorka struggled past the rear hatches and lurched for the mast. A wave crashed into the bow. Then another. Senya did not move. Salty lather streamed down her cloak and whipped away into the wind.

Delsorka heard singing as he staggered forward. A woman's voice, weaving through the crashing cacophony of the storm. The sound was gentle, delicate, and soft yet somehow audible over the waves and wind.

Senya's voice.

She swayed with the movements of the boat, her eyes closed. She sang, and the mist swirled around her. She almost disappeared as another wave hit the bow. Still she sang.

Delsorka lumbered toward her. *Very dangerous at sea,* he heard Ghellan's voice in his head. *Could bring forth things that we cannot fathom, even accidentally.*

He shouted her name, but Senya stood motionless. The mist drifted. She slipped in and out of view with the swirling air. For a moment, he lost sight of her completely. Sea spray and fog shrouded the bow. Then the mist opened and she was there, standing as before. Delsorka struggled toward her. Anchoring a second safety cord to the main line at the mast, he stumbled with the loose end in hand.

Her song grew louder. The sound challenged the storm, its words and melody penetrating the wind. The next wave tossed the ship upward, and Delsorka went down to one knee. The power was lesser now, nothing like mere minutes before, as if the storm was quickly losing a battle that nobody on board could see.

Senya sang, and the waves lessened. The fog thickened, but the wind backed away and settled. Her body drifted in and out of view. The waves diminished further, coming at them now with no spray, no power, no punch. The rolling deck of the *Siege Runner* pitched and then settled and calmed. Delsorka strode forward with the safety line. He reached for Senya's waist as a sudden wave crashed against the bow.

The heaving deck drove him back. Delsorka stumbled and fell, sliding backward to the base of the mast.

Senya sang on. The song came from inside him then, like the whisper of a distant lover or his mother's lullaby drifting in from some forgotten memory. The voice of a sister he never had. All the wind and roaring water became static and calm, the *Runner* held motionless above the stale sea.

Senya's song rose to a light crescendo before drifting away into the misty sky. Delsorka shook off the water. He stood to rush back to the stem and get the safety line secured to her. Even though it had strangely settled into stillness, sudden violent storms like this were always dangerous. He took a step, and his heart dropped.

Senya was gone.

PART FIVE

❧ 47 ❧

CRASSICA SENT four men into Raedwin's tower chamber in front of her. All ropy arms and powerful hands, they lunged and drove his body to the floor. Raedwin struggled to make their work as difficult as he could manage, twisting and punching, but none of it mattered. Soon enough, he succumbed. The men bound his wrists, shoved him onto the bed, and secured the bindings to the frame. As Crassica had directed, the men said nothing, asked no questions, and answered none.

She offered no announcement or greeting. Raedwin lay for a long second in stunned silence. Crassica gave him a cold smile and nodded at each of the guards. One placed a bowl on a side table in the alcove next to Raedwin's chair and set a clean cloth alongside. Retreating to the stairwell, they secured the door behind them.

She knew Raedwin would love to ask what she had done with Sadahlia, and why Katliga. What purpose and gain any of this treatment would serve. He would offer whatever he could for his paltry love's freedom or, short of that, attack with fists and curses for what Crassica had done. He clearly wanted to scream. What he likely wanted most was to beat her body back into the Crosslands right here, and be done with her.

But of course Raedwin would know better than all of that. He would know that pleading or fighting would both be pointless. Crassica would do whatever she wanted, and it would not matter what Raedwin said or did. His nonsensical ego would try to explain, try for some release, but none of it would get him anywhere in the end. Not with her.

Wordless, Crassica went to the alcove and sat. Her body moved slowly.

277

Stilted. She had grown so much weaker of late, since those horrible miscreants had choked off her easy access to Amaris. Thankfully, Ghellan had devised other options, other methods to keep her going.

Sunlight slid across the side of her head as she bent forward. Unstopping a small vial, she poured a stream of pale blue liquid into the bowl. Soaking the rag, she lifted it to gently pat the back of her head before sitting back in the shadows. A renewed energy flushed through her tingling skin.

"Tell me," she said, her voice quietly sinister. "Do you ever dream, my sweet?"

Raedwin pulled his arms tight against the restraints. He likely did often dream of leaving this tower, of undoing all the things Crassica had done, and of course he would nightly dream of Sadahlia, but he said nothing. The lad found no reason to play her lovely little game.

She shifted her gaze to the wide western window. "I wonder, do you ever dream of death? Or have you engineered a machine to take you past even that? Death scares most men, but perhaps not you?"

"I will find her, that much I promise," he hissed. "I will get out of this tower, and I will do whatever it takes, at whatever cost. I will find her."

Crassica squeezed the rag against her skin. Her vitality surged. "There are worse places for you than this, my sweet. Be wise and remember that." She wrung the rag hard in the bowl. Dripping sounds echoed through the cold room.

The smell of the liquid began to fill the room—cinnamon, with an acrid undertone. Raedwin would know that smell.

This isn't water in this bowl, is it, my sweet?

Crassica smiled in spite of herself. She had wondered herself how liquefied Amaris would be possible even when Ghellan first proposed it. If the crystalline salts were melted, nobody could touch it—yet his new method allowed her to massage it directly into her skin, which gave her so much energy while using so little of the vital resource. The smoke of Amaris allowed Crassica steady control over her body and helped orchestrate the actions of all her Vallahnir, but as a liquid, the power escalated. After the destruction of her beloved mine, this extra useful application had immediately become essential to her. She needed every ounce for her later purposes.

"I have truly built something here, have I not?" she said at length. "I can breathe your air. I can see your light. I can suffer your wounds. Yet I can still be banished from this world, the same as any other person. Where is the fairness? Where is the justice?"

Light slipped over Crassica's bare pale skin. She sat without moving for a long time. "And yet I fade," she said quietly. "Here, I am only weakness. Dependent upon tools and machinations. In the Crosslands, I was eternal..."

"You're welcome to go back there if you like."

She stiffened at his sharp words. "You say you seek the truth. That you're looking for some deeper knowledge. Well, this is my truth. This false body of mine withers, and my grip is loosening. Amaris has allowed me to sustain myself for years, decades even, to continue on with this self-made body, but you have broken that cycle now, haven't you? You have brought me great difficulty, my sweet. You and your little band of ruffians. And now, time is no longer with me."

Raedwin had very little to say about any of this.

"But hope remains." She gave him a cold smile. "Hope for both of us. As we speak, your sister is on her way to us."

Raedwin's jaw clenched. He let out a sharp and mirthless laugh. "You are wrong."

Crassica's brow raised in mock surprise. "Am I? You think Delsorka sails her north to Faeroen instead of here? Is that what you think?"

Raedwin strained against his bindings. What a fool this simple boy had been. His beloved sister had tried to warn him, but he had not much listened, had he? He never quite listened. Not exactly. He had assumed Senya was safely away, and he had left it at that. Crassica had counted on it. She allowed herself another smile.

"To be born at sea is no small thing," she said. "One becomes uniquely connected to the world in a manner very different from others." She lifted the rag from the bowl and twisted the fibers. "Water is actually the key, you know. The one element we Vallahnir cannot tolerate is also the one element that makes up most of life. Without water, one cannot live. And without being truly alive, no Vallahnir can embrace it." Cupping her hands in the bowl, she sprinkled the liquid over her bare head, fingers gently dancing as each touch gave a prickling tingle to her delicate skin. "And yet Senya comes. Borne on the very waters which gave her life, bringing us a fresh new hope for birth."

Raedwin's teeth gritted against one another in silence. Crassica pinched her brow and cocked her head, as if discovering a novel idea. "I wonder, have you ever heard your sister sing?" she asked abruptly, aiming the question like a barb, like an arrow of thought from a place unexpected yet clear and pure. "I am afraid, my sweet, that our dear Senya has put voice to certain music while at sea—a particular kind of song better left to those who know how to wield it. And as I am sure you know, certain music holds deep powers. Such actions cannot be taken lightly. Her power awakens. Your sister redefines the boundaries of beauty, even now."

"If you've done something to her," Raedwin growled, his voice low, "I swear by all the Knowing..."

"Oh, do not worry yourself, my sweet. Soon brother and sister shall be reunited in glory, as I have said. And then our true convergence can begin."

Raedwin seethed. Both fists clenched as he struggled against the restraints. Finally, he gave up, shaking his head. "May the full fire of all four hells take you," he cursed.

Crassica slowly allowed a cold smile to creep across her face. "You say such kind things, my sweet. Do you not want our little family to all be together, here in your newly permanent home?"

Raedwin did not answer. He never had any proper answer to give. Such a waste. Soon he turned his face to the wall and spoke no more.

Crassica reached, and the Hermit of Montcarsel responded. Together they watched the four Vallahnir climb slowly through the forest. They had served their purpose well. Each day away from the Valle d'Brasti had made them stronger, had clearly taught them how to walk more freely among the living—their gait more measured and assured, sturdier and more confident. They ascended the tower stairs in silence.

Crassica directed the Hermit to lead the Vallahnir to the top floor, open to the misty morning air. They stood next to one another, motionless bodies becoming almost one with the stone. A curious and unnatural mist gathered around them, filling the spaces between. The lead Vallahnir began to sing, her voice penetrating the wet air and pulling the fog in close. Crassica joined her voice with theirs, channeled through the throat of the Hermit himself. The air thickened. Soon all four were lost from view. The song diminished, and then much like the sudden manner in which the fog had arrived, it began to lift. The cloud dissipated. The top floor of the crumbling tower of Montcarsel stood roofless and clear. Crassica herself withdrew as well, leaving the Hermit alone once again.

☙ 48 ❧

SQUARE WINDOWS wrapped the full stern of the *Siege Runner*, lining the entire back wall of Delsorka's cabin. A commanding view of the following sea. The captain paced from side to side, while Maddon stood with his back to the bulkhead. Next to a writing desk in the corner sat the strange necromancer—Ghellan, they'd said his name was. He held a penetrating stare on Senya, increasing her discomfort by the minute.

"There has been a frantic search," the necromancer offered, his slippery voice attempting in vain to remain calm. "We've been trying to find you. We thought you went overboard in the storm."

"Nobody said *overboard*," Maddon insisted. "Nobody saw her go *over* anything. I said she was there, and then she was gone. Into the mist and the storm. Gone."

Delsorka stopped and shook his head. "We thought we lost you," he said gently to Senya. "I saw you disappear. Maddon saw. Anybody on deck saw. At least five of us. You came out in the middle of the storm, strolled up to the bow, started singing, and disappeared. Right into the mist. Just like that."

A few had seen her go, but most had not. Some of the louder ones had proclaimed her a true seaborn goddess who'd lifted herself from the deck and commanded the wind and waves to halt. In trade, she had given herself over to the Knowing. Others claimed she'd been swallowed whole by the gale, and this tranquility was an apology offered by the sea gods themselves.

She didn't argue with any of their stories. The whole thing just confused her.

"I tried to get a lifeline on you," Delsorka continued. "But you vanished before I could. And then the storm just... stopped."

Senya shifted in her chair. She had no real explanation for any of this, and, even if she did, she didn't much care to offer one. Let them figure it out on their own.

The necromancer studied her with an unnerving hushed stillness, taking on some deeper form of observation, as if listening with his whole being. She refused to look at him. She'd had enough of his kind already.

"Describe the song to me again," he said to Delsorka. "You say she was singing?"

"I don't really know how to describe it. It was her voice, light and slow, like it came from inside my own head. Cut right through the noise of the storm."

"And you say she disappeared during this song?"

"Ask anybody who was out here. They all saw. She was there, and then she was gone. That's the only way I can tell it."

"I was asleep," Senya said, her voice steady, repeating again what she'd already explained more than once. "In my cabin."

Ghellan's brow furrowed into deep worry and concern. "Senya," he said gently. "Tell me what you know of the *Saolweald*."

Disturbing tattoos lined both of his eyes, rising to wrap his forehead. What could a necromancer possibly know of the Lifesong?

"How much did your good Brohndai father teach you?"

Senya's father had taught her many things over the years, variations of the Lifesong among them—songs to help living things grow, to ease disease out of a young calf or a goat's kid or to speed the healing of a child. Things this charlatan would know nothing about. Many of the songs had been helpful at times, useful for giving her garden a boost or maybe for some extra coin when things got tight, but mostly they were just pretty. Sometimes when she would sing, not intending to use the Lifesong itself exactly but singing to enjoy the sound, a little bit would sneak its way in without her intending. She didn't ever really control it. Her mind would wander, and she could feel the power come.

"That was a long time ago," she said and left it at that.

Veins bulged along Delsorka's forehead. "I need you to speak plainly, boneshaker," he growled at Ghellan. "I've had just about enough of your wordplay. I don't think you exactly know what you're doing, so get to an explanation for all of this. And do it fast."

Ghellan sat back. "Much in the way the Vallahnir are versed in the music of death, the Brohndai hold the rhythms and vibrations of life. The *Saolweald*, or the Lifesong, as it is called in plain speech, is crafted from the deepest languages of the Way, ringing notes in those same vibrations. It touches the breath of the Knowing herself and has certain suggestive powers. It can be used to persuade, if one desires to do so."

He paused and let out a long sigh, clearly annoyed by needing to explain such basic principles to simple laymen. "Normally it is a tool of guidance and nothing more. Use of it for control is possible, but of course such use would be against the Brohndai Way."

The four of them sat in silence. Ghellan held his gaze on Senya with a relentless steadiness. Shouts echoed from the deck above as the crew restored the ship to working order.

"I don't know if I buy what you're selling," Delsorka said slowly, his voice nearly a snarl. "Doing a job is one thing, but putting my boat at risk for all this shit you're hiding is quite another. You set up that cage down in the hold and told me none of this could happen. That all of it was fine. And Crassica herself left all these details out. I don't like it. I don't like any of this."

"I did not realize she possesses quite this level of power." Ghellan's voice was so low he seemed to speak to nobody but himself. He glanced at Delsorka. "She may have gone inside a deeper styling of the Lifesong and conversed with the sea herself. Something like a sorcerer's trance. At that level, the *Saolweald* could theoretically be used to persuade elementals along with the living. Theoretically. Which would stand to reason if she'd had the deeper training of the Brohndai Elders and would maybe explain the calming of the storm. But her disappearance is another thing entirely."

Delsorka watched Senya, obviously trying to gauge her reaction, to get a sense of what she might be thinking. She gave him nothing. "And your little fancywork down in the hold?" he said to Ghellan. "Tremendously successful all that turned out to be."

"The birdcage does indeed appear to have been less effective than I'd hoped. Which brings me back to my question." He shifted to Senya. "How much do you remember learning of the Lifesong? And how much have you used it in the past?"

Senya did not move. The sea outside the window remained calm and steady, so abrupt after the intensity of the storm. She kept quiet. Her past didn't matter to these men, no matter what she might have to say. And whatever had happened in her life before Pentmore had happened to a different person anyway. Everything now was new.

"And the dreams," Ghellan added quietly. "The strange and powerful dreams you've been having. Like the one you had just now…"

Senya shifted uneasily. How could he know about her dreams? Healers and necromancers were about as opposite as anything could be in this world. They never much liked to speak to one another and definitely never shared information. But this one was clearly more than some simple carnival sorcerer.

"I never said anything about dreams," she said in a low voice.

All her life, men like Ghellan had stared at her as if she were some kind of prize, a specimen for study, some sort of trophy. And Ghellan was worse than most. He watched her with a salacious hunger, as if he'd just found a special toy for play. A fresh pet, bringing him novel games.

"Your vivid dream, just before you woke," he said. "This was not the first of its kind, was it?"

She glanced at him and then snapped her eyes to the floor.

"Describe these dreams for me," he urged.

The steadiness of the sea swirled around her. She pressed her mouth into a thin unbroken line. "No, thank you."

The dreams were fairly ordinary anyway. No need to go into them. Most were nothing remarkable and needed no insight. But a few others were different. More vivid. Alive. Colors and textures would become living things, with voices and stories all their own, more real than anything she had ever known. Trees and stones and rivers would speak to her as if they knew her—like old friends coming together after a long time away. When those appeared, it was like she was inside the truth of things. More real than her waking world. Once in a while they were helpful, but mostly they were useless.

"You saw something this time," Ghellan probed. "Here on the ship. Tell me. What did you see?"

She reached for a nearby tankard and drew in a long swallow of water. Setting it down, she looked at the three men in turn. All watching her. Waiting. Their eyes were different now, filled with an anxious defensiveness.

Here she was, back to being the freak. The gleeman's sideshow on full display. An oddity. One whose talents were to be used but also feared. Delsorka appeared especially concerned. She could sense him. Mostly he was angry with Ghellan, but his unease reverberated to Crassica as well. Whatever deal he'd made with her, Senya was sure this was more than he'd bargained for.

"I was walking through a blue grassland of rolling hills," she said at length, slowly, with reluctance. "The air was clear and fresh, like from a recent rain. It felt like I was going somewhere important, like I was being pulled forward or urged toward something. I thought maybe Raedwin was there. I called his name. I thought I heard him answer, way in the distance, but when I tried to see, a woman was there, right there, as if she'd been following me. Or maybe she lived there. She was tall. Very old and wise. Her eyes were the brightest blue, almost white. I asked if she'd heard my brother just then. She said she could sometimes hear words from the childhood of the earth, from the bones of the rainfall and the bright songs of the sunshine, but she had not heard my brother. She said he was somewhere else but that it would be good for me to find him."

We all must find our brothers and sisters, she said. *The missing parts of ourselves. Rivers return to the sea from whence they came. It is the Way of things.*

"She would not let me pass. I tried to move around her, but every way I turned, she blocked me. Just stood there. Unmovable but gentle—like my mother used to be. She didn't want me to go. She wanted to talk some more. Too much time had passed since we'd seen one another, she said. Since I'd been taken from her. Taken to the other side."

Senya had told the woman she must be mistaken. They'd never met before. She needed to find her brother. He might be in trouble.

"The woman smiled and said she did remember Raedwin, but he was not a child of hers. Not like her daughters. Not like me. Her eyes brightened, and then her whole head shone like the sun. I heard shouts and stomping. And then I woke up lying in my hammock—with all of you running around on the deck. Like I told you."

A silence fell in the room. Ceiling timbers creaked as men worked overhead, running lines and repairing the damaged rigging.

"Hells," Delsorka breathed. "You've got some real juice in you, don't you, little sister?"

Ghellan stroked the left braid of his beard. "This is a power beyond what I have ever seen before," he said idly. "There has been an unlocking. A rift of some kind."

Senya wanted to agree with him, to scream in his face that of course there had been an unlocking, and they were at fault, him and all the others—first in Pentmore, then in the Hallonath, and after that in Corregidon. And now here at sea. Cevellica and Korsta had started it—and now the ocean's life had brought something new. She looked Ghellan dead in the eye.

"None of you understand what is coming for you," she said quietly. She had not meant it to sound like a threat, only a fact. But she was fine with how sinister it came out. Let them understand the threat if they may. Let it be the truth.

Delsorka nodded. "Good to know," he said flatly.

Ghellan shook his head. "The ability to wield the Lifesong unknowingly, while asleep, is far deeper than I would have thought possible…"

"Like I suspected," Delsorka said to him. "You don't much know what you're doing, do you, conjureman?"

"This, if you don't mind my saying, is quite intriguing…"

"Intriguing?" The captain let out a scoffing grunt. "*Intriguing*? Yes, I do mind you saying that. I absolutely mind. That's a load of nonsense. I don't give a shit or a sheck what you find *intriguing*, boneshaker. Not on my boat."

Ghellan ignored him. "For the time being, we should take additional… cautionary measures. The birdcage must be strengthened, to begin with…"

"I blame you for this, Ghellan," Delsorka snapped. "Let me make that much clear. Crassica as well. Both of you are to blame for bringing me into whatever this is and for whatever you've done here. I plan to have words with our Vallahnir master in due time, but as for you, you'll be spending the rest of this voyage down in the hold." He turned to his first mate, pointing at Ghellan. "Maddon, I want this one in shackles. Chain him next to Senya's cabin. Bring him food or water from time to time if you like, but he can shit in his pants where he lies, for all I care."

The captain went to Senya with a look of ache and conflict in his face. For a long moment she watched the word *sorry* form on his lips, but the sound never came. He turned back to the sorcerer. "If anything else happens to her, or to any of my crew, you'll be the first to get tossed overboard."

And with that, Delsorka stormed out of his own cabin.

49

THE *SUMMERHAWK* was barely a day out of Donasberth when her top watch cried out, sighting a single ship on the horizon, directly behind. A two-master under full cloth, apparently tracking their exact course. Brogan stood idly at the taffrail. For two full days, the southern sky ahead had been dominated by a massive storm, with clear skies at their stern. The unseasonal winds had pushed toward the storm, driving down from the north. So unusual for this time of year. But without warning, the strange foul weather had suddenly lifted and disappeared, with no apparent shift in the northerly wind. Nobody on board had ever seen a storm like that arrive so fast or vanish so abruptly. The whole crew was already uneasy.

Freógan stood beside Brogan in silence. Kaetas joined them. She slid open her spyscope and drew focus to scan the horizon.

"She's got up every patch of canvas she's able," the captain muttered. "Plus a bedsheet or two, from the looks of it. Rigged square and fast. She'll be able to harness far more downwind speed than the *Hawk*. She'll close this gap in no time."

"Out to beat all hells," Freógan agreed. "And light on the hull, by the speed of her." He squinted into the distance, studying the pursuit. "I'd say anyone with coin enough to hire kidnappers back in Donny Bay could just as easily send a tall ship after us, packed with assassins or whatever else to keep us from following. Maybe one or two actual sailors as well."

Kaetas had ordered the *Summerhawk* to keep well offshore and out of sight of land, and they'd been doing their best to remain hidden in the vast open sea. After the distant storm had melted away, the skies had parted, and the breeze held. A good omen, if not for the unnaturalness of the whole affair.

Kaetas clapped her spyscope closed and stiffened. Sunlight threw rippling patches over the pitted ocean. Rigging creaked above their heads. They watched in silence for a time as the pursuing sails billowed in the steady breeze. Kaetas glanced up to survey the stream of the *Summerhawk*'s telltales, their slant against the wind, and the shape of her sails.

"We'll never outrun a square rig downwind," she muttered, a deep furrow creasing her brow. "We don't have enough cloth."

"And they've got a good stretch of daylight left."

Kaetas tapped the spyscope against the palm of her hand. "This may get pinchy, Fre. It's not likely that boat's out here for a chat. Let's push out a whisker pole and see if an extra wing'll get us anything."

"Aye." Freógan relayed the order down. Men scurried to the foredeck and began lashing the clip base of a pole to the mast.

"Hells," Kaetas muttered. "If this breeze would swing around to the south where it's supposed to be this time of year, we could come up nice and tight to the wind, while our new square rig girlfriend out there'd have to slog back and forth, climb the wind ladder on tack after tack. She'd have a hell of a time catching up."

She brought the spyscope to her eye and then clapped it closed again. "But not when this hellscursed breeze is right up our backsides." The pursuit had already come close enough to be watched with the naked eye. Tall and white, her sails stretched round and full. The stern of the *Hawk* lifted and settled as a large wave rolled underneath.

"Narrow beam," Freógan said. "Probably deep-keeled. Fast as anything, but she won't be able to maneuver like we can."

"As if that really matters out here." Kaetas stood watching the pursuit before giving a reluctant shake of her head. "All right, Fre," she said, her voice heavy. "Let's get the triggerfish mounts ready."

"Aye, Cap." The first mate's voice came crisp and firm.

Brogan followed Freógan into the dark of the *Summerhawk*'s hold. Filtered daylight swung in lazy shafts over wooden casks, grain sacks, and heavy crates. They strode ahead toward the bow, nimbly weaving past a row of tall clay jars. Freógan crouched over a long wax-coated crate and slapped open the iron clamp lock. He lifted the lid.

Three long bundles lay lengthwise, wrapped tightly in oilcloth. "These little sweethearts don't much care for water," he said. "Or the sun, for that matter." Each bundle was easily as long as a man and half again as wide at the head, tapering to nearly a point at the end. "Everybody said it was a waste of space to keep one of these aboard a ship, let alone three. But sealed up in here, they stay nice and dry." Freógan untied the bindings of one bundle and peeled away the oilcloth.

Brogan had never seen an instrument as elegant and deadly as the weapon before him—something akin to a six-foot crossbow. A set of wooden planks encased the firing end, holding thick torsion springs of sinew. An iron crank sat at the small end of the firing trough.

Freógan grinned at him. "Ever seen one of these before? A Kalldonian Barker. Leftover genius from the late empire. Landers call them scorpions, but sailors call them triggerfish." He heaved the massive weapon onto one edge of the case. "Springs tighten when she's drawn and unleash all four hells when loosed."

They lifted the weapon together. Brogan gripped the heavy body and lashed it to the capstan carry hook. Freógan signaled the hands above to haul it up. The triggerfish rose and swung flashing in the shafted sunlight. The *Hawk* heaved over another swell. Together they grabbed a second.

"They get all the more effective when you add a little Kortugan Fire," Freógan said. "And we've got plenty of that packed down here as well." They retrieved and lashed the second for raising.

"Still full of surprises, Freógan my friend," Brogan said. He lashed the third to be hauled up. "I'll give you that."

They returned to the top deck. A scramble of sailors crouched at the bow to fasten the last triggerfish to the bulwarks. The other two waited along the stern. Each swung easily, mounted to a free motion joint with plenty of room to aim at any angle. Polished bronze and oiled wood shone in the sun.

The sails of the pursuing ship bellied out full and white, less than a mile distant. Brogan could just make out people on her deck. Several archers crowded her rigging and both masthead watch decks.

"We're nearly in her wind shadow," Brunby reported. "She'll have us dead in the water soon enough if we keep this course."

"Okay," Kaetas said. "Looks like it's time. Get the Fire up here, and let's get some warning shots ready. See if she's interested in what we have to show."

Freógan barked orders down to the main deck. Two men spun the capstan to hoist a sturdy chest from the hold, grabbed bronze handles at each end, and hauled it up the steps to the quarterdeck. Kaetas swung open the heavy lid. At least twenty thin sausage-like bags filled the chest, each stuffed with a dull green sludge. She slowly inspected the bags, running her fingers along each length.

"There be our little secret sister," Brunby said to Brogan with a grin. "Kortugan Fire, stuffed all trim and neat into links of cow belly. Cap'n there devised the method herself. Those spicy sausages get lashed to spears, and we light em up. Usually makes for a hell of a short fight."

Kaetas closed the lid and stood with a satisfied nod. Two sailors laid out a series of short wooden spears, each almost five feet long, with sharpened tips and wide feathered tails. Outsized arrows, made for giants.

Kaetas held the spyscope to her eye and studied the pursuing boat. Her jaw clenched. "Range?" she called.

"I'd make it five furlongs," Freógan replied from the taffrail. "Maybe a little less."

"I'd second that, yes. Let's load some blanks. Aim for that nice little carving she's got sticking out front. Wipe that smile off her hellscursed face."

The men at the two stern triggerfish cranked their winches. Both bow arms bent as the firing carriages pulled back. Twisted sinew creaked and groaned in protest. With the weapons fully drawn, they set the firing pins and dropped a naked spear into each trough.

"On your call, Fre," Kaetas said.

"Starboard ready!" the massive bearded man cried. "Loose!"

The triggerfish erupted with a sound of snapping iron, sinew, and wood—a weapon of bone and truth giving voice to fluid song. Brogan barely saw the projectile launch. He'd never seen anything fly that fast. The dark spear made a smooth arc over the liquid distance to the pursuing ship and splashed to the side of her bow.

"Port!" cried Freógan. "Loose!"

The second triggerfish clapped with a loud iron snap. The huge spear streaked across and easily perforated the small foresail of the pursuing ship before splashing into the sea off her starboard bulwarks.

"Load!" cried Freógan.

"All right," Kaetas muttered, spyscope to her eye. "Let's see if that got anybody's attention."

Three archers at the masthead of the pursuing ship loosed in return, only to find the arrows from their longbows splash down less than half the reach to the *Hawk*, even with the wind at their backs. Kaetas dropped the spyscope and shook her head. "Another example, if you please."

Freógan cried out the order, and two more triggerfish spears let loose. The first hit with a crack and bounced away from the ship's bow, while the second glanced off a spar. Kaetas raised the spyscope to her eye. The pursuing ship made no move to turn away. A few of the more confident archers raised their longbows high, trying for distance. Their arrows splashed far short, utterly harmless.

"Determined, aren't they." Kaetas dropped the spyscope and sighed. She shook her head. "Nobody ever believes." She glanced back at the flurry of activity on the quarterdeck. Two sailors stoked a small iron brazier behind the mizzenmast. "All right," she said. "Let's get this dance started. Brunby, I need you up front, if you please."

"Aye." The old bosun grinned. He leapt down the sheer steps to the main deck.

Kaetas shouted an order to bring the *Summerhawk* up into the wind. Senya would have to wait. They needed to deal with this threat first and would get back southward in due course. Sails tightened and booms swung as the deck planks and hull complained. The *Hawk* circled eastward back toward the Cellenway coast, continuing around to northeast by north. The pursuing ship altered course directly into their path.

"We can't shoot Kortugan Fire with the wind blowing into our rigging," Kaetas explained to Brogan. "Can't risk any sparks flying back at us. So we need to sail into the wind as tightly as we can and shoot off our backside. That's the only way this trick works."

"They'll try to cut us off."

"They'll try, yes, but the *Hawk* is tricky. She sails differently from what most in the North are used to, and that glorified merchant over there is likely to misjudge us. Many have. Not many survive it."

As the wind came over the *Hawk*'s beam and then across her bow, the distance between her and the other ship closed quickly.

"But," Kaetas added in a more measured tone, "part of why nobody is dumb enough to try this stunt is because you can just as easily blow yourself to the Everlife if you don't do it exactly right." She shook her head with a grin. "So we're gonna be real careful. Once we slip past, she can't follow us tight into the wind. We'll have a clear shot. And then, with the wind at our bow, we can rain Kortugan Fire down on her all day long."

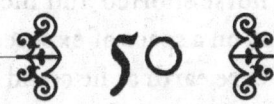

50

FOUR KNOCKS came to Raedwin's door, as promised, sooner than he'd dared hope. The door opened and stood ajar, but nobody entered. No voices called for him. Raedwin took in an uncertain breath and rose.

The stairs were empty. He retrieved a fresh torch from its bronze wall brace and descended, continuing below ground, down steps drilled into living bedrock. He passed into hallways and tunnels and turned toward the heart of the Keep, in the direction of the pit. Moving quickly past the cages and instruments of discarded misery, he soon reached the hallway on the far side, heading westward. The narrow tunnel led straight and true, its walls smooth and well-crafted. The air was drier here, less trapped and compressed than under the rest of the Keep. He moved quickly. The passage soon ended at a wide round room, its ceiling reaching to a dizzying height. A narrow stairway climbed the entire sheer expanse of wall.

Springing up the stairs, Raedwin crossed into an abandoned basement storeroom at the top. Empty barrels lay broken apart in the far corner, with scraps of rat-strewn burlap nearby. He made his way up a final series of steps into the moonless starlight. Outside. Free.

The waiting horse appeared to be healthy and strong. Raedwin approached and ran his hand along her flank. A stout shortsword sat in a scabbard strapped to the saddle, and a water gourd hung from the pommel. A bedroll and oilskin food pouch were tucked securely alongside.

He quickly untied the reins and mounted. Urging the horse south, he sought to avoid the open causeway, seeking out low and hidden folds of land. He held his body against the horse's back as they crested a rise, hiding as best he could against any shadowed profile. As soon as enough distance had passed, he slowed the horse to a stop.

This was as good a spot as any. He would not have the benefit of places rich with energies left by the Old Ones, like the symbol-carved hills east of the Keep, but the earth itself would help. The best he could do for now. Maybe it would be enough.

He dismounted. The horse snorted and flicked her tail. Crouching low, Raedwin placed a palm on a space of exposed granite and pushed his other hand as deeply into bare earth as he could manage.

Senya, he called. Driving his thoughts northward, he reached across the sea to Brinsfallon, and north to Stronaway and Montroath. Past the Horn. Seeking Faeroen.

Senya, he called.

No answer came. No sense of her anywhere. Nothing moving northward along the Great Brinsfallon Way, nor up in Stronhaven.

But then, a flicker. A sense came to him, little more than a heartbeat. Heavily blocked and caged. Floating. With reverberations of the Lifesong, somewhere off the Cellenway coast, moving south. A resonant wake left behind in the water.

Something had happened. Delsorka must've gotten to her, like Crassica had said. Maybe Senya had passed Lophlyn already. Maybe she was inside the Gulf of Dunnen, on her way south to the Valle d'Brasti.

His sister was indeed coming here after all.

Raedwin rose, brushing himself off. He had to move fast. Mounting again, he spun the horse to the west.

"All right," he said into her ear as he gripped the reins. "We've got work to do. You know the way to Katliga?"

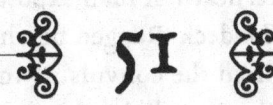

51

"BRUNBY!" KAETAS shouted to the foredeck. "What's your call?"

The bosun glanced up at the streaming telltales and surveyed the *Hawk*'s sail shape. "She can go five points closer, I'd say."

"Five points closer up, Privos," Kaetas called to the helmsman. "And hold her there."

Privos acknowledged the order and gave the wheel a slight turn. The *Hawk* swung a bit farther north, tighter into the wind. The deck heeled as the pursuit came at them.

"When you're ready, Brun!" Kaetas called. "She'll be on us soon enough."

Brunby barked orders on the foredeck. The men at the forward trigger-fish scrambled to crank and load the weapon. Kaetas called for everybody out of the rigging and for shields to be laid along the port bulwarks. Her voice was loaded with a fresh gravity. Men scrambled across the deck. A handful down in the hold handed up a mismatched series of various fighting shields. Some displayed sigils of houses long since shattered, and some showed forgotten remnants of families scattered across all the Inner Islands. A few boasted no signs at all. Most were pocked and marked with split clefts and arrow divots.

The pursuing ship came nearly head-on. She pointed a line directly for the *Summerhawk*'s port bow, as if on course to ram her. The first arrows came in a vague spread across the sky, loosed more for distance and angle than a focused attempt to kill. They fell among the *Hawk*'s rigging and sails, clattering across the open foredeck. A few stuck hard in the planks and shields.

The *Hawk*'s forward triggerfish cracked a report, sending a heavy spear out low and hard. Shrieks echoed as the shaft wreaked havoc across the deck of the other ship.

The *Summerhawk* kept her course northeast by north, heeling hard and sailing fast and straight. Her portside shield wall offered a sliver of protection to those huddled underneath. A man exposed against the mainmast howled and collapsed to the deck. Ragged fletching quivered in his side. Brogan flew to him and lifted the convulsing man as two more arrows clattered across the deck. Carrying him to the hatch, Brogan lowered the man down to the relative safety of the lower deck.

The pursuing ship came on, as did her arrows. Brogan crouched against the shield wall to wait for more wounded. A man struggled to bind his own leg, huddled underneath the quarterdeck steps. Blood streamed from his torn thigh.

"Loose!" Brunby cried, and the *Hawk*'s forward triggerfish responded again. The shaft arced over the space between boats and tore through sail and rigging alike, ripping cloth and rope away. Minor damage, and mostly ineffective. The pursuing ship closed in. As she drew near, she circled into the wind to come alongside. Several men armed with heavy crossbows scrambled along her starboard side. One shot into the air, launching a hooked anchor over the short distance between the ships, trailing a long heavy rope behind. The hook landed on the deck of the *Hawk* forward of the mainmast and slid to catch against the bulwarks. The rope snapped taut. Two more hooks came in and caught on various pieces of deck hardware, rigging, and rail.

Brogan was at the ropes in an instant. His bright shortsword flashed as he hacked at the taut braids. Arrows flew around him. Still he hacked. The first rope snapped. Then the second. The pursuing ship hurled heavy stones from a small deck-mounted trebuchet, crashing through the rigging. One caught an unlucky man with an ugly punching sound across his temple. He collapsed to the deck. Another smashed a wide hole in the portside shield wall and shattered a man's leg in the process.

Brogan chopped through the third rope. The *Hawk* heeled again and powered forward. Two more hook anchors flew in but found no solid purchase on the quarterdeck. He rushed to the head-struck man splayed on the deck. Blood spread from behind his head. Rolling him over to inspect the wound, Brogan found that most of his face was missing, depressed into a purple-gray mass with toothy fragments of white skull bone exposed. This one was gone.

Brogan pushed the dead man's body against the mainmast and lashed it fast. The last thing anybody needed was a corpse sliding around a blood-slippery deck. Freógan cried for the triggerfish to keep firing.

"Steady on!" shouted Kaetas from the stern. "Steady on! She's almost past!"

The pursuing ship had indeed misjudged speed and distance and would cross behind them by a wide margin. She could not pinch the wind as tightly as the *Summerhawk*, as Kaetas had said. Both taffrail triggerfish sent out a volley of spears. Crashes and screams sounded in return.

Passing the stern, the pursuing ship started to clear eastward. Arrows flew. Archers lined her rails and clung to her rigging and stood in the top decks. With a sudden cry, Privos slumped away from the wheel of the *Summerhawk* and collapsed to the deck. Two heavy fletchings protruded from his bleeding back. The wheel spun, and the *Hawk*'s bow slipped uselessly up into the wind. Her sails flapped empty, and she quickly limped to a crawl. More arrows flashed across her quarterdeck. Kaetas leapt to the wheel and cranked it back to proper position. The *Hawk* swung back to true. Her sails filled. She regained power and heeled over, shoving headlong through the swells.

Brogan jumped up the sheer steps to the quarterdeck and knelt next to Privos. One arrow protruded from his right shoulder blade, and the second from the side of his lower back. The young man moaned with pain. Brogan quickly snapped off both arrow shafts. Privos winced. An arrow buried itself in the planks next to him. Crouching to hoist the smaller man over his shoulder, Brogan made his way down to the main deck, lowering him to healers in the hold.

The gap grew as the pursuing ship sailed farther to the east, unable to draw the *Hawk*'s tight line upwind. Arrows grew more sporadic, and soon they would be out of range altogether.

"Brunby!" Kaetas called as a feebly shot arrow crashed to the deck next to her feet. "Get up here and get the fire ready! She's about to come around!"

Two men lowered a square of sailcloth to soak in the frothy sea off the stern. They hoisted it dripping back on board, spreading it on the deck planks behind the wheel. Brunby strode up to the quarterdeck. With cautious care, he removed several thin bladders of Kortugan Fire and laid them on the wet sailcloth. He lashed the first casing to the middle of a waiting spear. A balled-up wad of oiled pitch sat at the base of the long steel broadhead. A flying torch, ready for lighting. Brunby started lashing a second.

The pursuing ship swung toward the north and then tacked through to the northwest. She lined a course to pass westward behind them, struggling to stay close enough to get back into arrow range. She would have to climb the wind ladder to stay in the fight at all, as long as the *Summerhawk* sailed north, into the wind. The taffrail triggerfish launched its last naked spear, and the men quickly cranked the firing carriage back to load. Sporadic arrows flew in among them.

"Hold fast," Kaetas called. "Not until she comes across our stern."

Soon Brunby had seven shafts waiting on the soaked sailcloth. Narrow bladders of Kortugan Fire sat glistening along the bodies of the loaded spears. Brunby lifted one with great care and laid it into the firing trough of the nearest triggerfish. He moved to load the second.

"Steady and hold," Kaetas called.

The pursuing ship neared the wake of the *Hawk*. Kaetas glanced up to check wind direction, sail shape, and airflow over the telltales. They'd need to shoot off the starboard side to make sure the wind wouldn't push any fire back their way. Another volley of arrows clattered across the quarterdeck.

The pursuit passed the stern.

"There's our mark, Fre!" Kaetas called. "We're clear. Light her up!"

Freógan snapped out a few quick orders. A sailor dipped a small iron torch into the brazier near the mizzenmast and lit the tip of the starboard spear.

"Loose when you're ready," Freógan called.

The men swung the triggerfish, aimed, and loosed. The weapon clapped its fierce wood and iron release. A ball of flame sparked across the sky, leaving chunks of burning material in its path. The spear splashed in the sea close behind the pursuing ship. Flames spread over the water, erupting across the surface and discharging a column of billowing black smoke into the air.

"Holy hells," Brogan muttered. "It really does burn on water."

Brunby grinned. "The legends you've heard are true," the old bosun said. "Nothing can put out Kortugan Fire." He ducked as a small volley of arrows came in. "That's why we make a point of being ever so very careful when we use it."

"Loose!" Freógan called. The second triggerfish launched in a flurry of flame, arcing across the space between the ships. Fire exploded on the starboard bow, splashing furious orange flames over her foredeck and into her rigging. Screams from the other ship. Freógan called for a reload.

The men at the triggerfish cranked and loosed a second set of flaming spears. The first crashed across the quarterdeck and stern, lighting the wheel and taffrail immediately ablaze. The second hit forward of her middle, right below the bulwarks. A splatter of Kortugan Fire gushed across her hull. A man squealed a shrieking yell, his clothing sprouting flame and smoke. He slapped at himself in a frantic panic and fell backwards over the rail into the burning sea.

"Loose again," Freógan called, and two more flaming spears launched. The first fell short, its fire spreading harmlessly over the water in front of the ship's bow. The second split her foresail almost in half. Fire ate across both pieces of heavy canvas. Chunks of flaming sail fell windward down to the deck and rigging, spreading the fire yet farther. More screams from the deck. Almost the entire ship was engulfed in flame. Nobody worked her wheel.

The doomed ship swung and drifted, slipping head to wind, dead in the water. She drifted away from the *Hawk*. Men splashed buckets on flames and over the sails and rigging in a desperate attempt to hold her together. Two men jumped overboard.

"One last set," Kaetas ordered. "And then she's done."

A final pair of flame-filled spears launched into the burning ship. A towering column of black smoke reached into the northern sky as the sun drifted toward the horizon in the west. Three more men dove into the sea, one with his back ablaze.

"Hold," called Kaetas. "That's enough."

The men at the triggerfish relaxed their weapons as the carnage unfolded. Huge angry flames poured upward from the cracking ship and fed a cloud of black smoke surging into the sky. One of the spars collapsed with a heavy crash to the deck. Then another. The last few wails died away. No life could be left on board.

Silence crept across the deck of the *Summerhawk*. No great sense of victory pervaded. No gratitude flared. Ugliness gushed forth from the disintegrating ship behind them as they took on the onerous burden of lives they had extinguished only a moment before. Sailors much like themselves. Men and women on the other side of some odious transaction in a darkened room somewhere, easy money exchanged days before by indifferent superiors deciding their fate.

"Freógan," Kaetas called. "Ready us to come about. Bring her across the wind and get us out of here. I want a damage and casualty report as soon as we're able." She glanced at the evening sky. "We have two or three hours of light left. Get us clear of this wreckage before any of this fire comes back to bite us."

52

THE KIND of place Raedwin sought could usually be found alongside riverbanks or near docks and shaded warehouses in parts of cities that lived and sang only in the night, where smoke and refuse choked away unwary wanderings in flagrant daylight. The kind of place where pleasure and pain waited on either end of a whispered transaction. Cool, forgotten corners that allowed one to hide—from other people, from the law, or even from one's own self.

Raedwin led his horse across the river. Beggars lined both stone embankments, this bridge being Katliga's central link between Kalldon to the south and Darizi to the north. Water glittered over white pebbles below the teeming din. Stepping off the dusty high street on the far bank, he passed Kalldonian concrete buildings with fired brick faces. Woven baskets hung in high dark windows, scattered among dangling vines. Men stood smoking in the shadows.

The place should be right here. Manka had been specific, and Raedwin had memorized and repeated the details. A red tiled landing with a blue oaken door. A black and white archway over the street, east of the watchtower and before the Temple of the Wayward Sun. But nothing resembled Manka's landmarks. The streets shifted in imperceptible ways and defied direction, crossing at odd angles that he couldn't quite understand.

Raedwin stopped and took his bearings again. Long poles reached from shopfront tops to grip awnings of rough-spun canvas, offering pools of shade in the glaring streets. Bins of firewood sat next to baskets of grain below hanging tendrils of dried meats. A stonemason chipped at a grave marker nearby.

He must have missed a turn, gotten off the proper path, and found himself in the wrong place. Perhaps he should go back to the eastern gate again and retrace his steps.

"You seek the Alabaster Dove," a man's quiet voice came from over his shoulder. Raedwin turned to find a hooded figure cloaked all in white, standing uncomfortably close and yet facing away, idly examining fruits in a shopfront bin.

"Do I...?" Raedwin said with hesitation.

"Do not speak directly to me. Not here. I am known in this city."

Raedwin took a step away, leading the horse out of the bustling flow of people and wares. The man followed casually along the shopfronts.

"You are Raedwin of the North," the man said after a time, barely audible, still facing away.

"Maybe," Raedwin answered. "Maybe not."

The man chuckled quietly. "You must realize you are not difficult to spot. How many sons of a Brohndai do you see leading a frothy horse through these streets? A horse recently run hard for some distance, perhaps from as far away as the Valle d'Brasti...?"

Maybe this was Manka's man. The connections ran deep and true. If this had been Crassica's hand, they'd have grabbed and taken him without hesitation, no matter who witnessed it.

"Black light shines from the mountains of the west," he offered.

"And so it shines as well from within one's own soul," the man answered correctly.

So it was Manka's man. He stepped away and strolled down a shaded side alley. Raedwin followed, drawing the horse behind. The tall stone walls slanted inward, pinching away the blazing sky. Dark windows frowned over unlit torch mounts. Long flower braids hung from a doorway, their red flow like a frozen waterfall of blood. After a time, the man stopped and turned to Raedwin, pulling the hood from his head to reveal a burn-scarred brown face. Piercing dark eyes under a shock of curling black hair.

"You seek the Alabaster Dove," the man said again.

"Is she alive?"

"Yes, she is alive. As much as her kind is able to be."

Three hogs grunted at some scraps in a gutter. A burdened donkey struggled past, heaped over with sacks of bolt cloth and an assortment of misshapen craft. An aging jacktender followed, prodding with a long thin pole.

"It is a wicked place you desire to go," the man said after the jacktender had passed. "Where she is held... is not easy. I can take you there, but you are unlikely to find it pleasing."

"I didn't come here for pleasure."

The man led Raedwin through side streets away from the crowds. Arched windows loomed overhead, their unlit interiors hidden from the street. Smoke drifted from meats searing on heated iron plates. Soon they came to a narrow doorway set into a tiled wall painted with blue and black flowers—leftover beauty from some lost prior purpose. The man stopped and offered to hold Raedwin's horse.

"This is the exit for the place you seek, and therefore better for secret entry," he said. "It is still morning and so is mostly unguarded. Many patrons have not yet arrived. You should find your work easier by entering this way."

"You're not coming?"

"It is important that your horse remains here, ready to ride. Leaving the city with your prize might prove more difficult than you anticipate."

Raedwin took a step toward the door in the seething heat. He stopped and turned back to the man. "What is your name?"

The man's dark eyes glittered. "We do not have names here, Raedwin of the North—none that should be known or ever repeated."

Raedwin stepped through the door and plunged into darkness. He waited. The low glow of lamps showed a long hallway lined with doors. Somewhere a man moaned with pleasure.

A sagging crone stepped from a doorway and let out a yell at the sight of Raedwin. She disappeared down the hall. Raedwin rushed after her. Painted faces of pleasuregirls appeared and vanished. Doors slammed closed. The crone's cries died away.

A man stepped from the shadows and barred Raedwin's path. Pinched face like a trapped rat. "Excuse me," he said in the sharp accent of the Baked Plains nomads far to the south. "This is not a proper entrance." He reached to take Raedwin's arm. "You must go back and..."

Raedwin jerked his arm away. "Where is she?"

"There are many women in this house... to which *she* do you refer?" The man grabbed at Raedwin's arm again. "Perhaps if you go back and..."

Raedwin spun and slammed him against the wall. The rat-faced man fumbled quickly for a thin curved blade. Raedwin rammed the pommel of his sword into his mouth, and the man collapsed. His body fell against the wall into an awkward, crumpled heap.

"Are you the one running the show around here?"

The now toothless man sputtered and went silent.

The crone returned and lunged at Raedwin, brandishing a long dagger. Raedwin jumped back. Her blade flashed. The man on the floor let out a groan as the woman waved her dagger, passing it back and forth through the air in front of her. Raedwin grabbed her wrist. He drove her back and pushed her arm up, pinning it against her chest. The dagger fell away. He held her throat against the wall.

"Where is she?" Raedwin demanded. "The *Alabaster Dove*?"

The woman stuttered and let out a stream of incomprehensible words in some local Katligan dialect.

"Where is she?" Raedwin repeated.

The woman continued to bellow, shook her head, and repeated the same incoherent phrases.

"Who's in charge? Who runs this place?"

The woman pointed down the hall. Raedwin released her. She slid down the wall and crawled toward the crumpled rat-faced man, whimpering questions as she reached to stroke his matted hair.

Raedwin strode toward the shadows at the far end of the hallway and stopped. A short set of stairs led down into a torchlit chamber of hanging curtains. He could narrowly make out the corner of something resembling a drink-serving station. Voices and low music flickered from somewhere beyond. A second set led up into lamplight.

Raedwin bounded upward and found a long hallway at the top of the stairs. A face ducked away as a door to the side closed. The hallway ended at a wooden door with no apparent handle. Raedwin approached with caution and then stopped. He listened. Another cry came from downstairs, possibly the old crone again. Then silence. Raedwin raised a boot and kicked at the door, which flew inward, slamming against its own hinges, one of which shattered and left the door askew against the wall.

A pale man sat behind an oaken desk. His jowls hung soft and plump over a scarlet collar. A loose-fitting jerkin draped from his shoulders. Shining black hair lay in long thin lines backward from his forehead to a thick fleshy neck.

"The door was open," the man said. "There was no need to..."

"Where is she?"

The man gave a lascivious grin. "So the lover of Death finally comes."

"Where is she?"

"You are not one for kindness, are you? Such things like using front doors, embracing common formalities like knocking, showing respect...?"

"Where is she?"

"One finds things so much easier when one shows respect."

"If you've harmed her, you will see my respect."

"Harm is such a relative thing..." The man drew his ample fingers across the polished surface of the desk, sliding several papers into a leather folding case.

"Where is she? I'm getting tired of asking..."

"You, my lover friend, seek our Alabaster Dove, no?"

"Her name is Sadahlia."

"And in seeking her, you propose to storm into places that do not welcome you, entering through transgressive ways, breaking things and destroying doors, to demand her release? To fulfill your purpose? Surely you understand that we are equipped here to defend ourselves against the rabble. Against unsavory actions from our patrons."

"Where is she?"

The brothelkeeper gathered the leather case and set it into an alcove beside the desk. "What if I were to tell you that she no longer wished to remain among the living and has since returned to the Crosslands without you?"

"I would damn you to all four hells."

"Or perhaps she has achieved a full understanding of her existence here among us and simply no longer wishes for silly trysts with her dark lover from the North."

"You will tell me where you have her, or I will cut that fat head from your waste of a body and find her myself."

The man grinned. His teeth glowed yellow in the low light. He tapped the desktop and shrugged, holding his palms out wide. "But, my lover friend, she has gone from this place. I do not have what you seek..."

"Where is she?"

"You may go and see for yourself. Hidden steps to your lover's former chambers lead down from this very room, yet you will find that she is gone."

"Where have you taken her?"

"I have taken her nowhere. Perhaps she has gone home? Perhaps the men who generously brought her to us have retrieved her back into the arms of the master herself?"

"Is she still alive?"

"There is no need for your histrionics."

"Is. She. Still. Alive?"

The man's jowls bulged as he nodded. "She lived when she was taken from here. That is all I know."

Raedwin glanced around him. "And where's her room? Where are these stairs?"

The man lifted his sizable bulk from the chair and reached to slide open a hidden panel along the wall behind his desk. Stairs led downward into darkness.

"You may see," the man purred. "But will seeing allow you to know?"

Raedwin pushed the man forward to the top of the stairs and yanked a torch from the wall. "All right," he ordered. "Let's take a walk."

"You are determined to find your doom, aren't you?" the man muttered. He spun on his heel and started down the stairs, striding a tight spiral into the earth. Raedwin followed with sword in hand. The guts of the city connected here through dripping caverns housing sewer chambers and watery refuse.

After a time, they came to a wide cistern with a stone pathway circling the central basin. Spent torches hung limply on the walls. Raedwin's own flickering light glinted across a shining black pool several feet below. A narrow wooden bridge reached in a long arc over the cistern to an open cage suspended over the water.

Raedwin urged the man ahead of him over the bridge. The empty cage held a generous bed in the middle, along with an elegant writing desk in the corner.

"You see?" the man said. "She is gone."

"Yeah, well..." Raedwin said as he shoved the brothelkeeper off the bridge. The man splashed and resurfaced and shouted curses and plagues upon Raedwin, pulling three separate languages into the tirade. Raedwin ignored him. His torch guttered and wrestled with the shadows. He rushed back to the stairs, leaving the screaming brothelkeeper behind in darkness. The circular path led him back to the surface and the doorway outside, to his horse, and to the blinding full light of day.

53

SADAHLIA'S RETURN had been quick and simple. They'd bound her hands again and led her to a waiting carriage before hauling her at speed over the long miles between Katliga and the Valle d'Brasti. Now she lay again suspended in an iron cage over water, deep in the quarries below the Keep. Somewhat smaller than the one under the streets of Katliga, this was a carefully fashioned version of the same, with an ornate set of bars that had probably served as an aviary in a former life. Curtains hung at all four corners beside the lavish bed, allowing for a thin semblance of privacy, though nobody would come to see her. Not here, kept hidden from the world, deep under Crassica's own home.

Still no word of Raedwin. Did they have him, or had he gotten away? Was he here in the Keep? Or lost somewhere in the wilderness?

Steps on stone echoed through the halls above, drawing near—maybe coming to her chamber, her cage, her newly exalted bedroom. Torchlight spilled into the vaulted chamber, reflecting off the pool below.

"Good evening, your worship," came the voice of Lanius. "It's so nice to have you back home."

He strode over the short bridge to her cage, confident in his movements, in his place in this world, in his ability to move at will, anywhere at any time.

"Our princess of the Crosslands," he said. "Untouchable. Unknowable. So elevated, so lauded for all these long years living here among us, and yet now here you are, reduced to this." He shook his head. "So shameful.

Tragic, I would say. Yet admittedly I was beginning to enjoy the extra coin you were making me in Katliga."

He held keys on a chain, brushing their brass tips against the iron mechanism of the lock. He let them hang inches out of reach. "A man deserves respect in his own house, you know. And yet you never quite saw fit to utter my name, did you? Not here in these halls, not for all these years. Perhaps you would like to utter it now? Ask for forgiveness? For release? Death, perhaps? Then maybe you could go and find your lover. I wonder... is he there already, in the Crosslands, passing through to the Underworld without you?" Lanius looked down at the glistening pool under the bridge, as if pondering some deeper truth that could only be found there.

"When darkness finally falls," he said after a long moment. "To whom does a lonely Vallahnir pray? Who hears the call when an agent of Death herself wishes to be heard? Who listens when she cries out in fear or pain?"

Sadahlia rose without words and stepped to the iron bars. She said nothing.

"Does she call upon the Knowing?" Lanius continued. "Even after all of this, after all her transgressions, all her failings. Or does she call out for Crassica, her living and sovereign queen, also born of the immeasurable Crosslands herself? Does she beg for Her High Honor's kind and generous mercy?"

In silence, Sadahlia drew the thick bloodred curtain closed, concealing the bars, the locked door, and the coldly grinning face of Lanius on the other side.

"We of course can't have you simply dying on us, can we?" he called. "That little escape trick would not do, would it, my dear Sadahlia? That would not do at all."

She did the same with the remaining curtains, effectively blocking away the world outside her plush aviary and the guttering, mocking torchlight of Lanius along with it.

❧ 54 ❧

AFTER TWELVE days locked in the hold of a ship at sea, Senya was almost glad to be locked in a carriage for the ride overland instead. Still a prisoner, at least now she could look out the windows and watch the teeming streets of Kalldon pass by. Delsorka rode alongside her. Polished wood and finely wrought brass adorned the carriage interior. Plush curtains hung beside the windows. Something in the engineering of the wheels and axles kept their ride exceptionally smooth. Maybe Raedwin himself had designed it.

Ghellan had wanted to join as well, but the captain had thankfully refused. After the storm, he'd clearly wanted no more of that strange necromantic sorcerer. Despite everything else, Delsorka did seem to care at least a little bit about Senya, in his own way. It was all less than ideal, but at least he'd wanted to make her as comfortable as he could during the remainder of the voyage. He'd come to her cell countless times asking after her comfort, apologizing over and again for the lack of view, the stale air, and her general confinement. Occasionally he brought maps to let her know their position and course, as well as what they were expecting from the weather.

Maybe he wanted to ensure she didn't do anything else that might sink his ship underneath him.

Senya had appreciated the updates but barely listened. She'd mostly thought of Raedwin and her inability to see him, to find him, or to feel his presence. Ghellan had done something to strengthen her confinement aboard the ship, and now the blockage around this carriage was strong as well. Probably orchestrated by Crassica herself. Did she hold a veil over all of central Kalldonia?

She wondered if Kaetas and Brogan had left Donasberth or if they would try to follow her. Did they know where she'd been taken? Most likely not. Most likely she was on her own. This would be her fight from here on out, in a foreign land, unable to see or connect to anything.

The day cleared, and the sun drifted behind. A brisk wind rose some time after they crossed the Mondini River. The speed they made would quickly break most horses down, but they never slowed. Senya worried for them. Late in the evening, an ancient and partially ruined citadel came into view, with a soaring Keep perched on the bluffs above. Senya counted five towers, or what remained of them, with a sixth peering out from the far side. The ruins of a seventh appeared to have given violent birth to an iron spire holding a glass scepter aloft. Black smoke rose from a few stout chimneys scattered among the lower buildings below the massive Keep.

The carriage passed through the crumbling shell of a great gate. Inside, activity swarmed around a small courtyard. The number of people surprised her. She'd pictured Raedwin alone in a solitary windswept tower on some distant barren hill, but this place was bustling, full of workers and servants. Craftspeople of all kinds.

The carriage came to a stop. Delsorka alighted and offered his hand to Senya. His calloused grip bore a raw strength that held surprising gentleness and grace. He gave a low, formal bow. "Welcome to the Valle D'Brasti," he said. "Home to Her High Honor Crassica the White, and, of course, your dear brother Raedwin."

After a quick and quiet word with one of the hosts, Delsorka led her past several structures, some used as homes and workplaces and some clearly left to ruin. Several armed men walked with her, two to either side, and a few others behind. Their path took them across an arching stone bridge into the Keep above.

She reached for Raedwin, letting herself float beyond her body to listen, searching for his beating heart, the warmth of his blood shared with hers, and the strength of his voice. But she felt nothing. No presence, no pulse. The blockage was stronger here, in Crassica's own stronghold.

Where could he be?

But then a glimmering flare came to her, burning somewhere deep below her feet, buried beneath layers of stone and bedrock. Not Raedwin exactly, but something connected, a candle in a vast and empty chamber. A resolute yearning, like a fleeting dream reaching out to her with a sense of unshakable hope.

And then it was gone.

Well, at least that was a start. A little something to go on.

Soon they came to a carved door, the wood worn by time and weather. As they approached, it opened from within, seemingly of its own accord. Delsorka lit a lamp and led Senya down a winding stone stair that spilled into an underground hallway. Elegant marble graced the floor. Kalldonian pine lined both walls, with iron pillars bracing the vaulted stone ceiling.

The hallway widened as they descended a set of marble steps, leading to an imposing entrance at the far end. A strange bronze mouth mounted to the wall on one side. Delsorka stopped midway at a beautifully carved door and opened it to enter a small but well-appointed room. A large oaken table dominated the center, spread with a great feast. A roaring fire in the hearth.

"Apparently they figure you're hungry." Delsorka strode past the table. He threw open a second door to reveal another comfortable space. A feather bed crouched against the wall, with a dressing stool and armoire to one side. A small oil lamp gave the windowless space a welcoming glow.

"Well, here you are," he said. "Make yourself comfortable. Feel free to eat whatever you want in there. I'm sure somebody will be along shortly to see to the rest of your needs."

"Do you know where my brother is?"

"Sadly, no. I only met him once, and I don't know where he spends his time. But I'm sure you'll see him soon enough."

And with that, he gave his leave and departed.

Senya sat on the edge of the bed. A washbasin and mirror stood against the far wall, and a set of gowns hung on a rack in the corner. She tried to concentrate now that she was alone and resting, tried to sense her brother's presence and seek him out again. But the entire Keep and citadel all seemed empty. Even the faint glimmer below was now subdued, almost missing entirely.

Hunger suddenly overcame her. She couldn't recall when she'd last eaten—before or after they'd docked in Kalldon? Back aboard the *Siege*

Runner, she had not eaten her fill. The smells in the hold and the motion of the ship hadn't offered the most pleasant dining experience. She rose and swung open the heavy door.

The table remained spread with food, yet a seated woman now waited at the far end—or rather the pale simulacrum of one. All bloodless angles and bones, she was hairless, similar to Cevellica, but glimmering with a clean purity as if some strange artifice lay upon her. She pressed long fingers onto the table and rose as Senya stepped into the room.

"You must be famished from your journey," the woman said, gesturing to the table overflowing with food. A keen sparkle danced in her sharp blue eyes. "Please, sit and eat."

Senya stiffened. "Crassica," she said flatly.

The woman sat. She gave a wide cold smile. "You say my name like an accusation."

"That depends on the condition of my brother. Where is he?"

Lifting a silver goblet from the table, Crassica held it in a toast to Senya and took a small sip of its contents. The smell of cinnamon wafted through the room. "You have doubtless heard many stories about me." A small quiver lit across her lip. "Not all of them are true."

Senya moved toward the table. "Was any of it true? Was he ever here at all?"

Crassica set the goblet on the table. "Of course he was here. He has been here for many years. You will see him soon enough." Her voice came with a frosty sweetness. "But for now, a lovely meal awaits."

Senya glanced at the food. Steam rose from a freshly roasted chicken. A wheel of cheese sat to one side, with salads and exotic fruits. A bottle of red Kalldonian wine. "I would like to see my brother first."

A flash of annoyance flew across Crassica's face, overtaken by a benevolent and toothy smile. "Sadly, your brother is not well. I cannot take you to him just yet. We are waiting to find the proper moment, and the situation is complicated." She gestured again at the food. "Please. First, eat. Take your time. To swallow a mouthful of fine wine quickly and without regard to quality or origin is to miss the point entirely. Such is the same with life, do you not agree?"

Senya sat but did not reach for the food.

"I am glad to finally meet you, of course," Crassica continued. "We have awaited this moment with great anticipation. I do apologize for the uncomfortable precautions my people were forced to take on your journey.

All for your own safety, you see. You have yet to master the Lifesong, and such powers, unbridled as they are, could be dangerous for all involved."

"What is your plan?" Senya broke in, not hiding the edge in her voice.

Crassica gripped the goblet's base and shifted its position on the table, as if considering her next words. She lifted and drew in another small sip. "You are the living connection between the eternal power of the Knowing and the fallible, temporal existence of man," she said, lowering the goblet. "You are the key. You and your brother both."

"What did you do to him?"

"The proper question is, what did he do to himself? What did he do to me? Did he show respect for the things I offered? Did he understand the rules of his position?"

"Rules? What rules?"

Crassica closed her eyes. A pained look blazed over her face. "He came here of his own desire. And stayed by choice." She glanced at the goblet on the table in front of her, examining it with a turn, as if only now discovering its worth. "Your brother is most ambitious. I have done nothing to him that he has not engaged in voluntarily. His path belongs to him alone, as does whatever reckoning may come."

"He came to you to learn. But what have you taught him exactly? He offered you much of his life. How much of yours did you offer to him?"

Crassica grinned. A gleam came into her eye. "So much alike, you and our beloved Raedwin are. Both full of such spark and passion. So lovely to witness."

"Where is he?"

"Please do not mistake my meaning. We are all saddened by our sweet Raedwin's struggles. He has indeed become locked inside his dreams and has created a fantasy that is separate from reality, so all of that is, unfortunately, true. And this fantasy of his has led him to..." She drifted off and drank from the goblet again, her lips tightening with the strength of whatever was in it. "His current, most unfortunate position."

Senya sat back and said nothing. She studied the creature across from her. What were the limits to her power? How easily could she control things she wasn't expecting? Quietly, Senya began to hum. She pulled at the threads of the Lifesong, seeking a voice to bring forth with the right melody and rhythm.

The hum became a song, seeking its identity, its living spirit.

Crassica burst out in a broad laugh. "Oh, my dear sweet Senya," she cried, shaking her head. "You bold child!" She waved a dismissive hand. "The *Saolweald* has no place here, especially with your lack of experience."

Senya let the song die away. Estranged in a hostile land, she was suddenly struck by her daunting vulnerabilities.

All manner of benevolence left Crassica's face. Her jaw clenched as she clearly struggled to subdue a rising anger. "Your own father was unsatisfied with his position in the fabric of the Knowing, much like me." Her voice came in a low growl. "He and I share a broken truth in that way. We both found the limits of the Knowing to be too restrictive, too similar to incarceration, a sentence for a crime never committed, feeble rules for those with no imagination."

Senya watched Crassica's almost glowing icy blue eyes. "You are nothing like my father," she said.

Crassica's hand shook as she raised the goblet again, either from rage or weakness. Maybe a combination of both. She drank with a frantic desire, as if seeking something far beyond what the strange pungent liquid could possibly provide. "One must truly understand oneself in order to know others," she said, slowly setting the goblet back on the table. "Go backward to find the path forward. See the earth in order to know the stars. Are these not the paths of your precious father's Brohndai Way? Water defines the land, and darkness shows the power of light."

Senya did not answer. She surveyed the table as she calmed herself. Steel tumblers glinted in the firelight. Metal serving trays overflowed with fruits, and a glass ewer of water stood alongside. The cutlery shone. She realized there were no attendants in the room. No protection. The two of them were alone.

With a table full of knives.

"What, then, is my true purpose to be?" Crassica continued. "I will tell you. It is this: to be. To live. That is all. How can you argue against this?" A fresh light sparkled in her eyes. "When one's true embodiment is death, then the only thing remaining to discover is birth."

Senya let out a scoffing laugh. "That is where you are wrong," she snapped. "Some things are never meant to be discovered, not by the likes of you. This is not your world. You are owed nothing—not by me, and not by anybody else. Yes, your body is false, but so are you, and so is your hope."

She rose, putting both palms onto the table. She leaned forward and held her eyes on Crassica. "I'm finally waking up," she said. "Maybe I can't quite control all of what you've unleashed on me just yet, but I'm a fast learner. Every move you make brings me closer. From your clown act up in Pentmore to your Vallahnir in the Hallonath. And that second-rate necromancer on Delsorka's ship. All of it. Each piece you give is making me stronger."

Crassica grinned. "Yes, my sweet Senya. But your true purpose yet awaits…"

"You can try to hold me here and tie me down or use whatever you think will own me, but hear this. It will never happen."

Crassica pinched away a look of false confusion. "But why would you say such a thing? I speak of pure beauty here."

With a single fluid movement, Senya yanked a long carving knife from the roast chicken and dove for Crassica's throat. She would end this here and now, quickly and cleanly. She would end Crassica. There would be time enough to find Raedwin once the confusion of this twisted Vallahnir's veil was lifted.

But her body froze. Her hand refused to go forward.

Crassica slowly drank from her goblet and closed her eyes. Senya felt no hand, no exertion, no binding force. No sorcery she could see or sense. She simply could not move any closer.

Senya, Crassica whispered without moving her mouth. *My child, my soon-to-be mother. Sister to the sea herself. In time, you will come to understand.*

Panic lit through Senya. *My soon-to-be mother.* What could that possibly mean? She shuddered at the thought. Whatever manner of Dark Arts this twisted Vallahnir had achieved—whatever level of power she'd wielded just to be here—likely unlocked untold deviances along with it. Senya hoped never to know what those were.

Crassica set the goblet down in silence.

Senya took a step back, the movement easy and clear. She could retreat, but she could not advance. Her hand let loose, and the knife dropped to the floor. "That," she managed through clenched teeth, "will never happen."

Crassica raised a finger. A simple gesture. "If you insist." Her voice turned deeper, with an unspoken force underneath. The outer door burst open and a pair of men marched into the room. Each took Senya by the arm and escorted her backward, gently but firmly, into her cell.

"You must rest, my sweet," Crassica called. "Both of us have much for which to prepare."

55

LEAVING THE causeway as the sun was setting, Raedwin turned east over dry grassland hills south of the Valle d'Brasti. He rode hard through the night. At first light, he followed a broad wash upward through foothills before it surrendered to the western edge of the forest. A morning breeze picked up, bringing with it a bittersweet pinch of pine.

He kept on, riding over a stony ridge and down a wooded, rocky ravine. The ground fell sharply. Dawn swelled in the eastern sky. They'd taken Sadahlia back to the Keep, that much he knew, so maybe Senya was there as well. Or maybe she was still at sea. At the very least, she was somewhere hidden. Each time he tried to reach for her, searching and probing with whatever connections he could grasp, nothing appeared.

Crassica's hold over the Valle d'Brasti hummed with fresh hostility, a pulsing discord that reverberated for miles around. Even with his knowledge of the Keep's concealed channels and secret passages, there'd be no way to get in, find both of them, and get back out alive.

At least not alone.

Ignorant of the forms of forest tracking, he could not tell for sure if the path he followed would get him where he needed to be. Soon he was forced to guide the horse sideways across the slope until he found a well-used trail among the trees. A series of towering monoliths loomed on either side of the track, as if the forest itself had erected ancient standing stones in its own silent honor.

Suddenly a shout echoed. A number of figures moved to block the narrow path ahead, while a handful more cut off his retreat. Jehndai, all of them. Nimble bodies and fluid movements. Several others came into view atop the monoliths, creating a tight ring around him. Raedwin reined his horse to a stop. The ravine fell silent.

An especially tall individual at the front held a long pike decorated with several animal skins. Black paint covered half his face. He raised a hand in greeting.

"Come not," he warned in a high voice. "No closer."

Many stood freely among the trees. Each held a longbow nearly as tall as themselves, and some wore slat armor woven with precision and skill. Carved wooden helmets and greaves. Metal bracers. They stared at Raedwin with wide black eyes set in narrow faces. Deeply sunken cheeks and high cheekbones.

"You have an enemy beyond the edge of this forest," Raedwin called. "And I need your help against her. Against Crassica."

At the sound of the name, a tense murmur flew through the group. Several fidgeted with their weapons, clearly agitated. A few whispered to one another. The leader held up his pike, and the group quieted. "The Shaper," he called, letting the weapon settle. "Not welcome." A flicker of agreement. Some clicked the base of their longbows on the stones. The leader gestured to the space behind Raedwin, as if to brush him away. "You must to go back."

Raedwin slowly dismounted and stepped toward the leader. Several of the others bristled, their bodies stiffening. Those on the stones widened their stance and nocked arrows, razored broadheads aimed at Raedwin's heart.

"I have seen the mine," Raedwin said. "I was with those who destroyed it and freed your people." He held his palms open. "Your enemy is also my enemy."

The leader smiled, revealing sharp amber-colored teeth. He spoke to the entire group, translating Raedwin's words. Their faces remained skeptical. Those with bent bows relaxed but kept their aim. The leader turned back to Raedwin. The Jehndai closest to him bent and whispered into his ear. The leader remained poised, watching Raedwin as they spoke to one another in their own splintered language.

"If I had gifts," Raedwin pleaded, "I would give them to you. But Crassica has taken everything. I am no true warrior, but I will give you everything I can. I will fight until my last breath to be free of her. That much I can promise. But I could really use your help."

At length the leader cocked his head in thought. He nodded and stepped forward. Reaching out to touch Raedwin's cheek, he rubbed at the skin, tugging to see if the swarthy flesh was true. He considered something silently to himself. Holding up his hand, he addressed the group, his eyes on each of the Jehndai in turn as he spoke. Some bobbed heads in agreement, while others showed clear contempt and concern. Several more spun away almost immediately, vanishing among the trees. One leapt onto Raedwin's horse and deftly took up the reins. He began to ride slowly down the trail.

"You will come with us," the lead Jehndai said to Raedwin. "You must answer to the Elder for what you ask."

Raedwin followed. He was in no real position to argue.

The lithe pale-furred creatures moved with an effortless grace as they led him down the slope over two more ridges and into a small sheltered valley. The sun passed into late evening, and distant mountains glowed orange against the purple sky. Water poured over a narrow falls as they descended a misty path to the edge of a deep pool. Cool air drifted through a grove of giant orange-barked trees nestled along the stony beach. Torchlight flickered among the trunks. Voices echoed. Then something like laughter. Cookfires brought the scent of roasted meats with a rich aroma that Raedwin had never before experienced.

Wooden platforms ringed each massive trunk high overhead. Rope bridges reached from platform to platform, creating an interconnected village suspended among the trees. A fine moss grew over much of the open space, the base of each trunk a patchwork blanket of green. Something of a central path made its way northward. A loose and haunting song floated eerily through the grove.

One of the Jehndai secured Raedwin's horse to a low branch while another motioned for him to follow. Soon they arrived at a modest clearing in the center of the grove. A raised dais of stone with a large wooden chair dominated the space. Intricate carvings of unnamed beasts climbed the legs and arms of the chair, twisting alongside anguished men and women before rising to a pale likeness of Crassica at the high back. A manufactured vengeful goddess, watching over the glade.

An aged Jehndai, wearing a heavy bearskin robe, lounged in the chair. His hollow wizened face gave a youthful sparkle to his large black eyes under an elegant circlet of silver. The loose gray fur of his body was dulled with time and experience, a thin beard dangling from his chin. He offered a smile as Raedwin entered the grove.

"I know of you," the Elder said, his voice crisp and clear. "You are the one they call Raedwin, of the far North. You have done us a great service at a place of immense pain and anguish for our people. So I bid you welcome." He sat back, relaxed. "We unfortunately have little hospitality to offer you. Perhaps food and drink, some rest, but we must know more about what you seek in order to judge the quality of your purpose in these woods."

"I need your help against our common enemy, against the one who brought your people the pain and anguish of which you speak, and still does. I need your help against Crassica."

The Elder stiffened. His face darkened and pinched as the sound of the name fell hard into the space between them.

"We do not speak the name of the Shaper in this grove," he warned. "You will not do so again."

"My apologies." Raedwin bowed his head. "The Shaper... has taken..." he said at length, taking his time to begin carefully. "In the Sevenfold Keep she holds two women... who matter more to me than my own life. I cannot free them on my own. I need the help of the Jehndai."

The Elder grimaced. "Our ancestors were born of blade and furnace under the very Keep of which you speak, seven generations ago. The pain of the Shaper is known and felt among us."

"Your pain is why I've come to you. She has to pay for the things she's done." Raedwin did his best to express everything that boiled inside him. Crassica, Senya, Sadahlia. Not a plan exactly, but a hope. Where he'd been, and where he was going. There was before, and then there was after—the middle ground no longer mattered. Seeing Sadahlia's empty cage in the sewer tunnels of Katliga had broken something in him, and he was not sure the wound of it could ever be truly mended. And now Crassica held his sister as well—he was sure of it. He had seen the spectacle of the Vallahnir master's wrath, and such a stain was not easily washed away. He had to end the struggle.

"The Shaper cannot continue," he said firmly. "I will throw myself against her walls alone if I have to. I'll spend my final drop of blood to break her if it comes to that. But I won't get very far on my own."

The Elder cocked his head to the side and considered this for a long moment. "So you propose to spill Jehndai blood instead, to help infiltrate her lair and retrieve your... prizes."

"I wish to spill the Shaper's blood, not the Jehndai's."

"Yet there will be consequences. Ones that the Jehndai will bear, not you. It is no small thing you ask."

Raedwin made every effort to hold his voice steady. "We all bear her consequences, either way. The Shaper bleeds malice into everything she does..."

"Evil is everywhere in this world. Why should this one matter more than any other?"

"It was her arrogance and greed that brought you unspeakable pain."

"And yet we live because of her."

"It was her need to control and dominate that has caused your long and difficult history of bondage and abuse. Your torture, your imprisonment."

"But now we are free."

"Free to hide and live in fear?"

The Elder opened his arms in a gesture of broad welcome. "We give great thanks to you for what you have done," he said. "But the love you speak of is a strange and twisted thing, practiced between the fateful and the delirious. Does this now call for more blood?"

"True freedom does."

"You and the Vallahnir with whose heart you are entangled both grapple for a connection, but neither of you realize the risk in such a thing. Your path is fragile and tenuous, yet you continue on, oblivious to the threat you pose. You entwine, despite the serious and immediate dangers at hand. You create imbalance, inviting the possibility to perhaps someday lose... everything."

Raedwin tried to find a rebuttal but instead found himself standing in dumb silence. He had no real answer for the stark truth.

The Elder pointed directly at him, and a sharpness came into his voice. "You are without balance, my child. I have seen you from the edge of our trees, and I have watched your actions from afar. You strive for evidence of the Hand of the Knowing upon the land, seeking for some hidden artifact, some lost moment undiscovered by all others, some working of the world's machinery that will allow you to glimpse a deeper truth underneath all things. But this is a futile wish. One cannot fully understand the Knowing—a thing both known by all who seek and truly unknowable by anyone."

"But hope remains for us to be better than our past selves," Raedwin said. "We just need a chance."

"Just a chance," the Elder repeated. His eyes glittered as he smiled and shook his head. "You are a wandering soul, Raedwin of the North. I know this. I have seen it. And you come to this place as part of your many journeys, your seeking of truth, and perhaps as part of your search for justice. But destruction and renewal are both essential parts of the Knowing. Cycles repeat, and they repeat once again. Even these trees have seen the arguments of many lost men. Births and deaths have come and gone, unions and dissolutions, laughter as well as tears. Humankind is a pattern long repeated. Hope begets desire, and desire fosters violence. The violence then brings devastation and despair, which in turn creates a catalyst for new hope. You all tinker with the details, but the story remains the same. Always. Perhaps you don't realize the error of what you seek. Perhaps you have lost your way. Many have done so."

"Does hiding out here give you the peace you long for? A true and lasting peace?"

"You search for your own true home as well, the same as us. A place you have yet to find. Only in our true home will any of us find the peace we seek."

"My home is with Sadahlia. And my sister and I will find a way together. We were so close once. I'll find a way to right the wrongs I've done. This is our chance for a new kind of balance."

The Elder sat back, reflecting upon something unspoken between them. A bond of sorts. Or maybe a rift. At length he raised his head, as if assessing and judging the lives and strengths of the branches overhead.

"Your heart is connected to both the living and the dead," he said at last, bringing his gaze back to Raedwin. "Born broken. I have never seen such a thing in all my life. So I invite you to stay with us here. Be well, and live. Embrace the quietude. Solace. Forget the troubled place from which you have escaped. The forest will give everything you need. Find your balance here."

"What happens when the Shaper decides it's time, and she comes to end me, as well as all of you? What then?"

"You ask for war."

"I ask for an end to her control."

"For your own purposes."

Raedwin opened his mouth to continue but held his words. All of this hung in some unseen balance that was delicate and tenuous at best. He'd never been good at negotiation. That was his sister's arena.

"I am alone," he said at last, holding the Elder's steady gaze. "And I can't get them out on my own. But I will die trying if I have to."

The Elder considered this. He leaned forward, eyes narrowed. "Why have you never come to us before? For years upon years the Shaper has worked our people to death in her trench of horrors. Have we not been neighbors all this time? Why does this offer of friendship arise only now, from your desperation?"

"I've learned a lot lately."

"The Jehndai are not here to teach you anything more."

"But maybe I'm here to teach you. You fight her forces all along your borders, all the time, more and more every day. I can help you, the same as you can help me."

The Elder sat back, a deep crease furrowing his brow. He idly stroked his thin beard, deep in thought, eyes unfocused on the space between them. "There is truth in what you say, I do admit," he said after a time. "Even before the Shaper lost her ability to dig and destroy the earth, she sent many men to penetrate our forest and take from among our people. More and more, as you have said, shrouded in the secret silence that such men keep. They come with violence in their hearts and blood on their hands. They kill and take, and then they come again.

"A number of Jehndai have already lost their lives to blades of the Shaper's men," the Elder explained. "Their skirmishes have grown intense in the last few days, and as a people we have found it necessary to retreat deeper into the trees, far from our traditional reach.

"Because of this, some wish to break our promise with the trees and go to seek revenge and retribution, to avenge the brothers and sisters we have lost. Many already wish to rise in strength and bring destruction to the Shaper. But I have urged them to remain here. To remain hidden. Remain safe."

"There's no safety in hiding. Not if she is coming for you."

The Elder stiffened. He nodded slowly. "Love is strong with you, which is honorable. Perhaps the Jehndai wish to share in your truth. But how does Raedwin of the North propose that we can help? The Sevenfold Keep is not a place for us. The Shaper's halls are unknown. What you desire will cause much new pain. How do you answer for this?"

"The skill and strength of your people," Raedwin offered, "coupled with my knowledge of the Shaper's Keep. Together, we would be a formidable force."

"Yet many will die."

"How many will die if you do nothing?"

"None of us will live forever."

Raedwin's body tensed. The Elder's words came not as an allegation but as a simple fact. Maybe the Elder had already made up his mind. Maybe he had known everything about Raedwin and what had been going on, even before he'd come wandering among these trees. "A sacrifice now will gain you lives," he said. "And a future. For both of us. A future beyond whatever she decides we're allowed."

The singing elsewhere in the grove died away as darkness fell. At length the Elder smiled kindly, his face holding a deep and unfathomable sadness. "In truth," he said at last, with resignation in his voice, "the dry tinder within the hearts of the Jehndai have indeed called for the spark you bring for quite a long time. I cannot deny. And I see our moment has finally arrived, along with yours, whether any of us want the coming bloodshed or not. Whether any of us are ready or not, the Shaper's time must come to an end. And that end is now."

The Elder stood from his wooden chair and drew himself to full height, addressing the other Jehndai assembled as much as he did Raedwin. "So we will join with you in this effort, Raedwin of the North," he said. "The seven clans of the Jehndai shall converge at last as one people, one voice, and one weapon. The Shaper has started us down this road, and we will finish it, together."

He brought his gaze to Raedwin and held his eyes for a long moment. "There will be brutal and savage death on the road ahead. Is our gentle friend from the distant North ready for such action?"

Raedwin shifted his body forward. "For Senya and for Sadahlia, I'm ready for anything."

The Elder nodded, considering. When he spoke again, his voice was lower and more measured. "In all of this, you must remember one thing: Gain and loss cannot exist without one another. Profit requires a forfeiture.

Such is the Way of Balance. Loss allows one to someday hold true reward deep in one's heart, where it cannot be broken, not ever. One must fully understand the sharp beauty of loss and the bitter lessons it may offer. Only then may the rewards come. Do not ever forget that."

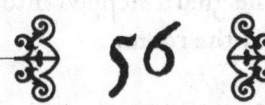

56

SENYA ROSE from the bed. Had she fallen asleep? She thought only a few minutes had passed, but something remained off. Foggy. Out of balance. She opened the door. Servants had cleared the table and completely cleaned the room. The fire had died to coals. Clearly she'd been out for hours. So strange, this place. Disorienting and confusing.

She continued to the outer door. Maybe if she wandered a bit, walked the halls of the Keep and learned the paths of the citadel, she could find some answers. Maybe she'd stumble upon somebody who could help her. At any rate, some fresh air would help. She could stroll a little and let her thoughts drift.

The door was locked.

She tried it again, worked the handle, felt the strength of it.

"I'm sorry. You are not to leave your rooms," a man called from the other side. "But please rest assured. You are plenty safe here."

More furious than dismayed, she turned away and stoked the coals of the dead fire. Timid flames emerged from fresh embers, growing to a modest blaze. A few bed pillows propped into a chair wrapped in her own cloak created a passable image of a huddled figure next to the hearth.

She called for the guard. "Something's not right," she claimed. "I don't feel well. Could you please enter for a moment and help me?"

"I'll send for somebody," the guard replied through the door.

"No, no, it's not that..." she stammered. "I just need help... moving this chair..."

A pause. "Moving a chair?"

"To be closer to the fire. This... underground... it's cold..."

"Perhaps place more wood on the coals..."

"Yes, I know... I just... can you please help? I'm not strong enough to move it..."

After a long silent moment, a key rang brightly against the lock. The mechanism slid and turned, and the door swung open. Bright torchlight spilled in from the hall. The guard stepped into the doorway and stood, adjusting to the dim light of the room.

Now. Come on...

He moved toward the huddled figure at the fire.

Senya cracked a candlestick sharply against the man's temple, dropping him to the floor. She dragged his limp body back into her bedchamber. After binding his hands and gagging his mouth, she wondered if even this was too gentle, if anything short of death was less than the need at hand. But she let the thought go. She pulled out his long dagger and boot knife, slipping both into her belt.

Moving from shadow to shadow, she made her way down the torchlit hallway. She reached for Raedwin again, perhaps with a futile, flailing effort, searching for something—anything—to guide her. Maybe all of this was in vain. She wanted so badly to call out for him, but the strength of Crassica's veil pulsed through everything, reverberating through the air itself, confusing any attempts to connect.

But then that same strange beacon again. A glimmer far below, barely more than a quivering flash. It wasn't like Raedwin exactly, but it was something clearly connected to him. A shining sliver of hope deep underneath the Keep.

She crept along the corridor, keeping to shadows and looking for a way down. A pair of armed sentries made their presence known well before she came upon them. Backing behind a column and pressing her body against the wall, she held still. The men passed unsuspecting. Taking a side passageway, they soon disappeared. After a time, Senya came to a set of stairs leading down. Pulling a torch from a wall-mounted sconce, she descended into darkness.

Whispers flashed in her ears. Raedwin's voice. The sound echoed through the halls, without form or source. Maybe it was only in her mind, something from her childhood memories transplanted to this alien Keep by her simple desire to find him, but an image came as well, through her brother's own eyes. A pale, naked woman lying next to him. Strikingly beautiful. Hairless, with sparkling blue eyes.

A Vallahnir—the same one from her vision back in Pentmore.

Senya stumbled. The image broke apart and vanished. She caught herself against the wall. The whispers disappeared, as well as the flickering sense of hope and longing they'd brought to her.

Emotions had surged in that short moment. Whispers and truths. A powerful love, along with fear and disgust at needing to hide. A feeling she knew well enough herself. Raedwin had shared much with this Vallahnir—Senya could sense it completely.

She kept on, more cautious now. A short while later, the stairs opened into a cavernous room with an open cistern in the center. She was close. Circling the water, she found no immediate passage beyond this room, but the sparkling sense of hope had come from underneath, somewhere deeper yet.

A sound rang out, iron on iron, echoing through the halls. Nothing moved. A tiny drip reverberated in the cistern. The flash of hope came again, somewhere directly below.

And then she saw—an opening barely more than a hidden crack in the wall. Ducking to enter, she found that the portal opened onto yet another set of narrow steps leading down. Senya descended. The passage soon devolved into a coarse and brutally carved tunnel, more remnant of an ancient mine shaft than anything like a proper passage.

The source was down there somewhere ahead, reaching without words and without thought, crying maybe for Raedwin or maybe blindly beckoning to any who could hear, sending out hope and pain blended together in final desperation. Senya drew the long dagger she'd taken from the guard and proceeded slowly.

At last she came to a vaulted chamber lit by a single wall-mounted oil lamp. An ornate iron cage hung over a deep pool of black water, with a wooden bridge leading to its door. A bed sat in the cage, lavishly appointed yet shoved askew with intentional disarray. On the bed lay the Vallahnir Senya had seen from Raedwin's own eyes.

She stirred and sat up. Blinked. Surprise flashed over her face. "Senya," she said. "You've come."

Senya gave a crisp bow of her head. "Sadahlia." The name came to her lips without effort, having arrived unbidden through Raedwin's own lingering memories. This woman in front of her had come from the realm of death, her provenance in the Crosslands, like Crassica and Cevellica and all the others, but this was the one. Raedwin's love. She was real. Her fate was tied to his. Senya saw the clarity of it. Her brother had connected with this particular Vallahnir in some true way, and that was all she needed for now.

The Vallahnir rose and stepped to the edge of the cage. "How are you here? How did you find this place?"

Senya paused for a moment, uncertain how to answer. "I don't know," she managed. "I heard you... and I saw you together with Raedwin..."

"Where is he? What have they done with him?"

Senya moved toward the bridge. "I don't think he's here. I can't sense him anywhere."

Sadahlia stepped back from the iron bars and sat on the edge of the bed. "He must have gotten out..." She quickly told of their plans to flee north together, their hope of finding Senya and warning her not to come. Their failed meeting at the farmhouse.

"So how do we find him?"

Sadahlia shook her head. "You should go alone. Your chances are better that way."

"I can't leave you here. I've felt what you mean to him."

"There really isn't much of a choice."

"We can do this together."

Sadahlia stood and stepped again to the edge of her iron cage. "They're dangerous, those who locked me in this place... They are..." She trailed off, unable to finish.

"You don't know what I've been through to get here."

Sadahlia thought for a moment. "There are only two keys to this cage that I have seen. Crassica holds one on a chain around her neck, which makes it impossible to get. And the other..." Her voice failed and she shook her head again. "The other is held by a man called Lanius. He is less careful than Crassica but much more dangerous. If you can get to his room while he's away, he probably keeps it in there somewhere."

"So Lanius it is, then."

Sadahlia put her hand to the iron. "Listen to me. Lanius is dangerous.

Maybe the most dangerous person in this Keep besides Crassica herself. He is not one to be played with."

Senya gave a cold grin. "Well, lucky for us, I'm not playing. So where do I find his room?"

Senya hurried up the stairs. Sadahlia had explained that Lanius lived in a series of sparse rooms adjacent to the courtyard. She had done her best to explain the way. A complex maze of tunnels would serve to cover her movements, but the rest would be up to Senya.

She emerged from the stairs. Following Sadahlia's instructions, she headed toward the cellars of the bake house near the backside of the granary. A face flashed in a doorway as Senya hurried past but disappeared as she froze and spun to look. Drawing her dagger again, she kept on. Soon she came upon a series of rooms that served as storage under the kitchens. Past them she would find a heavy door with iron bracing. This would lead to a set of steps upward into Lanius's chambers.

A dark shape flashed in the corner of her vision again. Senya spun and found nothing. She waited. Nothing came. She turned to continue on.

The arms that grabbed her seemed too massive to be human, too hairy and thick as they smothered her body, lifting her from the floor. Hands groped for her wrists as she struggled. She flipped her dagger without thinking and drove it upward behind her, easily cleaving leather and skin and ramming deep into her attacker's abdomen. She stabbed again. A pained gasp exploded in her ear, and the arms fell away. Senya hit the ground. She whirled on her feet and slashed with the dagger, splitting open the huge man's throat.

Two more men came at her from the shadows on either side. The first one lunged. Senya cut upward across his wrist, and blood sprayed from the deep laceration. The second received two quick gashes across his face before he backed away as well. They attempted a second attack, but Senya spun easily. Then they stood waiting, a stalemate set before them. The first attacker lay on the floor breathing wetly, his life spilling over the stone in silence.

A last man emerged from the shadows at the far side of the hallway, holding a long thin dagger. He was dressed entirely in black, his long blond hair stark and white against the darkness. Deep-set eyes sparkled over his narrow nose. He regarded the scene before him, the first huge attacker lying motionless, the second panting harshly as he gripped his gushing wrist, the third clutching his badly wounded face. Senya stood central to the space, owning the struggle for the moment.

A thin malicious grin crawled across the newcomer's face. "My dear, dear Senya," he said in a low, menacing voice. "Such a willful, mutinous little girl. So much like your brother you are…"

Senya said nothing. She found no point in speaking to men such as these, ones who followed money or lust for power or whatever else held this place together. She waited, blade in hand.

"Oh, I'm sorry…" the man said. "I've not introduced myself." He gave a mock formal bow. "I am called Lanius. And nobody wanders the tunnels of this Keep without my permission."

Lanius gestured to the other two men, who immediately backed away. A leader passing silent orders to his acolytes, allowing the master to do his work. "You have been to see our fair pet below. Which is, of course, forbidden. And perhaps devious promises were passed between the two of you, shared poisons of fate that will lead you both into the sad providence of wickedness."

Senya stiffened and held her arm straight toward this man, this lurking menace, pointing the tip of her wet blade at his face. "Where is my brother," she said in a measured tone, not so much a question as an order—a command for disclosure, from one empowered speaking to a subordinate held before her.

Lanius laughed, the sharp sound so bright and foreign to this dark place. "My dear girl," he said. "Your brother is long gone. He has not been in this Keep for some time now."

She lunged at him without a sound, diving for his exposed throat. Her cleverly timed leap was shockingly quick, yet Lanius dodged and then stepped into her path, swiping his blade crosswise to parry her charging dagger. He laughed again as she backed away.

"Our dance together begins at last! How exciting!" He pivoted calmly away from her, arms open, prowling catlike along the chamber walls, his blade shining in one hand. "Your brother proved quite foolish in the end, you know. So ignorant of the larger picture. Ungrateful and foolish both."

She came at him again, but Lanius dodged and stepped into her thrust.

Grabbing her wrist with his free hand, he pulled her toward his body. The smell of onions and old bread filled her nose. He held his dagger high as the other two men rushed in, grabbing and binding her arms and ankles with speed and deftness.

The men hoisted her, struggling and screaming. Lanius pulled a long strip of cloth across her mouth. She gagged and bit as the cloth slipped between her teeth. Striking out as best she could with every bit of fury she had, Senya punched with fists and arms and kicked with her legs. But held fast by two sets of thick arms, she quickly tired. Soon she succumbed.

"Ungrateful," Lanius said again as he watched her settle to her fate, "and foolish both."

The men carried her away into darkness.

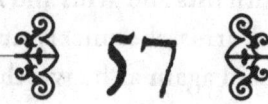

57

AFTER THE clash with the ship out of Donasberth, the *Summerhawk* quickly passed the Blastonbree Islands and reached the Lophlyn coast in quick order, but the Gulf of Dunnen frustrated all their efforts at any kind of speed. So they made a quick plan. With these shifty winds, it might take three extra days to reach the mouth of the Mondini by sail, and after that they'd have the long upriver haul to Katliga. Not ideal when in a hurry. Instead, Brogan would go ashore as soon as possible with Kaetas and a handful of her best fighters. They'd cut due east across Kalldonia, making directly for the Valle d'Brasti over fifty or sixty leagues of open grasslands. Maybe they'd try to find some horses. Freógan would continue south with the *Hawk*, and as soon as the ship was secure in port, he would join Kaetas and Brogan's little band with most of the remaining crew.

Finally, a small deserted cove northwest of Darizi presented itself. "That one'll do," Kaetas said, spyscope to her eye. "That'll do nicely." She clapped the scope closed and barked orders to bring the *Summerhawk* in close to the surf and get the launch in the water.

They rowed hard through the frothing breakers to a stony beach. Kaetas and Brogan and the few select sailors gave goodbyes, cinched gear straps to secure various weapons to their bodies, and began their hike up a watery cleft in the bluff, leaving the safety of the sea behind.

They held a quick pace through the evening. Strange southern stars peeked from the night sky while tall, narrow trees stood in sparse groves, marking their stealthy passage. The darkened country lay open and wide, flowing grasslands shining in the early moonlight. No one spoke. Skeletons of once-proud homes rose from the gray land. The moon swung tall over their heads, offering uneasy guidance as they jogged eastward. Hours passed.

Near dawn they approached a wide valley with lush grasses coming golden with early hints of the sun. Cows dotted the landscape. A large stone house stood among several whitewashed buildings, their red clay roofs warming to the morning. A few scattered Kalldonian herders watched from afar. Olive trees and almond groves graced the rolling hills on the far side.

A pair of women on horseback rode out from the nearby bunkhouse to meet this strange group of travelers bristling with weaponry, having arrived without invitation or any clear purpose.

"Your weapons," the taller of the two women called as they approached. "Please remove them." The riders spread to opposite sides, ringing and hemming them in. "If you do not mean us harm, you have no need for such things."

Kaetas studied the horsewomen as they circled. "What's to say you don't mean harm to us?"

The lead rider's mount shifted, tail flicking. "You are free to turn around and go back from where you came," she said. "Or you may lay down arms and come with us. The choice is yours."

Brogan removed his sword and bow and set them at his feet. Kaetas gestured to the sailors and proceeded to remove her own as well.

Once disarmed, they spoke briefly with the riders. Brogan explained their desire to purchase horses in order to speed their journey eastward. The women nodded and said little. The taller one motioned for the group to follow. She circled her horse and descended toward the valley and the bunkhouse while the other rider gathered the weapons in a blanket and followed.

As they approached the small compound of buildings, the leader dismounted and called for Kaetas and Brogan to join her. She led them into a kitchen. The others waited outside. An old man stood at a wide sink and washed fruit in preparation of the morning meal.

"Wait here," the lead rider said. She disappeared farther into the house. The man at the sink took no notice of their arrival and ignored their lingering presence behind him. After a moment a woman entered, tall and stout-boned with graying hair tied in an elegant wrap behind her sturdy head.

"Please," she said with a gesture of invitation to the doorway. "Come. Sit."

Brogan followed Kaetas into the spacious main room. Light spilled through open east-facing windows. Wooden beams braced the ceiling between whitewashed plaster. The woman watched them carefully as they sat at a long oak table in the center. She moved to sit opposite. Producing a hammered tin box of dried rustica leaf, she packed the bowl of a long thin pipe in silence.

"Which of you," she said at length, "is the leader?"

Kaetas and Brogan exchanged glances. "We don't exactly have a leader," Brogan said.

The woman rose and walked to an iron stove against the wall. Hinges cried as she opened its door. Reaching for a lighting stick, she lit the tip and brought the flame to the bowl of her pipe. The leaf glowed with her breath. She swung the protesting door closed and turned back to the table.

"One must have a leader," she said. "Decisions must be made, courses drawn, and discipline meted out to the group." She stepped back to her chair and sat.

"Now that we're ashore, we work together."

The woman tilted her head. "*Now that we're ashore*. So you have come by sea." She trained her gaze on Kaetas. "You are the sea captain, then. The queen of all worlds while the land is water underneath your hull. And you," she said to Brogan, "are the leader here. He who speaks first."

"Well, I wouldn't say ..."

"You have come overland from the sea and you wish to rest your tired feet and perhaps acquire some of my horses."

"We're in a hurry," Kaetas said.

"I have many horses. Some are fine and elegant creatures of grace and beauty. Others are weak and wild. Some have a lust for speed and endurance in their blood, while others simply wish to eat grass and become fat." She studied her two guests in turn. "Will you be able to offer proper judgment of horses in order to be worthy of ones such as those I may offer?"

"I'm no true horseman," Brogan replied. "But I can ride. I've seen fine ones and poor ones and can give a halfway decent assessment between one and the other."

The woman smoked. "This land has seen many of your kind," she said. "Men seeking glory. Wealth. Perhaps ownership of place. Men seeking opportunities outside their nature, looking to become more than they were before. Is this you? Are you of this kind?"

"We only need to pass through," Kaetas offered. "Nothing more."

"You wish to pass through, as with the lightness of wind in your sails. And yet what consequence is left upon the land with your passing? You bring weapons here to our home. Weapons upon weapons. Your knives themselves carry knives."

Brogan sat back and studied the woman. Smoke trailed from her pipe in graceful curls upward to the wood-beamed ceiling. She gave the impression of being wholly formed from the land itself, burnished by the sun and the repeated struggles of this long-disputed country.

Kaetas broke the silence. "We are heading for the Valle d'Brasti."

The woman raised her eyebrows as she drew from her pipe. "Ah, the Valley of the Brave," she said with an exhale. "And why would one go there? Such a place as that offers little to sailors of the North. It was a place of ruin even before the storied days of lofty emperors."

"We have business to attend to, and time is short. So we would like to purchase some horses to make that journey a little faster."

The woman nodded and smoked as she considered this. "Do you know of this place? The Valley of the Brave? It is a place of quarrels and arguments. Differences of opinion. There is a woman there, a woman of shining white with a gleaming smooth head like a living moon. A woman beyond a woman but also less than one."

"Her name is Crassica," Brogan said.

"Ahh." The woman pointed her pipe at him. "You know of this woman-not-woman, then."

"A little."

"She is not a creature with whom one engages in games. She has power and influence and yet remains hidden. Those who work for her are unsavory. Much is said, but very little is known. She does not often venture forth from her many crumbling towers but has a great and mysterious reach that is hidden from view."

"That sounds about right."

"I myself am indifferent," the woman continued. "I care little about masters of ancient keeps near the far mountains, so long as they remain there. But clearly you must know much of what I speak. And yet you do not travel as emissaries of peace, do you? Armed and determined you come, with burdensome purpose. I nearly had my riders shoot from the rooftops rather than speak to you, such was your presentation."

"Thanks for not doing that," Kaetas said. "Our business with Crassica is our own, but we could likely use a pointer or two on how to get there quickly."

"Getting there is of no issue," the woman said. "One travels eastward to the great Via Kalldonia and then follows the causeway south to Darizi. From there, the road eastward will bring one to the Valle d'Brasti at the seat of the mountains."

"Through Darizi, then."

"One need not enter the city, of course. Especially when one is astride fine Kalldonian horses..."

"How much?" Brogan asked.

The woman turned and watched him for a moment. She smiled thinly and cocked her head toward Kaetas. "Your man asks *how much*, as if a crude transaction with a whore is about to take place. He is uncouth and rude. But then again, he is a man. From the North. So such things are to be expected."

"I don't mean to offend," Brogan offered. "I just thought we could get to the point of the matter."

The woman nodded and considered him. "How many horses do you require?"

"There are five of us. Maybe we could double up and make it with three...?"

"To the Valle d'Brasti? This is not an easy thing. How accomplished are your riders?"

Brogan turned to Kaetas. The captain's head swayed side to side as she considered. "They're great sailors and solid fighters," she admitted. "But maybe not so good on the backs of horses."

"Five horses, then," the woman said. "A fair number."

Brogan produced the leather pouch he'd taken so long ago from the Vallahnir back in the Hallonath. He opened the drawstring and laid the contents on the table, separating the Kalldonian gold pieces from the silvers and pushing the Brinsfallon bronzes aside. The remaining sheckers he ignored.

The woman leaned back and studied Brogan and Kaetas both. A wry smile crept across her sun-burnished face. Smoke from her pipe curled upward through the air. "You are serious travelers," she said, "with a serious purpose. And you say time is of the essence, so let us not mince. You show maybe enough money for three or four plain horses that will be acceptable for your objective. They will be easy and kind and will be steady mounts for your purpose. But they will not be the finest of animals. They will not have determination nor driving motivation. They will lack spirit. Their speed will be less than ambitious."

"They'd be better than walking," Kaetas added. "By a long shot."

The woman smoked. "But clearly your need shows cause for more than this, yes? So with the money you have put onto the table here before us, I offer you this: you may use five of my very best Kalldonian palfreys, geldings with spirit and ambition and a lust for speed. But you may only use, not own. I will send three of my riders as guides. They will show the way quickly to the Valle d'Brasti and help you to approach in stealth or to announce your arrival, however you prefer. Then, once arrived, they will gather these fine animals and return them here to me."

"That's a lot of money for a simple hire."

"That is my offer. I risk horses of a worth at least ten times the money you've displayed to me. They will serve your intentions with great advantage, and this will be of benefit to us both."

Brogan glanced at Kaetas, who simply shrugged. This was as good a deal as any and certainly their best shot at getting to Senya as fast as they could.

Brogan agreed. He and the woman spat and shook. They stood, and the woman smiled. She gestured toward the kitchen.

"But first," she said, "you and your sailors must eat. One cannot properly choose fine animals on empty stomachs."

The horses indeed were all beautiful Kalldonians—tall and elegant, with wide lined faces and large eyes. Brogan had never seen any of quite this quality. Their snouts were narrower than those in the North, their muzzles almost too small for their foreheads. Their lean and refined bodies were clearly suited to enduring long journeys at speed, but for sailors not used to riding, the pace set by their expert guides quickly became brutal. Shock reverberated through flesh and bone alike, for Brogan as well as those less attuned to riding.

They rode east into the morning sun, their shadows reaching behind them toward the sea in long, beckoning surges. The land dried out and emptied. A dark gravel of black lava showed between clumps of golden grass. Trees became scarce, as if life itself retreated under the harsh Kalldonian sun. Over time, the sailors appeared to grow used to the different strides, and with the help of their guides, they learned to flex above the saddle.

The day drew on. From time to time their guides motioned for them to lie belly flat against their horses to avoid being spotted against the expanse of sky, while other times they called for a full run over open ground. On one occasion they stopped completely to let the horses blow and stand, pulling idly at the stark grass. And then they ran again.

By late afternoon the horses were stumbling, and their guides directed all to dismount and walk for a time. The lead guide was tautly built, with a rawboned strength to her body. She kept her black hair pulled away from her deeply tanned, sand-colored face. They watered in a small wash. Along a steep ridge on the far side, a group of sheepherders watched them with an eye for defense of their stock, of their position, of their withered and worn land. The leader called for the group to mount again, and they moved on.

Night fell as the low green valley of the Dophini River came into view. They dipped into a small vale and made camp, spreading blankets over the cracked soil. Strange southern stars slid across the night sky as a soft breeze came easily and briskly out of the west, pushing at their small fire. The flames danced and contorted, reaching ever eastward as if drawn toward the Valle d'Brasti, yearning to join some fresh new hell that waited there.

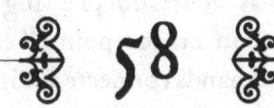

58

SENYA WOKE with a powerful ache in her head. She found herself lounging in a wire mesh chair, mostly submerged in a strange room-sized bath. A thick and viscous liquid, pale blue and lightly sparkling, the temperature of blood, covered everything up to her face. She caught the faint scent of cinnamon.

She remembered Lanius and his men carrying her back to her cell. They'd provided food and water and then left her alone, locking the outer door behind them. She had stood and paced the room for hours. All attempts to reach or connect with Raedwin or bring out any kind of force in her voice had failed. Useless and futile. So powerless. Lost. Finally, she'd given in to hunger and sat to eat.

That was the last thing she remembered.

Light from the full moon streamed down from the strange room's high glass dome, illuminating the wide bath. Iron columns curved overhead, bracing the walls of the triangular room like ribs in the belly of some great stone beast. Three fires roared in hearths at each corner. The thick liquid around her lay placid and still, yet all of it was somehow alive, heaving with a slow and silent energy.

"The preparation is complete," came a man's voice to her left. "The womb is prepared."

Senya turned to find Ghellan, the sorcerer from Delsorka's ship, lying back in a wire chair the same as hers, submerged in the same strange blue bath. The sorcerer's bare palm was pressed loosely against her own, with a sleeve of some artificial snakeskin binding them together. From their wrapped wrists, the sleeve covered the length of his arm from shoulder to hand and stretched over her own arm as well—binding her wrist and wrapping her shoulder. She tried to pull away and break the touch but found the sleeve secure.

"The circle has been cast," came a woman's voice to her right. "The moon is full. She honors us with her pale light."

Crassica lounged in an identical wire mesh chair on Senya's other side, her left arm wrapped as well, palm pressing Senya's right hand. The three of them were situated in a three-pointed star, with heads near one another. Their outstretched hands connected skin to skin, bound together inside the snakeskin sleeves.

Senya pulled harder at the material, struggling to force a rupture along its length. Finally, she tore it open.

"Calm yourself, my sweet," Crassica urged. "It is important you remain composed as we finish. A mother must be delicate with her new child."

Yanking her hand away from Crassica's and then her other from Ghellan, Senya struggled to rip and peel away the remaining sleeve bindings. "What is this?" she said, her lips thick and listless. Her fingers felt sluggish and numb. Raising a dripping hand to her forehead, she found a delicate webwork of metal ringing her head. Wires ran to matching circlets on both Crassica and Ghellan as well. She tried to sit up but failed. "What are you doing?"

"From man and woman will come the body of a child," Ghellan called out, speaking as if reciting some ritual. "And from the Crosslands itself rises the spirit."

Senya tugged at the crown, managing to shove it off and away. Her vision blurred. For a moment she floated and sank at the same time. Her body went still and shifted into something else entirely, as if all this time the simple flesh had been foreign to her true self. She lay back in the metal mesh of the chair, fighting to regain control.

"There is no need for melodramatic tantrums," Crassica said gently. "We have completed a great beginning tonight, the first of three vital rituals. This is a time of beauty and fulfillment."

Senya stared at the ceiling and the moonlight beyond. A circle of lit candles ringed the basin around her, surrounding their strange shared pool. Regaining some of her strength and control, she reached to pull the last remains of the snakeskin sleeve clear.

Painted inscriptions crawled up her arm and shoulder, crossing toward her neck. Symbols of dark sorcery, things well outside her comprehension. Where had they come from? She dropped the sleeve into the pool.

Wire mesh flexed with Senya's weight as she sat up. The bath's milky liquid moved along with her, caressing her skin as if welcoming her, beckoning onward.

"Tonight we couple with the Knowing," Crassica said. "You are the vessel, and we are the spark. The first step on a beautiful journey, for all of us. You are now imbued with my own essential essence, new and vital powers. You have become a Daughter of the Crosslands, a Mother of Vallahnir, and a Speaker to the Dead."

The room swam, and Senya's vision blurred. The fires in the four corners of the room crackled and spat. She gripped the edge of the chair, struggling to hold herself upright.

"This is our time," Crassica said, unmoving. "Yours and mine. I am the wellspring who will become your child. Once we reach the deep darkness of the new moon, we shall complete my transference. Ghellan will provide the seed to form the empty vessel—a living container awaiting this very chamber, these very chairs, the light of the fresh full moon in one month's time. That which is now Crassica will fall away, and the child will then be full, to be born anew, thoroughly and truly alive. Even the Knowing herself will be brought to understand this excellent and vital joining. And it begins tonight."

Senya willed the room to focus and brighten. She glanced at the stone basin, the steps at the edge. Crassica's naked body in the milky bath. Scars marked the ancient Vallahnir's bare chest.

"Hear what I say, my sweet." Crassica's voice carried a new weight. "The time for the Elders is past. It is now time for mortals, for those who walk the earth, for those who are born to die. The age of humankind has truly begun at last, and I must fully be part of it."

She reached out, but Senya pulled her hand away. Ghellan began to chant in a low voice, almost a whisper. Closing her eyes, Crassica called for the north and the distant waters of the Mirrorwater. She summoned the east and its mountain winds. The ancient power of birth in the Blackmere far to the south. At last, she gazed up at the expanse of glass overhead, the shining moon, and called for the western oceans to awaken and come forth to bless the child to be.

Senya steadied herself against the metal frame of the chair and rose, fighting to hold her balance. Crassica's words came thick and gruff, with a harsh rasp to them, as if the sounds themselves were not for human throats to form. This, Senya knew, was the language of the Crosslands, of the binding of life to death and the joining of birth to the eventual passing of all living souls.

"The beginning is complete," Ghellan proclaimed. "In preparation for many glories to come."

Senya tried to step forward, but her body failed to answer. Her legs refused to move. Her balance shifted. She fell forward, face down into the shimmering blue bath. The milky liquid caught and folded her into its warm and living embrace. Wrestling for space to breathe, Senya slipped sideways and rolled onto her back.

The room spun. Stars glimmered in a distant night sky, holding forth over earth and fire, water and stone, rising in the east and setting in the west.

Senya dreamed. Her body was her own once more. She soared through vast latticed windows at the top of a strange iron tower, flying over forests and snow-covered peaks. She sang. The sun followed her. Its voice rose in response, weaving songs to celebrate the day. Then they fell together, she and the sun, plunging deep into the sea. They swam and sang and emerged nearly as one.

She lay somewhere in the middle of a vast hall. Massive fires blazed in the corners, giving neither warmth nor comfort, their hearths carved of stone in the fashion of upturned cheeks and lips. Crassica's spidery fingers traced several markings on Senya's chest.

You are very tired, she said, her voice so gentle. So kind.

Yes, Senya answered. *Yes, I am.*

Sleep then, my sweet. Just sleep. You must save yourself for the true transference to come.

The mouthlike fires spoke in the tongues of ancients and spilled forth a sudden heat that lit across her toes. Crassica's coarse voice whispered in Senya's ear that together they were making new dawns and new revelations. Together they would be as one. Brohndai and Vallahnir, at long last, joined together with humankind to form the great final dream of the Knowing upon the living earth.

PART SIX

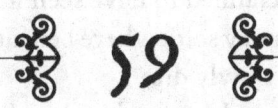

59

THE COVER of darkness had long been Delsorka's friend, offering plenty of stealth for whatever task required secrecy. Darkness allowed one to pass unseen and, with some skill, unheard. Daylight was often so harsh and determined, so unforgiving. Night permitted knowledge to be gained and certain kinds of business to be done cleanly.

Delsorka had known Crassica for a long time. He'd seen her devise quite a few strange schemes over the years, both against or aligned with warlords and villains in Katliga and Kalldon, or up in Corregidon—each entwined in their own violent struggles. She'd conceived plots designed to manipulate petty kings and princes. Some were laid for the benefit of local townsfolk, and some were hostile to them. Some had been brilliant, and some much less than so. Through all of them, Delsorka could usually get a pretty strong sense of what the pale old master was up to, even if only vaguely. Most of the time she shored up her own strength, corrected wrongs that were done to her, all to make sure everybody in her long reach knew well enough to leave her alone. Let the scorpion lie in her Sevenfold Keep, and go about life in her shadow.

But this business with Senya was different. This girl was a mystery. Delsorka still couldn't quite wrap his head around why Crassica had worked so hard to send the *Siege Runner* all the way to Brinsfallon to bring her down here. Kidnapping some miscreant or malcontent was one thing, but Senya clearly had done nothing to Crassica. And that unnatural storm with its placid aftermath was not a thing he could easily let go. Senya was worth more than all this. Something about the whole business didn't smell quite right.

And where had her brother gotten off to? The kid had been gone for far too long. Whispers said he'd fallen for one of Crassica's girls—that first one, the one called Sadahlia. That one was trouble if trouble was ever made flesh. Apparently, they'd been caught together, and the rumors held that Crassica had banished both of them to the Underworld with a flash of lightning. Some claimed to have seen it happen. Others asserted they'd both been walled away somewhere beneath the Keep, inches apart. Listening to one another slowly die.

Nonsense or not, rumors happened in this place for a reason. Delsorka himself was responsible for bringing Senya here and for putting her in danger. He needed to understand the reasons, if there were any, and maybe take back what he had done, if what he had done was wrong.

He bounded up the stairs quickly, winding through bedrock and into the skeleton of the high iron tower. With Senya isolated like this, Crassica could control who saw her, who came and went, and whether she was free to roam the halls or not. Delsorka had put a few coins in the right hands to make sure the sentries all took a break at the same time. The Keep stood vacant, guardians and workers all strangely missing.

Delsorka kept to the shadows. The Valle d'Brasti was not a place he really trusted, and the Keep even less so. Plenty of passages slipped between hidden spaces, connecting hidden rooms to hidden paths, offering those who knew the code an entire system of secret movement. Shifting corridors and changing doors. The walls themselves all told lies. Delsorka knew none of it and could only see half the story. This was nothing like being at sea.

At the tower's peak, the stairs ended at a thick oaken door. He knocked quietly. No answer. He knocked again, and a muffled noise came from inside. A reply of sorts, maybe an invitation to enter, but he could not be sure. Delsorka hesitated a moment, glanced over his shoulder at the empty stairway behind him, and entered.

Senya lay on a bed in the middle of the room, her eyes slack and staring at the ceiling. Her breathing came short and shallow. A glisten of sweat covered her brow.

"Who's there?"

Delsorka came to the bed. "Senya," he said. "It's Captain Delsorka..."

"How did you get in here?" she rasped. "The door is locked..."

"Money can open all kinds of doors," he assured her.

She closed her eyes and shook her head. "They know I can't move anyway, so where would I go?"

Delsorka glanced around the room. An array of windows dominated the far end. Empty desks lined two other walls. "This is your brother's workshop," he said. "Have you spoken to him?"

She swallowed thickly. Her voice came dry and tight. "No," she said. "They won't..."

A plate of untouched food sat next to the bed with a pitcher of fresh water. A pair of oil lamps gave good light to the room. Her bedding was ample and clean, and the quality attested to her being more guest than prisoner, yet the elements did not add up. This was a makeshift arrangement, hastily thrown together.

"What have they done to you?"

She shook her head. "I don't know. There was a strange pool... some kind of ritual..." She trailed off. "Crassica... and your necromancer, Ghellan..."

"He's not *my* necromancer."

A dark painted marking lined her exposed forearm. Delsorka examined a series of strange characters up to her shoulder. Fury laced through him. That godscursed conjureman and his meddling again. There was so much here Delsorka did not understand. Crassica gave him nothing. Why all the mysteries? What was she up to? None of his past deals with her had ever directly involved any of these sorcerers. Never involved necromancy. Why hold Senya here in this tower, her brother's tower of all places, and keep her drugged or under some incantation or whatever twisted thing Ghellan had worked up? Delsorka hated being the last to know. He rose and gently stroked Senya's hand.

"All right," he said. "I need to poke around some more. See what I can figure out. Something doesn't ring right around here."

"Can you find my brother for me?"

"I can try," he said. "But for now, get some rest. And be careful eating whatever they're giving you."

Lanius stepped from the shadows into the torchlight of the hall and waited. Delsorka had been remarkably clumsy tonight for a man with a reputation of doing plenty of dark things for the master. His first mistake, of course, had been trusting the wrong servants. Underlings were not so versed in the inner machinery of secrets. People talked. They whispered. They showed their thoughts and intentions in ways that were quite public, even when done in private. That gaggle of idiots frequently made this an easy game to play. Lanius simply had to watch and listen. When those who lived and labored in the quiet corners of the Keep displayed what they knew in unsuspecting ways, he saw, and he heard. Like when the guard of the Keep had evaporated. Telltale signs of action afoot. Raedwin had escaped because Lanius hadn't been in the Keep at the time—a mistake he would not allow to be repeated. Tonight, he would tend to business properly.

Lanius had never quite trusted Delsorka, in spite of all the times they'd worked alongside one another. That sailor cared too much about the stories behind the jobs he did. He pondered the big picture, about what it all added up to, rather than just doing his job and doing it well. Empathy was not a good trait in certain professions.

Tonight, for instance, Delsorka had shown himself to be far too interested in the reasons behind Crassica's plans and actions. That much was obvious. He'd probably fallen in love with the girl on that boat of his. That would be the most likely cause. Things happened at sea. There could be other motivations for sure—money, power, ownership of things—but simple infatuation is what took most men down. Lanius found the whole show to be rather entertaining. Crassica, of course, saw Delsorka's overly meddlesome focus on Senya as a frank betrayal and was not amused, but Lanius enjoyed a good laugh now and again.

The poor sailor had been mistaken in so many ways. Shadowed corridors were clearly not his place of business. Delsorka had emerged from his rooms immediately after the guard disappeared, moving from shadow to shadow and thinking himself unseen. But Lanius had followed at a comfortably hidden distance. Perhaps at sea Delsorka would prove a fearsome adversary, but here in the master's Keep he was unequal to the elements of stealth. Together they had danced in this manner through various passages for some time, until Delsorka finally arrived at the stairs to the iron tower. To Raedwin's workshop. To Senya.

Lanius smiled to himself. *Here is your story, my dear Delsorka. Watch and learn. Here is the narrative that you yourself helped create. Read the signs and understand. Perhaps the world shall make itself clearer to you now.*

Lanius almost felt sorry for him. After many years of service, his life would come to a sad conclusion tonight. Delsorka himself would end tonight. When orders were questioned, outcomes debated, or the reasonings examined, then the entire structure of a civilized existence would come apart. This could not be allowed to happen. Crassica would surely agree. Rogue elements, especially ones as capable and dangerous as Delsorka, must be checked in their path and dealt with immediately and without argument. In these matters Lanius was solely the master's tool. Nothing more, and nothing less. He understood his role as a keen weapon kept at the ready. There were to be no questions, no doubts, no parley with chance, and never more than one way forward.

Crassica had been furious when Lanius had mentioned the likely turning of Delsorka. But he'd assured her this lesion would not be allowed to fester. Crassica was not to worry. Lanius would deal with the matter, and deal with it swiftly.

Delsorka emerged into the hall, returning from Raedwin's tower. His face showed all the story Lanius needed—a look of defeat and concern, of plans to take his newly beloved girl away from all of this. To make the world brighter for him and his daring new love. Lanius stepped out of the shadows.

Delsorka stopped short. His face passed through a series of acknowledgments, from surprise to acceptance to shock of sudden understanding.

"Lanius," he said crisply.

"Captain."

"Why are you here?"

"I believe you know why I am here."

"Do I?"

"All this time," Lanius said, "I thought you and I held the same understanding of our roles in this world and the necessity of remaining on our assigned paths. When one deviates, there are consequences."

"Things change."

"Do they? Does anything ever really change?"

"Do you know what's going on up there?"

"It is not my place to know. Nor is it yours."

"She's just a girl."

"A woman, you mean," Lanius corrected. "Older than both of us."

"And that makes it okay?"

"You show a lack of trust. A lack of belief in Her High Honor's truth."

"I need to talk to Crassica. I need to understand."

Lanius drew his dagger and held it at his side. "Crassica does not speak to traitors."

Delsorka drew his own stout knife. "So this is what it's come to?"

"You yourself have brought us here, to this very moment, and yet you ask."

"You're going to allow her to do whatever she wants?"

"It is not my place to allow or disallow what the master requires. Nor is it yours. We are weapons in an arsenal. Nothing more, and nothing less."

"You always were heartless, Lanius."

The Sword Hand gave a cold thin smile. "And you, my dear Delsorka, have always been soft and weak."

Delsorka stepped toward him, his movements slow and calm, almost casual. Lanius waited. Delsorka was, of course, still dangerous. This was not a man one confronted too quickly, too justly, in that risky egotistical manner of duelists and fair-minded fools. This was a man who must be done quickly and cleanly, with misdirection and confusion, as an assassin would. Already Lanius had probably allowed himself too much play.

Delsorka feinted a lunge and Lanius shifted into his path to press the sailor's movements against the wall. He brandished the dagger. Delsorka backed away.

"We should talk about this," Delsorka said. "Before things get too... permanent."

"We are talking. These are words we use..."

"We both serve Crassica. This is nonsense."

"You mean to say we both formerly served the same master. Clearly such is not the case anymore."

Delsorka feinted a slash upward. Lanius deftly sidestepped and brought his dagger cleanly across Delsorka's chest. A noisy hiss came from the doomed man's mouth. Delsorka attempted another thrust. Lanius cut along his exposed forearm and passed on to the side of his abdomen. Delsorka spun to slash backhanded and Lanius bent his body away, cutting him again on the chest, upward to his shoulder. Delsorka grunted. He brandished his blade with good balance and body position, yet he found nothing but air. Lanius cut him again across the gut.

"There have been others, you know," Lanius said. "Those who thought they could come here and take from the master and then leave again with their lives. None fared very well." He stepped back and crouched on his haunches as if to warm himself from a hidden campfire.

Each of Delsorka's breaths came with a struggle. Blood spread through his linen shirt in several places. Lanius watched the sailor's eyes in that dim subterranean light and found new fear—fear and weakness of a sort that had not seemed possible in this man's face. Perhaps Delsorka had come at last to an understanding of this place, the point at which his death was ultimately to come.

Delsorka made a last lunge to escape Lanius barring his path. He swept his blade to parry a thrust by his killer, but his movements were slowed by injury, by dimness of eyesight, and by the cruel measure of fate that holds one man to be faster than another. Lanius swept him aside and burst upward from his crouch, bringing his dagger upward across Delsorka's neck, releasing all blood, air, and life to the outside world. He pressed hard, and then let the limp body of Delsorka slide from his blade down the wetness of the wood-paneled wall to lay in a misshapen heap at his feet.

Lanius stood for a moment and waited. No movement came, no final breath, no words. The sound of guttering torches flickered through the hall. He wiped his dagger on the dead man's shirt, stood, and walked away to locate a custodian of these halls to request prompt removal of this disgusting mess.

❧ 60 ❧

OVER THE years, many had fought against Crassica. They had risen as individuals or banded together in groups to claim control over her. Some had won small victories, caused minor pains or annoyances, but many more had lost. Most had lost bitterly. Victory and defeat alike had taken a toll on her self-made body. Scars crossed her pale skin in many places. Assassins' blades had left long marks from her time among the emperors of Kalldonia. Burns and slash wounds from struggles among petty thieving men in the chaos that followed. Perhaps she was a horror to behold. Or perhaps she remained pure and beautiful, her flesh sourced from the waters of the sea and the binding firmaments of the earth, from sunlight and stone woven into one. Who was to tell? She allowed few to truly see her and fewer still to have the complete view.

And yet she fought on. She burned through her dwindling store of Amaris, pulling its liquid power through her as she strengthened and spread her reach. The last of it would bring an end to everything.

Seeing through the eyes of her nine remaining Vallahnir, she watched as they moved through the forest east of her citadel with a keenly honed awareness. Together they represented the greatest concentration of Vallahnir ever seen outside the Valle d'Brasti, a force of great power and reckoning by any stretch of the imagination.

A band of armed men strode alongside them. Three score, or perhaps four, these men would do what the Vallahnir themselves were not well-versed in doing—wield the weapons of this world to quick and devastating

scattered among the untouched Vallahnir. Moans and cries of pain died away into silence.

As the last man fell, scores of the creatures emerged from the trees. Their numbers seemed impossible. Perhaps two hundred, perhaps more. They drew a wide circle around the remaining Vallahnir and moved closer. Crassica urged them to pulse forth the Sharpness, but to no avail. These strange killers remained unconcerned as they closed in.

One of the creatures stepped forward and raised his bow. Several of the others did the same. Their leader cried out in the singing language of the Jehndai, and together as one, they loosed their arrows.

The nine Vallahnir dropped to the ground, as if the strings of life holding each upright were all suddenly severed. Crassica's vision flickered and blinked as the Jehndai rushed forward to finish off the bodies with their quick flashing blades.

"Remember," she heard Raedwin call to them from some distance away. "First the heads, and then fire."

They cut with wrath and vengeance, tearing the bodies of the Vallahnir to shreds while others among them gathered fuel. Crassica's vision pinched away into nothingness.

To lose nine of her beloved Vallahnir Sisters, all in the same moment, crushed the very air from Crassica. Bodies banished from this plane, spirits sent back into the Crosslands to remain shapeless and formless for all time yet to come. This was an agony like nothing she had ever experienced since emerging into this weak and pale body. The piercing shock nearly split her asunder.

Twelve had emerged from the Crosslands to stand alongside her, and yet now only one remained. All gone, save for one faithless traitor.

How could such a thing be possible? How could scores of heavy fighting men and nine powerful Vallahnir be crushed in a single moment? Crassica struggled to steady herself as she limped down the last few steps to Sadahlia's chamber with its iron cage dangling over the glistening black pool. A lone oil lamp burned in its mount against the wall. She pressed a hand against the damp wall as she entered the dripping cell.

"Sadahlia," she called softly. "My dear sweet Sister, what has become of us?" She stepped closer and sat on a stone bench beside the pool.

Only one remained.

Sadahlia stirred on her makeshift bed. "Get out," she moaned. "Leave me alone."

A shiver went through Crassica, not from cold but from some final, deep weakness of flesh that she found new and vaguely concerning. "This enterprise was not born of ignoble dreams," she said to the empty pool. Drawing an uncertain hand across the smoothness of her bare head, she wavered for a brief moment, here in this darkest of places, before recovering.

"I am so close," Crassica said, her voice rising, regaining footing.

Sadahlia propped herself up, her eyes glittering with rage. "Either free me, or go and die someplace else." She turned away and lay back down.

Crassica sat up straighter, her pallid fingers stroking the edge of the bench. "I remain Crassica the White, despite this cruel wave of destruction Raedwin has brought upon us. I remain the One Before and the One Beyond. This… even this… will not vanquish me."

Sadahlia remained facing the far wall. "I truly wish that were not the case."

Crassica watched her, the first Sister of the Great Gathering, the spearhead of her hope, her grand dream, the promise of what could yet come. "You think you have found victory this day," she said. "That your feeble allies have won."

Sadahlia rose and shifted to look upon her master, eyes burning with hatred. "Do I look happy to you?"

"This will end worse for you than it will for me."

"As long as your end comes, I'll be fine."

Crassica rose, a new energy filling her fragile frame. "I gave you so much, you ungrateful child. I provided your life, your home, and indeed your love. And this is how you repay the debt?"

"I would pay you with more pain and regret, but my accounts seem to have all run dry."

"You were the first. You were the belief in what could be done, what we could achieve together, the greatness of life brought forth from the Crosslands. And yet look at you now. The last of them all. The final Sister, now nothing more than a bruised picture of betrayal and deceit."

"A mirror of she who brought me here."

"There's nobody left to protect you, Sadahlia, not anymore. With our beloved Sisters gone, we have nothing left here to guard against that foolish child's incursions. Nothing but you, and the focus of his desires. Raedwin is coming, that much I know. He is coming for you. And so I will be here for him. I will lie in wait and I will watch and I will see each of his impotent attempts, and then I will strike. This will be the end of him and of you as well. That much I can assure you."

Sadahlia watched her former master and friend, her past colleague and partner. "What you say to me now, much like everything you have ever said to me before, is steeped in lies, delusions, and mistruths. My Raedwin will come, yes, but he will not come in a way you will expect. Your methods will deceive you and your own eyes will blind you, and that is how you will find your end. Maybe here, in this very room."

Crassica allowed herself a humorless smile. "I must leave you now, my sweet Sadahlia, for the last time. Where I am going, you cannot follow. What I am doing, you cannot be part of. Not now, and not ever again."

Closing her eyes, Sadahlia drew her knees up to her chest and wrapped her arms around her body. When she spoke again, her voice was steady and strong. "Before you go, I have a wish for you," she said. "I wish for you a wandering and diminished nothingness, with no shape or form, and no memory of ever having lived. I wish for you to be forgotten. With nobody left to remember you. No birth, no life, and no descendants. Tossed out beyond the Crosslands into the Everdark for all time yet to come."

Crassica straightened as she stood. She moved to leave and then turned back for a final look. "I cannot help you, Sadahlia, not anymore. There was a time in which I could. Alas, even very recently. But the choices you have made belong to you and you alone. You have brought these struggles upon yourself. Here you shall remain to deal with them all. I am sorry for this. Truly sorry. But a million sorrowful regrets cannot change the truth. You are broken, and there is nothing I can do to fix what will happen to you."

Crassica turned away from her former apprentice and friend, her past colleague and partner, and stepped into the black mouth of the waiting stairway.

❦ 61 ❦

SENYA'S VISION lit with images, disjointed and vivid. Dawn was coming slowly, as if taking its precious time to acknowledge the day's events set before it. Stars winked out one by one, clinging to the darkness they left behind. The horizon boldened to gray. Her vision followed Raedwin as he moved quickly through folded lands east of the Keep. Three tall pale-furred creatures followed, all bristling with weapons. Steel glinted in the low light, and powerful longbows flashed stark and white against the predawn sky.

The clear image of her brother awakened Senya, lifting her cloudy grogginess. Her perception began to clear. She watched as they approached the Valle d'Brasti, weaving through hidden shadowed creases in the land.

Crassica had blundered yet again, unlocking yet more power within her. Senya held the full Sight now, like the Vallahnir master herself.

The Sight.

Raedwin, she reached. *I'm here.*

He stopped and glanced behind, clearly confused.

Raedwin, she reached again. *I'm here. In the Keep.*

Senya?

Yes. I'm here. I'm in your tower…

She could sense him piecing together his sister being in his own workshop, a thought both incongruous and strange, even after everything.

What has she done to you? he said. *Are you safe?*

None of us are safe.

She's been trying to coax you here. I don't know why. I never understood it. Something about our blood—yours and mine. But there is nothing for either of us here. There never really was.

And there never will be. She wanted to tell him of her struggles to find him—beginning first with the Vallahnir's message in Posselhead—of the Hallonath, of Brogan and their journey to Corregidon, of each piece of her strange new awakening power. But there was no time, not now.

Find me in the tower, she called. *Crassica has done nothing that can't be undone. We have to go after her together. She has too much power for either of us to confront alone. We have to be together.*

Sadahlia is somewhere in the Keep.

Yes, she's underground, deep in the tunnels. They have her caged, over water...

She could feel his emotions surge. Anger and hope churned at one another, fighting for dominance before he subdued them both into calm and controlled focus.

Okay, he said at last. *I'm coming to get you.*

62

THE SEVENFOLD KEEP loomed overhead with no signs of life save a few trails of smoke from early cookfires in the lower courtyards. Raedwin's tower, his former workshop of iron and glass, glittered in the half-light. It reached into the sky, a symbol of his broken past and the shattered promises of what could've been, housed in an oversized sky-bound jewel box.

And Senya up there, imprisoned. Waiting too long already.

Raedwin knew from experience there would be no watchmen at the windows, nobody paying attention to protect against direct assault. Confident in the fear her reputation produced, Crassica was never one to worry over creating a bastion for defense. This was no fortress, not anymore.

As planned, the Jehndai horde began their diversion with noise. Raedwin watched from a distance as the first group stormed the ruins of the gate, a cacophony of howling battle cries throwing up a cloud of stony dust to hide numbers and conceal the scores that raced in behind. Such things were most successful when they were loud, fast, and confusing.

Fire followed. Jehndai in the vanguard carried a blazing torch in each hand and set alight anything that would burn—hay piles, wooden crates, roof thatch. They kissed the citadel with flame, moving westward away from the Keep toward the lower gardens and stables.

The servants and residents of the citadel took up arms to meet the onslaught and defend their homes. Some were trained fighters, but most were not. None gave ground without a fight. Rejected by the rest of the world, they'd come to live in a place that would finally fully accept them.

They stood firm and struck back with whatever weapons they could find, fought with pikes and shortswords, with arrows and knives, and with an assortment of tools normally used for hunting or cooking. The central cluster of stone buildings quickly locked down into a fortified redoubt amid the dust-strewn bodies of the dead. Those armed with whatever could aim and shoot stood at shattered windows and sent volley after volley into the shrieking Jehndai. The invaders took cover and returned arrow for arrow. Some found their targets while others clattered uselessly against stone.

Smoke billowed from the burning piles of detritus along the north wall. A few smaller structures belched out flames. Shrieks and cries met one another from each side as the barrage settled to a standstill.

A second wave of Jehndai poured through the gate then, as silent and swift as the first had been deafening and deliberate. They swept upward to the east, gaining purchase through the Keep's breached west wall near the base of Raedwin's tower. Death came quickly to anyone they encountered. As they penetrated and climbed the northwest corner, an archer stopped at every open window to cover the lower citadel as well as the inner courtyard. Others flew to occupy the opposite tower for the same deadly purpose.

The time for death had come to the Valle d'Brasti, and the end of Crassica's reign. There would be no more corrupted births in agony, no more Jehndai to endure the torturous manipulations of her degenerate hand. The time had come for revenge.

Raedwin quickly led three elite Jehndai into the ruined village below the bluffs under the eastern foundations of the Keep. They made their way to the same derelict house from which he'd escaped days before. Dipping inside, they descended with footfalls echoing through the abyss. They paused for a brief moment to light torches before continuing downward, directly into the bowels of the Keep.

Raedwin knew that so much of what Crassica did was for the mind—to move it, to know it, to control it. Her body was so weak at times, but charming the minds around her meant she neatly controlled her entire world. And Amaris, of course, helped to fuel that control.

So how would that all play out? Surely she would've thought about what imprisonment would mean to Sadahlia and how it would make her feel. And of course she would've anticipated Raedwin coming to find his love. She would've considered their shared hopelessness, Raedwin's sense of necessity, his torment and desperation. So what message would she send? What twisted logic would she use to torture him? Where would she hold his love?

He'd pondered all these questions and more during these past few days in the forest. But all of his ruminations, his thoughts and efforts, became so vague and hopeless now that he was here. In truth, Sadahlia could be almost anywhere. Senya had said she was underground, deep in the tunnels, but this warren of mazes and twisting corridors could be used in a myriad of confusing ways. He had never explored certain depths. And suspended over water? Raedwin knew of no water under the Keep other than the cistern, which had no height above to allow suspension of an iron cage.

Crassica, of course, would want to keep Sadahlia secure, keep her away from the eyes of the servants, and so many hidden spaces down here could easily be suited to hold somebody against her will. With an irony that split his gut, Raedwin knew it was really Sadahlia herself who would best know where Crassica would hold her. If only he could ask.

With the three Jehndai at his side, he first tried the cistern underneath the Keep, to be sure, which did prove fruitless. Then the cavernous cells and corridors around the great tortured Pit, after which he retraced some of the lesser passages northward under the armory and the smithy, searching all the chambers and strange ruined rooms as well as several side halls. Nothing. Then, under the northwest tower, they tried an arcade that led nearly to the surface. Still nothing. Twice they had to retreat and duck into shadows to avoid being spotted.

He did not have time for this. Soon the Jehndai horde would tear this whole citadel apart, and the world would close in around him.

As he led the Jehndai past the pit one last time, past the dusty evidence of lingering tortures and nightmares, Raedwin gestured for the three of them to gather close. They needed to forget Sadahlia for the moment and get to Senya first. His sister was right—all of them would be stronger together. So he would go straight to the heart. Together with the Jehndai, he would make his way through the tunnels near where Crassica slept in order to access the lone stairway to the tower. They would need to keep silent and kill anybody who discovered them.

"And if we run into Crassica along the way," he said, mostly to himself, "then we can put an end to this whole business all that much faster."

63

BROGAN AND KAETAS saw the smoke long before they reached the Valle d'Brasti. As they made their approach, a pillar of black billowed in the distance, churning as it rose into the wide Kalldonian sky. Chaos unfolded before them. The lower compound was almost completely engulfed in flame. Men and women darted among the burning structures, brandishing an incongruous array of makeshift weapons. Several tall ghostly creatures appeared as well, armed with pikes and elegant longbows, leaping with grace and agility, vaguely human but clearly something else entirely.

"This," the lead guide said finally, "is where we leave you. We can go no farther."

Flaming arrows flew downward from two of the Keep's towers, lighting fresh flames inside the walls, feeding the massive fire. Brogan and Kaetas dismounted along with the other sailors and gathered their weapons, strapping gear tightly to be ready for movement and action. Secrecy wasn't much of an issue anymore.

"Probably for the better," Kaetas said to Brogan. "Taking a ship already in chaos tends to be easier than trying to sneak aboard when everything's calm and quiet."

They took leave of their guides and followed the causeway toward the ancient fortress. Nothing gave evidence of an organized assault—no siege engines lined the walls, and no armies surrounded the citadel. It was as if the entire compound was devouring itself whole from the inside out.

They approached the remains of the northern gate, keeping out of sight as best they could. Men and women hacked with axes and pitchforks, and a few used blunt wooden clubs. The strange ghostly besiegers worked them over with arrows. A lone horse emerged from the flames and galloped blindly into the dry hills behind them.

An armed man crawled away from the scene through the grass, a bloody arrow shaft jutting from his thigh. He raised a hand to Brogan and Kaetas, mumbling incoherent pleas for mercy.

"They came from the forest," the man panted. "Like demons out of the trees…"

"We're looking for a girl," Brogan said. "Small. Orange eyes and dark brown skin. Black hair. Name of Senya."

The man panted in short gulps, closed his eyes, and lay back.

"She'd be hard to miss," Brogan added. "Would've arrived a few days ago, maybe with a sailor named Delsorka."

"Please," the man said, twitching in pain. His shaky hand reached for the arrow shaft.

Kaetas and one of the sailors bent to the man's thigh. She took hold of the shaft.

"Where is the girl?" Brogan asked gently.

The man winced. "She was up in that tower… when all this started," he wheezed. "The iron one… where Raedwin used to work…"

"Raedwin? That's her brother. Where is he?"

"Her brother?" The man's eyes went wide. He fell back into the grass. "Hells," he muttered. "That was his sister…"

Kaetas gestured to the sailor, who peeled away the man's bloody pantleg. Brogan urged him to keep talking. Kaetas quickly shoved the arrow shaft clear. The man hissed and wheezed. The sailor deftly wrapped his wound with a long strip of cloth, securing it tightly.

"Thank you," the man managed.

"Where is Raedwin?"

He gathered himself and shook his head, gesturing vaguely at the walls and the destruction around them. "This," he said weakly. "All this shit is him."

"Tell us where to find the girl."

"Four of us had orders to stand guard at the tower entrance, just before the assault," he said. "But I have no idea where she'd be now."

Brogan glanced at Kaetas, and they shared a silent nod between them.

They thanked the man and gave him a drink. Ensuring that his fresh bandage was secure and the bleeding stemmed, they gave him a spare waterskin and left him to his fate in the grass.

The chaos grew oddly quiet once they were inside the walls. The body of a man with an arrow through his neck sat near the remains of the gate, bent forward as if paying silent homage to their triumphant entry. Flames cracked and spat from a blazing hay pile nearby. A half-burned dog scrambled past.

Shouting erupted from somewhere in the lower compound. Brogan led Kaetas and her sailors in a crouching run over a narrow stone bridge into the upper Keep. The iron tower rose before them, its base an improbable union of iron and stone woven with an elegant orchestration of materials and engineering. The Keep's courtyard lay immediately beyond the tower, with series of stout buildings and a vast doorway looming on the far side. Anxious soldiers emerged and scurried across the courtyard to the bridge, joining the fray below.

The sailors of the *Hawk* kept an eye out for pursuit as Kaetas and Brogan searched for any kind of door in the base of the tower. At length they agreed to split up. There was no sense in all of them trying to do the same thing. They didn't know for sure if Senya was in the tower. Speed mattered now more than anything. The game had changed. Brogan would figure out how to get in and see what was up top, while Kaetas and her sailors would check the buildings and try to find Raedwin. They would meet back here as fast as they could.

Brogan watched Kaetas and her sailors go. They located a doorway in one of the nearby structures and disappeared inside. He turned back to the iron and stone puzzle beside him, surveyed the base again, and glanced around for any obvious opening.

"Okay," he muttered as he circled to his original position near the bridgehead. "So how do I get inside this thing?"

64

"I DON'T KNOW how many are out there," Lanius said, his voice calm and measured. "But enough to prove difficult to hold at bay for long."

Crassica leafed through the parchments in front of her—sections of the citadel, plans of structures and maps of the underground tunnels. She paused at a diagram of the Keep with its towers and courtyards, its grand hall and throne room all clustered to the east.

Had Raedwin chosen to destroy everything rather than rescue his many loves? His work? All that he cherished? His beloved Sadahlia? His sister even...?

A sudden realization gripped her. She clutched the side of the table and stumbled to her chair. She sat.

"Senya..." she muttered to herself.

Raedwin could not have come for his sister. There was no way he knew Senya was here. He would have joined with those ungrateful Children out in the forest, inciting this ridiculous rebellion, and he would storm the Valle d'Brasti to find Sadahlia—all without knowing what he was really doing, what was actually at risk.

Reaching to retrieve a small glass vial, she let a single drop of her last Amaris reserves fall into a chalice of wine. So little remained—time and Amaris both.

"This is nothing new," Lanius assured her. "Those freaks in the forest have been gathering for some time. You know that."

Crassica raised the chalice and drank. She closed her eyes and shook her head. "This has nothing to do with them. This is all Raedwin."

There was no way the Children would have put all this together without him. She had seen. He had fomented their passion with that nonsense at the mine, sparked this intense frenzy, and provoked their eager hearts. And now they had brought that inferno to her door.

She needed to leave. She would have to abandon her beloved Keep and leave nearly everything behind. But if Raedwin was focused on Sadahlia, then she could use his blindness against him. She could find some leverage to counter their whole effort, use Senya and Sadahlia both, without any of them knowing the truth.

"We remain within reach, my Lanius," Crassica muttered, her voice rising and regaining strength. She sat up straighter. "Raedwin will, of course, seek his cherished lover, but..."

She stood again and looked over the table, searching the parchments to find one specific sheet. She pulled a plan that showed the various tunnels below the Keep, the maze of passages, their sizes and arrangements, scanning for which ones led to secret exits. "Where are your men? That elite group you spoke of."

"Right outside, keeping these doors secure."

Crassica nodded and settled into herself. Steady. "Okay. That is good." Her confidence began to return. "We will fashion a defense, here and here." She pointed at breaches in the Keep's walls where they adjoined the citadel below, ordering him to set his men in a perimeter. "The citadel below can burn, but see to it that no Jehndai passes into this place. We cannot allow them inside."

"And what of Sadahlia?"

"What of her? She is below, where she belongs. We will use her as the delicious bait that she is. We will use Raedwin's own foolishness to defeat this silly incursion of his."

"And if he gets to her first?"

"He cannot have her! He will have nothing!" Crassica slammed a fist on the table. "This is exactly why I needed him brought to heel before! I created his power, and he owes it to me. He cannot be allowed to leave this place alive." She glared at Lanius, enraged. "He has caused all of this, and now he is threatening everything. He will not have Sadahlia. They die first. All of them."

Crassica sat down again, collecting herself. She reached a wavering hand to the chalice and brought the rim to her lips. "Shortly, I will descend to Sadahlia," she said. "The bait is laid, and the trap shall spring. I want

367

Raedwin close to his goal so I can watch his eyes dim in the last few seconds while I destroy him."

A sly grin slid across Lanius's face, laced with a deep and respectful affection for brutal strength. "I understand," he said quietly.

"After you ready your men and devise a plan to your satisfaction, you must go to the tower. Check on Senya and see that she is secure. Ensure that Raedwin cannot get to her. I will join you when all of this is finished. Send for Ghellan. We shall complete the transference without delay."

She lifted the chalice and drank slowly, letting her eyes drive into Lanius. Her voice came cold and flat as she finished. "Do not let me regret having left my prize up in that tower alone."

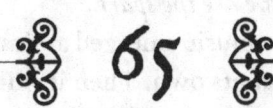

65

SENYA COULD almost hear Raedwin down in the tunnels. She could sense but not see. He was below somewhere, amid the fire and the desperate fighting. The shape of his path was vague and uncertain, obscured by whatever misdirection Crassica held over this place.

She needed to get out. To get to Raedwin and help direct him to Sadahlia. They needed to work together.

She tried the door. Locked. Always locked. She called for the guards. "I need... water."

No answer.

"Please, the smoke... I don't know that I'll be able to breathe in here much longer."

Whispers. Muted discussions on the other side of the door.

"Please... I just need some water. They've left nothing for me in here. Can you open the door?"

They gave no answer. She pleaded, to no avail. Nothing she said would garner any response. Senya crumpled to the floor and sat back against the wall. She closed her eyes, shaking with fury. All this time, all this distance, all the lives and death she'd seen to get here, and this would be the end of it. So close, and yet still so far away.

She boiled with rage, and then the rage shifted into something else. Something new. Words and phrases flickered at the back of her mind, only now coming within reach. Her left eye pulsed and twitched, a strange, invigorated prickle forming directly behind it.

She may be blocked from much of her innate power of healing, the familiar voice she'd held and used all her life, but she had gained something else in the bargain of this place, something new—something with a power all its own, sprung forth from the swirling darkness of the Crosslands.

A gift from Crassica. A power with which to destroy.

Senya eased into crafting sound out of this feeling, the trembling urges of escape crying out from the back of her mind, invigorated and relentless.

You are the vessel, and we are the spark.

She began to sing. The music emerged at first as nothing more than a low anguished moan, all on its own. Then it shifted and curled, forming a new involuntary hymn. Notes marked themselves against one another into a slow, coursing melody. Almost a chant. A strange, fresh power joined and took control. The voice was not hers, yet she followed and let it create its own particular path.

A Mother of Vallahnir. A Speaker to the Dead.

Fear and terror could be her weapons now, if she wanted them—the gift they called the Sharpness. She could lance the hearts of men with a thought. She could use this new offering to bring every one of these walls down around her, if she allowed it.

The lock in the door slid open, and the first guard entered. He turned to Senya, his face a mask of shock and fear, the face of a man with no control over his own movements. Senya sang on. The second guard entered as well.

She stood and went to them, her tiny frame a fraction of their size. Fear coursed around both men in a swirling shimmer she could almost see. The color of white-hot pain. Twin songs came to her at once—the new voice of the Vallahnir, swirling and ready, but then another emerged as well. A renewed life for her Brohndai blood churned and argued against the Vallahnir, the cycling river of all living things, unlocked and raw. The old fought to hold off the new. She could almost see the guards' weaknesses, touch hidden wounds in need of tending. Her own fear entwined with that of these two men, struggling for supremacy, becoming a new kind of weapon.

The Sharpness.

The power lit out from her, swirling and pummeling the guards.

You did this to me, she said softly without speaking, the words forming in both their minds without any sound from her mouth. *All of you.*

The Sharpness pulled at their fear, shaped it, drove it inward. The rigid bodies of the men shook as she crushed the breath from their chests.

You opened powers from a wound that may never heal, she whispered. *And I am sorry, but this is how it must end.*

The first man wanted to speak, to open his mouth and scream, but Senya only wished for quiet. For a gentle finish. For all the pain everywhere in the world to stop. She put the palm of her free hand to his cheek, deep brown on white, warm on cold. A tear made its way down her cheek, and she wiped it away with the back of her hand. Both guards crumpled to the floor. Neither of them moved again.

Her song died away into the echoes of the fighting far below.

She knelt between the bodies, making sure both were dead. "I'm sorry," she whispered. "I am truly sorry."

Pulling a shortsword from the first guard's scabbard, she rose and went to the window. Nearly all of the lower citadel was already in flames. The fire reached up the brush-choked slope to the crumbled walls of the Keep itself, searching for new fuel. The courtyard below was mostly empty. The majority of the fighting flared along the gaps of the breached walls, the Keep's guard holding strong. There was no sign of Raedwin nor of Crassica.

With sword in hand, Senya left the room.

❦ 66 ❧

BROGAN CREPT along the underground passage, on the alert for any sound or movement. Making his best guess for getting inside the tower, he worked his way inward and down, first to the north and then back to the west. At long last he came to a wood-paneled hallway leading to the entrance of an iron stairwell. Two heavily armed guards stood to either side. A prisoner of great value must be up those stairs, important enough to post two armed guards here, well underground, while the outside world burned in chaos.

Brogan dropped the first with an arrow through his throat. The second barely had time to turn before he fell beside the first. Brogan stepped toward the opening.

"The hero has arrived," a voice came from behind him. "At last."

A wiry man emerged from the shadows of a side corridor. Narrow nose and dark eyes. Thin, but powerfully built, his long blond hair almost menacing in its loose array.

Brogan drew and nocked another arrow, holding tense on the bowstring. "Where is Senya?"

The man's upper lip curled into a sinister smile. "Is brandishing one's weapon the proper way to introduce oneself to his host? Especially after you display such rudeness to my men?"

"She's a friend of mine, and she's leaving with us."

The man stepped sideways, gazing at the ceiling as if considering. "Friends are important indeed. A vital thing in life. But where are the rest of your friends, I wonder? Here we are together, you and I alone, and we must ask ourselves, where are our compatriots? Our brothers- and sisters-in-arms. Perhaps they are engaged with one another elsewhere? Perhaps even now their steel meets steel…"

Brogan never saw the blade appear. One moment the man's hands were free, and in the next a long thin dagger was there, glinting in the torchlight. Brogan drew the bow fully and loosed.

The man was fast. Very fast. In a blink, he ducked the arrow and came low and close to Brogan, passing the dagger twice across his chest. Brogan fended the first with the empty bow, but the second caught him deeply above the right shoulder. He stumbled backward. Falling from his grip, the bow clattered across the stone floor. Brogan drew his sword.

"At times like these, I do truly enjoy my work," the man said. He stepped slowly along the far wall, more casually than circumstances would dictate. "But you trespass here, which perhaps in your mind is heroic and admirable. However, this is a gross transgression that cannot be left unpunished."

Brogan stepped forward and flaunted his sword in a quick feint and then passed the blade across the man's chest. Almost inhuman in flexibility, the man dodged most of the blow but caught a bit of edge along his forearm. With no reaction to the cut, he stepped forward and slashed Brogan twice along his ribs.

Instinctively grabbing his side, Brogan's fingers came away wet with his own blood. He lunged again, but this man anticipated everything. The killer twisted to the side and drove his own blade, opening Brogan's forearm in a long gash. Stepping back, he stalked along the far wall. The man's movements remained measured and controlled. "There have been others, you know," he said. "Those who had the mistaken impression they could trespass here and leave again with their lives. But none fared very well in that endeavor…"

"Lanius!" A second man emerged from a side passage. "This is no time for your incessant chatter." Necromantic tattoos covered much of the bald man's forehead and upper face. "Finish this, and let's get to the tower!" A narrow beard fell in twin braids over his sturdy leather armor. The man held a strange twisted staff with a glass ball wired to a notch at its peak. Thick bluish liquid sloshed inside.

Lanius grinned at Brogan. "Ghellan here does not enjoy my games, but without entertainment, what joy is there in life?"

Brogan sprang at Lanius again, but the one he called Ghellan raised his staff and gave a strange and guttural shout. Brogan's body froze. He stumbled. A piercing, abject terror suddenly consumed him—a pure and clear panic. The sorcerer began to chant. A flurry of remembrances washed over Brogan—all the times he had almost died but had not, all the ways he had been afraid of death, the power of that fear to alter what he had done and how he had lived his life. How small and futile such worries had been. Almost insulting and sad now to have wasted all that energy on all those fears, when this was how he would actually die in the end—and this small ordinary dagger the thing that would finally kill him.

Brogan held up his sword, wavering and loose, nearly useless in a paralyzed grip. Lanius stepped toward him. Brogan's heart pounded. As fast as he could manage, he spun and stumbled toward Ghellan. With so little command over his body, he needed to break that sorcerer's hold, or this whole thing was already over. Ghellan easily dodged the clumsy strike. Brogan attempted again, but the panic coursing through him slowed and blunted his actions. Lanius followed with a charge low and sideways. Brogan was able to block the first strike but then missed as the dagger opened his thigh to the bone. He faltered. Lanius came again and cut his hand nearly through. Brogan's sword fell to the floor. He stumbled back, somehow remaining on his feet.

A thin smile slid across Lanius's face. He put a foot on the sword's pommel and pulled it, grinding along the stone floor, to rest against the wall behind him.

"Things have become grave for the hero," he mocked. "Grave indeed."

Brogan gave no answer. Pulling a long knife from his boot, he held it in his off hand, his wounded arm tight across his belly.

"The hero still believes he can win this day. He believes that maybe he will walk freely from this place with his life still in hand. And yet the thirsty stone already drinks his blood."

Brogan attempted a feeble attack again but was cut twice more along his ribs. He backed away, holding his torn arm against the new wounds.

"So perhaps now it is time to make deals," Lanius taunted. "Would you like to barter with us? How much would you offer for your sword? It is dear to you, I am sure. A past is shared between a man and his blade, like lovers. Together you've met various victims in your heroic past. Sword and man together, opening gateways to the Crosslands for poor unfortunate souls."

Brogan did not answer, his energy waning. The loss of blood dulled his reactions and clouded his mind. He shifted his arm against his belly, cuts adjoining cuts, blood cooling on his clothing.

Ghellan continued chanting, but his voice became lost to Brogan as Lanius came in close again. Barely able block the blade and with two more cuts across his chest, Brogan fell to his knees, eyes going slack. Lanius stepped away.

Brogan saw his daughter then—Glenna lying in a bed next to him telling the story of her latest nightmare, gripping the ragged scrap of cloth that served as her beloved blanket. Brogan held her close and whispered that everything would be okay. He was there. Her mother was there. Everything remained all right in the world.

But the girl would not accept that. She was suspicious of the simplicity of such answers. Nothing could be that easy. She smiled nonetheless, always the dutiful daughter. Shifting her tiny body to the side, she pulled her worn blanket to her cheek. Her young green eyes sparkled in the low light as she gazed into the distance, into the nightmare she'd left behind, into the space next to the bed of her careful parents, and into the future beyond all of this. She let out a small sigh and blinked. Maybe she saw more than her father ever knew, more than he could ever have possibly understood. Or maybe she saw this, her father's last moments—this hallway, this place, the corridors of this strange, ugly Keep, and this twisted creature of malice creeping toward him, dagger waiting in his pale grip.

Or maybe Glenna had known more than she saw. Maybe she had known that none of this would last forever, the bad as well as the good, the blissful ease of family, with plentiful food and a safe life. Somewhere out there, past where her small tired gaze could reach, past this room and these walls, this valley or these mountains, somewhere out there she knew, and had known all along, that no matter what any of them did, death was coming for them.

Just then, music began to form deep in Brogan's mind. Weaving through his ears, the sound seemed to come from his own inner hope as well as from somewhere outside, from both before and after he was born. A song of his daughter, his wife, and maybe a song of all mothers and sisters. His fear eased. He caught his breath.

Lanius paused, confused. He glanced at Ghellan. Was this strange new shift the sorcerer's doing? The song continued, from everywhere and nowhere at the same time. A woman's voice, light and beautiful, a voice both familiar and forever unknowable.

Senya.

She emerged at the base of the iron stairwell, nearly motionless. She stood and sang, her eyes closed and face lowered. Her body remained rigid, as if a brown crystalline shard of the earth's own core had quietly appeared on the steps, swathed in scarlet.

Lanius turned to take in this strange new threat, this lilting assault holding such unexpected strength.

"Senya!" Ghellan cried, breaking his chant. "You... cannot!" The sorcerer's breath pinched away and became labored. His face contorted in rage and fear. "How...?" These last few words dragged out nearly soundless, buried inside his smothered throat.

Lanius took a threatening step toward Senya, blade in hand, but struggled with the effort, as if the air itself held him back. Senya shuddered. A shock wave blurred the air and burst with a flash through the room. Lanius stumbled back. He nearly lost his dagger. Ghellan fell to the ground, his mouth open and gaping, seeking a breath that refused to come. His body lurched, foam slipping from the corner of his lips.

Brogan found himself suddenly free of the sorcerer's paralyzing grip. A fresh new energy surged through his body. He dove for his bow. Ghellan's skin purpled quickly with the lack of air, crushed away by this recent and surprising power. His eyes paled and drifted, losing focus.

Lanius propelled himself forward, moving awkwardly with each forced step. Senya made no reaction. She sang on, her eyes closed. Wavering on his knees, Brogan fumbled with blood-covered fingers to grab an arrow. Lanius lunged at Senya, crashing into her and pulling her body across the bottom steps onto the hallway floor. He managed to wrap one wiry arm under her chin, choking off her air. The song fell away.

Brogan finally managed to nock an arrow and draw. Lanius pressed his dagger point to Senya's neck. "Not today," he hissed at Brogan. "Not now, not here."

Senya's mouth fell open as she struggled, unable to breathe. Her eyes flashed wide. Both arms flailed behind her, trying uselessly to tear at Lanius.

"The hero is not thinking straight," Lanius taunted as he tightened the choke hold. "Perhaps his wounds have slowed his mind. He must drop his bow or risk losing the life of this girl—while he takes his time to consider..."

Brogan held firm, his strength nearly gone. A lingering sense of Senya's song danced the corridor with a life all its own.

"Does the hero not understand, I wonder? And all of this for what? This *friend*? Does the hero know what his place is in this drama? Friend or suitor or lover... which of these is..."

Lanius's voice erupted into a scream as Brogan's arrow ripped his elbow apart. His dagger flipped free and loose against the wall, flashing in the torchlight. Senya slipped from his shattered arm and gasped.

Brogan dove for the dagger, as did Lanius. Bloodied hands slipped and grabbed. Lanius found purchase first, but Brogan used his body to pin him, driving into his wounded elbow. Lanius cried out again as he fought to bring the blade to bear. Brogan forced his hand inward, using both wounded arms to shove the blade down and in, slipping the point between Lanius's ribs. The killer spat and shouted curses as Brogan slowly used his weight, crushing against one good arm, shoving the blade, pushing again and again into the killer's chest, driving the steel clean through to the floor. Blood spilled over the polished marble. Soon Lanius settled and went still. The hallway fell silent.

Steps away, Ghellan lay staring blankly at the ceiling, his lifeless mouth open, no longer striving for breath that would never come again.

Brogan struggled to hold himself upright on his knees, his own inner voice urging him not to lie down.

Don't lie down, and don't go to sleep. Stay up, and stay alive.

Senya rose and came to him. Brogan coughed and stared blankly down. His clothing was bloodied, torn and shredded, holding little of its former shape. She knelt beside him.

"How did you get here? Is Kaetas with you?"

Exhaustion hit him with an icy wave. His body collapsed sideways into her as the room swam. Straining to breathe, he submitted to resting his head against her arm.

"Hey," she said. "Stay with me."

His eyes lost focus. The hallway grew dim as his breathing slowed.

Senya began a low chant, a new song this time, weightless and pure. A Brohndai song of healing. A sense of goodness and hope surged through Brogan. Quickly ripping long strips of cloth from Ghellan's cloak, Senya bound his arm and thigh and then secured his midsection.

"Stay with me," she urged.

He held silent, clutching his belly to help stanch the bleeding in the fading light. He shivered, his body so cold. So heavy and dull. Yet somehow Senya's song warmed and lifted from within.

"Good to see you... again." His voice fell flat on the cold and bloody floor, echoing into nothing. The final sound of his words tumbled away as if useless, presiding over the unlistening ears of the newly dead. At last, he drifted off.

67

AS RAEDWIN led the Jehndai toward the iron bones of his tower, he felt none of the old pull of this place, none of its easy allure, none of the thirsty calls for learning, for knowledge and discovery. The memory of his workshop high in the tower no longer held its former fascination. Soon all of this would be gone, left to die in the darkness. And good riddance to it all.

A familiar odor wafted through the air—the strange spice of sweat and steel, along with freshly spilled blood. He rounded a corner and stopped, waving the Jehndai back. Two guards lay dead on either side of the doorway leading to his tower. Crumpled against the far side of the passage was Lanius, or what remained of him. And the sorcerer Ghellan also lay in a distorted heap of cloth nearby, dead eyes staring into nothing.

A woman was there as well, crouched over a badly wounded man on the ground, deftly binding cuts and quelling his bleeding.

Senya. At last.

Raedwin held for a long moment, watching his sister here in this hallway, so slight and graceful in her scarlet linen shift. She sang quietly to the man on the ground, trying to keep as quiet as she could.

Raedwin approached and knelt next to her. She turned and leapt at him, throwing her arms around his neck and crying his name as she held him. Gone was her hushed control, her muted stealth, her careful steps. Her cries rang through the claustrophobic halls as she pulled him tight to her.

"I'm here," he comforted. "We're here, together. We're going to be okay." He pressed his forehead to hers, this twin of his, this sister of sisters, this connection to all his history, his life. Something struck him as he did so, something new. A power radiated from her that he'd never felt before. He'd have to ask about that later.

Glancing past his shoulder, Senya gave a start as she caught sight of the three Jehndai behind him. Each moved forward slowly, focused on the two bodies crumpled in the corner, warily watching for movement.

"They're with me," Raedwin assured. "They have far more against Crassica than either of us ever will."

He pointed to the set of strange arcane markings lining both of her arms. "What happened here? What have they done?"

She stammered out something about Crassica and some preparation ritual. Ghellan was involved. Preparation for Crassica's transference, in two weeks' time. Her words came out in fits and starts with speculation and half guesses, but none of it quite made sense. He told her not to trouble herself trying to explain. They would talk about it later, in safety.

"This place is finished," he said.

They held one another again, and she fell into sobbing against his shoulder. She settled and pulled away, wiping tears from her cheeks. "We have to go," she said. "They will have heard. Crassica is still around here somewhere."

Raedwin stood. "I need to find Sadahlia first. I already searched the tunnels..."

"They have her in a cage underneath the cistern."

"Underneath? How...?"

Senya went to the body of Lanius and drew a crude set of keys from his belt, handing them over. "We'll need those."

She crouched next to the man on the ground. "Brogan," she said. "I'm sorry, but we need to go." She pulled his torso up and slid an arm under his thigh. She leaned back and took his full weight, struggling to stand with his body over her shoulder. She stumbled as she picked up a sword from the floor.

"What are you doing?" Raedwin scolded her as he stepped forward. "Let me help."

"I've got him." She set her feet and strode heavily toward the doorway leading down. The Jehndai stepped aside.

"Senya..."

"You're wasting time. Let's go."

"Hold on a second," Raedwin urged. "Let me carry him. We can do this better together."

Senya stopped. She turned to him. "Raedwin, I love you. You're my brother. You have no idea what I've been through to find you. And I want to get out of here as fast as we can." She shifted Brogan on her shoulder. "But you can either wait here and talk about it, or you can shut up and follow me."

She continued down the stairs without waiting for an answer. Raedwin shook his head and followed.

"Oh, and hey," she said and spun again to face him. "Stop trying so hard to get yourself into all this trouble. I won't have you leaving me behind again."

As they reached the cistern, an energy flickered in the depths below, dim and weak. Raedwin had not noticed it before. He directed the three Jehndai to stand guard near the entrance, urging them to keep silent. Senya laid Brogan on the ground, keeping him as protected as possible.

Senya took Raedwin to a crack in the wall. He knew Sadahlia was down there, her very beacon of life burning against the bedrock. He stepped into the blackness and headed down the wet stone stairs. Senya followed.

The descent took an eternity before they came at last to a small cavern. A single oil lamp gave unsettled light to the dim chamber.

Sadahlia knew it was him. She knew it was not the guards this time, nor Crassica, nor that bastard Lanius. She knew it was Raedwin. She could almost pull his presence toward her as the torchlight surged from the stairwell. When he finally appeared, she could not help but gasp.

He had found her. Even here, her love had come at last.

Raedwin rushed over the small bridge to her cage and fumbled with a bloody set of keys. He looked thin. Damaged. Like he'd been ill for weeks. His face and clothing were dirty and cut in a few places. Blood marred his knee. He shoved the key into the lock and swung open her iron prison.

She jumped to him and pulled him close. She began to cry. She did not tell him of the vision she'd just had in which she'd found him dead, once again, and how she'd stumbled across his lifeless body in a darkened chamber similar to this one. She'd tried to wake him. Screamed and held him and cried in ways she hadn't thought possible. She wanted to tell him she would've stayed here with him, even now, here in this cage in this room over this sinister blackwater pool, if that was the only way for them to be together. With him, she would stay anywhere. They could make friends with the rats and the worms. But she simply held him close and said nothing.

"I should've brought you some flowers." Raedwin laughed with a nervous happiness.

"There is no need for such things," she whispered. "Flowers are for the dead. We don't need symbols and nonsense like that anymore." They had each other now, and that was all that either of them needed. She glanced back at the empty cage with all of its rudeness and crude strengths, rendered now as so much nothing. Raedwin led her over the narrow bridge to the stone ledge that served as a landing.

Senya stood there, waiting. She smiled. "I told you we were in this together."

"A woman of her word." Sadahlia nodded. "I like that."

Shouts erupted far above them, reverberating down the narrow passage. A clash of metal echoed in the distance. The fighting had gotten close indeed.

68

CRASSICA KEPT to the shadows as she descended the stairs. No need to rush and risk exposure. Raedwin would return with his prize soon enough, and then her real task would begin. The boy, of course, had no real training in swords or daggers or any proper manner of blade, but Crassica knew well enough that he still held plenty of fighting skill. She needed to be very careful. Despite Raedwin being no true killer, he remained dangerous, especially paired with Sadahlia in shared desperation. One should never underestimate cornered prey. And three of those ridiculous mischief-makers from the forest were down here as well. No easy matter, those ones. Deft in their movements, and utterly serious in their ability to kill. Crassica blamed herself for not spending more effort on keeping all of these hideous *Children* well encased in chains. She would tend to them when this current nonsense was over.

Amaris surged through her body, giving the tingling buzz of lightning in a cage. Ghellan had assured her direct ingestion, undiluted, should last for an hour or more. It would steady her body and grant her speed. Sharper reflexes. Potent focus. Keen precision with a blade.

An hour would be far more than necessary.

From out of sight in the stairwell, safely tucked in the dark, Crassica made whimpering noises and then let silence fall. She scraped her dagger against stone. A scrape, a tap, and then nothing.

One of the Children stepped into the shadows to investigate. Even with the creature cautious and wary, Crassica sliced his throat in silence beyond the reach of torchlight. Almost too easy.

The second proved a bit more difficult. Alerted to the silence in the corridor, this one approached with more caution and deflected Crassica's strike in a way she had not anticipated. The creature shouted. An alarming noise both human and animal. Crassica brought her sword to bear, cracking blade for blade, letting Amaris flow through her arms, flashing to the tip of her steel. She was able to finish him quickly, albeit a little too loudly. She took the third immediately after the second, with much more fuss and racket than she would have preferred. But so be it. The outcome would be the same regardless, and now the chamber stood empty and silent. All three Sevenfold's Children lay dead in the dark stairwell, beyond the torchlight's reach. Crassica stepped back and waited in the shadows, burning with a cold blue fire in her blood.

Raedwin emerged a moment later, his traitorous lover in hand. Crassica could not help but grin as an icy fury rose in her. She watched as they paused together, taking in the empty room. All three of their deadly pets now missing.

Senya emerged to join them.

Crassica drew in a sharp breath. Her vision blurred for a moment, adrenaline heaving along with the Amaris. How had Senya come to be all the way down here? Why was she not up in the tower where she belonged? Where was Lanius? How had he let this happen?

She shook away the thought. Plenty of time to deal with that later. She would speak with him soon enough.

Senya rushed to the far side of the chamber and crouched in the darkness.

A fourth. A man on the ground Crassica had not noticed before. Clearly badly wounded, this one did not look to be long for this world—not without a very good healer, very soon. He must have come in with that other band of useless fools sneaking around upstairs. Probably the core of their feeble little rescue effort. Shamefully inept, all of them.

Crassica interrupted their reunion by scraping the tip of her sword along the stone floor. The sound grated the air and echoed through the torchlit chamber. Then silence. She watched as they shared unspoken glances of confusion between them. Dragging the sword again, spasmodic on the uneven stone, she let the shadows settle back into silence. Together Raedwin and Sadahlia stood with Senya. They said nothing.

"Raedwin…" Crassica called gently from the darkness with a cloying, mocking lightness. "Welcome home, my sweet…"

Raedwin's face fell as the full realization of their position hit him—of where they stood and why his three companions had gone missing. Crassica scraped the stone again, harder this time. The sound pierced through the dead space with a horrible grinding, as if to peel the very skin from their ears. "Raedwin…" she called again and gave a biting scrape with her blade.

Raedwin drew his sword and held it at his side. Of course he understood that this would be his time, his place, his chance. He would attempt to hold his own as any man would, glorious and sadly tragic as the case may be. But in the end, he would fail. That was assured.

Crassica stepped into the light.

"Your precious Sword Hand is gone," Raedwin called. "There's nobody left to help you."

Crassica allowed a menacing smile to creep across her face. "I am far more than those I keep around me, as you yourself can attest."

Senya stood to the side and shifted her weight. She remained oddly calm, whispering quietly to herself, crafting something of a song. "Crassica," she said, simple and flat, her voice low and deliberate.

There was something behind that sound. An odd vibration. Something underneath, very familiar but nothing Crassica had ever experienced in another person before, not for all her long years among the living. A rolling shiver lit her blood.

"Leave us be!" Sadahlia shouted. "Lanius is gone. Ghellan is gone. There's nothing left for you anymore. Go back to the Crosslands and leave us alone. There's no point in remaining."

Crassica smiled. "Oh, Sadahlia, you are so wrong," she said gently, as a mother to her firstborn child. "I cannot simply leave the three of you here, can I? That would not do at all. Senya and I have much work left to do. We have only begun the transference. The field has been prepared, but the seed has yet to be sown."

"Crassica," Senya repeated flatly. The sound echoed through the chamber and reverberated over the cistern, strangely outsized from Senya's small, quiet voice—as if she was calling to someone else. Something in the water ready to answer.

Crassica cocked her head to the side, momentarily intrigued. *That*, she thought, *was unexpected*.

Sadahlia crouched and pulled a dagger from Raedwin's boot and another from his belt. With a blade in each hand, she stepped away. "Keep her between us."

Crassica grinned and pulled a long knife with her off hand to pair with her sword. "Smart, as well as beautiful." She pointed the tip of her dagger at Sadahlia. "We did well there. You should hang on to that one. *A keeper*, as men say."

Raedwin charged, but Crassica held firm. Without moving, she blasted her Vallahnir Sharpness through him like a lance. She would bring this rude boy to his knees without a single blow, and she would force cries of mercy from his faithless mouth before his end came. Of that much she was certain.

But even with the heaving fire of Amaris surging through her, something was off. She sensed a blockage. The Sharpness rushed and seethed, but Raedwin came on.

The Sharpness did nothing.

Senya.

What had she done? Something in her voice...

Crassica slapped Raedwin's blade away at the last moment, feinted a strike, and forced him to jump back. Sadahlia lunged as well, but Crassica spun to block her, exposing herself to Senya, who rushed in, sword flashing. Crassica cracked each blade as she whirled, deflecting both separate blows, her charged reflexes blindingly quick. A dynamic conflagration of fueled power.

Crassica stepped back. Pivoting with arms out, she held blades at each of them in turn, keeping all three in front of her. She casually paced the edge of the room, sending forth the Sharpness in focused torrents. Still no reaction. No response.

So odd.

A resonance of sound licked at her ears, a flame at the edge of her vision, defeating all the energies she put forth.

Crassica let the Sharpness fall away, useless against whatever Senya's new threat posed. She would resort to Amaris and the quickness of blades in her hand. Keep it simple for now. She understood the ultimate calculus of moments such as these. Aiming her sword tip at Sadahlia, she held her eyes on Raedwin. "She is quite delicious, Is she not?" Crassica purred, letting the words hang. "So nimble."

Without warning, she went low in a blinking movement before stepping back, leaving Raedwin's thigh open and bleeding badly. He took in a sharp rasping breath, his free hand reflexively going to the wound. Blood flowed down his leg.

Sadahlia flinched, clearly wanting to go to him, to comfort him, to stanch the bleeding, but she held her ground and kept her eyes on Crassica.

"We have to all take her together," Sadahlia urged. "All three of us at the same time."

Raedwin steadied himself, slightly off-balance with his badly wounded leg.

Crassica laughed. She held her arms wide. "You are welcome to try. But of course, the effects of such actions are difficult to predict. Who knows what could happen? Many knives at play, with several razor edges flying. Uncontrolled fury. Whose blade will find which flesh?"

All three did come at her then, from opposite sides. Crassica stepped at an angle and crossed blades in a way that blocked all three. She barely had to move her feet.

Senya stepped back, lowering her sword. "Crassica," she whispered, her words barely audible—yet the sound easily reached Crassica's ears. "That is your name."

Crassica.

Raedwin held his thigh. Blood squeezed between tight fingers. He cursed again. "The Knowing will need to find a fresh new hell for you," he hissed. "Four will not be enough."

Crassica offered a smile. "Oh, my sweet, the Knowing is not quite ready for me yet. Not today anyway."

"Crassica," Senya whispered again.

Crassica cocked her head. What was she up to? Was she struggling to memorize the name of the woman who would kill her brother this day? Or was she creating a mantra of love for the child she would someday bear?

"Crassica," she repeated. "That is your name."

Repeated whispers flickered in the water, reaching and awakening anxious spirits. Energies of the long since lost.

Of course. *A Daughter of the Crosslands, and a Speaker to the Dead.*

Crassica had opened this particular door herself.

"Senya!" she called. "Great powers are stirring in you—we both know it. Wonderful things are happening already! But you are wild and loose. This is not the Way."

Senya stood motionless, her orange eyes ablaze.

"Do not go down this path," Crassica urged. "You must join me, my sweet. Learn how to wield it properly. Do not fight me!"

Crassica, whispered Senya's voice, this time from behind.

She whirled but found nothing.

"Crassica," Senya called aloud.

"We are not enemies! The two of us are mothers and daughters entwined as one! Your glorious new gifts need training. Control. You must not take this burden on alone!"

As she spoke, Raedwin and Sadahlia lunged as a pair, gauging the Vallahnir master's movements, pushing for a breach.

Crassica, the walls murmured.

"Senya!" she shouted. "You are not ready for what you are doing!"

Crassica, whispered the water of the cistern.

Raedwin lunged, feinting a thrust to the best of his ability and then spun with whatever remaining deftness his injured leg could provide, bringing his blade low to high in order to catch shoulder and neck alike. But Crassica, surprised though she was, still held the Amaris advantage. Catching the slash and knocking it aside, she stepped forward in the same movement and drove her dagger deep into Raedwin's chest. Cloth from her cloak fell across her victim's face as she hammered the blade between ribs, thrusting upward. Yanking it forth with a violent twist, she stepped back.

All air left Raedwin's body. He fell to a crouch and then toppled forward. His face hit the floor with a sickening thud.

Crassica, the stone and water called as one.

Senya dropped her sword and fell to her knees with her mouth open and silent. Sadahlia lunged at Crassica with a piercing scream, brandishing both daggers at once, but the master circled to meet her protege's onslaught blade for blade, managing to knock one from her hand. Charging forward, Crassica cracked her pommel against Sadahlia's temple. She fell limp to the floor. Her remaining dagger clattered harmlessly away.

Crassica, sighed the water again, alone. The sound echoed over stone, repeated by the air before dying into darkness.

Senya's eyes focused on the body of her brother and burned with a silent ferocity beyond anything Crassica had ever seen.

"Senya, my sweet," she said gently. "This was never my intention." She moved to stand before her. "I had wanted us all to be together. Like a family." She shook her head and clicked her tongue in a mocking scold. "But you have become so headstrong, so quickly. And now, you insist on these silly attempts to wield the power of—"

She was never able to finish the thought.

Senya, from her knees, thrust her sword upward from the floor to Crassica's belly just above the hip. Pushing her full blade knuckles deep, she splayed open the Vallahnir until steel met bone and then sliced outward across her chest. Crassica made almost no sound as sword and dagger both fell from her hands. Dropping to her own knees, she faced Senya—the two of them unexpected supplicants preparing for some fresh prayer in the bloodied space between them. Senya raised her blade and jammed it downward into the vulnerable space where neck met body, where the collarbone offered an open cradle for life to be released from body.

Crassica stared at her then, almost strangely proud of the surprise this tiny woman had dealt, this angel star of all her hope, herself only a lonely erstwhile queen of this Keep who had seen so few true surprises in such a long time, so few lessons offered in all these diligent years, finally and truly surprised. She reached vainly at the sword handle at her neck, fingers fumbling at the slippery wood under a thin spray of blood, gripping in vain at nothing but air. She gave no exhale, no whisper, no words, as she fell sideways and slumped backward. Crassica's hands dropped and lay open on the bloody stone. She did not move again.

Senya sprang toward Raedwin and knelt beside him. The one brother she would ever have in this life lay at a strange, uncomfortable angle, his dark hair matted with effort and blood. His face so gray. Only moments before, they'd both stood together in that cursed hallway upstairs under the tower. He'd been so flush with energy then, with the hope of rescue and the coming deliverance of all that he loved in this world. And yet now here he was. Here they both were. His tunic shredded from belly to chest, his thigh in tatters. The stone underneath him impossibly wet as his chest struggled to lift with each remaining breath.

"Did we..." he managed. "Get her?" His eyes grew dim and unfocused as his life quietly spilled forth.

"Raedwin," Senya said through choking tears. "Please..." She put her head to his neck and called his name again. "Don't go."

She held him, and he smiled weakly, the slightest twitch coming through.

"Okay." His voice cracked. "Deal."

PART SEVEN

69

BROGAN WOKE to the face of his long-dead wife. For some reason, she'd pulled her hair back and tied it into a ball of loose red turbulence, and she was gazing down at him from some floating lofty height in a rough bedrock room. Her skin glowed in the torchlight. Strange. He must've gone to some fine and lovely place, some distant removal from his mud-soaked life. A place where he could breathe easily and take in the morning light. Let everything else fall away. At last.

"Brogan?" she said.

A sharp need powered through him, an urge to stand and go to her, to hold her and believe that nothing had ever happened up in those high mountain valleys along the Elrune, both of them living, back in another place and another time, the two of them and their daughter together once again. They could renew the man he'd been in the cold wash of a new connection. Or a fresh beginning. A rebirth.

"Hey. Can you hear me?"

But this. Not quite Dahlwea's voice...

Brogan slowly became aware of solid details, real things, his mouth hanging open, movement in the corner of his eye, and the fact that this woman was not actually his long-dead wife. This was somebody else. Someone close. The details swam in an uncertain liquid of some deeper truth that he could not quite locate.

This was not Dahlwea.

Her sister. *Kaetas*.

What was Kaetas doing here? Wait. Where was he?

He blinked. The room was unfamiliar, strange and hard, with cold stone under his back. Was he on the floor? Why was he on the floor? His head throbbed. Kaetas bent over him and spoke, but the sound came all muffled and confusing to his ears.

"Brogan. Can you hear me?"

Cold stone, but also wet. Blood everywhere. His blood...?

"Welcome back."

A lone guttering torch showed a dark opening in the jagged wall, barely more than a wide crack, leading to shadows. Brogan turned. The body of a Vallahnir lay nearby. Small and frail. Her severed head resting within the twisted fringes of her own cloak.

Was that Crassica? Had they made it at last? The generational matriarch of their troubled world, cast aside like so much bloody laundry.

Senya was there as well, crouching over a man with features much like her own. That must be Raedwin. At long last, they'd found him. Blood glistened in the flickering light, pooling in a meandering arc away from his chest to seek low points of the uneven floor. If that was indeed Raedwin, he did not look good. All this way, all their efforts, all these lives spent, only to have it come to this. Failure. Brogan watched him recline in the arms of a Vallahnir, pale and motionless.

Wait. *Another* Vallahnir?

But this one was not like the others. Something was different about her. Something new. He would have to ask about that. She rocked quietly, sobbing heavily as she held him.

Other creatures huddled over Brogan and Raedwin both, the same as those outside. Working quickly and deftly alongside Senya and Sadahlia, they used sinew and cloth to close lacerations and fasten bandages over gashes. They cleaned skin and wiped brows. Senya urged Raedwin to stay with her, to keep breathing. Stay awake.

"Sorry it took us so long to find you," Kaetas said. "We got a little lost."

Her face was so like Dahlwea's—allowing no lies or misleading assurances, no simplistic, naive hope for anything but the truth. All of their efforts had fallen short. Their long journeys and struggles, all the bloodshed they'd seen, had finally come to little more than this—to Raedwin's end and Brogan himself bloody and nearly dead as well.

Brogan tried to acknowledge, but his body refused to cooperate. Unable to move, he closed his eyes and slipped back into a dreamless sleep.

"Again," Sadahlia implored, urging Raedwin to repeat the words, the phrasings, the punctuations of tone and timbre, sound and manipulations in the arcane language of the Vallahnir.

"I..." he gasped. "Don't think..."

"You can," she assured. "You have to. Please." And she said the words again, coarse and earthy with a rich, smoky sound, wrapped inside existence itself.

Raedwin repeated. Timidly and weakly, but correctly.

Sadahlia held his body in her arms, rocking gently as she whispered encouragement, holding her tears at bay while Raedwin managed the words with a struggle, his voice nearly lost. "Again," she said softly.

Fire raged in the lower citadel, climbing toward its chance to rise and devour the Keep itself. Senya began to cry as Sadahlia spoke the words again.

"I'm... sorry..." Raedwin wheezed. "I tried to fix it..."

Senya reached and touched his cold and clammy cheek. "Hush," she whispered.

Raedwin repeated the words again, but then paused. His eyes flashed wide. He tensed and lifted his back from the floor, then settled. His face relaxed. His body went limp. He quietly finished the phrasing as his eyes slipped closed. All he had ever been in this life or would ever become, all the things he'd ever said or done, failed or accomplished, won or lost, high or low or somewhere in between, all of it, simply ended. Senya called to him. She threw herself onto him and cried his name. Her brother's eyes remained open, seeking no further vision, holding no sight, unfocused, seeing nothing that remained in this living world.

Sadahlia urged Raedwin to repeat the phrasings again, yet she knew the futility of her request, the uselessness of it all—this life, this grand experiment of hers, the love she'd thought would be easy to hold for all the rest of her days upon this earth. All of it, gone.

Still, hope remained. The words she had given to him, the phrases blocking his entry into the Crosslands, of binding Vallahnir to man, these words could indeed make possible what she was about to do and what she was about to give. Not even Senya would be able to heal him. Healing was the mode of the Brohndai, not the Vallahnir, but this was a wound beyond all of them. Sadahlia would not be able to hold life within his fragile body, at least not here. Even after all her decades striving to craft this body of hers, she remained an usher of the Crosslands, a simple minister of death. And as such, she still held great power granted by the Knowing, even now. Sadahlia could deny the reckoning now at hand, so long as she did so from the other side.

To hold Raedwin here, she had to first go back to the Crosslands.

So that was what she would do. Sadahlia would give the Knowing her blessed Balance right here and right now. She would return to the Crosslands voluntarily, whole and intact, so that Raedwin could live. She would push his living soul back into his badly wounded body, and hold him—keep him alive from the other side. Life would fill his body again, here in this godscursed place. He would carry on. She would release her living form and go back to the beginning, and there would be no silly games left to play between them, none from this day forward, forevermore.

She slipped from underneath his body and kneeled next to him, across from Senya. She drew a light chain over her head. A small green amulet dangled from it—a leaf with bright silver veins. Torchlight played on the glittering surface. She placed the amulet on Raedwin's chest and pulled the chain over his head. "Keep me with you," she whispered, her face close to his. "Always."

She reached for his sword. Placing the pommel in a crease of the hard stone floor, she pushed the tip into the soft folds of her own belly, and fell forward. The blade slid in easily. Pain came, yet this pain was merely physical—weak and small when compared to the cries already tearing at her heart.

Senya glanced up and shouted, diving to stop her, but Sadahlia shoved herself farther onto the sword, pulling Raedwin to her and embracing her love, her life, her simple belief that these things could truly be more than weak vessels of blood and bone, of fragile air and the uncertain voice of water.

Senya cried out, not yet understanding the true finality of what Sadahlia had done, her whispered words of release, of countering entry into this life, words to exit this body and this world, severing the delicate ties she'd crafted to bind herself to the impermanent clay of life.

Sadahlia let the sword twist, driving into and through her, ensuring that this body of hers would never draw another breath in the sentient world. She chanted a quick succession of guttural phrases. All air and life escaped her well-crafted container, this corporeal portrait of her truth, becoming little more than an empty vessel left withering in a cascade of dust and spent dreams.

The linen sheet so recently covering her mortal self fluttered, settling without shape as it fell empty over Raedwin's lifeless body. Senya laid her head on her brother's silent chest, weeping on the cold stone floor.

Raedwin drifted in and out of sleep. This was sleeping, wasn't it? Such a strange kind. Sadahlia lay next to him. The milky expanse of her body rose and fell with the slightest of movements. He could reach out and touch her, sprawled naked across a vast landscape of fur blankets and linen sheets, yet somehow he knew both of them were already lost.

The world beyond the expansive reach of this bed fell away into nothingness. How long had he been lying here? So confusing, this place. Senya had come to the Valle d'Brasti, had been drawn or dragged, and she was here, somewhere deep in the Keep. He had seen her. They had fought side by side, together, and then they had laughed and cried, and then they had descended into the deep to free Sadahlia. And then...

Crassica.

Sleeping in silence, Sadahlia held position, blocking him, confining him to this strange bed. He pulled her close. Her body harbored far more heat than his own, and yet she grew colder. The waking world so long ago now, so far away. He pondered her breathing for a long time, her body, and the slowly diminishing beat of her weakening heart.

70

THE FIRE BURNED and gathered fury as Senya helped the Jehndai hurriedly carry Brogan and Raedwin's lifeless body through the lower reaches of the quarries to a cave-mouth exit in the cliffside. It burned as Kaetas directed the formation of a rudimentary camp beside the causeway to Katliga. It burned all through the night and continued into the morning.

Before escaping, a few of the Jehndai dragged Crassica's headless body up to the burning Great Hall and heaved it onto a flaming pile of timbers. They tossed her head into the inferno of the lower citadel. For a brief moment they watched the separated parts burn, offering songs of release and departure as well as chanting curses of hatred and banishment. The master of this Keep, the architect of their entire existence, the hated cause of generations of pain, was finally and truly finished.

Former residents who were able enough had already fled into the surrounding countryside. Those too wounded or otherwise without capacity to flee allowed themselves to be cared for by the Jehndai. The people's erstwhile enemies turned out to be quite deft in the various arts of healing, even to enemies of their own.

Senya sat alone in the long grass beside Raedwin's body and watched the distant flames, answers to silent questions hidden in the unfathomable remoteness of the burning Keep. She had so little left to give, her body so dry and spent, yet the tears still came. Her brother's body lay beside her, her one true friend, her always and forever. A world without Raedwin was a world she could not understand. There was no her without him, not since the very beginning. Holding his face, she let her forehead drop to his shoulder and gave in to sobbing. If she'd been able, she would've pushed clean through to the ground and allowed her head to crack open like a fragile robin's egg and release whatever new powers she may hold, all the memories of laughter and light her brother had given her over their long lives together, all the images of their mother and father with them, and any thought of this place, this hellscursed place and everything it had ever stood for along with everything it had taken from them, her pain slipping free and returning to the Knowing from whence it had once come.

A few of the Jehndai kneeled in the grass nearby and sang a mournful ballad of loss for Raedwin and for their own fallen kin. Others built a pyre for the dead on a rise some distance away. Senya washed the body of her lost brother before wrapping him carefully in a death shroud of the cleanest cloth she could muster from the wreckage. She called his name and sang a song of quiet release, of goodbye and welcome both, her voice weaving through the smoke and breeze.

An ancient Jehndai approached her slowly, his movements tentative and respectful. Thin and regal, he wore something of a beard. A silver circlet ringed his head, and the others gave him deference. Clearly the clan Elder. He sat beside her and did not speak for a long time. Careful and measured, as if approaching a wounded animal, he reached to Senya and traced the strange markings on her arm.

"You must allow me to remove these," he said gently. "They are not to be trusted."

She turned to him and nodded weakly, unable yet to manage words. The Elder massaged the markings with oils and herbs and a small rough cloth until they were gone. Finished, he sat next to her in silence. The Keep blazed in the distance.

"Every day the sun goes away," Senya said quietly, "and we somehow believe that it'll be back again. But what if it doesn't come back?"

The Elder did not answer. Distant flames reflected in his black eyes.

"What if darkness is the way the world remains?"

Several Jehndai around them sang softly. Their lament settled to a sad and plaintive end. After a time, the Elder drew in a long breath. "Alas, nothing lasts," he said. "The deepest darkness, as well as the light. Water destroys earth and stone alike, air feeds the flames, and earth in turn will quench the fire."

Senya ran her hand through the grass, idly watching the movement of the blades against her fingers. "We make a place inside ourselves for those we love, full of all our memories of the past. Our hope for the future. A place to be together. But what is any of that hope worth? Hope is a place open to invasion, just like any other. Anything can come in and kill it with bloodshed or break it down or burn it all away. And then we're left with nothing. A space filled only with pain. Even the memories hurt."

They sat together in silence for a long time. "Forward is the only way, no matter what comes," the Elder said quietly, almost to himself. "Our lives burn in a line, which moves uniquely forward. One cannot go back along this line. Behind us is nothing but charred dust..." His voice trailed away. A massive part of the Keep's western wall collapsed.

A new song of the Jehndai began, floating into the evening. "But your line is not yet lost, dear Senya," the Elder said. "This is simply a turn. You will find that there is deep healing yet to come, perhaps in unexpected ways."

Senya shook her head. How was she supposed to heal from this? What could she do now? All her focus had been on coming to this place, on finding Raedwin, on her goal of being together with him once again, and now that focus was gone. She had no North Star. There was no wayfinder, no star taker to navigate home from here. She'd lived for years apart from Raedwin, with the solace and knowledge that he was out there somewhere. On his own or with others. Still out there. A lifetime's stout foundation built by their long years with one another, and now everything they had built was gone.

Finally, the Elder rose and stood. Smoke billowed into the evening sky. "The world moves on around us," he said to Senya. "And we are left with the choices ahead, not behind. Nothing more and nothing less. You hold great powers within you, some ancient and some very new, yet the two are in conflict with one another. I believe you know that. You must be careful. And so I wish you peace and wellness in your days to come." He gave his leave and stepped away to examine the wounds of others.

Senya lay back in the grass. Powers in conflict. Powers she never asked for nor ever wanted. She was no hero. She had never intended to be one. Heroes were made of song and stone and unbreakable will. She had never been any of that. People wanted things from their heroes. They had expectations. Senya had long since stopped trying to live up to such things—new powers, old powers, or no power of any kind at all.

Brogan regained consciousness just after dawn. He spoke and was able to smile, even laughing a little. Senya tended to him, freshly binding his wounds with strips cut from salvaged clothing. He watched her as she worked.

"What happened to your eye?" he asked, a hesitance to his voice.

"What do you mean?"

"The color. It's off. Your left eye…"

She wrapped his arm and pulled the bandage tight, securing the ends with a knot. A strange prickle had indeed begun to itch at the back of her eye even while she had still been locked high in Raedwin's tower. Barely noticeable. She'd done her best to ignore it.

"I'm sure it's nothing," she said.

But since leaving the Keep, the prickle had already become more than nothing. A tingling itch, pulsing with her blood. Over the last day or so, her vision seemed to have shifted as well. Light now formed around living bodies, showing a dancing sheen. Color energy she'd never seen before. Some were larger, some smaller.

"What did she do to you?" Brogan asked quietly, nearly a whisper.

Senya shook her head. She cleaned and bound the wound on his thigh. She had no real answer. She had no idea what was happening to her and mostly did not want to know.

"We are here, and Crassica is gone. That's something to hold on to. At least for today."

The Jehndai offered to guide them all to their hidden vale, safe in the confines of the forest. Brogan was clearly not ready for a long journey to Katliga, and especially not for a much longer one at sea. Not yet at least. But among the Jehndai, they could spend all the time needed to rest and heal. They would bring Raedwin's body along as well, to provide a resting place of great honor under the trees.

Kaetas directed the fashioning of sturdy stretchers to carry Brogan and the rest of the wounded, as well as a drag litter for Raedwin's body. Freógan should have docked in Katliga by now and with any luck would've made quick work of it. She sent two of her sailors with a message of their plan. Freógan was to remain in Katliga and keep most of the *Summerhawk* crew near at hand to begin provisioning for a return journey north. Kaetas and Brogan would join them once the wounded man was well enough for the journey.

The next morning, they followed the remains of a Kalldonian road eastward up the far rim of the valley, slipping through a broken crease in a low ridge. The Jehndai's long legs kept easy pace over the splintered paving stones, despite carrying several wounded. After a time, the road disintegrated to little more than a wide path, and at times even less than that.

Hours passed. They climbed into the face of the rising sun, and their path broke apart into a broad country of unyielding stony earth. They held course due east. Light fell and the moon showed full and cold. Making camp on the banks of a small creek, they laid the wounded out between warming fires. The Jehndai set a watch. Soon the healthy and wounded alike fell asleep to the distant mournful wail of a lone wolf crying unanswered into the purple night.

Far behind them, the Valle d'Brasti burned. In the end, the fire would rage for over three full days. It would find every timber, every wood-paneled wall, every linen and tapestry, every scrap of carpeted floor, and all the planks underneath. The greatest library in all of Kalldonia, perhaps in all the known world outside of Yesteralen or Faeroen Island, would fuel the heart of the blaze with its dry, hungry pages. Stone would crumble where missing beams no longer supported the structure. Flint would crack and shatter with the heat, and in places even the iron would melt. The once proud and fearsome Valle d'Brasti with its magnificent Sevenfold Keep would collapse to nothing more than a blackened and charred ruin. None but the exceptionally brave or insane would ever come again to comb through its storied remains.

71

RAEDWIN'S EYES suddenly flew wide at dawn the third day away from the Keep. He pulled in a deep gasp, grunting and wheezing. Senya cried out in shock and amazement beside his drag litter. Her brother flailed and gripped her arm, pulling her to him.

Fresh vigor coursed through his body, limp and cold only moments before. Senya's mouth fell open. Words failed as Raedwin's chest heaved. His surging energy narrowly provided enough strength for each breath to follow the one before. He uttered hideous and awkward noises beneath the forming of language, like an animal becoming human, struggling to regain control over his freshly living body. Turning to Senya, he called her name, wheezing and settling as he blinked awake.

"Where...?" he whispered hoarsely.

What was she seeing? *How was he alive?* Was this some new depths of necromancy? Or a dream wrapped inside her own fleeting nightmare? Some strange secret sorcery? His eyes fixed on his sister for a long moment, his mouth open, clearly struggling to find new words.

"Where is..." he said at last. "Sadahlia?"

Senya shook her head. "She's—" and her voice broke. A rushing sound flooded her ears. "She's... gone," she finally managed, realizing then that the brutal sacrifice Sadahlia had made was not the futile and foolish act it had seemed but rather the sole and heroic reason Raedwin now breathed. Somehow Sadahlia had obstructed his fall into the Crosslands and forced his life back here, returning him to his living body.

Raedwin shuddered and closed his eyes. He shook his head. A lone tear slid down his dirty cheek. He reached for Senya, taking her hand in his and falling asleep again as his revived body slowly recovered.

The Elder offered his guests a strange milky tea as they arrived in the grove. Fashioning a pair of pine-bough beds inside a simple structure, several Jehndai crafted a rudimentary House of Healing for both Raedwin and Brogan. Every able body then attended to the construction of a traditional welcome fire in the central clearing. Night fell, and the blaze sent orange light rippling through the trees. Raedwin and Senya sat in silence some distance away, watching the Jehndai chant and dance around the fire.

"I saw her," Raedwin said weakly. "I was with her. Just after... when I...." He took in a shaky breath, as if the words themselves could cause the fragile image to disappear. "I knew Crassica had won, and both of us were lost, but Sadahlia was right there with me. In a white bed. She was asleep beside me."

He held her amulet to his chest, rotating it over and around with his fingertips. One corner of the silver edge was bent away, twisted during her struggle with Crassica. "I can feel her," he said at length. "Wherever she's gone to, she's still with me."

Senya reached out and took his hand, holding his arm in hers. "I suspect she always will be."

He nodded with timid hope. She knew then that her brother was not yet ready for the lingering pain this loss would bring—a pain that would likely follow him for all the rest of his living days. He had found something there in the Valle d'Brasti, something real and true, something close to what he might've called a home, and now all of it was gone. But he was alive now, and for that she cried with happiness. He was broken and would remain so for a long time to come, but he was alive. The imperfect joy of half victories.

Before she spoke her next words, Senya felt herself beginning to want the very thing she'd urged her brother to leave behind—the seeking of keys, ways of unlocking secrets of the world. Visions of hidden truths, and the mysteries of her new voice.

"If Sadahlia and the others did it once," she said slowly, "maybe there's a way..." She trailed off, unable to fully give credence to her brother's hope, as well as her own, lest both prove too weak and tenuous for words. Death was just a door, after all. The passing from branch to root in the Great Circle of the Everliving Tree, open and ready. Offering fresh light for the living. Maybe it would be possible to find her again. Someday, somehow.

"Maybe," Raedwin agreed with hesitance, his life and body both so broken and weak.

She smiled. "Or maybe that'd be looking for more trouble to get ourselves into."

Her brother let out a small, tired laugh. "Maybe." He glanced around at the towering majestic Kalldonian pines gracing the grove. "Maybe we just stick around here for a while."

She rested her head against his shoulder. "Okay," she whispered. *Maybe* was probably the best they could live with for now. They sat in silence together for a long time, watching the flames.

"Change can come hard," she said at last. "Or it can come easy. But change will always come, like Father used to say. I guess we might as well embrace it as best we can."

A call rang out in the darkness from the edge of the grove. An answer sounded from the far side. A third from another edge. Maybe to signify that night had fully arrived and the clan was well and fed. No danger lurked outside the safe and happy confines of their hidden suspended world.

Or maybe the signal and the fire both told of something else—maybe they meant the opposite. Maybe they meant the true dawn of the Jehndai had come at last. Danger and violence lurked forever outside the massive trees of their newly exposed, fragile home, and this was the start of their final summons. Their long hunger for retribution had come to an end, but perhaps the real fighting was soon to begin.

Life in the grove settled into something resembling a new normal. Senya spent most of her time in the rudimentary House of Healing tending to her brother and Brogan each day. Their wounds remained clean and healing steadily. She also helped the Jehndai with food and crafting better sleeping pallets for all the newcomers, even climbing a tree to harvest wild honey, singing away the stings of several bees.

Days passed. The Jehndai honored Senya with her own shelter lofted among the trees, the largest in the grove aside from the Elder's own. A wide wooden platform with a modest structure nestled against the trunk. A small hearth built into the outer wall. In the evenings, she took to sitting at the platform's edge and watching the Jehndai in their own proud homes spread high through the grove, dancing light splashing from trunk to trunk. Faint music in the distance.

Soon Brogan proudly began to walk the grove under his own power, heavily bandaged, unsteady with his movements. Nearly a week after arriving in the grove, he followed Senya and Kaetas up the narrow path beside the waterfall, looping back to sit and stare at the beauty of the large black pool below.

"That's twice now you've patched me up with your magic Brondy touch," he quipped. "Not many left in the world who can claim that."

"I'm glad I could help," she said. "For a bit there, I wasn't so sure I had it in me anymore." In truth, since coming to the Jehndai grove, she'd returned to being more completely herself than she'd felt in years. Yet something tugged at her, something not yet knowable. An awakening, deep in her spirit she could not yet fully see.

Raedwin was healing astonishingly fast as well—maybe because of Senya's continued efforts, maybe his Brohndai blood, or maybe something else entirely.

Kaetas and Brogan and the remaining sailors of the *Summerhawk* gave their goodbyes seven days after arriving in the grove. They'd gotten word that Freógan had procured a cart at the Valle d'Brasti for Brogan to ride the rest of the way to Katliga, so they'd decided it was time to go. Brogan straightened and tried to stand tall and proud, giving Senya a strong, true smile.

"Being around Kaetas here is about the closest thing to home I've got left in this world," he said. "So I figure that's my path for now."

Kaetas flushed. "Careful," she said. "We'll end up making you a full crew member. I could use a good cabin boy to bark at."

They all laughed and embraced and spoke to one another in hesitant tones, as if any misspoken words could cause harm to the fragile threads of life that remained between them.

Senya mixed a series of poultices and salves for Brogan, carefully explaining their use. Kaetas, alongside him, listened carefully. Some of the salves were to be applied daily, others hourly, all with fresh dressings at specified intervals, all of it important for his quick and complete recovery.

"You put your life on the line for me," she said. "The least I can do is help get you better as best I can."

Brogan smiled and thanked her. He glanced around at the grove, the suspended structures among the branches, the several Jehndai watching them. "Looks like you're the one out on the edge of nowhere now," he said finally. "In a forest filled with strange creatures of myth and legend."

She returned the smile. "I wouldn't have it any other way."

Kaetas promised to get Brogan safely back to Brinsfallon without fail, maybe all the way to Corregidon. "If, of course, I haven't burned every remaining bridge I had left in the city."

Taking both of Senya's hands in hers, she held firm as she looked into her eyes. "You belong at sea," she said at length. "Not tucked away out here in the mountains." A fact of strength, almost some claim against doing anything other than sail away with her.

Senya loved the sea, of course, but there would be other times for such things. "Maybe we'll end up seeing one another sooner than you think. Only the Knowing can tell."

"Well, don't take forever." Kaetas grinned, her mouth curling unevenly with a small crease to the left of her lips. "The rest of us don't live as long as a Brohndai."

Senya watched them both as they walked away, Brogan limping with his new walking stick and the captain's flaming hair loose and unruly against all futile attempts to subdue it with various ties and bindings.

Several days later, she climbed to an outcropping of stone along a tall ridge at the edge of their tiny valley. She sat. The sun descended over dusky rolling hills beyond the reach of the forest. She'd taken up this position many times since coming here, gazing out over the land toward the sea beyond sight, watching the day descend into evening. Mountains stood dignified and imposing over her shoulder to the east, rising in ridge after ridge of weather-hewn stone. Glaciated peaks braced against one another, their impenetrable weight ascending into the glittering distance. Light from the setting sun shone on their snowy slopes, turning the exposed summer stone to golden copper and blood-red rose.

Glancing down, only then did she notice her left hand seemed lighter than her right. Paler. As if a bit of her brown color had drained. The difference was subtle, narrowly apparent when she held skin against skin, like she'd been kneading a mound of dough one-handed. She wondered at it and tried to rub off whatever dust or liquid she'd gotten into, but nothing changed. Maybe she'd slept on it wrong.

She let it go and gazed over the grove below. The waterfall and pool. Warm evening sun haloed around a crown of flowers on a young Jehndai girl's head. Her simple dress, plain and well stitched. Soft gently loomed cloth. Her gleaming smile. The girl's dark eyes sparkled with mischief and tender caring, ablaze with opposing powers like two wrestling cats. She giggled and ran. Tree boughs waved in her honor with the breeze she left behind.

The girl's proud father stood alone at the edge of the pool and watched her go. He was one of the warriors who had been at the storming of the Sevenfold Keep, and he had been alongside Senya in the tunnels below during the aftermath. Injured in a fight with some of Lanius's men, he walked with a limp. His daughter would be home with her mother soon. Such a sweet girl, one of Senya's favorites.

Tonight there would be stewed rabbit waiting in a new iron pot over the fire. Fresh onions, carrots, and potatoes. Baked flatbread. A small portion of mead. Maybe there'd be enough mead for everybody. The girl would probably ask for music, as she often did. She would demand that somebody play for her. For everybody. Music to bind their worlds together.

Senya let out a sigh. She and Raedwin were safe here among the Jehndai. Safe together. This would be a good place to build a new life, away from the struggles and penetrating strife of Brinsfallon and the boneskins of the North. Out of sight of the rest of the world's judging eyes. Here they had what they needed. The soil was good. The air was clean and the water pure. Here they could stay. Maybe even be happy.

Her left eye twitched. That same prickling tingle. She tried to ignore it. Closing her eyes, she began to sing. The sound came easily in smooth, woven notes, almost without her asking—old friends as well as new, both urging her to come and play. The strains rose all on their own and wandered into a melody that rang in a wide echo over the forest, her long-held hopes and sadness joining in.

A mist gathered beyond the distant ridgelines guarding the valley, thickening quickly and sealing away the lands outside. Senya paid no heed. She concentrated on the song. The rest of the world would do whatever it did. She leaned against the exposed stone. Her mind drifted elsewhere, watching westward, seeking for any sense of threat that might be there.

None came. Still she sang. To the east, the purple tips of faraway mountains disappeared behind a wall of fog, while overhead the cloudless lavender sky opened to the evening's first sparkling stars.

Thanks for reading! Please leave a review.

IF YOU'VE enjoyed this book, please leave a review on Amazon, Goodreads, your favorite review site, or wherever you procured this copy. After sixteen years of writing, revising, sharing with friends, rewriting, sending to agents, getting rejection after rejection—and pondering those who ghosted entirely—rewriting yet again, hiring a development editor, deciding to go for it on my own, hiring a copy editor, and making all the last-minute tweaks and revisions, you are now holding the final result. All those late nights, early mornings, and missed events along the way have at last added up to something tangible. From here, its success is really up to you, truth be told. So please spread the word to any fans of epic fantasy you know—or anybody else you think might enjoy reading this book. Those of us in independent publishing could use all the help we can get, so word of mouth is absolutely vital. A little bit goes a long way. I'd really appreciate it.

Scan to review on Amazon:

Scan to review on Goodreads:

Sign up for my newsletter at briankerrbooks.com to stay in the know, be apprised of updates, or find out when new books are ready to launch.

Acknowledgements

OVER THE YEARS spent writing (and rewriting) this book, I've been heroically helped by a small army of assistance. Early readers endured preposterous, overlong versions, yet steadfastly gave very helpful insight and critique. I'm therefore eternally grateful to my early team: Alisa Jones, Chris Lazarek, Laurie and Ryan Haaland, Cody and Heather Sprague, Kristin Howe, Celestia Caredio, Luke Davais, Olivia Serrill, Seth English-Young, and Mike Pitt. Later readers helped immensely in getting this thing over the finish line, each in their own way, so my additional thanks to Nick Seid, Thom Hines, and Jennifer Wolfe.

A special level of gratitude goes to my lovely and stalwart editors, Susan Barnes and Laura Josephsen, who helped shape things up in so many ways.

I also want to give a special thanks to those who were instrumental in helping make my craft of writing a reality way back at the California College of the Arts in San Francisco (more years ago than I care to admit): John Laskey, Windsor Cooley, Ann Williams, Gloria Frym, and Martin Venezky, as well as Erin McCluskey, Josh Kamler, Amy Yuen, Youmna Chlala, and Brent Foster Jones, among so many others. You guys were sparks at the start of this fire.

Thanks to my family for enduring the nonsensically long hours spent poking away at this monster that never seemed to properly get finished, and to my parents for quietly believing this sort of thing was ever possible.

Lastly, and most completely, I want to thank my wife, Julie West, for always believing, always understanding, and always letting me know when the words weren't quite good enough—and the times when I've cut too much and lost the good stuff somewhere along the way. Thank you, my dear. You're still my favorite.

About the Author

BRIAN KERR lives in the misty wilds of the Pacific Northwest's urban/suburban divide with his wife and children. His day job is in branding, strategy, and graphic design. He has an MFA in Writing from the California College of the Arts in San Francisco, and loves peaty, salty, smoky single malt Scotch from Islay. Daughters of the Crosslands is his first novel.

@briankerrwrites

briankerrbooks.com

www.ingramcontent.com/pod-product-compliance
Lightning Source LLC
Chambersburg PA
CBHW010520100726
47903CB00011B/2833